THE WORLD OF O. HENRY

THE UNKNOWN QUANTITY

and other stories

THE WORLD OF O. HENRY

THE UNKNOWN QUANTITY

and other stories

HODDER AND STOUGHTON
LONDON SYDNEY AUCKLAND TORONTO

 First printed 1974. ISBN 0 340 17949 X. *Printed in Great Britain for Hodder and Stoughton Limited, St. Paul's House, Warwick Lane, London EC4P 4AH by Cox & Wyman Ltd, London, Fakenham and Reading*

Introduction

"Pull up the shades," he enjoined a nurse. "I don't want to go home in the dark."

O. Henry had been taken ill two days earlier in the Caledonian Hotel, New York: he died his sunny death at the age of forty-eight, departing as suavely as a character in one of his own stories. He'd been a lonely man, making do with acquaintances where others demand friends, twice married, and on his own reckoning the daily consumer of two quarts of whisky. He haunted the New York streets and bars, endlessly listening to the stories of other people's lives: the world was grist to his typewriter, and towards the end of his life he lived for nothing else.

He was born William Sydney Porter in Greensboro, N.C., in 1862, the son of a doctor whose practice of medicine took second place to his interest in perpetual motion. When he was three, William Sydney's mother died. At fifteen, he left school to work in an uncle's drug store, and a few years later he became a teller in the First National Bank in Austin. Summoned to stand trial for embezzlement, he fled—and at once became involved with Al and Henry Jennings, whose methods of extracting money from banks were swifter and more direct than months of patient appropriation.

He travelled to Mexico with thirty thousand dollars, the proceeds of a Jennings robbery, but having "knocked around with refugees and consuls" for some years, he returned to Austin and was awarded three years' incarceration in the Ohio State Penitentiary. Here, it seems, there was a prison guard named Orrin Henry, whom William Sydney Porter, small-town crook and model prisoner, immortalised as O. Henry.

There's the whiff of some bad, black joke about all that,

some wry O. Henry comment that wryly bore its final fruit twenty-odd years later when the citizens of Greensboro built the O. Henry Hotel in honour of their safely-dead reprobate. An extraordinary tribute this, and a rare one for a man of letters: in one grandiloquent American gesture it established him as the Henry Ford of the short story, and since that time his creations have to some extent shared the vicissitudes of the Tin Lizzie. O. Henry's collected works published in 1913 ran into twelve volumes. Once considered classics of their kind, they fell from grace when popular American magazines became fashionably sophisticated. But their decline and resurrection parallels the decline and resurrection of the short story itself, which is a starting point in any assessment of their quality.

O. Henry's stories are the stories people tell one another. They are anecdotes with a beginning, a middle and an end. It is the end that contains the punch or often the winning trick, and because of their construction a certain similarity carries from story to story. Like the stories of Saki and unlike those of, say, Thomas Hardy, they are true to the form: they could not, by any stretch of the Henry imagination, have been novels. Most of Hardy's could, and many of the fashionable short stories that have led the way since O. Henry's day are chapters from some unwritten novel rather than stories in their own right. Novels themselves during that same period have become shorter, more confused, and emptier of content.

But now, as the mid-seventies approach, the story and the novel are finding their length and their shape again. Frank O'Connor, one of the best short-story writers of this century, was an appallingly bad influence because what O'Connor could get away with lesser writers emphatically could not. This is all too patently true, far more so than the argument that magazine outlets for the short story dried up and in so doing almost killed it. What *did* seriously affect its health since the days when writers thrived on popular demand was the fashion for slight, formless little bits and pieces, addressed to an intelligentsia—O'Connor without the genius. To quote Alan Ross, who as the editor of the *London Magazine* did so much for the short story during its wilderness years by publishing stories that represented: "a necessary reaction against shapeless impressionism, against the post Denton Welch period in which china bric-a-brac and a young man's relationship with his mother appeared controlling forces." The story, in short, had become inbred, precious, self-consciously literary and often self-congratulatingly incomprehensible.

O. Henry is rather the opposite of all that, and those who seek to denigrate his works might perhaps consider them the contents of a cracker-barrel. There is an ordinariness about his ordinary people that could well be too much for those who require characters of a nobler cut. There is a precision about his plotting that may offend those who believe that plots have no place in art. But in his style and in the crisp naturalness of his dialogue and his wit there is little that anyone in full possession of senses and sensibility could object to. With the economy that is, above all, the essence of the thing he creates characters with real life in them and draws from their lips words that start the machinery of drama immediately moving. But it's his own prose, set in the succinct style of a primitive who's a comedian and a professional as well, that distinguishes most of his pages. And the familiar ring it sometimes has is because it has been endlessly imitated since the days when it was fresh and new.

> The first time my optical nerves were disturbed by the sight of Buckingham Skinner was in Kansas City. I was standing on a corner when I see Buck stick his straw-coloured head out of a third-story window of a business block and holler, "Whoa, there! Whoa!" like you would in endeavouring to assuage a team of runaway mules.
>
> I looked around; but all the animals I see in sight is a policeman, having his shoes shined, and a couple of delivery wagons hitched to posts. Then in a minute downstairs tumbles this Buckingham Skinner, and runs to the corner, and stands and gazes down the street either at the imaginary dust kicked up by the fabulous hoofs . . .
>
> "Was that your team broke away and run just now?"

I asks him, polite. "I tried to stop 'em," says I, "but I couldn't. I guess they're half-way back to the farm by now."

"Gosh blame them darned mules," says Strawtop, in a voice so good that I nearly apologized . . ."

Con-men, street-men, grafters, bar-flies, vaudeville players, soap kings, bread kings, scrub-women, dice-shakers, captains of adventure, girls who are strictly business, loiterers in Bogle's Chop House, where the pepper is tasteless and melancholy: the failings of all of them flow as the blood of the O. Henry world.

They have not lost their lustre and at a time when the short story can again hold up its head it seems right that, being so much part of the history of the form in America, they should again be presented. Their stories are one kind of story. They are not classic and they are not the only kind. But a renaissance is a varied movement, and I believe this present one would be incomplete without its O. Henry tribute.

William Trevor

Contents

THE WORLD OF O. HENRY

THE UNKNOWN QUANTITY

and other stories

1

The Unknown Quantity

THE poet Longfellow—or was it Confucius, the inventor of wisdom?—remarked:

Life is real, life is earnest;
And things are not what they seem.

As mathematics are—or is: thanks, old subscriber!—the only just rule by which questions of life can be measured, let us, by all means, adjust our theme to the straight edge and the balanced column of the great goddess Two-and-Two-Makes-Four. Figures—unassailable sums in addition—shall be set over against whatever opposing element there may be.

A mathematician, after scanning the above two lines of poetry, would say: "Ahem! young gentlemen, if we assume that X plus—that is, that life is real—then things (all of which life includes) are real. Anything that is real is what it seems. Then if we consider the proposition that 'things are not what they seem,' why——"

But this is heresy, and not poesy. We woo the sweet nymph Algebra; we would conduct you into the presence of the elusive, seductive, pursued, satisfying, mysterious X.

Not long before the beginning of this century, Septimus Kinsolving, an old New Yorker, invented an idea. He originated the discovery that bread is made from flour and not from wheat futures. Perceiving that the flour crop was short, and that the Stock Exchange was having no perceptible effect on the growing wheat, Mr. Kinsolving cornered the flour market.

The result was that when you or my landlady (before the war she never had to turn her hand to anything; Southerners accommodated) bought a five-cent loaf of bread you laid down an additional two cents, which went to Mr. Kinsolving as a testimonial to his perspicacity.

A second result was that Mr. Kinsolving quit the game with $2,000,000 prof—er—rake-off.

Mr. Kinsolving's son Dan was at college when the mathematical experiment in breadstuffs was made. Dan came home during vacation, and found the old gentleman in a red dressing-gown reading *Little Dorrit* on the porch of his estimable red-brick mansion in Washington Square. He had retired from business with enough extra two-cent pieces from bread buyers to reach, if laid side by side, fifteen times around the earth and lap as far as the public debt of Paraguay.

Dan shook hands with his father, and hurried over to Greenwich Village to see his old high-school friend, Kenwitz. Dan had always admired Kenwitz. Kenwitz was pale, curly-haired, intense, serious, mathematical, studious, altruistic, socialistic and the natural foe of oligarchies. Kenwitz had forgone college, and was learning watch-making in his father's jewellery store. Dan was smiling, jovial, easy-tempered and tolerant alike of kings and rag-pickers. The two forgathered joyously, being opposites. And then Dan went went back to college, and Kenwitz to his mainsprings—and to his private library in the rear of the jewellery shop.

Four years later Dan came back to Washington Square with the accumulations of B.A. and two years of Europe thick upon him. He took a filial look at Septimus Kinsolving's elaborate tombstone in Greenwood, and a tedious excursion through typewritten documents with the family lawyer; and then, feeling himself a lonely and hopeless millionaire, hurried down to the old jewellery store across Sixth Avenue.

Kenwitz unscrewed a magnifying glass from his eye, routed out his parent from a dingy rear room, and abandoned the interior of watches for outdoors. He went with Dan, and they sat on a bench in Washington Square. Dan had not changed much; he was stalwart, and had a dignity that was inclined to relax into a grin. Kenwitz was more serious, more intense, more learned, philosophical and socialistic.

"I know about it now," said Dan finally. "I pumped it out

of the eminent legal lights that turned over to me poor old dad's collection of bonds and boodle. It amounts to $2,000,000, Ken. And I am told that he squeezed it out of the chaps that pay their pennies for loaves of bread at the little bakeries around the corner. You've studied economics, Ken, and you know all about monopolies, and the masses, and octopuses, and the rights of labouring people. I never thought about those things before. Football and trying to be white to my fellow-man were about the extent of my college curriculum.

"But since I came back and found out how dad made his money I've been thinking. I'd like awfully well to pay back those chaps who had to give up too much money for bread. I know it would buck the line of my income for a good many yards; but I'd like to make it square with 'em. Is there any way it can be done, old Ways and Means?"

Kenwitz's big black eyes glowed fierily. His thin, intellectual face took on almost a sardonic cast. He caught Dan's arm with the grip of a friend and a judge.

"You can't do it!" he said, emphatically. "One of the chief punishments of you men of ill-gotten wealth is that when you do repent you find that you have lost the power to make reparation or restitution. I admire your good intentions, Dan, but you can't do anything. Those people were robbed of their precious pennies. It's too late to remedy the evil. You can't pay them back."

"Of course," said Dan, lighting his pipe, "we couldn't hunt up every one of the duffers and hand 'em back the right change. There's an awful lot of 'em buying bread all the time. Funny taste they have—I never cared for bread especially, except for a toasted cracker with the Roquefort. But we might find a few of 'em and chuck some of dad's cash back where it came from. I'd feel better if I could. It seems tough for people to be held up for a soggy thing like bread. One wouldn't mind standing a rise in broiled lobsters or devilled crabs. Get to work and think, Ken. I want to pay back all of that money I can."

"There are plenty of charities," said Kenwitz mechanically.

"Easy enough," said Dan, in a cloud of smoke. "I suppose I could give the city a park, or endow an asparagus bed in a hospital. But I don't want Paul to get away with the proceeds of the gold brick we sold Peter. It's the bread shorts I want to cover, Ken."

The thin fingers of Kenwitz moved rapidly.

"Do you know how much money it would take to pay back the losses of consumers during that corner in flour?' he asked.

"I do not," said Dan stoutly. "My lawyer tells me that I have two millions."

"If you had a hundred millions," said Kenwitz vehemently "you couldn't repair a thousandth part of the damage that has been done. You cannot conceive of the accumulated evils produced by misapplied wealth. Each penny that was wrung from the lean purses of the poor reacted a thousand-fold to their harm. You do not understand. You do not see how hopeless is your desire to make restitution. Not in a single instance can it be done."

"Back up, philosopher!" said Dan. "The penny has no sorrow that the dollar cannot heal."

"Not in one instance," repeated Kenwitz. "I will give you one, and let us see. Thomas Boyne had a little bakery over there in Varick Street. He sold bread to the poorest people. When the price of flour went up he had to raise the price of bread. His customers were too poor to pay it, Boyne's business failed and he lost his $1,000 capital—all he had in the world."

Dan Kinsolving struck the park bench a mighty blow with his fist.

"I accept the instance," he cried. "Take me to Boyne. I will repay his thousand dollars and buy him a new bakery."

"Write your cheque," said Kenwitz, without moving, "and then begin to write cheques in payment of the train of consequences. Draw the next one for $50,000. Boyne went insane after his failure and set fire to the building from which he was about to be evicted. The loss amounted to that much. Boyne died in an asylum."

"Stick to the instance," said Dan. "I haven't noticed any insurance companies on my charity list."

"Draw your next cheque for $100,000," went on Kenwitz. "Boyne's son fell into bad ways after the bakery closed, and was accused of murder. He was acquitted last week after a three years' legal battle, and the State draws upon taxpayers for that much expense."

"Back to the bakery!" exclaimed Dan impatiently. "The Government doesn't need to stand in the bread line."

"The last item of the instance is—come and I will show you," said Kenwitz, rising.

The socialistic watchmaker was happy. He was a millionaire-baiter by nature and a pessimist by trade. Kenwitz would assure you in one breath that money was but evil and corruption, and that your brand-new watch needed cleaning and a new ratchet-wheel.

He conducted Kinsolving southward out of the square and into ragged, poverty-haunted Varick Street. Up the narrow stairway of a squalid brick tenement he led the penitent offspring of the Octopus. He knocked on a door, and a clear voice called to them to enter.

In that almost bare room a young woman sat sewing at a machine. She nodded to Kenwitz as to a familiar acquaintance. One little stream of sunlight through the dingy window burnished her heavy hair to the colour of an ancient Tuscan's shield. She flashed a rippling smile at Kenwitz and a look of somewhat flustered inquiry.

Kinsolving stood regarding her clear and pathetic beauty in heart-throbbing silence. Thus they came into the presence of the last item of the Instance.

"How many this week, Miss Mary?" asked the watchmaker. A mountain of coarse grey shirts lay upon the floor.

"Nearly thirty dozen," said the young woman cheerfully. "I've made almost $4. I'm improving, Mr. Kenwitz. I hardly know what to do with so much money." Her eyes turned, brightly soft, in the direction of Dan. A little pink spot came out on her round, pale cheek.

Kenwitz chuckled like a diabolic raven.

"Miss Boyne," he said, "let me present Mr. Kinsolving, the son of the man who put bread up five years ago. He thinks he would like to do something to aid those who were inconvenienced by that act."

The smile left the young woman's face. She rose and pointed her forefinger toward the door. This time she looked Kinsolving straight in the eye, but it was not a look that gave delight.

The two men went down into Varick Street. Kenwitz, letting all his pessimism and rancour and hatred of the Octopus come to the surface, gibed at the moneyed side of his friend in an acrid torrent of words. Dan appeared to be listening, and then turned to Kenwitz and shook hands with him warmly.

"I'm obliged to you, Ken, old man," he said vaguely—"a thousand times obliged."

"Mein Gott! you are crazy!" cried the watchmaker, dropping his spectacles for the first time in years.

Two months afterward Kenwitz went into a large bakery on lower Broadway with a pair of gold-rimmed eyeglasses that he had mended for the proprietor.

A lady was giving an order to a clerk as Kenwitz passed her.

"These loaves are ten cents," said the clerk.

"I always get them at eight cents up-town," said the lady. "You need not fill the order. I will drive by there on my way home."

The voice was familiar. The watchmaker paused.

"Mr. Kenwitz!" cried the lady heartily. "How do you do?"

Kenwitz was trying to train his socialistic and economic comprehension on her wonderful fur boa and the carriage waiting outside.

"Why, Miss Boyne!" he began.

"Mrs. Kinsolving," she corrected. "Dan and I were married a month ago."

2

A Cosmopolite in a Café

At midnight the café was crowded. By some chance the little table at which I sat had escaped the eye of incomers, and two vacant chairs at it extended their arms with venal hospitality to the influx of patrons.

And then a cosmopolite sat in one of them, and I was glad, for I held a theory that since Adam no true citizen of the world has existed. We hear of them, and we see foreign labels on much luggage, but we find travellers instead of cosmopolites.

I invoke your consideration of the scene—the marble-topped tables, the range of leather-upholstered wall seats, the gay company, the ladies dressed in demi-state toilets, speaking in an exquisite visible chorus of taste, economy, opulence or art, the sedulous and largess-loving *garçons*, the music wisely catering to all with its raids upon the composers; the *mélange* of talk and laughter—and, if you will, the Würzburger in the tall glass cones that bend to your lips as a ripe cherry sways on its branch to the beak of a robber jay. I was told by a sculptor from Mauch Chunk that the scene was truly Parisian.

My cosmopolite was named E. Rushmore Coglan, and he will be heard from next summer at Coney Island. He is to establish a new "attraction" there, he informed me, offering kingly diversion. And then his conversation rang along parallels of latitude and longitude. He took the great, round world in his hand, so to speak, familiarly, contemptuously, and it seemed no larger than the seed of a Maraschino cherry in a table-d'hôte grape fruit. He spoke disrespectfully of the equator, he skipped from continent to continent, he derided the zones, he mopped up the high seas with his napkin. With a wave of his hand he would speak of a certain bazaar in

Hyderabad. Whiff! He would have you on skis in Lapland. Zip! Now you rode the breakers with the Kanakas at Kealaikahiki. Presto! He dragged you through an Arkansas post-oak swamp, let you dry for a moment on the alkali plains of his Idaho ranch, then whirled you into the society of Viennese archdukes. Anon he would be telling you of a cold he acquired in a Chicago lake breeze and how old Escamila cured it in Buenos Ayres with a hot infusion of the *chuchula* weed. You would have addressed the letter to "E. Rushmore Coglan, Esq., the Earth, Solar System, the Universe," and have mailed it, feeling confident that it would be delivered to him.

I was sure that I had at last found the one true cosmopolite since Adam, and I listened to his world-wide discourse fearful lest I should discover in it the local note of the mere globe-trotter. But his opinions never fluttered or drooped; he was as impartial to cities, countries and continents as the winds or gravitation.

And as E. Rushmore Coglan prattled of this little planet I thought with glee of a great almost-cosmopolite who wrote for the whole world and dedicated himself to Bombay. In a poem he has to say that there is pride and rivalry between the cities of the earth, and that "the men that breed from them, they traffic up and down, but cling to their cities' hem as a child to the mother's gown." And whenever they walk "by roaring streets unknown" they remember their native city "most faithful, foolish, fond; making her mere-breathed name their bond upon their bond." And my glee was roused because I had caught Mr. Kipling napping. Here I had found a man not made from dust; one who had no narrow boasts of birthplace or country, one who, if he bragged at all, would brag of his whole round globe against the Martians and the inhabitants of the Moon.

Expression on these subjects was precipitated from E. Rushmore Coglan by the third corner to our table. While Coglan was describing to me the topography along the Siberian Railway the orchestra glided into a medley. The concluding air was "Dixie", and as the exhilarating notes tumbled forth they were almost overpowered by a great clapping of hands from almost every table.

It is worth a paragraph to say that this remarkable scene can be witnessed every evening in numerous cafés in the City of New York. Tons of brew have been consumed over theories to account for it. Some have conjectured hastily that all Southerners in town hie themselves to cafés at nightfall. This applause of the "rebel" air in a Northern city does puzzle a little; but it is not insolvable. The war with Spain, many years' generous mint and water-melon crops, a few long-shot winners at the New Orleans race-track, and the brilliant banquets given by the Indiana and Kansas citizens who compose the North Carolina Society, have made the South rather a "fad" in Manhattan. Your manicure will lisp softly that your left forefinger reminds her so much of a gentleman's in Richmond, Va. Oh, certainly; but many a lady has to work now—the war, you know.

When "Dixie" was being played a dark-haired young man sprang up from somewhere with a Mosby guerrilla yell and waved frantically his soft-brimmed hat. Then he strayed through the smoke, dropped into the vacant chair at our table and pulled out cigarettes.

The evening was at the period when reserve is thawed. One of us mentioned three Würzburgers to the waiter; the dark-haired young man acknowledged his inclusion in the order by a smile and a nod. I hastened to ask him a question because I wanted to try out a theory I had.

"Would you mind telling me," I began, "whether you are from——"

The fist of E. Rushmore Coglan banged the table and I was jarred into silence.

"Excuse me," said he, "but that's a question I never like to hear asked. What does it matter where a man is from? Is it fair to judge a man by his post-office address? Why, I've seen Kentuckians who hated whisky, Virginians who weren't descended from Pocahontas, Indianians who hadn't written a novel, Mexicans who didn't wear velvet trousers with silver dollars sewed along the seams, funny Englishmen, spend-thrift Yankees, cold-blooded Southerners, narrow-minded

Westerners, and New Yorkers who were too busy to stop for an hour on the street to watch a one-armed grocer's clerk do up cranberries in paper bags. Let a man be a man and don't handicap him with the label of any section."

"Pardon me," I said, "but my curiosity was not altogether an idle one. I know the South, and when the band plays 'Dixie' I like to observe. I have formed the belief that the man who applauds that air with special violence and ostensible sectional loyalty is invariably a native of either Secaucus, N.J., or the district between Murray Hill Lyceum and the Harlem River, this city. I was about to put my opinion to the test by inquiring of this gentleman when you interrupted with your own—larger theory, I must confess."

And now the dark-haired young man spoke to me, and it became evident that his mind also moved along its own set of grooves.

"I should like to be a periwinkle," said he, mysteriously, "on the top of a valley, and sing too-ralloo-ralloo."

This was clearly too obscure, so I turned again to Coglan.

"I've been around the world twelve times," said he. "I know an Esquimau in Upernavik who sends to Cincinnati for his neckties, and I saw a goat-herder in Uruguay who won a prize in a Battle Creek breakfast-food puzzle competition. I pay rent on a room in Cairo, Egypt, and another in Yokohama all the year round. I've got slippers waiting for me in a tea-house in Shanghai, and I don't have to tell 'em how to cook my eggs in Rio de Janeiro or Seattle. It's a mighty little old world. What's the use of bragging about being from the North, or the South, or the old manor-house in the dale, or Euclid Avenue, Cleveland, or Pike's Peak, or Fairfax County, Va., or Hooligan's Flats or any place? It'll be a better world when we quit being fools about some mildewed town or ten acres of swampland just because we happened to be born there."

"You seem to be a genuine cosmopolite," I said admiringly. "But it also seems that you would decry patriotism."

"A relic of the stone age," declared Coglan warmly. "We are all brothers—Chinamen, Englishmen, Zulus, Patagonians, and the people in the bend of the Kaw River. Some day all this petty pride in one's city or state or section or country will be wiped out, and we'll all be citizens of the world, as we ought to be."

"But while you are wandering in foreign lands," I persisted, "do not your thoughts revert to some spot—some dear and——"

"Nary a spot," interrupted E. R. Coglan flippantly. "The terrestrial, globular, planetary hunk of matter, slightly flattened at the poles, and known as the Earth, is my abode. I've met a good many object-bound citizens of this country abroad. I've seen men from Chicago sit in a gondola in Venice on a moonlight night and brag about their drainage canal. I've seen a Southerner on being introduced to the King of England hand that monarch, without batting his eyes, the information that his grand-aunt on his mother's side was related by marriage to the Perkinses, of Charleston. I knew a New Yorker who was kidnapped for ransom by some Afghanistan bandits. His people sent over the money and he came back to Kabul with the agent. 'Afghanistan?' the natives said to him through an interpreter. 'Well, not so slow, do you think?' 'Oh, I don't know,' says he, and he begins to tell them about a cab-driver at Sixth Avenue and Broadway. Those ideas don't suit me. I'm not tied down to anything that isn't 8,000 miles in diameter. Just put me down as E. Rushmore Coglan, citizen of the terrestrial sphere."

My cosmopolite made a large adieu and left me, for he thought that he saw someone through the chatter and smoke whom he knew. So I was left with the would-be periwinkle, who was reduced to Würzburger without further ability to voice his aspirations to perch, melodious, upon the summit of a valley.

I sat reflecting upon my evident cosmopolite and wondering how the poet had managed to miss him. He was my discovery and I believed in him. How was it? "The men that breed from them they traffic up and down, but cling to their cities' hem as a child to the mother's gown."

Not so E. Rushmore Coglan. With the whole world for his——

My meditations were interrupted by a tremendous noise

and conflict in another part of the café. I saw above the heads of the seated patrons E. Rushmore Coglan and a stranger to me engaged in terrific battle. They fought between the tables like Titans, and glasses crashed, and men caught their hats up and were knocked down, and a brunette screamed, and a blonde began to sing "Teasing".

My cosmopolite was sustaining the pride and reputation of the Earth when the waiters closed in on both combatants with their famous flying wedge formation and bore them outside, still resisting.

I called McCarthy, one of the French *garçons*, and asked him the cause of the conflict.

"The man with the red tie" (that was my cosmopolite), said he, "got hot on account of things said about the bum sidewalks and water supply of the place he come from by the other guy."

"Why," said I, bewildered, "that man is a citizen of the world—a cosmopolite. He——"

"Originally from Mattawamkeag, Maine, he said," continued McCarthy, "and he wouldn't stand for no knockin' the place."

3

The Brief Début of Tildy

If you do not know Bogle's Chop House and Family Restaurant it is your loss. For if you are one of the fortunate ones who dine expensively you should be interested to know how the other half consumes provisions. And if you belong to the half to whom waiters' checks are things of moment, you should know Bogle's, for there you get your money's worth—in quantity, at least.

Bogle's is situated in that highway of *bourgeoisie*, that boulevard of Brown-Jones-and-Robinson, Eighth Avenue. There are two rows of tables in the room, six in each row. On each table is a castor-stand, containing cruets of condiments and seasons. From the pepper cruet you may shake a cloud of something tasteless and melancholy, like volcanic dust. From the salt cruet you may expect nothing. Though a man should extract a sanguinary stream from the pallid turnip, yet will his prowess be balked when he comes to wrest salt from Bogle's cruets. Also upon each table stands the counterfeit of that benign sauce made "from the recipe of a nobleman in India."

At the cashier's desk sits Bogle, cold, sordid, slow, smouldering, and takes your money. Behind a mountain of toothpicks he makes your change, files your check, and ejects at you, like a toad, a word about the weather. Beyond a corroboration of his meteorological statement you would better not venture. You are not Bogle's friend; you are a fed, transient customer, and you and he may not meet again until the blowing of Gabriel's dinner horn. So take your change and go—to the devil if you like. There you have Bogle's sentiments.

The needs of Bogle's customers were supplied by two waitresses and a Voice. One of the waitresses was named

Aileen. She was tall, beautiful, lively, gracious and learned in persiflage. Her other name? There was no more necessity for another name at Bogle's than there was for finger-bowls.

The name of the other waitress was Tildy. Why do you suggest Matilda? Please listen this time—Tildy—Tildy. Tildy was dumpy, plain-faced, and too anxious to please to please. Repeat the last clause to yourself once or twice, and make the acquaintance of the duplicate infinite.

The Voice at Bogle's was invisible. It came from the kitchen, and did not shine in the way of originality. It was a heathen Voice, and contented itself with vain repetitions of exclamations emitted by the waitresses concerning food.

Will it tire you to be told again that Aileen was beautiful? Had she donned a few hundred dollars' worth of clothes and joined the Easter parade, and had you seen her, you would have hastened to say so yourself.

The customers at Bogle's were her slaves. Six tables full she could wait upon at once. They who were in a hurry restrained their impatience for the joy of merely gazing upon her swiftly moving, graceful figure. They who had finished eating ate more that they might continue in the light of her smiles. Every man there—and they were mostly men—tried to make his impression upon her.

Aileen could successfully exchange repartee against a dozen at once. And every smile that she sent forth lodged, like pellets from a scatter-gun, in as many hearts. And all this while she would be performing astounding feats with orders of pork and beans, pot roasts, ham-and, sausage-and-the-wheats, and any quantity of things on the iron and in the pan and straight up and on the side. With all this feasting and flirting and merry exchange of wit Bogle's came mighty near being a salon, with Aileen for its Madame Récamier.

If the transients were entranced by the fascinating Aileen, the regulars were her adorers. There was much rivalry among many of the steady customers. Aileen could have had an engagement every evening. At least twice a week someone took her to a theatre or to a dance. One stout gentleman whom she and Tildy had privately christened "The Hog" presented her with a turquoise ring. Another one known as

"Freshy," who rode on the Traction Company's repair wagon, was going to give her a poodle as soon as his brother got the hauling contract in the Ninth. And the man who always ate spareribs and spinach and said he was a stockbroker asked her to go to "Parsifal" with him.

"I don't know where this place is," said Aileen while talking it over with Tildy, "but the wedding-ring's got to be on before I put a stitch into a travelling dress—ain't that right? Well, I guess!"

But, Tildy!

In steaming, chattering, cabbage-scented Bogle's there was almost a heart tragedy. Tildy with the blunt nose, the hay-coloured hair, the freckled skin, the bag-o'-meal figure, had never had an admirer. Not a man followed her with his eyes when she went to and fro in the restaurant save now and then when they glared with the beast-hunger for food. None of them bantered her gaily to coquettish interchanges of wit. None of them loudly "jollied" her of mornings as they did Aileen, accusing her, when the eggs were slow in coming, of late hours in the company of envied swains. No one had ever given her a turquoise ring or invited her upon a voyage to mysterious distant "Parsifal".

Tildy was a good waitress, and the men tolerated her. They who sat at her tables spoke to her briefly with quotations from the bill of fare; and then raised their voices in honeyed and otherwise-flavoured accents, eloquently addressed to the fair Aileen. They writhed in their chairs to gaze around and over the impending form of Tildy, that Aileen's pulchritude might season and make ambrosia of their bacon and eggs.

And Tildy was content to be the unwooed drudge if Aileen could receive the flattery and the homage. The blunt nose was loyal to the short Grecian. She was Aileen's friend; and she was glad to see her rule hearts and wean the attention of men from smoking pot-pie and lemon meringue. But deep below our freckles and hay-coloured hair the unhandsomest of us dream of a prince or a princess, not vicarious, but coming to us alone.

There was a morning when Aileen tripped in to work with

a slightly bruised eye; and Tildy's solicitude was almost enough to heal any optic.

"Fresh guy," explained Aileen, "last night as I was going home at Twenty-third and Sixth. Sashayed up, so he did, and made a break. I turned him down, cold, and he made a sneak; but followed me down to Eighteenth, and tried his hot air again. Gee! but I slapped him a good one, side of the face. Then he give me that eye. Does it look real awful, Til? I should hate that Mr. Nicholson should see it when he comes in for his tea and toast at ten."

Tildy listened to the adventure with breathless admiration. No man had ever tried to follow her. She was safe abroad at any hour of the twenty-four. What bliss it must have been to have had a man follow one and black one's eye for love!

Among the customers at Bogle's was a young man named Seeders, who worked in a laundry office. Mr. Seeders was thin and had light hair, and appeared to have been recently rough-dried and starched. He was too diffident to aspire to Aileen's notice; so he usually sat at one of Tildy's tables, where he devoted himself to silence and boiled weakfish.

One day when Mr. Seeders came in to dinner he had been drinking beer. There were only two or three customers in the restaurant. When Mr. Seeders had finished his weakfish he got up, put his arm around Tildy's waist, kissed her loudly and impudently, walked out upon the street, snapped his fingers in the direction of the laundry, and hied himself to play pennies in the slot machines at the Amusement Arcade.

For a few moments Tildy stood petrified. Then she was aware of Aileen shaking at her an arch forefinger, and saying:

"Why, Til, you naughty girl! Ain't you getting to be awful, Miss Slyboots! First thing I know you'll be stealing some of my fellows. I must keep an eye on you, my lady."

Another thing dawned upon Tildy's recovering wits. In a moment she had advanced from a hopeless, lowly admirer to be an Eve-sister of the potent Aileen. She herself was now a man-charmer, a mark for Cupid, a Sabine who must be coy when the Romans were at their banquet boards. Man had found her waist achievable and her lips desirable. The sudden and amatory Seeders had, as it were, performed for her a miraculous piece of one-day laundry-work. He had taken the sackcloth of her uncomeliness, had washed, dried, starched and ironed it, and returned it to her sheer embroidered lawn—the robe of Venus herself.

The freckles on Tildy's cheeks merged into a rosy flush. Now both Circe and Psyche peeped from her brightened eyes. Not even Aileen herself had been publicly embraced and kissed in the restaurant.

Tildy could not keep the delightful secret. When trade was slack she went and stood at Bogle's desk. Her eyes were shining; she tried not to let her words sound proud and boastful.

"A gentleman insulted me to-day," she said. "He hugged me around the waist and kissed me."

"That so?" said Bogle, cracking open his business armour. "After this week you get a dollar a week more."

At the next regular meal when Tildy set food before customers with whom she had acquaintance she said to each of them modestly, as one whose merit needed no bolstering:

"A gentleman insulted me to-day in the restaurant. He put his arm around my waist and kissed me."

The diners accepted the revelation in various ways—some incredulously, some with congratulations; others turned upon her the stream of badinage that had hitherto been directed at Aileen alone. And Tildy's heart swelled in her bosom, for she saw at last the towers of Romance rise above the horizon of the grey plain in which she had for so long travelled.

For two days Mr. Seeders came not again. During that time Tildy established herself firmly as a woman to be wooed. She bought ribbons, and arranged her hair like Aileen's, and tightened her waist two inches. She had a thrilling but delightful fear that Mr. Seeders would rush in suddenly and shoot her with a pistol. He must have loved her desperately; and impulsive lovers are always blindly jealous.

Even Aileen had not been shot at with a pistol. And then Tildy rather hoped that he would not shoot at her, for she was always loyal to Aileen; and she did not want to overshadow her friend.

At four o'clock on the afternoon of the third day Mr. Seeders came in. There were no customers at the tables. At the back end of the restaurant Tildy was refilling the mustard pots and Aileen was quartering pies. Mr. Seeders walked back to where they stood.

Tildy looked up and saw him, gasped, and pressed the mustard spoon upon her heart. A red hairbow was in her hair; she wore Venus's Eighth Avenue badge, the blue bead necklace with the swinging silver symbolic heart.

Mr. Seeders was flushed and embarrassed. He plunged one hand into his hip pocket and the other into a fresh pumpkin pie.

"Miss Tildy," said he, "I want to apologize for what I done the other evenin'. Tell you the truth, I was pretty well tanked up or I wouldn't of done it. I wouldn't do no lady that a-way when I was sober. So I hope, Miss Tildy, you'll accept my 'pology, and believe that I wouldn't of done it if I'd known what I was doin' and hadn't of been drunk."

With this handsome plea Mr. Seeders backed away, and departed, feeling that reparation had been made.

But behind the convenient screen Tildy had thrown herself flat upon a table among the butter chips and the coffee cups, and was sobbing her heart out—out and back again to the grey plain wherein travel they with blunt noses and hay-coloured hair. From her knot she had torn the red hair-bow and cast it upon the floor. Seeders she despised utterly; she had but taken his kiss as that of a pioneer and prophetic prince who might have set the clocks going and the pages to running in fairyland. But the kiss had been maudlin and unmeant; the court had not stirred at the false alarm; she must for evermore remain the Sleeping Beauty.

Yet not all was lost. Aileen's arm was around her; and Tildy's red hand groped among the butter chips till it found the warm grasp of her friend's.

"Don't you fret, Til," said Aileen, who did not understand entirely. "That turnip-faced little clothes-pin of a Seeders ain't worth it. He ain't anything of a gentleman or he wouldn't ever of apologized."

4

Telemachus, Friend

RETURNING from a hunting trip, I waited at the little town of Los Piños, in New Mexico, for the south-bound train, which was one hour late. I sat on the porch of the Summit House and discussed the functions of life with Telemachus Hicks, the hotel proprietor.

Perceiving that personalities were not out of order, I asked him what species of beast had long ago twisted and mutilated his left ear. Being a hunter, I was concerned in the evils that may befall one in the pursuit of game.

"That ear," said Hicks, "is the relic of true friendship."

"An accident?" I persisted.

"No friendship is an accident," said Telemachus; and I was silent.

"The only perfect case of true friendship I ever knew," went on my host, "was a cordial intent between a Connecticut man and a monkey. The monkey climbed palms in Barranquilla and threw down coconuts to the man. The man sawed them in two and made dippers, which he sold for two *reales* each and bought rum. The monkey drank the milk of the nuts. Through each being satisfied with his own share of the graft, they lived like brothers.

"But in the case of human beings, friendship is a transitory art, subject to discontinuance without further notice.

"I had a friend once, of the entitlement of Paisley Fish, that I imagined was sealed to me for an endless space of time. Side by side for seven years we had mined, ranched, sold patent churns, herded sheep, took photographs and other things, built wire fences, and picked prunes. Thinks I, neither homicide nor flattery nor riches nor sophistry nor drink can make trouble between me and Paisley Fish. We was friends an amount you could hardly guess at. We was friends in business, and we let our amicable qualities lap over and season our hours of recreation and folly. We certainly had days of Damon and nights of Pythias.

"One summer me and Paisley gallops down into these San Andrés mountains for the purpose of a month's surcease and levity, dressed in the natural store habiliments of man. We hit this town of Los Piños, which certainly was a roof-garden spot of the world, and flowing with condensed milk and honey. It had a street or two, and air, and hens, and a eating-house; and that was enough for us.

"We strikes the town after supper-time, and we concludes to sample whatever efficacy there is in this eating-house down by the railroad tracks. By the time we had set down and pried up our plates with a knife from the red oil-cloth, along intrudes Widow Jessup with the hot biscuit and the fried liver.

"Now, there was a woman that would have tempted an anchovy to forget his vows. She was not so small as she was large; and a kind of welcome air seemed to mitigate her vicinity. The pink of her face was the *in hoc signo* of a culinary temper and a warm disposition, and her smile would have brought out the dogwood blossoms in December.

"Widow Jessup talks to us a lot of garrulousness about the climate and history and Tennyson and prunes and the scarcity of mutton, and finally wants to know where we came from.

"'Spring Valley,' says I.

"'Big Spring Valley,' chips in Paisley, out of a lot of potatoes and knuckle-bone of ham in his mouth.

"That was the first sign I noticed that the old *fidus Diogenes* business between me and Paisley Fish was ended for ever. He knew how I hated a talkative person, and yet he stampedes into the conversation with his amendments and addendums of syntax. On the map it was Big Spring Valley; but I had heard Paisley himself call it Spring Valley a thousand times.

"Without saying any more, we went out after supper and set on the railroad track. We had been pardners too long not to know what was going on in each other's mind.

"'I reckon you understand,' says Paisley, 'that I've made up my mind to accrue that widow woman as part and parcel in and to my hereditaments for ever, both domestic, sociable, legal, and otherwise, until death us do part.'

"'Why, yes,' says I. 'I read it between the lines, though you only spoke one. And I suppose you are aware,' says I, 'that I have a movement on foot that leads up to the widow's changing her name to Hicks, and leaves you writing to the society column to inquire whether the best man wears a japonica or seamless socks at the wedding!'

"'There'll be some hiatuses in your programme,' says Paisley, chewing up a piece of a railroad tie. 'I'd give in to you,' says he, 'in 'most any respect if it was secular affairs, but this is not so. The smiles of woman,' goes on Paisley, 'is the whirlpool of Squills and Chalybeates, into which vortex the good ship Friendship is often drawn and dismembered. I'd assault a bear that was annoying you,' says Paisley, 'or I'd endorse your note, or rub the place between your shoulder-blades with opodeldoc the same as ever; but there my sense of etiquette ceases. In this fracas with Mrs. Jessup we play it alone. I've notified you fair.'

"And then I collaborates with myself, and offers the following resolutions and bye-laws—

"'Friendship between man and man,' says I, 'is an ancient historical virtue enacted in the days when men had to protect each other against lizards with eighty-foot tails and flying turtles. And they've kept up the habit to this day, and stand by each other till the bellboy comes up and tells them the animals are not really there. I've often heard,' I says, 'about ladies stepping in and breaking up a friendship between men. Why should that be? I'll tell you, Paisley, the first sight and hot biscuit of Mrs. Jessup appears to have inserted a oscillation into each of our bosoms. Let the best man of us have her. I'll play you a square game, and won't do any underhanded work. I'll do all of my courting of her in your presence, so you will have an equal opportunity. With that arrangement I don't see why our steamboat of friendship should fall overboard in the medicinal whirlpools you speak of, whichever of us wins out.'

"'Good old hoss!' says Paisley, shaking my hand. 'And I'll do the same,' says he. 'We'll court the lady synonymously, and without any of the prudery and bloodshed usual to such occasions. And we'll be friends still, win or lose.'

"At one side of Mrs. Jessup's eating-house was a bench under some trees where she used to sit in the breeze after the south-bound had been fed and gone. And there me and Paisley used to congregate after supper and make partial payments on our respects to the lady of our choice. And we was so honourable and circuitous in our calls that if one of us got there first we waited for the other before beginning any gallivantery.

"The first evening that Mrs. Jessup knew about our arrangement I got to the bench before Paisley did. Supper was just over, and Mrs. Jessup was out there with a fresh pink dress on, and almost cool enough to handle.

"I sat down by her and made a few specifications about the moral surface of nature as set forth by the landscape and the contiguous perspective. That evening was surely a case in point. The moon was attending to business in the section of sky where it belonged, and the trees was making shadows on the ground according to science and nature, and there was a kind of conspicuous hullabaloo going on in the bushes between the bullbats and the orioles and the jack-rabbits and other feathered insects of the forest. And the wind out of the mountains was singing like a jew's harp in the pile of old tomato cans by the railroad track.

"I felt a kind of sensation in my left side—something like dough rising up in a crock by the fire. Mrs. Jessup had moved up closer.

"'Oh, Mr. Hicks,' says she, 'when one is alone in the world, don't they feel it more aggravated on a beautiful night like this?'

"I rose up off of the bench at once.

"'Excuse me, ma'am,' says I, 'but I'll have to wait till Paisley comes before I can give a audible hearing to leading questions like that.'

"And then I explained to her how we was friends cinctured by years of embarrassment and travel and complicity, and how we had agreed to take no advantage of each other in any of the more mushy walks of life, such as might be fomented by sentiment and proximity. Mrs. Jessup appears to think serious about the matter for a minute, and then she breaks into a species of laughter that makes the wild-wood resound.

"In a few minutes Paisley drops around, with oil of bergamot on his hair, and sits on the other side of Mrs. Jessup, and inaugurates a sad tale of adventure in which him and Pieface Lumley has a skinning match of dead cows in '95 for a silver-mounted saddle in the Santa Rita valley during the nine months' drought.

"Now, from the start of that courtship I had Paisley Fish hobbled and tied to a post. Each one of us had a different system of reaching out for the easy places in the female heart. Paisley's scheme was to petrify 'em with wonderful relations of events that he had either come across personally or in large print. I think he must have got his idea of subjugation from one of Shakespeare's shows I see once called *Othello*. There is a coloured man in it who acquires a duke's daughter by disbursing to her a mixture of the talk turned out by Rider Haggard, Lew Dockstader, and Dr. Parkhurst. But that style of courting don't work well off the stage.

"Now, I give you my own recipe for inveigling a woman into that state of affairs when she can be referred to as '*née* Jones.' Learn how to pick up her hand and hold it, and she's yours. It ain't so easy. Some men grab at it so much like they was going to set a dislocation of the shoulder that you can smell the arnica and hear 'em tearing off bandages. Some take it up like a hot horseshoe, and hold it off at arm's length like a druggist pouring tincture of asafoetida in a bottle. And most of 'em catch hold of it and drag it right out before the lady's eyes like a boy finding a baseball in the grass, without giving her a chance to forget that the hand is growing on the end of her arm. Them ways are all wrong.

"I'll tell you the right way. Did you ever see a man sneak out in the back yard and pick up a rock to throw at a tomcat that was sitting on a fence looking at him? He pretends he hasn't got a thing in his hand, and that the cat don't see him, and that he don't see the cat. That's the idea. Never drag her hand out where she'll have to take notice of it. Don't let her know that you think she knows you have the least idea she is aware you are holding her hand. That was my rule of tactics; and as far as Paisley's serenade about hostilities and misadventure went, he might as well have been reading to her a time-table of the Sunday trains that stop at Ocean Grove, New Jersey.

"One night when I beat Paisley to the bench by one pipeful, my friendship gets subsidized for a minute, and I asks Mrs. Jessup if she didn't think a 'H' was easier to write than a 'J'. In a second her head was mashing the oleander flower in my buttonhole, and I leaned over and—but I didn't.

"'If you don't mind,' says I, standing up, 'we'll wait for Paisley to come before finishing this. I've never done anything dishonourable yet to our friendship, and this won't be quite fair.'

"'Mr. Hicks,' says Mrs. Jessup, looking at me peculiar in the dark, 'if it wasn't for but one thing, I'd ask you to hike yourself down the gulch and never disresume your visits to my house.'

"'And what is that, ma'am?' I asks.

"You are too good a friend not to make a good husband,' says she.

"In five minutes Paisley was on his side of Mrs. Jessup.

"'In Silver City, in the summer of '98,' he begins, 'I see Jim Bartholomew chew off a Chinaman's ear in the *Blue Light Saloon* on account of a cross-barred muslin shirt that—what was that noise?'

"I had resumed matters again with Mrs. Jessup right where we had left off.

"'Mrs. Jessup,' says I, 'has promised to make it Hicks. And this is another of the same sort.'

"Paisley winds his feet around a leg of the bench and kind of groans.

"'Lem,' says he, 'we been friends for seven years. Would you mind not kissing Mrs. Jessup quite so loud? I'd do the same for you.'

"'All right,' says I. 'The other kind will do as well.'

"'This Chinaman,' goes on Paisley, 'was the one that

shot a man named Mullins in the spring of '97, and that was——'

"Paisley interrupted himself again.

"'Lem,' says he, 'if you was a true friend you wouldn't hug Mrs. Jessup quite so hard. I felt the bench shake all over just then. You know you told me you would give me an even chance as long as there was any.'

"'Mr. Man,' says Mrs. Jessup, turning around to Paisley, 'if you was to drop in to the celebration of mine and Mr. Hick's silver wedding, twenty-five years from now, do you think you could get it into that Hubbard squash you call your head that you are *nix cum rous* in this business? I've put up with you a long time because you was Mr. Hicks's friend; but it seems to me it's time for you to wear the willow and trot off down the hill.'

"'Mrs. Jessup,' says I, without losing my grasp on the situation as fiancé, 'Mr. Paisley is my friend, and I offered him a square deal and a equal opportunity as long as there was a chance.'

"'A chance!' says she. 'Well, he may think he has a chance; but I hope he won't think he's got a cinch, after what he's been next to all the evening.'

"Well, a month afterward me and Mrs. Jessup was married in the Los Piños Methodist Church; and the whole town closed up to see the performance.

"When we lined up in front, and the preacher was beginning to sing out his rituals and observances, I looks around and misses Paisley. I calls time on the preacher. 'Paisley ain't here,' says I. 'We've got to wait for Paisley. A friend once, a friend always—that's Telemachus Hicks,' says I. Mrs. Jessup's eyes snapped some; but the preacher holds up the incantations according to instructions.

"In a few minutes Paisley gallops up the aisle, putting on a cuff as he comes. He explains that the only dry-goods store in town was closed for the wedding, and he couldn't get the kind of a boiled shirt that his taste called for until he had broke open the back window of the store and helped himself. Then he ranges up on the other side of the bride, and the wedding goes on. I always imagined that Paisley calculated as a last chance that the preacher might marry him to the widow by mistake.

"After the proceedings was over we had tea and jerked antelope and canned apricots, and then the populace hiked itself away. Last of all Paisley shook me by the hand and told me I'd acted square and on the level with him, and he was proud to call me a friend.

"The preacher had a small house on the side of the street that he'd fixed up to rent; and he allowed me and Mrs. Hicks to occupy it till the ten-forty train the next morning, when we was going on a bridal tour to El Paso. His wife had decorated it all up with hollyhocks and poison ivy, and it looked real festal and bowery.

"About ten o'clock that night I sets down in the front door and pulls off my boots a while in the cool breeze, while Mrs. Hicks was fixing around in the room. Right soon the light went out inside; and I sat there a while reverberating over old times and scenes. And then I heard Mrs. Hicks call out, 'Ain't you coming in soon, Lem?'

"'Well, well!' says I, kind of rousing up. 'Durn me if I wasn't waiting for old Paisley to——'

"But when I got that far," concluded Telemachus Hicks, "I thought somebody had shot this left ear of mine off with a forty-five. But it turned out to be only a lick from a broom-handle in the hands of Mrs. Hicks."

5

The Handbook of Hymen

'TIS the opinion of myself, Sanderson Pratt, who sets this down, that the educational system of the United States should be in the hands of the weather bureau. I can give you good reasons for it; and you can't tell me why our college professors shouldn't be transferred to the meteorological department. They have been learned to read; and they could very easily glance at the morning papers and then wire in to the main office what kind of weather to expect. But there's the other side of the proposition. I am going on to tell you how the weather furnished me and Idaho Green with a elegant education.

We was up in the Bitter Root Mountains over the Montana line prospecting for gold. A chin-whiskered man in Walla-Walla, carrying a line of hope as excess baggage, had grubstaked us; and there we was in the foothills pecking away, enough grub on hand to last an army through a peace conference.

Along one day comes a mail-rider over the mountains from Carlos, and stops to eat three cans of greengages, and leave us a newspaper of modern date. This paper prints a system of premonitions of the weather, and the card it dealt Bitter Root Mountains from the bottom of the deck was "warmer and fair, with light westerly breezes."

That evening it began to snow, with the wind strong in the east. Me and Idaho moved camp into an old empty cabin higher up the mountain, thinking it was only a November flurry. But after falling three foot on a level it went to work in earnest; and we knew we was snowed in. We got in plenty of firewood before it got deep, and we had grub enough for two months, so we let the elements rage and cut up all they thought proper.

If you want to instigate the art of manslaughter just shut two men up in a eighteen by twenty-foot cabin for a month. Human nature won't stand it.

When the first snowflakes fell me and Idaho Green laughed at each other's jokes and praised the stuff we turned out of a skillet and called bread. At the end of three weeks Idaho makes this kind of a edict to me. Says he—

"I never exactly heard sour milk dropping out of a balloon on the bottom of a tin pan, but I have an idea it would be music of the spears compared to this attenuated stream of asphyxiated thought that emanates out of your organs of conversation. The kind of half-masticated noises that you emit every day puts me in mind of a cow's cud, only she's lady enough to keep hers to herself, and you ain't."

"Mr. Green," says I, "you having been a friend of mine once, I have some hesitations in confessing to you that if I had my choice for society between you and a common yellow, three-legged cur pup, one of the inmates of this here cabin would be wagging a tail just at present."

This way we goes on for two or three days, and then we quits speaking to one another. We divides up the cooking implements, and Idaho cooks his grub on one side of the fireplace and me on the other. The snow is up to the windows, and we have to keep a fire all day.

You see me and Idaho never had any education beyond reading and doing "if John had three apples and James five" on a slate. We never felt any special need for a university degree, though we had acquired a species of intrinsic intelligence in knocking around the world that we could use in emergencies. But, snow-bound in that cabin in the Bitter Roots, we felt for the first time that if we had studied Homer or Greek and fractions and the higher branches of information we'd have had some resources in the line of meditation and private thought. I've seen them Eastern college fellows working in camps all through the West, and I never noticed but what education was less of a drawback to 'em than you would think. Why, once over on Snake River, when Andrew McWilliam's saddlehorse got the botts, he sent a buckboard ten miles for one of these strangers that claimed to be a botanist. But that horse died.

One morning Idaho was poking around with a stick on top of a little shelf that was too high to reach. Two books fell down to the floor. I started toward 'em, but caught Idaho's eye. He speaks for the first time in a week.

"Don't burn your fingers," says he. "In spite of the fact that you're only fit to be the companion of a sleeping mud-turtle, I'll give you a square deal. And that's more than your parents did when they turned you loose in the world with the sociability of a rattlesnake and the bedside manner of a frozen turnip. I'll play you a game of seven-up, the winner to pick up his choice of the books, the loser to take the other."

We played; and Idaho won. He picked up his book, and I took mine. Then each of us got on his side of the house and went to reading.

I never was as glad to see a ten-ounce nugget as I was that book. And Idaho looked at his like a kid looks at a stick of candy.

Mine was a little book about five by six inches called *Herkimer's Handbook of Indispensable Information.* I may be wrong, but I think that was the greatest book that ever was written. I've got it to-day; and I can stump you or any man fifty times in five minutes with the information in it. Talk about Solomon or the New York *Tribune*! Herkimer had cases on both of 'em. That man must have put in fifty years and travelled a million miles to find out all that stuff. There was the population of all cities in it, and the way to tell a girl's age, and the number of teeth a camel has. It told you the longest tunnel in the world, the number of the stars, how long it takes for chicken-pox to break out, what a lady's neck ought to measure, the veto powers of Governors, the dates of the Roman aqueducts, how many pounds of rice going without three beers a day would buy, the average annual temperature of Augusta, Maine, the quantity of seed required to plant an acre of carrots in drills, antidotes for poisons, the number of hairs on a blonde lady's head, how to preserve eggs, the height of all the mountains in the world, and the dates of all wars and battles, and how to restore drowned persons, and sunstroke, and the number of tacks in a pound, and how to make dynamite and flowers and beds, and what to do before the doctor comes—and a hundred times as many things besides. If there was anything Herkimer didn't know I didn't miss it out of the book.

I sat and read that book for four hours. All the wonders of education was compressed in it. I forgot the snow, and I forgot that me and old Idaho was on the outs. He was sitting still on a stool reading away with a kind of partly soft and partly mysterious look shining through his tan-bark whiskers.

"Idaho," says I, "what kind of a book is yours?"

Idaho must have forgot, too, for he answered moderate, without any slander or malignity.

"Why," says he, "this here seems to be a volume by Homer K. M."

"Homer K. M. what?" I asks.

"Why, just Homer K. M.," says he.

"You're a liar," says I, a little riled that Idaho should try to put me up a tree. "No man is going round signing books with his initials. If it's Homer K. M. Spoopendyke, or Homer K. M. McSweeney, or Homer K. M. Jones, why don't you say so like a man instead of biting off the end of it like a calf chewing off the tail of a shirt on a clothes-line?"

"I put it to you straight, Sandy," says Idaho, quiet. "It's a poem book," says he, "by Homer K. M. I couldn't get colour out of it at first, but there's a vein if you follow it up. I wouldn't have missed this book for a pair of red blankets."

"You're welcome to it," says I. "What I want is a disinterested statement of facts for the mind to work on, and that's what I seem to find in the book I've drawn."

"What you've got," says Idaho, "is statistics, the lowest grade of information that exists. They'll poison your mind. Give me old K. M.'s system of surmises. He seems to be a kind of a wine agent. His regular toast is 'nothing doing', and he seems to have a grouch, but he keeps it so well lubricated with booze that his worst kicks sound like an invitation to split a quart. But it's poetry," says Idaho, "and I have sensations of scorn for that truck of yours that tries to convey sense in feet and inches. When it comes to explaining the instinct of philosophy through the art of nature, old K. M. has got your man beat by drills, rows, paragraphs, chest measurement, and average annual rainfall."

So that's the way me and Idaho had it. Day and night all the excitement we got was studying our books. That snowstorm sure fixed us with a fine lot of attainments apiece. By the time the snow melted, if you had stepped up to me suddenly and said: "Sanderson Pratt, what would it cost per square foot to lay a roof with twenty by twenty-eight tin at nine dollars and fifty cents per box?" I'd have told you as quick as light could travel the length of a spade-handle at the rate of one hundred and ninety-two thousand miles per second. How many can do it? You wake up 'most any man you know in the middle of the night, and ask him quick to tell you the number of bones in the human skeleton exclusive of the teeth, or what percentage of the vote of the Nebraska Legislature overrules a veto. Will he tell you? Try him and see.

About what benefit Idaho got out of his poetry book I didn't exactly know. Idaho boosted the wine agent every time he opened his mouth; but I wasn't so sure.

This Homer K. M., from what leaked out of his libretto through Idaho, seemed to me to be a kind of a dog who looked at life like it was a tin can tied to his tail. After running himself half to death, he sits down, hangs his tongue out, and looks at the can and says—

"Oh, well, since we can't shake the growler, let's get it filled at the corner, and all have a drink on me."

Besides that, it seems he was a Persian; and I never hear of Persia producing anything worth mentioning unless it was Turkish rugs and Maltese cats.

That spring me and Idaho struck pay ore. It was a habit of ours to sell out quick and keep moving. We unloaded on our grubstaker for eight thousand dollars apiece; and then we drifted down to this little town of Rosa, on the Salmon River, to rest up, and get some human grub, and have our whiskers harvested.

Rosa was no mining camp. It laid in the valley, and was as

free of uproar and pestilence as one of them rural towns in the country. There was a three-mile trolley line champing its bit in the environs; and me and Idaho spent a week riding on one of the cars, dropping off of nights at the *Sunset View Hotel*. Being now well read as well as travelled, we was soon *pro re nata* with the best society in Rosa, and was invited out to the most dressed-up and high-toned entertainments. It was at a piano recital and quail-eating contest in the city hall, for the benefit of the fire company, that me and Idaho first met Mrs. De Ormond Sampson, the queen of Rosa society.

Mrs. Sampson was a widow, and owned the only two-storey house in town. It was painted yellow, and whichever way you looked from you could see it as plain as egg on the chin of an O'Grady on a Friday. Twenty-two men in Rosa besides me and Idaho was trying to stake a claim on that yellow house.

There was a dance after the song-books and quail bones had been raked out of the hall. Twenty-three of the bunch galloped over to Mrs. Sampson and asked for a dance. I side-stepped the two-step, and asked permission to escort her home. That's where I made a hit.

On the way home says she—

"Ain't the stars lovely and bright to-night, Mr. Pratt?"

"For the chance they've got," says I, "they're humping themselves in a mighty creditable way. That big one you see is sixty-six billions of miles distant. It took thirty-six years for its light to reach us. With an eighteen-foot telescope you can see forty-three millions of 'em, including them of the thirteenth magnitude, which, if one was to go out now, you would keep on seeing it for twenty-seven hundred years."

"My!" says Mrs. Sampson. "I never knew that before. How warm it is! I'm as damp as I can be from dancing so much."

"That's easy to account for," says I, "when you happen to know that you've got two million sweat-glands working all at once. If every one of your perspiratory ducts, which are a quarter of an inch long, was placed end to end, they would reach a distance of seven miles."

"Lawsy!" says Mrs. Sampson. "It sounds like an irrigation ditch you was describing, Mr. Pratt. How do you get all this knowledge of information?"

"From observation, Mrs. Sampson," I tells her. "I keep my eyes open when I go about the world."

"Mr. Pratt," says she, "I always did admire a man of education. There are so few scholars among the sap-headed plug-uglies of this town that it is a real pleasure to converse with a gentleman of culture. I'd be gratified to have you call at my house whenever you feel so inclined."

And that was the way I got the goodwill of the lady in the yellow house. Every Tuesday and Friday evenings I used to go there and tell her about the wonders of the universe as discovered, tabulated, and compiled from nature by Herkimer. Idaho and the other gay Lutherans of the town got every minute of the rest of the week that they could.

I never imagined that Idaho was trying to work on Mrs. Sampson with old K. M.'s rules of courtship till one afternoon when I was on my way over to take her a basket of wild hog-plums. I met the lady coming down the lane that led to her house. Her eyes was snapping, and her hat made a dangerous dip over one eye.

"Mr. Pratt," she opens up, "this Mr. Green is a friend of yours, I believe."

"For nine years," say I.

"Cut him out," says she. "He's no gentleman!"

"Why, ma'am," says I, "he's a plain incumbent of the mountains, with asperities and the usual failings of a spendthrift and a liar, but I never on the most momentous occasion had the heart to deny that he was a gentleman. It may be that in haberdashery and the sense of arrogance and display Idaho offends the eye, but inside, ma'am, I've found him impervious to the lower grades of crime and obesity. After nine years of Idaho's society, Mrs. Sampson," I winds up, "I should hate to impute him and I should hate to see him imputed."

"It's right plausible of you, Mr. Pratt," says Mrs. Sampson, "to take up the curmudgeons in your friend's behalf; but it don't alter the fact that he has made proposals to me sufficiently obnoxious to ruffle the ignominy of any lady."

"Why, now, now, now!" says I. "Old Idaho do that! I could believe it of myself sooner. I never knew but one thing to deride in him; and a blizzard was responsible for that. Once while we was snowbound in the mountains he became a prey to a kind of spurious and uneven poetry, which may have corrupted his demeanour."

"It has," says Mrs. Sampson. "Ever since I knew him he has been reciting to me a lot of irreligious rhymes by some person he calls Ruby Ott, and who is no better than she should be, if you judge by her poetry."

"Then Idaho has struck a new book," says I, "for the one he had was by a man who writes under the *nom de plume* of K, M."

"He'd better have stuck to it," says Mrs. Sampson, "whatever it was. And to-day he caps the vortex. I get a bunch of flowers from him, and on 'em is pinned a note. Now, Mr. Pratt, you know a lady when you see her; and you know how I stand in Rosa society. Do you think for a moment that I'd skip out to the woods with a man along with a jug of wine and a loaf of bread, and go singing and cavorting up and down under the trees with him? I take a little claret with my meals, but I'm not in the habit of packing a jug of it into the brush and raising Cain in any such style as that. And of course he'd bring his book of verses along too. He said so. Let him go on his scandalous picnics alone! Or let him take his Ruby Ott with him. I reckon she wouldn't kick unless it was on account of there being too much bread along. And what do you think of your gentleman friend now, Mr. Pratt?"

"Well, 'm," says I, "it may be that Idaho's invitation was a kind of poetry, and meant no harm. Maybe it belonged to the class of rhymes they call figurative. They offend law and order, but they get sent through the mails on the ground that they mean something that they don't say. I'd be glad on Idaho's account if you'd overlook it," says I, "and let us extricate our minds from the low regions of poetry to the higher planes of fact and fancy. On a beautiful afternoon like this, Mrs. Sampson," I goes on, "we should let our thoughts dwell accordingly. Though it is warm here, we should remember that at the equator the line of perpetual frost is at an altitude of fifteen thousand feet. Between the latitudes of forty degrees and forty-nine degrees it is from four thousand to nine thousand feet."

"Oh, Mr. Pratt," says Mrs. Sampson, "it's such a comfort to hear you say them beautiful facts after getting such a jar from that minx of a Ruby's poetry!"

"Let us sit on this log at the roadside," says I, "and forget the inhumanity and ribaldry of the poets. It is in the glorious columns of ascertained facts and legalized measures that beauty is to be found. In this very log we sit upon, Mrs. Sampson," says I, "is statistics more wonderful than any poem. The rings show it was sixty years old. At the depth of two thousand feet it would become coal in three thousand years. The deepest coal mine in the world is at Killingworth, near Newcastle. A box four feet long, three feet wide, and two feet eight inches deep will hold one ton of coal. If an artery is cut, compress it above the wound. A man's leg contains thirty bones. The Tower of London was burned in 1841."

"Go on, Mr. Pratt," says Mrs. Sampson. "Them ideas is so original and soothing. I think statistics are just as lovely as they can be."

But it wasn't till two weeks later that I got all that was coming to me out of Herkimer.

One night I was waked up by folks hollering "Fire!" all around. I jumped up and dressed and went out of the hotel to enjoy the scene. When I seen it was Mrs. Sampson's house, I gave forth a kind of yell, and I was there in two minutes.

The whole lower storey of the yellow house was in flames, and every masculine, feminine, and canine in Rosa was there, screeching and barking and getting in the way of the firemen. I saw Idaho trying to get away from six firemen who were holding him. They was telling him the whole place was on fire downstairs, and no man could go in it and come out alive.

"Where's Mrs. Sampson?" I asks.

"She hasn't been seen," says one of the firemen. "She sleeps upstairs. We've tried to get in, but we can't, and our company hasn't got any ladders yet."

I runs around to the light of the big blaze, and pulls the Handbook out of my inside pocket. I kind of laughed when I felt it in my hands—I reckon I was some daffy with the sensation of excitement.

"Herky, old boy," I says to it, as I flipped over the pages, "you ain't ever lied to me yet, and you ain't ever throwed me down at a scratch yet. Tell me what, old boy, tell me what!" says I.

I turned to "What to do in Case of Accidents," on page 117. I run my finger down the page, and struck it. Good old Herkimer, he never overlooked anything! It said—

"Suffocation from Inhaling Smoke or Gas.—There is nothing better than flax-seed. Place a few seed in the outer corner of the eye."

I shoved the Handbook back in my pocket, and grabbed a boy that was running by.

"Here," says I, giving him some money, "run to the drug store and bring a dollar's worth of flaxseed. Hurry, and you'll get another one for yourself. Now," I sings out to the crowd, "we'll have Mrs. Sampson!" And I throws away my coat and hat.

Four of the firemen and citizens grabs hold of me. It's sure death, they say, to go in the house, for the floors was beginning to fall through.

"How in blazes," I sings out, kind of laughing yet, but not feeling like it, "do you expect me to put flax-seed in a eye without the eye?"

I jabbed each elbow in a fireman's face, kicked the bark off of one citizen's shin, and tripped the other one with a side hold. And then I busted into the house. If I die first I'll write you a letter and tell you if it's any worse down there than the inside of that yellow house was; but don't believe it yet. I was a heap more cooked than the hurry-up orders of broiled chicken that you get in restaurants. The fire and smoke had me down on the floor twice, and was about to shame Herkimer, but the firemen helped me with their little stream of water, and I got to Mrs. Sampson's room. She'd lost conscientiousness from the smoke, so I wrapped her in the bedclothes and got her on my shoulder. Well, the floors wasn't as bad as they said, or I never could have done it—not by no means.

I carried her out fifty yards from the house and laid her on the grass. Then, of course, every one of them other twenty-two plaintiffs to the lady's hand crowded around with tin dippers of water ready to save her. And up runs the boy with the flax-seed.

I unwrapped the covers from Mrs. Sampson's head. She opened her eyes and says—

"Is that you, Mr. Pratt?"

"S-s-sh," says I. "Don't talk till you've had the remedy."

I runs my arm around her neck and raises her head, gentle, and breaks the bag of flax-seed with the other hand; and as easy as I could I bends over and slips three or four of the seeds in the outer corner of her eye.

Up gallops the village doc. by this time, and snorts around, and grabs at Mrs. Sampson's pulse, and wants to know what I mean by such sandblasted nonsense.

"Well, old Jalap and Jerusalem oak-seed," says I, "I'm no regular practitioner, but I'll show you my authority, anyway."

They fetch my coat, and I get out the Handbook.

"Look on page 117," says I, "at the remedy for suffocation by smoke or gas. Flax-seed in the outer corner of the eye, it says. I don't know whether it works as a smoke consumer or whether it hikes the compound gastro-hippopotamus nerve into action, but Herkimer says it, and he was called to the case first. If you want to make it a consultation there's no objection."

Old doc. takes the book and looks at it by means of his specs. and a fireman's lantern.

"Well, Mr. Pratt," says he, "you evidently got on the wrong line in reading your diagnosis. The recipe for suffocation says: "Get the patient into fresh air as quickly as possible, and place in a reclining position." The flax-seed remedy is for "Dust and Cinders in the Eye," on the line above. But, after all——"

"See here," interrupts Mrs. Sampson, "I reckon I've got something to say in this consultation. That flax-seed done me more good than anything I ever tried." And then she raises up her head and lays it back on my arm again, and says: "Put some in the other eye, Sandy dear."

And so if you was to stop off at Rosa to-morrow, or any other day, you'd see a fine new yellow house, with Mrs. Pratt, that was Mrs. Sampson, embellishing and adorning it. And if you was to step inside you'd see on the marble-top centre table in the parlour *Herkimer's Handbook of Indispensable Information*, all re-bound in red morocco, and ready to be consulted on any subject pertaining to human happiness and wisdom.

6

The Making of a New Yorker

BESIDES many other things, Raggles was a poet. He was called a tramp; but that was only an elliptical way of saying that he was a philosopher, an artist, a traveller, a naturalist and a discoverer. But most of all he was a poet. In all his life he never wrote a line of verse; he lived his poetry. His Odyssey would have been a Limerick, had it been written. But, to linger with the primary proposition, Raggles was a poet.

Raggles's speciality, had he been driven to ink and paper, would have been sonnets to the cities. He studied cities as women study their reflections in mirrors; as children study the glue and sawdust of a dislocated doll; as the men who write about wild animals study the cages in the Zoo. A city to Raggles was not merely a pile of bricks and mortar, peopled by a certain number of inhabitants; it was a thing with a soul characteristic and distinct; an individual conglomeration of life, with its own peculiar essence, flavour and feeling. Two thousand miles to the north and south, east and west, Raggles wandered in poetic fervour, taking the cities to his breast. He footed it on dusty roads, or sped magnificently in freight cars, counting time as of no account. And when he had found the heart of a city and listened to its secret confession, he strayed on, restless, to another. Fickle Raggles!—but perhaps he had not met the civic corporation that could engage and hold his critical fancy.

Through the ancient poets we have learned that the cities are feminine. So they were to poet Raggles; and his mind carried a concrete and clear conception of the figure that symbolized and typified each one that he had wooed.

Chicago seemed to swoop down upon him with a breezy suggestion of Mrs. Partington, plumes and patchouli, and to disturb his rest with a soaring and beautiful song of future promise. But Raggles would awake to a sense of shivering cold and a haunting impression of ideals lost in a depressing aura of potato salad and fish.

Thus Chicago affected him. Perhaps there is a vagueness and inaccuracy in the description; but that is Raggles's fault. He should have recorded his sensations in magazine poems.

Pittsburg impressed him as the play of *Othello* performed in the Russian language in a railroad station by Dockstader's minstrels. A royal and generous lady this Pittsburg, though—homely, hearty, with flushed face, washing the dishes in a silk dress and white kid slippers, and bidding Raggles sit before the roaring fireplace and drink champagne with his pigs' feet and fried potatoes.

New Orleans had simply gazed down upon him from a balcony. He could see her pensive, starry eyes and catch the flutter of her fan, and that was all. Only once he came face to face with her. It was at dawn, when she was flushing the red bricks of the banquette with a pail of water. She laughed and hummed a chansonsette and filled Raggles's shoes with ice-cold water. Allons!

Boston construed herself to the poetic Raggles in an erratic and singular way. It seemed to him that he had drunk cold tea and that the city was a white, cold cloth that had been bound tightly around his brow to spur him to some unknown but tremendous mental effort. And, after all, he came to shovel snow for a livelihood; and the cloth, becoming wet, tightened its knots and could not be removed.

Indefinite and unintelligible ideas, you will say; but your disapprobation should be tempered with gratitude, for these are poets' fancies—and suppose you had come upon them in verse!

One day Raggles came and laid siege to the heart of the great city of Manhattan. She was the greatest of all; and he wanted to learn her note in the scale; to taste and appraise and classify and solve and label her and arrange her with the other cities that had given him up the secret of their individuality. And here we cease to be Raggles's translator and become his chronicler.

Raggles landed from a ferry-boat one morning and walked into the core of the town with the blasé air of a cosmopolite. He was dressed with care to play the rôle of an "unidentified man". No country, race, class, clique, union, party, clan or bowling association could have claimed him. His clothing, which had been donated to him piece-meal by citizens of different height, but same number of inches around the heart, was not yet as uncomfortable to his figure as those specimens of raiment, self-measured, that are railroaded to you by transcontinental tailors with a suit-case, suspenders, silk handkerchief and pearl studs as a bonus. Without money —as a poet should be—but with the ardour of an astronomer discovering a new star in the chorus of the Milky Way, or a man who has seen ink suddenly flow from his fountain pen, Raggles wandered into the great city.

Late in the afternoon he drew out of the roar and commotion with a look of dumb terror on his countenance. He was defeated, puzzled, discomfited, frightened. Other cities had been to him as long primer to read; as country maidens quickly to fathom; as send-price-of-subscription-with-answer rebuses to solve; as oyster cocktails to swallow; but here was one as cold, glittering, serene, impossible as a four-carat diamond in a window to a lover outside fingering damply in his pocket his ribbon-counter salary.

The greetings of the other cities he had known—their home spun kindliness, their human gamut of rough charity, friendly curses, garrulous curiosity and easily estimated credulity or indifference. This city of Manhattan gave him no clue; it was walled against him. Like a river of adamant it flowed past him in the streets. Never an eye was turned upon him; no voice spoke to him. His heart yearned for the clap of Pittsburg's sooty hand on his shoulder; for Chicago's menacing but social yawp in his ear; for the pale and eleemosynary stare through the Bostonian eyeglass—even for the precipitate but unmalicious boot-toe of Louisville or St. Louis.

On Broadway, Raggles, successful suitor of many cities, stood, bashful, like any country swain. For the first time he experienced the poignant humiliation of being ignored. And when he tried to reduce this brilliant, swiftly changing, ice-cold city to a formula he failed utterly. Poet though he was, it offered him no colour, no similes, no points of comparison, no flaw in its polished facets, no handle by which he could hold it up and view its shape and structure, as he familiarly and often contemptuously had done with other towns. The houses were interminable ramparts loopholed for defence; the people were bright but bloodless spectres passing in sinister and selfish array.

The thing that weighed heaviest on Raggles's soul and clogged his poet's fancy was the spirit of absolute egotism that seemed to saturate the people as toys are saturated with paint. Each one that he considered appeared a monster of abominable and insolent conceit. Humanity was gone from them; they were toddling idols of stone and varnish, worshipping themselves and greedy for, though oblivious of, worship from their fellow graven images. Frozen, cruel, implacable, impervious, cut to an identical pattern, they hurried on their ways like statues brought by some miracles to motion, while soul and feeling lay unaroused in the reluctant marble.

Gradually Raggles became conscious of certain types. One was an elderly gentleman with a snow-white short beard, pink unwrinkled face and stony sharp blue eyes, attired in the fashion of a gilded youth, who seemed to personify the city's wealth, ripeness and frigid unconcern. Another type was a woman, tall, beautiful, clear as a steel engraving, goddess-like, calm, clothed like the princesses of old, with eyes as coldly blue as the reflection of sunlight on a glacier. And another was a by-product of this town of marionettes—a broad, swaggering, grim, threateningly sedate fellow, with a jowl as large as a harvested wheatfield, the complexion of a baptized infant and the knuckles of a prize-fighter. This type leaned against cigar signs and viewed the world with frappéd contumely.

A poet is a sensitive creature, and Raggles soon shrivelled in the bleak embrace of the undecipherable. The chill, sphinx-like, ironical, illegible, unnatural, ruthless expression of the city left him downcast and bewildered. Had it no heart? Better the woodpile, the scolding of vinegar-faced housewives at back doors, the kindly spleen of bartenders behind provincial free-lunch counters, the amiable truculence of rural constables, the kicks, arrests and happy-go-lucky chances of the other vulgar, loud, crude cities than this freezing heartlessness.

Raggles summoned his courage and sought alms from the populace. Unheeding, regardless, they passed on without the wink of an eyelash to testify that they were conscious of his existence. And then he said to himself that this fair but pitiless city of Manhattan was without a soul; that its inhabitants were manikins moved by wires and springs, and that he was alone in a great wilderness.

Raggles started to cross the street. There was a blast, a roar, a hissing and a crash as something struck him and hurled him over and over six yards from where he had been. As he was coming down like the stick of a rocket the earth and all the cities thereof turned to a fractured dream.

Raggles opened his eyes. First an odour made itself known to him—an odour of the earliest spring flowers of Paradise. And then a hand soft as a falling petal touched his brow. Bending over him was the woman clothed like the princess of old, with blue eyes, now soft and humid with human sympathy. Under his head on the pavement were silks and furs. With Raggles's hat in his hand and with his face pinker than ever from a vehement burst of oratory against reckless driving, stood the elderly gentleman who personified the city's wealth and ripeness. From a near-by café hurried the by-product with the vast jowl and baby complexion, bearing a glass full of a crimson fluid that suggested delightful possibilities.

"Drink dis, sport," said the by-product, holding the glass to Raggles's lips.

Hundreds of people huddled around in a moment, their faces wearing the deepest concern. Two flattering and gorgeous policemen got into the circle and pressed back the overplus of Samaritans. An old lady in a black shawl spoke loudly of camphor; a newsboy slipped one of his papers beneath

Raggles's elbow, where it lay on the muddy pavement. A brisk young man with a notebook was asking for names.

A bell clanged importantly, and the ambulance cleared a lane through the crowd. A cool surgeon slipped into the midst of affairs.

"How do you feel, old man?" asked the surgeon, stooping easily to his task. The princess of silks and satins wiped a red drop or two from Raggles's brow with a fragrant cobweb.

"Me?" said Raggles, with a seraphic smile. "I feel fine."

He had found the heart of his new city.

In three days they let him leave his cot for the convalescent ward in the hospital. He had been in there an hour when the attendants heard sounds of conflict. Upon investigation they found that Raggles had assaulted and damaged a brother convalescent—a glowering transient whom a freight train had sent in to be patched up.

"What's all this about?" inquired the head nurse.

"He was runnin' down me town," said Raggles.

"What town?" asked the nurse.

"Noo York," said Raggles.

7

The Day Resurgent

I CAN see the artist bite the end of his pencil and frown when it comes to drawing his Easter picture; for his legitimate pictorial conceptions of figures pertinent to the festival are but four in number.

First comes Easter, pagan goddess of spring. Here his fancy may have free play. A beautiful maiden with decorative hair and the proper number of toes will fill the bill. Miss Clarice St. Vavasour, the well-known model, will pose for it in the "Lethergogallagher", or whatever it was that Trilby called it.

Second—the melancholy lady with upturned eyes in a framework of lilies. This is magazine-covery, but reliable.

Third—Miss Manhattan in the Fifth Avenue Easter Sunday parade.

Fourth—Maggie Murphy with a new red feather in her old straw hat, happy and self-conscious, in the Grand Street turnout.

Of course, the rabbits do not count. Nor the Easter eggs, since the higher criticism has hard-boiled them.

The limited field of its pictorial possibilities proves that Easter, of all our festival days, is the most vague and shifting in our conception. It belongs to all religions, although the pagans invented it. Going back still further to the first spring, we can see Eve choosing with pride a new green leaf from the tree *ficus carica*.

Now, the object of this critical and learned preamble is to set forth the theorem that Easter is neither a date, a season, a festival, a holiday nor an occasion. What it is you shall find out if you follow in the footsteps of Danny McCree.

Easter Sunday dawned as it should, bright and early in its place on the calendar between Saturday and Monday. At

5.24 the sun rose, and at 10.30 Danny followed its example. He went into the kitchen and washed his face at the sink. His mother was frying bacon. She looked at his hard, smooth, knowing countenance as he juggled with the round cake of soap, and thought of his father when she first saw him stopping a hot grounder between second and third twenty-two years before on a vacant lot in Harlem, where the La Paloma apartment-house now stands. In the front room of the flat Danny's father sat by an open window smoking his pipe, with his dishevelled grey hair tossed about by the breeze. He still clung to his pipe, although his sight had been taken from him two years before by a precocious blast of giant powder that went off without permission. Very few blind men care for smoking, for the reason that they cannot see the smoke. Now, could you enjoy having the news read to you from an evening newspaper unless you could see the colours of the headlines?

"'Tis Easter Day," said Mrs. McCree.

"Scramble mine," said Danny.

After breakfast he dressed himself in the Sabbath morning costume of the Canal Street importing house dray chauffeur—frock-coat, striped trousers, patent leathers, gilded trace chain across front of vest, and wing collar, rolled-brim derby and butterfly bow from Schonstein's (between Fourteenth Street and Tony's fruit stand) Saturday night sale.

"You'll be goin' out this day, of course, Danny," said old man McCree, a little wistfully. "'Tis a kind of holiday, they say. Well, it's fine spring weather. I can feel it in the air."

"Why should I not be going out?" demanded Danny in his grumpiest chest tones. "Should I stay in? Am I as good as a horse? One day of rest my team has a week. Who earns the money for the rent and the breakfast you've just eat, I'd like to know? Answer me that!"

"All right, lad," said the old man. "I'm not complainin'. While me two eyes was good there was nothin' better to my mind than a Sunday out. There's a smell of turf and burnin' brush comin' in the windy. I have me tobaccy. A good fine day and rist to ye, lad. Times I wish your mother had larned to read, so I might hear the rest about the hippopotamus—but let that be."

"Now, what is this foolishness he talks of hippopotamuses?" asked Danny of his mother, as he passed through the kitchen. "Have you been taking him to the Zoo? And for what?"

"I have not," said Mrs. McCree. "He sets by the windy all day. 'Tis little recreation a blind man among the poor gets at all. I'm thinkin' they wander in their minds at times. One day he talks of grease without stoppin' for the most of an hour. I looks to see if there's lard burnin' in the fryin' pan. There is not. He says I do not understand. 'Tis weary days, Sundays, and holidays, and all, for a blind man, Danny. There was no better nor stronger than him when he had his two eyes. 'Tis a fine day, son. Injoy yeself ag'inst the morning. There will be cold supper at six."

"Have you heard any talk of a hippopotamus?" asked Danny of Mike, the janitor, as he went out the door downstairs.

"I have not," said Mike, pulling his shirt sleeves higher. "But 'tis the only subject in the animal, natural and illegal lists of outrages that I've not been complained to about these two days. See the landlord. Or else move out if ye like. Have ye hippopotamuses in the lease? No, then?"

"It was the old man who spoke of it," said Danny. "Likely there's nothing in it."

Danny walked up the street to the Avenue and then struck northward into the heart of the district where Easter—modern Easter, in new, bright raiment—leads the pascal march. Out of towering, brown churches came the blithe music of anthems from the choirs. The broad sidewalks were moving parterres of living flowers—so it seemed when your eye looked upon the Easter girl.

Gentlemen, frock-coated, silk-hatted, gardeniaed, sustained the background of the tradition. Children carried lilies in their hands. The windows of the brown-stone mansions were packed with the most opulent creations of Flora, the sister of the Lady of the Lilies.

Around a corner, white-gloved, pink-gilled and tightly buttoned, walked Corrigan, the cop, shield to the kerb. Danny knew him.

"Why, Corrigan," he asked, "is Easter? I know it comes

the first time you're full after the moon rises on the seventeenth of March—but why? Is it a proper and religious ceremony, or does the Governor appoint it out of politics?"

"'Tis an annual celebration," said Corrigan, with the judicial air of the Third Deputy Police Commissioner, "peculiar to New York. It extends up to Harlem. Sometimes they has the reserves out at One Hundred and Twenty-fifth Street. In my opinion 'tis not political."

"Thanks," said Danny. "And say—did you ever hear a man complain of hippopotamuses? When not specially in drink, I mean."

"Nothing larger than sea turtles," said Corrigan, reflecting, "and there was wood alcohol in that."

Danny wondered. The double, heavy incumbency of enjoying simultaneously a Sunday and a festival day was his.

The sorrows of the hand-toiler fit him easily. They are worn so often that they hang with the picturesque lines of the best tailor-made garments. That is why well-fed artists of pencil and pen find in the griefs of the common people their most striking models. But when the Philistine would disport himself, the grimness of Melpomene, herself, attends upon his capers. Therefore, Danny set his jaw hard at Easter, and took his pleasure sadly.

The family entrance of Dugan's café was feasible; so Danny yielded to the vernal season as far as a glass of bock. Seated in a dark, linoleumed, humid back room, his heart and mind still groped after the mysterious meaning of the springtime jubilee.

"Say, Tim," he said to the waiter, "why do they have Easter?"

"Skiddoo!" said Tim, closing a sophisticated eye. "Is that a new one? All right. Tony Pastor's for you last night, I guess. I give it up. What's the answer—two apples or a yard and a half?"

From Dugan's Danny turned back eastward. The April sun seemed to stir in him a vague feeling that he could not construe. He made a wrong diagnosis and decided that it was Katy Conlon.

A block from her house on Avenue A he met her going to church. They pumped hands on the corner.

"Gee! but you look dumpish and dressed up," said Katy. "What's wrong? Come away with me to church and be cheerful."

"What's doing at church?" asked Danny.

"Why, it's Easter Sunday. Silly! I waited till after eleven expectin' you might come around to go."

"What does this Easter stand for, Katy?" asked Danny gloomily. "Nobody seems to know."

"Nobody as blind as you," said Katy with spirit. "You haven't even looked at my new hat. And skirt. Why, it's when all the girls put on new spring clothes. Silly! Are you coming to church with me?"

"I will," said Danny. "If this Easter is pulled off there, they ought to be able to give some excuse for it. Not that the hat ain't a beauty. The green roses are great."

At church the preacher did some expounding with no pounding. He spoke rapidly, for he was in a hurry to get home to his early Sabbath dinner; but he knew his business. There was one word that controlled his theme—resurrection. Not a new creation; but a new life arising out of the old. The congregation had heard it often before. But there was a wonderful hat, a combination of sweet-peas and lavender, in the sixth pew from the pulpit. It attracted much attention.

After church Danny lingered on a corner while Katy waited, with pique in her sky-blue eyes.

"Are you coming along to the house?" she asked. "But don't mind me. I'll get there all right. You seem to be studyin' a lot about something. All right. Will I see you at any time specially, Mr. McCree?"

"I'll be around Wednesday night as usual," said Danny, turning and crossing the street.

Katy walked away with the green roses dangling indignantly. Danny stopped two blocks away. He stood still with his hands in his pockets, at the kerb on the corner. His face was that of a graven image. Deep in his soul something stirred so small, so fine, so keen and leavening that his hard fibres did not recognize it. It was something more tender than the April day, more subtle than the call of the senses, purer and deeper-rooted than the love of woman—for had he not turned away from green roses and eyes that had kept him chained for a year? And Danny did not know what it was. The preacher, who was in a hurry to go to his dinner, had told him, but Danny had had no libretto with which to follow the drowsy intonation. But the preacher spoke the truth.

Suddenly Danny slapped his leg and gave forth a hoarse yell of delight.

"Hippopotamus!" he shouted to an elevated road pillar. "Well, how is that for a bum guess? Why, blast my skylights! I know what he was driving at now.

"Hippopotamus! Wouldn't that send you to the Bronx? It's been a year since he heard it; and he didn't miss it so very far. We quit at 469 B.C., and this comes next. Well, a wooden man wouldn't have guessed what he was trying to get out of him."

Danny caught a crosstown car and went up to the rear flat that his labour supported.

Old man McCree was still sitting by the window. His extinct pipe lay on the sill.

"Will that be you, lad?" he asked.

Danny flared into the rage of a strong man who is surprised at the outset of committing a good deed.

"Who pays the rent and buys the food that is eaten in this house?" he snapped viciously. "Have I no right to come in?"

"Ye're a faithful lad," said old man McCree, with a sigh. "Is it evening yet?"

Danny reached up on a shelf and took down a thick book labelled in gilt letters, "The History of Greece". Dust was on it half an inch thick. He laid it on the table and found a place in it marked by a strip of paper. And then he gave a short roar at the top of his voice, and said:

"Was it the hippopotamus you wanted to be read to about then?"

"Did I hear ye open the book?" said old man McCree. "Many and weary be the months since my lad has read it to me. I dinno; but I took a great likings to them Greeks. Ye left off at a place. 'Tis a fine day outside, lad. Be out and take rest from your work. I have gotten used to me chair by the windy and me pipe."

"Pel-Peloponnesus was the place where we left off, and not hippopotamus," said Danny. "The war began there. It kept something doing for thirty years. The headlines says that a guy named Philip of Macedon, in 338 B.C., got to be boss of Greece by getting the decision at the battle of Cher-Cheronaea. I'll read it."

With his hand to his ear, rapt in the Peloponnesian War, old man McCree sat for an hour, listening.

Then he got up and felt his way to the door of the kitchen. Mrs. McCree was slicing cold meat. She looked up. Tears were running from old man McCree's eyes.

"Do ye hear our lad readin' to me?" he said. "There is none finer in the land. My two eyes have come back to me again."

After supper he said to Danny: "'Tis a happy day, this Easter. And now ye will be off to see Katy in the evening. Well enough."

"Who pays the rent and buys the food that is eaten in this house?" said Danny angrily. "Have I no right to stay in it? After supper there is yet to come the reading of the battle of Corinth, 146 B.C., when the kingdom, as they say, became an integral portion of the Roman Empire. Am I nothing in this house?"

8

The Fifth Wheel

THE ranks of the Bed Line moved closer together; for it was cold, cold. They were alluvial deposit of the stream of life lodged in the delta of Fifth Avenue and Broadway. The Bed Liners stamped their freezing feet, looked at the empty benches in Madison Square whence Jack Frost had evicted them, and muttered to one another in a confusion of tongues. The Flatiron Building, with its impious, cloud-piercing architecture looming mistily above them on the opposite delta, might well have stood for the tower of Babel, whence these polyglot idlers had been called by the winged walking delegate of the Lord.

Standing on a pine box a head higher than his flock of goats, the Preacher exhorted whatever transient and shifting audience the north wind doled out to him. It was a slave market. Fifteen cents bought you a man. You deeded him to Morpheus; and the recording angel gave you credit.

The Preacher was incredibly earnest and unwearied. He had looked over the list of things one may do for one's fellow-man, and had assumed for himself the task of putting to bed all who might apply at his soap-box on the nights of Wednesday and Sunday. That left but five nights for other philanthropists to handle; and had they done their part as well, this wicked city might have become a vast Arcadian dormitory, where all might snooze and snore the happy hours away, letting problem plays and the rent man and business go to the deuce.

The hour of eight was but a little while past; sightseers in a small, dark mass of pay ore were gathered in the shadow of General Worth's monument. Now and then, shyly, ostentatiously, carelessly, or with conscientious exactness, one would step forward and bestow upon the Preacher small bills or silver. Then a lieutenant of Scandinavian colouring and enthusiasm would march away to a lodging-house with a squad of the redeemed. All the while the Preacher exhorted the crowd in terms beautifully devoid of eloquence—splendid with the deadly, accusive monotony of truth. Before the picture of the Bed Liners fades you must hear one phrase of the Preacher's—the one that formed his theme that night. It is worthy of being stencilled on all the white ribbons in the world.

"*No man ever learned to be a drunkard on five-cent whisky.*"

Think of it, tippler. It covers the ground from the sprouting rye to the Potter's Field.

A clean-profiled, erect young man in the rear rank of the bedless emulated the terrapin, drawing his head far down into the shell of his coat collar. It was a well-cut tweed coat; and the trousers still showed signs of having flattened themselves beneath the compelling goose. But, conscientiously, I must warn the milliner's apprentice who reads this, expecting a Reginald Montressor in straits, to peruse no further. The young man was no other than Thomas McQuade, ex-coachman, discharged for drunkenness one month before, and now reduced to the grimy ranks of the one-night bed seekers.

If you live in smaller New York you must know the Van Smuythe family carriage, drawn by the two 1,500-pound, 100-to-1-shot bays. The carriage is shaped like a bath-tub. In each end of it reclines an old lady Van Smuythe holding a black sunshade the size of a New Year's Eve feather tickler. Before his downfall Thomas McQuade drove the Van Smuythe bays and was himself driven by Annie, the Van Smuythe lady's maid. But it is one of the saddest things about romance that a tight shoe or an empty commissary or an aching tooth will make a temporary heretic of any Cupid-worshipper. And Thomas's physical troubles were not few. Therefore, his soul was less vexed with thoughts of his lost lady's maid than it was by the fancied presence of certain non-existent things that his racked nerves almost convinced him were flying, dancing, crawling, and wriggling on the asphalt and in the air above and around the dismal campus of the Bed Line Army. Nearly four weeks of straight whisky and a diet limited to crackers, bologna, and pickles often guarantees a psycho-zoological sequel. Thus desperate, freezing, angry, beset by phantoms as he was, he felt the need of human sympathy and intercourse.

The Bed Liner standing at his right was a young man of about his own age, shabby but neat.

"What's the diagnosis of your case, Freddy?" asked Thomas, with the freemasonic familiarity of the damned—"Booze? That's mine. You don't look like a panhandler. Neither am I. A month ago I was pushing the lines over the backs of the finest team of Percheron buffaloes that ever made their way down Fifth Avenue in 2·85. And look at me now! Say; how do you come to be at this bed bargain-counter rummage sale?"

The other young man seemed to welcome the advances of the airy ex-coachman.

"No," said he, "mine isn't exactly a case of drink. Unless we allow that Cupid is a bartender. I married unwisely, according to the opinion of my unforgiving relatives. I've been out of work for a year because I don't know how to work; and I've been sick in Bellevue and other hospitals four months. My wife and kid had to go back to her mother. I was turned out of the hospital yesterday. And I haven't a cent. That's my tale of woe."

"Tough luck," said Thomas. "A man alone can pull through all right. But I hate to see the women and kids get the worst of it."

Just then there hummed up Fifth Avenue a motor-car so splendid, so red, so smoothly running, so craftily demolishing the speed regulations, that it drew the attention even of the listless Bed Liners. Suspended and pinioned on its left side was an extra tyre.

When opposite the unfortunate company the fastenings of this tyre became loosed. It fell to the asphalt, bounded and rolled rapidly in the wake of the flying car.

Thomas McQuade, scenting an opportunity, darted from his place among the Preacher's goats. In thirty seconds he had caught the rolling tyre, swung it over his shoulder, and was trotting smartly after the car. On both sides of the avenue people were shouting, whistling, and waving canes at the red car, pointing to the enterprising Thomas coming up with the lost tyre.

One dollar, Thomas had estimated, was the smallest guerdon that so grand an automobilist could offer for the service he had rendered, and save his pride.

Two blocks away the car had stopped. There was a little, brown, muffled chauffeur driving, and an imposing gentleman wearing a magnificent sealskin coat and a silk hat on a rear seat.

Thomas proffered the captured tyre with his best ex-coachman manner and a look in the brighter of his reddened eyes that was meant to be suggestive to the extent of a silver coin or two and receptive up to higher denominations.

But the look was not so construed. The seal-skinned gentleman received the tyre, placed it inside the car, gazed intently at the ex-coachman, and muttered to himself inscrutable words.

"Strange—strange!" said he. "Once or twice even I, myself, have fancied that the Chaldean Chiroscope has availed. Could it be possible?"

Then he addressed less mysterious words to the waiting and hopeful Thomas.

"Sir, I thank you for your kind rescue of my tyre. And I would ask you, if I may, a question. Do you know the family of Van Smuythes living in Washington Square North?"

"Oughtn't I to?" replied Thomas. "I lived there. Wish I did yet."

The seal-skinned gentleman opened a door of the car.

"Step in, please," he said. "You have been expected."

Thomas McQuade obeyed with surprise but without hesitation. A seat in a motor-car seemed better than standing room in the Bed Line. But after the lap-robe had been tucked about him and the auto had sped on its course, the peculiarity of the invitation lingered in his mind.

"Maybe the guy hasn't got any change," was his diagnosis. "Lots of these swell rounders don't lug about any ready money. Guess he'll dump me out when he gets to some joint where he can get cash on his mug. Anyhow, it's a cinch that I've got that open-air bed convention beat to a finish."

Submerged in his greatcoat, the mysterious auto-mobilist seemed, himself, to marvel at the surprises of life. "Wonderful! amazing! strange!" he repeated to himself constantly.

When the car had well entered the crosstown Seventies it swung easily a half block and stopped before a row of high-stooped, brown-stone-front houses.

"Be kind enough to enter my house with me," said the seal-skinned gentleman when they had alighted.

"He's going to dig up, sure," reflected Thomas, following him inside.

There was a dim light in the hall. His host conducted him through a door to the left, closing it after him and leaving them in absolute darkness. Suddenly a luminous globe, strangely decorated, shone faintly in the centre of an immense room that seemed to Thomas more splendidly appointed than any he had ever seen on the stage or read of in fairy stories.

The walls were hidden by gorgeous red hangings embroidered with fantastic gold figures. At the rear end of the room were draped portières of dull gold spangled with silver crescents and stars. The furniture was of the costliest and rarest styles. The ex-coachman's feet sank into rugs as fleecy and deep as snowdrifts. There were three or four oddly shaped stands or tables covered with black velvet drapery.

Thomas McQuade took in the splendours of this palatial apartment with one eye. With the other he looked for his imposing conductor—to find that he had disappeared.

"B'gee!" muttered Thomas, "this listens like a spook shop. Shouldn't wonder if it ain't one of these Moravian Nights' adventures that you read about. Wonder what became of the furry guy."

Suddenly a stuffed owl that stood on an ebony perch near the illuminated globe slowly raised his wings and emitted from his eyes a brilliant electric glow.

With a fright-born imprecation, Thomas seized a bronze statuette of Hebe from a cabinet near by and hurled it with all his might at the terrifying and impossible fowl. The owl and his perch went over with a crash. With the sound there was a click, and the room was flooded with light from a dozen frosted globes along the walls and ceiling. The gold portières parted and closed, and the mysterious auto-mobilist entered the room. He was tall and wore evening dress of perfect cut and accurate taste. A Vandyke beard of glossy, golden brown, rather long and wavy hair, smoothly parted, and large, magnetic, orientally occult eyes, gave him a most impressive and striking appearance. If you can conceive a Russian Grand Duke in a Rajah's throne-room advancing to greet a visiting Emperor, you will gather something of the majesty of his manner. But Thomas McQuade was too near his *d t*'s to be mindful of his *p*'s and *q*'s. When he viewed this silken, polished, and somewhat terrifying host he thought vaguely of dentists.

"Say, doc," said he resentfully, "that's a hot bird you keep on tap. I hope I didn't break anything. But I've nearly got the williwalloos, and when he threw them 32-candle-power lamps of his on me, I took a snap-shot at him with that little brass Flatiron Girl that stood on the sideboard."

"That is merely a mechanical toy," said the gentleman with a wave of his hand. "May I ask you to be seated while I explain why I brought you to my house. Perhaps you would not understand nor be in sympathy with the psychological prompting that caused me to do so. So I will come to the point at once by venturing to refer to your admission that you know the Van Smuythe family, of Washington Square North."

"Any silver missing?" asked Thomas tartly. "Any joolry displaced? Of course I know 'em. Any of the old ladies' sunshades disappeared? Well, I know 'em. And then what?"

The Grand Duke rubbed his white hands together softly.

"Wonderful!" he murmured. "Wonderful! Shall I come to believe in the Chaldean Chiroscope myself? Let me assure you," he continued, "that there is nothing for you to fear. Instead, I think I can promise you that very good fortune awaits you. We will see."

"Do they want me back?" asked Thomas, with something of his old professional pride in his voice. "I'll promise to cut out the booze and do the right thing if they'll try me again.

But how did you get wise, doc? B'gee, it's the swellest employment agency I was ever in, with its flashlight owls and so forth."

With an indulgent smile the gracious host begged to be excused for two minutes. He went out to the sidewalk and gave an order to the chauffeur, who still waited with the car. Returning to the mysterious apartment, he sat by his guest and began to entertain him so well by his witty and genial converse that the poor Bed Liner almost forgot the cold streets from which he had been so recently and so singularly rescued. A servant brought some tender cold fowl and tea biscuits and a glass of miraculous wine; and Thomas felt the glamour of Arabia envelop him. Thus half an hour sped quickly; and then the honk of the returned motor-car at the door suddenly drew the Grand Duke to his feet, with another soft petition for a brief absence.

Two women, well muffled against the cold, were admitted at the front door and suavely conducted by the master of the house down the hall through another door to the left and into a smaller room, which was screened and segregated from the larger front room by heavy double portières. Here the furnishings were even more elegant and exquisitely tasteful than in the other. On a gold-inlaid rosewood table were scattered sheets of white paper and a queer, triangular instrument or toy, apparently of gold, standing on little wheels.

The taller woman threw back her black veil and loosened her cloak. She was fifty, with a wrinkled and sad face. The other, young and plump, took a chair a little distance away to the rear as a servant or an attendant might have done.

"You sent for me, Professor Cherubusco," said the elder woman wearily. "I hope you have something more definite than usual to say. I've about lost the little faith I had in your art. I would not have responded to your call this evening if my sister had not insisted upon it."

"Madam," said the professor, with his princeliest smile, "the true Art cannot fail. To find the true psychic and potential branch sometimes requires time. We have not succeeded, I admit, with the cards, the crystal, the stars, the magic formulae of Zarazin, nor the Oracle of Po. But we have at last discovered the true psychic route. The Chaldean Chiroscope has been successful in our search."

The professor's voice had a ring that seemed to proclaim his belief in his own words. The elderly lady looked at him with a little more interest.

"Why, there was no sense in those words that it wrote with my hands on it," she said. "What do you mean?"

"The words were these," said Professor Cherubusco, rising to his full magnificent height:

"'*By the fifth wheel of the chariot he shall come.*'"

"I haven't seen many chariots," said the lady, "but I never saw one with five wheels."

"Progress," said the professor—"progress in science and mechanics has accomplished it—though, to be exact, we may only speak of it as an extra tyre. Progress in occult art has advanced in proportion. Madam, I repeat that the Chaldean Chiroscope has succeeded. I can not only answer the question that you have propounded, but I can produce before your eyes the proof thereof."

And now the lady was disturbed both in her disbelief and in her poise.

"Oh, professor!" she cried anxiously—"When?—where? Has he been found? Do not keep me in suspense."

"I beg you will excuse me for a very few minutes," said Professor Cherubusco, "and I think I can demonstrate to you the efficacy of the true Art."

Thomas was contentedly munching the last crumbs of the bread and fowl when the enchanter appeared suddenly at his side.

"Are you willing to return to your old home if you are assured of a welcome and restoration to favour?" he asked, with his courteous, royal smile.

"Do I look bughouse?" answered Thomas. "Enough of the footback life for me. But will they have me again? The old lady is as fixed in her ways as a nut on a new axle."

"My dear young man," said the other, "she has been searching for you everywhere."

"Great!" said Thomas. "I'm on the job. That team of

dropsical dromedaries they call horses is a handicap for a first-class coachman like myself; but I'll take the job back, sure, doc. They're good people to be with."

And now a change came o'er the suave countenance of the Caliph of Bagdad. He looked keenly and suspiciously at the ex-coachman.

"May I ask what your name is?" he said shortly.

"You've been looking for me," said Thomas, "and don't know my name? You're a funny kind of sleuth. You must be one of the Central Office gumshoers. I'm Thomas McQuade, of course; and I've been chauffeur of the Van Smuythe elephant team for a year. They fired me a month ago for—well, doc, you saw what I did to your old owl. I went broke on booze, and when I saw the tyre drop off your whiz wagon I was standing in that squad of hoboes at the Worth monument waiting for a free bed. Now, what's the prize for the best answer to all this?"

To his intense surprise Thomas felt himself lifted by the collar and dragged, without a word of explanation, to the front door. This was opened, and he was kicked forcibly down the steps with one heavy, disillusionizing, humiliating impact of the stupendous Arabian's shoe.

As soon as the ex-coachman had recovered his feet and his wits he hastened as fast as he could eastward toward Broadway.

"Crazy guy," was his estimate of the mysterious automobilist. "Just wanted to have some fun kiddin', I guess. He might have dug up a dollar, anyhow. Now I've got to hurry up and get back to that gang of bum bed hunters before they all get preached to sleep."

When Thomas reached the end of his two-mile walk he found the ranks of the homeless reduced to a squad of perhaps eight or ten. He took the proper place of a new-comer at the left end of the rear rank. In the file in front of him was the young man who had spoken to him of hospitals and something of a wife and child.

"Sorry to see you back again," said the young man, turning to speak to him. "I hoped you had struck something better than this."

"Me?" said Thomas. "Oh, I just took a run around the block to keep warm! I see the public ain't lending to the Lord very fast to-night."

"In this kind of weather," said the young man, "charity avails itself of the proverb, and both begins and ends at home.

And now the Preacher and his vehement lieutenant struck up a last hymn of petition to Providence and man. Those of the Bed Liners whose windpipes still registered above 32 degrees hopelessly and tunelessly joined in.

In the middle of the second verse Thomas saw a sturdy girl with wind-tossed drapery battling against the breeze and coming straight toward him from the opposite sidewalk. "Annie!" he yelled, and ran toward her.

"You fool, you fool!" she cried, weeping and laughing, and hanging upon his neck. "Why did you do it?"

"The Stuff," explained Thomas briefly. "You know. But subsequently nit. Not a drop." He led her to the kerb. "How did you happen to see me?"

"I came to find you," said Annie, holding tight to his sleeve. "Oh, you big fool! Professor Cherubusco told us that we might find you here."

"Professor Ch—— Don't know the guy. What saloon does he work in?"

"He's a clearvoyant, Thomas; the greatest in the world. He found you with the Chaldean telescope, he said."

"He's a liar," said Thomas. "I never had it. He never saw me have anybody's telescope."

"And he said you came in a chariot with five wheels or something."

"Annie," said Thomas solicitously, "you're giving me the wheels now. If I had a chariot I'd have gone to bed in it long ago. And without any singing and preaching for a nightcap, either."

"Listen, you big fool. The Missis says she'll take you back. I begged her to. But you must behave. And you can go up to the house to-night; and your old room over the stable is ready."

"Great!" said Thomas earnestly. "You are It, Annie. But when did these stunts happen?"

"To-night at Professor Cherubusco's. He sent his automobile for the Missis, and she took me along. I've been there with her before."

"What's the professor's line?"

"He's a clearvoyant and a witch. The Missis consults him. He knows everything. But he hasn't done the Missis any good yet, though she's paid him hundreds of dollars. But he told us that the stars told him we could find you here."

"What's the old lady want this cherry-buster to do?"

"That's a family secret," said Annie. "And now you've asked enough questions. Come on home, you big fool."

They had moved but a little way up the street when Thomas stopped.

"Got any dough with you, Annie?" he asked.

Annie looked at him sharply.

"Oh, I know what that look means," said Thomas. "You're wrong. Not another drop. But there's a guy that was standing next to me in the Bed Line over there that's in a bad shape. He's the right kind, and he's got wives or kids or something, and he's on the sick-list. No booze. If you could dig up half a dollar for him so he could get a decent bed I'd like it."

Annie's fingers began to wiggle in her purse.

"Sure, I've got money," said she. "Lots of it. Twelve dollars." And then she added, with woman's ineradicable suspicion of vicarious benevolence: "Bring him here and let me see him first."

Thomas went on his mission. The wan Bed Liner came readily enough. As the two drew near, Annie looked up from her purse and screamed:

"Mr. Walter—oh—Mr. Walter!"

"Is that you, Annie?" said the young man weakly.

"Oh, Mr. Walter!—and the Missis hunting high and low for you!"

"Does mother want to see me?" he asked, with a flush coming out on his pale cheek.

"She's been hunting for you high and low. Sure, she wants to see you. She wants you to come home. She's tried police and morgues and lawyers and advertising and detectives and rewards and everything. And then she took up clearvoyants. You'll go right home, won't you, Mr. Walter?"

"Gladly, if she wants me," said the young man. "Three years is a long time. I suppose I'll have to walk up, though, unless the street-cars are giving free rides. I used to walk and beat that old plug team of bays we used to drive to the carriage. Have they got them yet?"

"They have," said Thomas feelingly. "And they'll have 'em ten years from now. The life of the royal elephantibus truckhorseibus is one hundred and forty-nine years. I'm the coachman. Just got my reappointment five minutes ago. Let's all ride up in a surface car—that is—er—if Annie will pay the fares."

On the Broadway car Annie handed each one of the prodigals a nickel to pay the conductor.

"Seems to me you are mighty reckless the way you throw large sums of money around," said Thomas sarcastically.

"In that purse," said Annie decidedly, "is exactly $11.85. I shall take every cent of it to-morrow and give it to Professor Cherubusco, the greatest man in the world."

"Well," said Thomas, "I guess he must be a pretty fly guy to pipe off things the way he does. I'm glad his spooks told him where you could find me. If you'll give me his address, some day I'll go up there myself, and shake his hand."

Presently Thomas moved tentatively in his seat, and thoughtfully felt an abrasion or two on his knees and elbows.

"Say, Annie," said he confidentially, "maybe it's one of the last dreams of the booze, but I've a kind of a recollection of riding in an automobile with a swell guy that took me to a house full of eagles and arc lights. He fed me on biscuits and hot air, and then kicked me down the front steps. If it was the *d t's*, why am I so sore?"

"Shut up, you fool," said Annie.

"If I could find that funny guy's house," said Thomas, in conclusion, "I'd go up there some day and punch his nose for him."

9

The Poet and the Peasant

THE other day a poet friend of mine, who has lived in close communication with nature all his life, wrote a poem, and took it to an editor.

It was a living pastoral, full of the genuine breath of the fields, the song of birds, and the pleasant chatter of trickling streams.

When the poet called again to see about it, with hopes of a beefsteak dinner in his heart, it was handed back to him with the comment:

"Too artificial."

Several of us met over spaghetti and Dutchess County chianti, and swallowed indignation with the slippery forkfuls.

And there we dug a pit for the editor. With us was Conant, a well-arrived writer of fiction—a man who had trod on asphalt all his life, and who had never looked upon bucolic scenes except with sensations of disgust from the windows of express trains.

Conant wrote a poem and called it "The Doe and the Brook". It was a fine specimen of the kind of work you would expect from a poet who had strayed with Amaryllis only as far as the florist's windows, and whose sole ornithological discussion had been carried on with a waiter. Conant signed this poem, and we sent it to the same editor.

But this has very little to do with the story.

Just as the editor was reading the first line of the poem, on the next morning, a being stumbled off the West Shore ferry-boat, and loped slowly up Forty-second Street.

The invader was a young man with light blue eyes, a hanging lip, and hair the exact colour of the little orphan's (afterward discovered to be the earl's daughter) in one of Mr.

Blaney's plays. His trousers were corduroy, his coat short-sleeved, with buttons in the middle of his back. One bootleg was outside the corduroys. You looked expectantly, though in vain, at his straw hat for ear-holes, its shape inaugurating the suspicion that it had been ravaged from a former equine possessor. In his hand was a valise—description of it is an impossible task; a Boston man would not have carried his lunch and law books to his office in it. And above one ear in his hair was a wisp of hay—the rustic's letter of credit, his badge of innocence, the last clinging touch of the Garden of Eden lingering to shame the gold-brick men.

Knowingly, smilingly, the city crowds passed him by. They saw the raw stranger stand in the gutter and stretch his neck at the tall buildings. At this they ceased to smile, and even to look at him. It had been done so often. A few glanced at the antique valise to see what Coney "attraction" or brand of chewing-gum he might be thus dinning into his memory. But for the most part he was ignored. Even the newsboys looked bored when he scampered like a circus clown out of the way of cabs and street-cars.

At Eighth Avenue stood "Bunco Harry", with his dyed moustache and shiny, good-natured eyes. Harry was too good an artist not to be pained at the sight of an actor overdoing his part. He edged up to the countryman, who had stopped to open his mouth at a jewellery store window, and shook his head.

"Too thick, pal," he said critically—"too thick by a couple of inches. I don't know what your lay is; but you've got the properties on too thick. That hay, now—why, they don't even allow that on Proctor's circuit any more."

"I don't understand you, mister," said the green one. "I'm not lookin' for any circus. I've just run down from Ulster County to look at the town, bein' that the hayin's over with. Gosh! but it's a whopper. I thought Poughkeepsie was some punkins; but this here town is five times as big."

"Oh, well," said "Bunco Harry", raising his eyebrows, "I didn't mean to butt in. You don't have to tell. I thought you ought to tone down a little, so I tried to put you wise. Wish you success at your graft, whatever it is. Come and have a drink, anyhow."

"I wouldn't mind having a glass of lager beer," acknowledged the other.

They went to a café frequented by men with smooth faces and shifty eyes, and sat at their drinks.

"I'm glad I come across you, mister," said Haylocks. "How'd you like to play a game or two of seven-up? I've got the keerds."

He fished them out of Noah's valise—a rare, inimitable deck, greasy with bacon suppers and grimy with the soil of cornfields.

"Bunco Harry" laughed loud and briefly.

"Not for me, sport," he said firmly. "I don't go against that make-up of yours for a cent. But I still say you've overdone it. The Reubs haven't dressed like that since '79. I doubt if you could work Brooklyn for a key-winding watch with that layout."

"Oh, you needn't think I ain't got the money," boasted Haylocks. He drew forth a tightly rolled mass of bills as large as a teacup, and laid it on the table.

"Got that for my share of grandmother's farm," he announced. "There's $950 in that roll. Thought I'd come into the city and look around for a likely business to go into."

"Bunco Harry" took up the roll of money and looked at it with almost respect in his smiling eyes.

"I've seen worse," he said critically. "But you'll never do it in them clothes. You want to get light tan shoes and a black suit and a straw hat with a coloured band, and talk a good deal about Pittsburg and freight differentials, and drink sherry for breakfast in order to work off phoney stuff like that."

"What's his line?" asked two or three shifty-eyed men of "Bunco Harry" after Haylocks had gathered up his impugned money and departed.

"The queer, I guess," said Harry. "Or else he's one of Jerome's men. Or some guy with a new graft. He's too much hayseed. Maybe that his—I wonder now—oh no, it couldn't have been real money."

Haylocks wandered on. Thirst probably assailed him again, for he dived into a dark groggery on a side-street and bought beer. Several sinister fellows hung upon one end of the bar. At first sight of him their eyes brightened; but when his insistent and exaggerated rusticity became apparent their expressions changed to wary suspicion.

Haylocks swung his valise across the bar.

"Keep that awhile for me, mister," he said, chewing at the end of a virulent claybank cigar. "I'll be back after I knock around a spell. And keep your eye on it, for there's $950 inside of it, though maybe you wouldn't think so to look at me."

Somewhere outside a phonograph struck up a band piece, and Haylocks was off for it, his coat-tail buttons flopping in the middle of his back.

"Divvy, Mike," said the men hanging upon the bar, winking openly at one another.

"Honest, now," said the bartender, kicking the valise to one side. "You don't think I'd fall to that, do you? Anybody can see he ain't no jay. One of McAdoo's come-on squad, I guess. He's a shine if he made himself up. There ain't no parts of the country now where they dress like that since they run rural free delivery to Providence, Rhode Island. If he's got nine-fifty in that valise it's a ninety-eight-cent Waterbury that's stopped at ten minutes to ten."

When Haylocks had exhausted the resources of Mr. Edison to amuse he returned for his valise. And then down Broadway he gallivanted, culling the sights with his eager blue eyes. But still and evermore Broadway rejected him with curt glances and sardonic smiles. He was the oldest of the "gags" that the city must endure. He was so flagrantly impossible, so ultra-rustic, so exaggerated beyond the most freakish products of the barnyard, the hayfield and the vaudeville stage, that he excited only weariness and suspicion. And the wisp of hay in his hair was so genuine, so fresh and redolent of the meadows, so clamorously rural, that even a shell-game man would have put up his peas and folded his table at the sight of it.

Haylocks seated himself upon a flight of stone steps and

once more exhumed his roll of yellow-backs from the valise. The outer one, a twenty, he shucked off and beckoned to a newsboy.

"Son," said he, "run somewhere and get this changed for me. I'm mighty nigh out of chicken feed. I guess you'll get a nickel if you'll hurry up."

A hurt look appeared through the dirt on the newsy's face.

"Aw, watchert'ink! G'wan and get yer funny bill changed yerself. Dey ain't no farm clothes yer got on. G'wan wit yer stage money."

On a corner lounged a keen-eyed steerer for a gambling-house. He saw Haylocks, and his expression suddenly grew cold and virtuous.

"Mister," said the rural one. "I've heard of places in this here town where a fellow could have a good game of old sledge or peg a card at keno. I got $950 in this valise, and I come down from old Ulster to see the sights. Know where a fellow could get action on about $9 or $10? I'm goin' to have some sport, and then maybe I'll buy out a business of some kind."

The steerer looked pained, and investigated a white speck on his left forefinger nail.

"Cheese it, old man," he murmured reproachfully. "The Central Office must be bughouse to send you out looking like such a gillie. You couldn't get within two blocks of a side-walk crap game in them Tony Pastor props. The recent Mr. Scotty from Death Valley has got you beat a cross-town block in the way of Elizabethan scenery and mechanical accessories. Let it be skiddoo for yours. Nay, I know of no gilded halls where one may bet a patrol wagon on the ace."

Rebuffed again by the great city that is so swift to detect artificialities, Haylocks sat upon the kerb and presented his thoughts to hold a conference.

"It's my clothes," said he; "durned if it ain't. They think I'm a hayseed and won't have nothin' to do with me. Nobody never made fun of this hat in Ulster County. I guess if you want folks to notice you in New York you must dress up like they do."

So Haylocks went shopping in the bazaars where men

spake through their noses and rubbed their hands and ran the tape line ecstatically over the bulge in his inside pocket where reposed a red nubbin of corn with an even number of rows. And messengers bearing parcels and boxes streamed to his hotel on Broadway within the lights of Long Acre.

At nine o'clock in the evening one descended to the sidewalk whom Ulster County would have forsworn. Bright tan were his shoes; his hat the latest block. His light grey trousers were deeply creased; a gay blue silk handkerchief flapped from the breast pocket of his elegant English walking-coat. His collar might have graced a laundry window; his blond hair was trimmed close; the wisp of hay was gone.

For an instant he stood, resplendent, with the leisurely air of a boulevardier concocting in his mind the route for his evening pleasures. And then he turned down the gay, bright street with the easy and graceful tread of a millionaire.

But in the instant that he had paused the wisest and keenest eyes in the city had enveloped him in their field of vision. A stout man with grey eyes picked two of his friends with a lift of his eyebrows from the row of loungers in front of the hotel.

"The juiciest jay I've seen in six months," said the man with grey eyes. "Come along."

It was half-past eleven when a man galloped into the West Forty-seventh Street police-station with the story of his wrongs.

"Nine hundred and fifty dollars," he gasped, "all my share of grandmother's farm."

The desk sergeant wrung from him the name Jabez Bulltongue, of Locust Valley Farm, Ulster County, and then began to take descriptions of the strong-arm gentlemen.

When Conant went to see the editor about the fate of his poem, he was received over the head of the office boy into the inner office that is decorated with the statuettes by Rodin and J. G. Brown.

"When I read the first line of 'The Doe and the Brook,'" said the editor, "I knew it to be the work of one whose life has been heart to heart with nature. The finished art of the line did not blind me to that fact. To use a somewhat homely comparison, it was as if a wild, free child of the woods and fields were to don the garb of fashion and walk down Broadway. Beneath the apparel the man would show."

"Thanks," said Conant. "I suppose the cheque will be round on Thursday, as usual."

The morals of this story have somehow gotten mixed. You can take your choice of "Stay on the Farm" or "Don't write Poetry".

10

Art and the Bronco

OUT of the wilderness had come a painter. Genius, whose coronations alone are democratic, had woven a chaplet of chaparral for the brow of Lonny Briscoe. Art, whose divine expression flows impartially from the finger-tips of a cowboy or a dilettante emperor, had chosen for a medium the Boy Artist of the San Saba. The outcome, seven feet by twelve of besmeared canvas, stood, gilt-framed, in the lobby of the Capitol.

The legislature was in session; the capital city of that great Western state was enjoying the season of activity and profit that the congregation of the solons bestowed. The boarding-houses were corralling the easy dollars of the gamesome law-makers. The greatest state in the West, an empire in area and resources, had arisen and repudiated the old libel of barbarism, law-breaking, and bloodshed. Order reigned within her borders. Life and property were as safe there, sir, as anywhere among the corrupt cities of the effete East. Pillow-shams, churches, strawberry feasts and *habeas corpus* flourished. With impunity might the tenderfoot ventilate his "stovepipe" or his theories of culture. The arts and sciences received nurture and subsidy. And, therefore, it behooved the legislature of this great state to make appropriation for the purchase of Lonny Briscoe's immortal painting.

Rarely has the San Saba country contributed to the spread of the fine arts. Its sons have excelled in the solider graces, in the throw of the lariat, the manipulation of the esteemed ·45, the intrepidity of the one-card draw, and the nocturnal stimulation of towns from undue lethargy; but, hitherto, it had not been famed as a stronghold of aesthetics. Lonny Briscoe's brush had removed that disability. Here, among the limestone rocks, the succulent cactus, and the drought-parched grass of that arid valley, had been born the Boy Artist. Why he came to woo art is beyond postulation. Beyond doubt, some spore of the afflatus must have sprung up within him in spite of the desert soil of San Saba. The tricksy spirit of creation must have incited him to attempted expression, and then have sat hilarious among the white-hot sands of the valley, watching its mischievous work. For Lonny's picture, viewed as a thing of art, was something to have driven away dull care from the bosoms of the critics.

The painting—one might almost say panorama—was designed to portray a typical Western scene, interest culminating in a central animal figure, that of a stampeding steer, life-size, wild-eyed, fiery, breaking away in a mad rush from the herd that, close-ridden by a typical cowpuncher, occupied a position somewhat in the right background of the picture. The landscape presented fitting and faithful accessories. Chaparral, mesquite, and pear were distributed in just proportions. A Spanish dagger-plant, with its waxen blossoms in a creamy aggregation as large as a water-bucket, contributed floral beauty and variety. The distance was undulating prairie, bisected by stretches of the intermittent streams peculiar to the region lined with the rich green of live-oak and water-elm. A richly mottled rattlesnake lay coiled beneath a pale green clump of prickly pear in the foreground. A third of the canvas was ultramarine and lake white —the typical Western sky and the flying clouds, rainless and feathery.

Between two plastered pillars in the commodious hallway near the door of the chamber of representatives stood the painting. Citizens and law-makers passed there by twos and groups and sometimes crowds to gaze upon it. Many—perhaps a majority of them—had lived the prairie life and recalled easily the familiar scene. Old cattlemen stood, reminiscent and candidly pleased, chatting with brothers of former camps and trails of the days it brought back to mind. Art critics were few in the town, and there was heard none of that jargon of colour, perspective, and feeling such as the East loves to use as a curb and a rod to the pretensions of the artist. 'Twas a great picture, most of them agreed, admiring the gilt frame—larger than any they had ever seen.

Senator Kinney was the picture's champion and sponsor. It was he who so often stepped forward and asserted, with the voice of a bronco-buster, that it would be a lasting blot, sir, upon the name of this great state if it should decline to recognize in a proper manner the genius that had so brilliantly transferred to imperishable canvas a scene so typical of the great sources of our state's wealth and prosperity, land—and —er—livestock.

Senator Kinney represented a section of the state in the extreme West—400 miles from the San Saba country—but the true lover of art is not limited by metes and bounds. Nor was Senator Mullens, representing the San Saba country, lukewarm in his belief that the state should purchase the painting of his constituent. He was advised that the San Saba country was unanimous in its admiration of the great painting by one of its own denizens. Hundreds of connoisseurs had straddled their broncos and ridden miles to view it before its removal to the capital. Senator Mullens desired re-election, and he knew the importance of the San Saba vote. He also knew that with the help of Senator Kinney—who was a power in the legislature—the thing could be put through. Now, Senator Kinney had an irrigation bill that he wanted passed for the benefit of his own section, and he knew Senator Mullens could render him valuable aid and information, the San Saba country already enjoying the benefits of similar legislation. With these interests happily dovetailed, wonder at the sudden interest in art at the state capital must, necessarily, be small. Few artists have uncovered their first picture to the world under happier auspices than did Lonny Briscoe.

Senators Kinney and Mullens came to an understanding in the matters of irrigation and art while partaking of long drinks in the café of the Empire Hotel.

"H'm!" said Senator Kinney, "I don't know. I'm no art critic, but it seems to me the thing won't work. It looks like the worst kind of a chromo to me. I don't want to cast any reflections upon the artistic talent of your constituent, Senator, but I, myself, wouldn't give six bits for the picture—

without the frame. How are you going to cram a thing like that down the throat of a legislature that kicks about a little item in the expense bill of six hundred and eighty-one dollars for rubber erasers for only one term? It's wasting time. I'd like to help you, Mullens, but they'd laugh us out of the Senate chamber if we were to try it."

"But you don't get the point," said Senator Mullens, in his deliberate tones, tapping Kinney's glass with his long forefinger. "I have my own doubts as to what the picture is intended to represent, a bullfight or a Japanese allegory, but I want this legislature to make an appropriation to purchase. Of course, the subject of the picture should have been in the state historical line, but it's too late to have the paint scraped off and changed. The state won't miss the money and the picture can be stored away in a lumber-room where it won't annoy anyone. Now, here's the point to work on, leaving art to look after itself—the chap that painted the picture is the grandson of Lucien Briscoe."

"Say it again," said Kinney, leaning his head thoughtfully. "Of the old, original Lucien Briscoe?"

"Of him. 'The man who', you know. The man who carved the state out of the wilderness. The man who settled the Indians. The man who cleaned out the horse thieves. The man who refused the crown. The state's favourite son. Do you see the point now?"

"Wrap up the picture," said Kinney. "It's as good as sold. Why didn't you say that at first, instead of philandering along about art. I'll resign my seat in the Senate and go back to chain-carrying for the county surveyor the day I can't make this state buy a picture calcimined by a grandson of Lucien Briscoe. Did you ever hear of a special appropriation for the purchase of a home for the daughter of One-Eyed Smothers? Well, that went through like a motion to adjourn, and old One-Eyed never killed half as many Indians as Briscoe did. About what figure had you and the calciminer agreed upon to sandbag the treasury for?"

"I thought," said Mullens, "that maybe five hundred——"

"Five hundred!" interrupted Kinney, as he hammered on his glass with a lead pencil and looked around for a waiter.

"Only five hundred for a red steer on the hoof delivered by a grandson of Lucien Briscoe! Where's your state pride, man! Two thousand is what it'll be. You'll introduce the bill and I'll get up on the floor of the Senate and wave the scalp of every Indian old Lucien ever murdered. Let's see, there was something else proud and foolish he did, wasn't there? Oh yes; he declined all emoluments and benefits he was entitled to. Refused his head-right and veteran donation certificates. Could have been governor, but wouldn't. Declined a pension. Now's the state's chance to pay up. It'll have to take the picture, but then it deserves some punishment for keeping the Briscoe family waiting so long. We'll bring this thing up about the middle of the month, after the tax bill is settled. Now, Mullens, you send over, as soon as you can, and get me the figures on the cost of those irrigation ditches and the statistics about the increased production per acre. I'm going to need you when that bill of mine comes up. I reckon we'll be able to pull along pretty well together that session and maybe others to come, eh, Senator?"

Thus did fortune elect to smile upon the Boy Artist of the San Saba. Fate had already done her share when she arranged his atoms in the cosmogony of creation as the grandson of Lucien Briscoe.

The original Briscoe had been a pioneer both as to territorial occupation and in certain acts prompted by a great and simple heart. He had been one of the first setters and crusaders against the wild forces of nature, the savage and the shallow politician. His name and memory were revered equally with any upon the list comprising Houston, Boone, Crockett, Clark, and Green. He had lived simply, independently, and unvexed by ambition. Even a less shrewd man than Senator Kinney could have prophesied that his state would hasten to honour and reward his grandson, come out of the chaparral at even so late a day.

And so, before the great picture by the door of the chamber of representatives, at frequent times for many days, could be found the breezy, robust form of Senator Kinney and be heard his clarion voice reciting the past deeds of Lucien Briscoe in connection with the handiwork of his grandson.

Senator Mullen's work was more subdued in sight and sound, but directed along identical lines.

Then, as the day for the introduction of the bill for appropriation draws nigh, up from the San Saba country rides Lonny Briscoe and a loyal lobby of cowpunchers, broncoback, to boost the cause of art and glorify the name of friendship, for Lonny is one of them, a knight of stirrup and chaparreras, as handy with the lariat and ·45 as he is with brush and palette.

On a March afternoon the lobby dashed, with a whoop, into town. The cowpunchers had adjusted their garb suitably from that prescribed for the range to the more conventional requirements of town. They had conceded their leather chaparreras and transferred their six-shooters and belts from their persons to the horns of their saddles. Among them rode Lonny, a youth of twenty-three, brown, solemn-faced, ingenuous, bow-legged, reticent, bestriding Hot Tamales, the most sagacious cow-pony west of the Mississippi. Senator Mullens had informed him of the bright prospects of the situation; had even mentioned—so great was his confidence in the capable Kinney—the price that the state would, in all likelihood, pay. It seemed to Lonny that fame and fortune were in his hands. Certainly, a spark of the divine fire was in the little brown centaur's breast, for he was counting the two thousand dollars as but a means to future development of his talent. Some day he would paint a picture even greater than this—one, say twelve feet by twenty, full of scope and atmosphere and action.

During the three days that yet intervened before the coming of the date fixed for the introduction of the bill the centaur lobby did valiant service. Coatless, spurred, weather-tanned, full of enthusiasm expressed in bizarre terms, they loafed in front of the painting with tireless zeal. Reasoning not unshrewdly, they estimated that their comments upon its fidelity to nature would be received as expert evidence. Loudly they praised the skill of the painter whenever there were ears near to which such evidence might be profitably addressed. Lem Perry, the leader of the claque, had a somewhat set speech, being uninventive in the construction of new phrases.

"Look at that two-year-old, now," he would say, waving a cinnamon-brown hand toward the salient point of the picture. "Why, dang my hide, the critter's alive. I can jest hear him, 'lumpety-lump,' a-cuttin' away from the herd, pretendin' he's skeered. He's a mean scamp, that there steer. Look at his eyes a-wallin' and his tail a-wavin'. He's true and nat'ral to life. He's jest hankerin' fur a cow-pony to round him up and send him scootin' back to the bunch. Dang my hide! jest look at that tail of his 'n a-wavin'. Never knowed a steer to wave his tail any other way, dang my hide if I did."

Jud Shelby, while admitting the excellence of the steer, resolutely confined himself to open admiration of the landscape, to the end that the entire picture received its meed of praise.

"That piece of range," he declared, "is a dead ringer for Dead Hoss Valley. Same grass, same lay of the land, same old Whipperwill Creek skallyhootin' in and out of them motts of timber. Them buzzards on the left is circlin' 'round over Sam Kildrake's old paint hoss that killed hisself overdrinkin' on a hot day. You can't see the hoss for that mott of ellums on the creek, but he's thar. Anybody that was goin' to look for Dead Hoss Valley and come across this picture, why, he'd jest light off 'n his bronco and hunt a place to camp."

Skinny Rogers, wedded to comedy, conceived a complimentary little piece of acting that never failed to make an impression. Edging quite near to the picture, he would suddenly, at favourable moments, emit a piercing and awful "Yi-yi!" leap high and away, coming down with a great stamp of heels and whirring of rowels upon the stone-flagged floor.

"Jeeming Christopher!"—so ran his lines—"thought that rattler was a gin-u-ine one. Ding baste my skin if I didn't. Seemed to me I heard him rattle. Look at the blamed, unconverted insect a-layin' under that pear. Little more, and somebody would a-been snake-bit."

With these artful dodges, contributed by Lonny's faithful coterie, with the sonorous Kinney perpetually sounding the picture's merits, and with the solvent prestige of the pioneer Briscoe covering it like a precious varnish, it seemed that the

San Saba country could not fail to add a reputation as an art centre to its well-known superiority in steer-roping contests and achievements with the precarious busted flush. Thus was created for the picture an atmosphere, due rather to externals than to the artist's brush, but through it the people seemed to gaze with more of admiration. There was a magic in the name of Briscoe that counted high against faulty technique and crude colouring. The old Indian fighter and wolf slayer would have smiled grimly in his happy hunting-grounds had he known that his dilettante ghost was thus figuring as an art patron two generations after his uninspired existence.

Came the day when the Senate was expected to pass the bill of Senator Mullens appropriating two thousand dollars for the purchase of the picture. The gallery of the Senate chamber was early pre-empted by Lonny and the San Saba lobby. In the front row of chairs they sat, wild-haired, self-conscious, jingling, creaking, and rattling, subdued by the majesty of the council hall.

The bill was introduced, went to the second reading, and then Senator Mullens spoke for it dryly, tediously, and at length. Senator Kinney then arose, and the welkin seized the bell-rope preparatory to ringing. Oratory was at that time a living thing; the world had not quite come to measure its questions by geometry and the multiplication table. It was the day of the silver tongue, the sweeping gesture, the decorative apostrophe, the moving peroration.

The Senator spoke. The San Saba contingent sat, breathing hard, in the gallery, its disordered hair hanging down to its eyes, its sixteen-ounce hats shifted restlessly from knee to knee. Below, the distinguished Senators either lounged at their desks with the abandon of proven statesmanship or maintained correct attitudes indicative of a first term.

Senator Kinney spoke for an hour. History was his theme—history mitigated by patriotism and sentiment. He referred casually to the picture in the outer hall—it was unnecessary, he said, to dilate upon its merits—the Senators had seen for themselves. The painter of the picture was the grandson of Lucien Briscoe. Then came the word-pictures of Briscoe's life set forth in thrilling colours. His rude and venturesome life, his simple-minded love for the commonwealth he helped to upbuild, his contempt for rewards and praise, his extreme and sturdy independence, and the great services he had rendered the state. The subject of the oration was Lucien Briscoe; the painting stood in the background, serving simply as a means, now happily brought forward, through which the state might bestow a tardy recompense upon the descendant of its favourite son. Frequent enthusiastic applause from the Senators testified to the well reception of the sentiment.

The bill passed without an opposing vote. To-morrow it would be taken up by the House. Already was it fixed to glide through that body on rubber tyres. Blandford, Grayson, and Plummer, all wheel-horses and orators, and provided with plentiful memoranda concerning the deeds of pioneer Briscoe, had agreed to furnish the motive power.

The San Saba lobby and its protégé stumbled awkwardly down the stairs and out into the Capitol yard. Then they herded closely and gave one yell of triumph. But one of them —Buck-Kneed Summers it was—hit the key with the thoughtful remark:

"She cut the mustard," he said, "all right. I reckon they're goin' to buy Lon's steer. I ain't right much on the parlyment'ry, but I gather that's what the signs added up. But she seems to me, Lonny, the argyment ran principal to grandfather, instead of paint. It's reasonable calculatin' that you want to be glad you got the Briscoe brand on you, my son."

That remark clinched in Lonny's mind an unpleasant, vague suspicion to the same effect. His reticence increased, and he gathered grass from the ground, chewing it pensively. The picture as a picture had been humiliatingly absent from the Senator's arguments. The painter had been held up as a grandson, pure and simple. While this was gratifying on certain lines, it made art look little and slab-sided. The Boy Artist was thinking.

The hotel Lonny stopped at was near the Capitol. It was near to the one o'clock dinner-hour when the appropriation had been passed by the Senate. The hotel clerk told Lonny that a famous artist from New York had arrived in town that day and was in the hotel. He was on his way westward to New Mexico to study the effect of sunlight upon the ancient walls of the Zuñis. Modern stone reflects light. Those ancient building materials absorb it. The artist wanted this effect in a picture he was painting and was travelling two thousand miles to get it.

Lonny sought this man out after dinner and told his story. The artist was an unhealthy man, kept alive by genius and indifference to life. He went with Lonny to the Capitol and stood there before the picture. The artist pulled his beard and looked unhappy.

"Should like to have your sentiments," said Lonny, "just as they run out of the pen."

"It's the way they'll come," said the painter man. "I took three different kinds of medicine before dinner—by the tablespoonful. The taste still lingers. I am primed for telling the truth. You want to know if the picture is, or if it isn't?"

"Right," said Lonny. "Is it wool or cotton? Should I paint some more or cut it out and ride herd a-plenty?"

"I heard the rumour during pie," said the artist, "that the state is about to pay you two thousand dollars for this picture."

"It's passed the Senate," said Lonny, "and the House rounds it up to-morrow."

"That's lucky," said the pale man. "Do you carry a rabbit's foot?"

"No," said Lonny, "but it seems I had a grandfather. He's considerable mixed up in the colour scheme. It took me a year to paint that picture. Is she entirely awful or not? Some say, now, that that steer's tail ain't badly drawed. They think it's proportioned nice. Tell me."

The artist glanced at Lonny's wiry figure and nut-brown skin. Something stirred him to a passing irritation.

"For Art's sake, son," he said, fractiously, "don't spend any more money for paint. It isn't a picture at all. It's a gun. You hold up the state with it, if you like, and get your two thousand, but don't get in front of any more canvas. Live under it. Buy a couple of hundred ponies with the money—I'm told they're that cheap—and ride, ride, ride. Fill your lungs and eat and sleep and be happy. No more pictures. You look healthy. That's genius. Cultivate it." He looked at his watch. "Twenty minutes to three. Four capsules and one tablet at three. That's all you wanted to know, isn't it?"

At three o'clock the cowpunchers rode up for Lonny, bringing Hot Tamales, saddled. Traditions must be observed. To celebrate the passing of the bill by the Senate the gang must ride wildly through the town, creating uproar and excitement. Liquor must be partaken of, the suburbs shot up, and the glory of the San Saba country vociferously proclaimed. A part of the programme had been carried out in the saloons on the way up.

Lonny mounted Hot Tamales, the accomplished little beast prancing with fire and intelligence. He was glad to feel Lonny's bowlegged grip against his ribs again. Lonny was his friend, and he was willing to do things for him.

"Come on, boys," said Lonny, urging Hot Tamales into a gallop with his knees. With a whoop, the inspired lobby tore after him through the dust. Lonny led his cohorts straight for the Capitol. With a wild yell, the gang endorsed his now evident intention of riding into it. Hooray for San Saba.

Up the six broad, limestone steps clattered the broncos of the cowpunchers. Into the resounding hallway they pattered, scattering in dismay those passing on foot. Lonny, in the lead, shoved Hot Tamales direct for the great picture. At that hour a downpouring, soft light from the second-storey windows bathed the big canvas. Against the darker background of the hall the painting stood out with valuable effect. In spite of the defects of the art you could almost fancy that you gazed out upon a landscape. You might well flinch a step from the convincing figure of the life-sized steer stampeding across the grass. Perhaps it thus seemed to Hot Tamales. The scene was in his line. Perhaps he only obeyed the will of his rider. His ears pricked up; he snorted. Lonny leaned forward in the saddle and elevated his elbows, wing-like. Thus signals the cowpuncher to his steed to launch himself full speed ahead. Did Hot Tamales fancy he saw a steer, red and cavorting that should be headed off and driven back to herd? There was a fierce clatter of hoofs, a rush, a gathering of steely flank muscles, a leap to the jerk of the bridle rein, and Hot Tamales, with Lonny bending low in the saddle to dodge the top of the frame, ripped through the great canvas like a shell from a mortar, leaving the cloth hanging in ragged shreds about a monstrous hole.

Quickly Lonny pulled up his pony, and rounded the pillars. Spectators came running, too astounded to add speech to the commotion. The sergeant-at-arms of the House came forth, frowned, looked ominous, and then grinned. Many of the legislators crowded out to observe the tumult. Lonny's cowpunchers were stricken to silent horror by his mad deed.

Senator Kinney happened to be among the earliest to emerge. Before he could speak Lonny leaned in his saddle as Hot Tamales pranced, pointed his squirt at the Senator, and said calmly:

"That was a fine speech you made to-day, mister, but you might as well let up on that 'propriation business. I ain't askin' the state to give me nothin'. I thought I had a picture to sell to it, but it wasn't one. You said a heap of things about Grandfather Briscoe that makes me kind of proud I'm his grandson. Well, the Briscoes ain't takin' presents from the state yet. Anybody can have the frame that wants it. Hit her up, boys."

Away scuttled the San Saba delegation out of the hall, down the steps, along the dusty street.

Half-way to the San Saba country they camped that night. At bedtime Lonny stole away from the camp-fire and sought Hot Tamales, placidly eating grass at the end of his stake rope. Lonny hung upon his neck, and his art aspirations went forth for ever in one long, regretful sigh. But as he thus made renunciation his breath formed a word or two.

"You was the only one, Tamales, what seen anything in it. It *did* look like a steer, didn't it, old hoss?"

11

A Chaparral Christmas Gift

THE original cause of the trouble was about twenty years in growing.

At the end of that time it was worth it.

Had you lived anywhere within fifty miles of Sundown Ranch you would have heard of it. It possessed a quantity of jet-black hair, a pair of extremely frank, deep-brown eyes, and a laugh that rippled across the prairie like the sound of a hidden brook. The name of it was Rosita McMullen; and she was the daughter of old man McMullen of the Sundown Sheep Ranch.

There came riding on red roan steeds—or, to be more explicit, on a paint and a flea-bitten sorrel—two wooers. One was Madison Lane, and the other was the Frio Kid. But at that time they did not call him the Frio Kid, for he had not earned the honours of special nomenclature. His name was simply Johnny McRoy.

It must not be supposed that these two were the sum of the agreeable Rosita's admirers. The bronchos of a dozen others champed their bits at the long hitching-rack of the Sundown Ranch. Many were the sheep's-eyes that were cast in those savannas that did not belong to the flocks of Dan McMullen. But of all the cavaliers, Madison Lane and Johnny McRoy galloped far ahead, wherefore they are to be chronicled.

Madison Lane, a young cattleman from the Nueces country, won the race. He and Rosita were married one Christmas day. Armed, hilarious, vociferous, magnanimous, the cowmen and the sheepmen, laying aside their hereditary hatred, joined forces to celebrate the occasion.

Sundown Ranch was sonorous with the cracking of jokes and sixshooters, the shine of buckles and bright eyes, the outspoken congratulations of the herders of kine.

But while the wedding feast was at its liveliest there descended upon it Johnny McRoy, bitten by jealousy, like one possessed.

"I'll give you a Christmas present," he yelled shrilly at the door, with his ·45 in his hand. Even then he had some reputation as an offhand shot.

His first bullet cut a neat underbit in Madison Lane's right ear. The barrel of his gun moved an inch. The next shot would have been the bride's had not Carson, a sheepman, possessed a mind with triggers somewhat well oiled and in repair. The guns of the wedding party had been hung, in their belts, upon nails in the wall when they sat at table, as a concession to good taste. But Carson, with great promptness, hurled his plate of roast venison and frijoles at McRoy, spoiling his aim. The second bullet, then, only shattered the white petals of a Spanish dagger flower suspended two feet above Rosita's head.

The guests spurned their chairs and jumped for their weapons. It was considered an improper act to shoot the bride and groom at a wedding. In about six seconds there were twenty or so bullets due to be whizzing in the direction of Mr. McRoy.

"I'll shoot better next time," yelled Johnny; "and there'll be a next time." He backed rapidly out the door.

Carson, the sheepman, spurred on to attempt further exploits by the success of his plate-throwing, was first to reach the door. McRoy's bullet from the darkness laid him low.

The cattlemen then swept out upon him, calling for vengeance, for, while the slaughter of a sheepman has not always lacked condonement, it was a decided misdemeanour in this instance. Carson was innocent; he was no accomplice at the matrimonial proceedings; nor had anyone heard him quote the line "Christmas comes but once a year" to the guests.

But the sortie failed in its vengeance. McRoy was on his horse and away, shouting back curses and threats as he galloped into the concealing chaparral.

That night was the birthright of the Frio Kid. He became the "bad man" of that portion of the State. The rejection of his suit by Miss McMullen turned him to a dangerous man. When officers went after him for the shooting of Carson, he killed two of them, and entered upon the life of an outlaw. He became a marvellous shot with either hand. He would turn up in towns and settlements, raise a quarrel at the slightest opportunity, pick off his man and laugh at the officers of the law. He was so cool, so deadly, so rapid, so inhumanly bloodthirsty that none but faint attempts were ever made to capture him. When he was at last shot and killed by a little one-armed Mexican who was nearly dead himself from fright, the Frio Kid had the deaths of eighteen men on his head. About half of these were killed in fair duels depending upon the quickness of the draw. The other half were men whom he assassinated from absolute wantonness and cruelty. Many tales are told along the border of his impudent courage and daring. But he was not one of the breed of desperadoes who have seasons of generosity and even of softness. They say he never had mercy on the object of his anger. Yet at this and every Christmastide it is well to give each one credit, if it can be done, for whatever speck of good he may have possessed. If the Frio Kid ever did a kindly act or felt a throb of generosity in his heart it was once at such a time and season, and this is the way it happened.

* * *

One who has been crossed in love should never breathe the odour from the blossoms of the ratama tree. It stirs the memory to a dangerous degree.

One December in the Frio country there was a ratama tree in full bloom, for the winter had been as warm as springtime. That way rode the Frio Kid and his satellite and co-murderer, Mexican Frank. The Kid reined in his mustang, and sat in his saddle, thoughtful and grim, with dangerously narrowing eyes. The rich, sweet scent touched him somewhere beneath his ice and iron.

"I don't know what I've been thinking about, Mex," he remarked in his usual mild drawl, "to have forgot all about a Christmas present I got to give. I'm going to ride over tomorrow night and shoot Madison Lane in his own house.

He got my girl—Rosita would have had me if he hadn't cut into the game. I wonder why I happened to overlook it up to now?"

"Ah, shucks, Kid," said Mexican, "don't talk foolishness. You know you can't get within a mile of Mad Lane's house to-morrow night. I see old man Allen day before yesterday, and he says Mad is going to have Christmas doings at his house. You remember how you shot up the festivities when Mad was married, and about the threats you made? Don't you suppose Mad Lane'll kind of keep his eye open for a certain Mr. Kid? You plumb make me tired, Kid, with such remarks."

"I'm going," repeated the Frio Kid, without heat, "to go to Madison Lane's Christmas doings and kill him. I ought to have done it a long time ago. Why, Mex, just two weeks ago I dreamed me and Rosita was married instead of her and him; and we was living in a house, and I could see her smiling at me, and—oh! h——l, Mex, he got her; and I'll get him—yes, sir, on Christmas Eve he got her, and then's when I'll get him."

"There's other ways of committing suicide," advised Mexican. "Why don't you go and surrender to the sheriff."

"I'll get him," said the Kid.

Christmas Eve fell as balmy as April. Perhaps there was a hint of far-away frostiness in the air, but it tingled like seltzer, perfumed faintly with late prairie blossoms and the mesquite grass.

When night came the five or six rooms of the ranch-house were brightly lit. In one room was a Christmas tree, for the Lanes had a boy of three, and a dozen or more guests were expected from the nearer ranches.

At nightfall Madison Lane called aside Jim Belcher and three other cowboys employed on his ranch.

"Now, boys," said Lane, "keep your eyes open. Walk around the house and watch the road well. All of you know the 'Frio Kid,' as they call him now, and if you see him, open fire on him without asking any questions. I'm not afraid of his coming around, but Rosita is. She's been afraid he'd come in on us every Christmas since we were married."

The guests had arrived in buckboards and on horseback, and were making themselves comfortable inside.

The evening went along pleasantly. The guests enjoyed and praised Rosita's excellent supper, and afterward the men scattered in groups about the rooms or on the broad "gallery", smoking and chatting.

The Christmas tree, of course, delighted the youngsters, and above all were they pleased when Santa Claus himself in magnificent white beard and furs appeared and began to distribute the toys.

"It's my papa," announced Billy Sampson, aged six. "I've seen him wear 'em before."

Berkly, a sheepman, an old friend of Lane, stopped Rosita as she was passing by him on the gallery, where he was sitting smoking.

"Well, Mrs. Lane," said he, "I suppose by this Christmas you've gotten over being afraid of that fellow McRoy, haven't you? Madison and I have talked about it, you know."

"Very nearly," said Rosita, smiling, "but I am still nervous sometimes. I shall never forget that awful time when he came so near to killing us."

"He's the most cold-hearted villain in the world," said Berkly. "The citizens all along the border ought to turn out and hunt him down like a wolf."

"He has committed awful crimes," said Rosita, "but—I—don't—know. I think there is a spot of good somewhere in everybody. He was not always bad—that I know."

Rosita turned into the hallway between the rooms. Santa Claus, in muffling whiskers and furs, was just coming through.

"I heard what you said through the window, Mrs. Lane," he said. "I was just going down in my pocket for a Christmas present for your husband. But I've left one for you, instead. It's in the room to your right."

"Oh, thank you, kind Santa Claus," said Rosita brightly.

Rosita went into the room, while Santa Claus stepped into the cooler air of the yard.

She found no one in the room but Madison.

"Where is my present that Santa said he left for me in here?" she asked.

"Haven't seen anything in the way of a present," said her husband, laughing, "unless he could have meant me."

* * *

The next day Gabriel Radd, the foreman of the X Q Ranch, dropped into the post-office at Loma Alta.

"Well, the Frio Kid's got his dose of lead at last," he remarked to the postmaster.

"That's so? How'd it happen?"

"One of old Sanchez's Mexican sheep-herders did it!—think of it! the Frio Kid killed by a sheepherder! The Greaser saw him riding along past his camp about twelve o'clock last night, and was so skeered that he up with a Winchester and let him have it. Funniest part of it was that the Kid was dressed all up with white Angora-skin whiskers and a regular Santy Claus rig-out from head to foot. Think of the Frio Kid playing Santy!"

12

In Mezzotint

THE doctor had long ago ceased his hospital practice, but whenever there was a case of special interest among the wards, his spirited team of boys was sure to be seen standing at the hospital gates. Young, handsome, at the head of his profession, possessing an ample income, and married but six months to a beautiful girl who adored him, his lot was certainly one to be envied.

It must have been nine o'clock when he reached home. The stableman took the team, and he ran up the steps lightly. The door opened, and Doris's arms were flung tightly about his neck, and her wet cheek pressed to his.

"Oh, Ralph," she said, her voice quivering and plaintive, "you are so late. You can't think how I miss you when you don't come at the usual hour. I've kept supper warm for you. I'm so jealous of those patients of yours—they keep you from me so much."

"How fresh and sweet and wholesome you are, after the sights I have to see," he said, smiling down at her girlish face with the airy confidence of a man who knows himself well beloved. "Now, pour my coffee, little one, while I go up and change clothes."

After supper he sat in the library in his favourite armchair, and she sat in her especial place upon the arm of the chair and held a match for him to light his cigar. She seemed so glad to have him with her; every touch was a caress, and every word she spoke had that lingering, loving drawl that a woman uses to but one man—at a time.

"I lost my case of cerebro-spinal meningitis to-night," he said gravely.

"I have you, and I don't have you," she said. "Your thoughts are always with your profession, even when I think you are most mine. Ah, well," with a sigh, "you help the suffering, and I would see all that suffer relieved or else like your cerebro—what is it?—patient, at rest."

"A queer case, too," said the doctor, patting his wife's hand and gazing into the clouds of cigar smoke. "He should have recovered. I had him cured, and he died on my hands without any warning. Ungrateful, too, for I treated that case beautifully. Confound the fellow. I believe he wanted to die. Some nonsensical romance worried him into a fever."

"A romance? Oh, Ralph, tell it to me. Just think! A romance in a hospital."

"He tried to tell it to me this morning in snatches between paroxysms of pain. He was bending backward till his head almost touched his heels, and his ribs were nearly cracking, yet he managed to convey something of his life story."

"Oh, how horrible," said the doctor's wife, slipping her arm between his neck and the chair.

"It seems," went on the doctor, "as well as I could gather, that some girl had discarded him to marry a more well-to-do man, and he lost hope and interest in life, and went to the dogs. No, he refused to tell her name. There was a great pride in that meningitis case. He lied like an angel about his own name, and he gave his watch to the nurse and spoke to her as he would to a queen. I don't believe I ever will forgive him for dying, for I worked the next thing to a miracle on him. Well, he died this morning, and—let me get a match—oh, yes, here's a little thing in my pocket he gave me to have buried with him. He told me about starting to a concert with this girl one night, and they decided not to go in, but take a moonlight walk instead. She tore the ticket in two pieces, and gave him one half and kept the other. Here's his half, this little red piece of pasteboard with the word 'Admit——' printed on it. Look out, little one—that old chair arm is so slippery. Hurt you?"

"No, Ralph. I'm not so easy hurt. What do you think love is, Ralph?"

"Love? Little one! Oh, love is undoubtedly a species of mild insanity. An over-balance of the brain that leads to an abnormal state. It is as much a disease as measles, but as yet, sentimentalists refuse to hand it over to us doctors of medicine for treatment."

His wife took the half of the little red ticket and held it up.

"Admit——" she said, with a little laugh. "I suppose by this time he's admitted somewhere, isn't he, Ralph?"

"Somewhere," said the doctor, lighting his cigar afresh.

"Finish your cigar, Ralph, and then come up," she said. "I'm a little tired, and I'll wait for you above."

"All right, little one," said the doctor. "Pleasant dreams!"

He smoked the cigar out, and then lit another.

It was nearly eleven when he went up stairs.

The light in his wife's room was turned low, and she lay upon her bed undressed. As he stepped to her side and raised her hand, some steel instrument fell and jingled upon the floor, and he saw upon the white countenance a creeping red horror that froze his blood.

He sprang to the lamp and turned up the blaze. As he parted his lips to send forth a shout, he paused for a moment, with his eyes upon his dead patient's half ticket that lay upon the table. The other half had been neatly fitted to it, and it now read:

ADMIT ONE

13

A Ramble in Aphasia

My wife and I parted on that morning in precisely our usual manner. She left her second cup of tea to follow me to the front door. There she plucked from my lapel the invisible strand of lint (the universal act of woman to proclaim ownership) and bade me take care of my cold. I had no cold. Next came her kiss of parting—the level kiss of domesticity flavoured with Young Hyson. There was no fear of the extemporaneous, of variety spicing her infinite custom. With the deft touch of long malpractice, she dabbed awry my well-set scarf-pin; and then, as I closed the door, I heard her morning slippers pattering back to her cooling tea.

When I set out I had no thought or premonition of what was to occur. The attack came suddenly.

For many weeks I had been toiling, almost night and day, at a famous railroad law case that I won triumphantly but a few days previously. In fact, I had been digging away at the law almost without cessation for many years. Once or twice good Doctor Volney, my friend and physician, had warned me.

"If you don't slacken up, Bellford," he said, "you'll go suddenly to pieces. Either your nerves or your brain will give way. Tell me, does a week pass in which you do not read in the papers of a case of aphasia—some man lost, wandering nameless, with his past and his identity blotted out—and all from that little brain-clot made by overwork or worry?"

"I always thought," said I, "that the clot in those instances was really to be found on the brains of the newspaper reporters."

Dr. Volney shook his head.

"The disease exists," he said. "You need a change or a rest. Court-room, office and home—there is the only route you travel. For recreation you—read law books. Better take warning in time."

"On Thursday nights," I said defensively, "my wife and I play cribbage. On Sundays she reads to me the weekly letter from her mother. That law books are not a recreation remains yet to be established."

That morning as I walked I was thinking of Doctor Volney's words. I was feeling as well as I usually did—possibly in better spirits than usual.

* * *

I awoke with stiff and cramped muscles from having slept long on the incommodious seat of a day coach. I leaned my head against the seat and tried to think. After a long time I said to myself: "I must have a name of some sort." I searched my pockets. Not a card; not a letter; not a paper or monogram could I find. But I found in my coat pocket nearly $3,000 in bills of large denomination. "I must be someone, of course," I repeated to myself, and began again to consider.

The car was well crowded with men, among whom, I told myself, there must have been some common interest, for they intermingled freely, and seemed in the best good-humour and spirits. One of them—a stout, spectacled gentleman enveloped in a decided odour of cinnamon and aloes—took the vacant half of my seat with a friendly nod, and unfolded a newspaper. In the intervals between his periods of reading, we conversed, as travellers will, on current affairs. I found myself able to sustain the conversation on such subjects with credit, at least to my memory. By and by my companion said:

"You are one of us, of course. Fine lot of men the West sends in this time. I'm glad they held the convention in New York; I've never been East before. My name's R. P. Bolder—Bolder & Son, of Hickory Grove, Missouri."

Though unprepared, I rose to the emergency, as men will when put to it. Now must I hold a christening, and be at once babe, parson and parent. My senses came to the rescue of my slower brain. The insistent odour of drugs from my companion supplied one idea; a glance at his newspaper, where my eye met a conspicuous advertisement, assisted me further.

"My name," said I glibly, "is Edward Pinkhammer. I am a druggist, and my home is in Cornopolis, Kansas."

"I knew you were a druggist," said my fellow-traveller affably. "I saw the callous spot on your right forefinger where the handle of the pestle rubs. Of course, you are a delegate to our National Convention."

"Are all these men druggists?" I asked wonderingly.

"They are. This car came through from the West. And they're your old-time druggists, too—none of your patent tablet-and-granule pharmashootists that use slot machines instead of a prescription desk. We percolate our own paregoric and roll our own pills, and we ain't above handling a few garden seeds in the spring, and carrying a sideline of confectionery and shoes. I tell you, Hampinker, I've got an idea to spring on this convention—new ideas is what they want. Now, you know the shelf bottles of tartar emetic and Rochelle salt Ant. et Pot. Tart. and Sod. et Pot. Tart.—one's poison, you know, and the other's harmless. It's easy to mistake one label for the other. Where do druggists mostly keep 'em? Why, as far apart as possible, on different shelves. That's wrong. I say keep 'em side by side so when you want one you can always compare it with the other and avoid mistakes. Do you catch the idea?"

"It seems to me a very good one," I said.

"All right! When I spring it on the convention you back it up. We'll make some of these Eastern orange-phosphate-and-massage-cream professors that think they're the only lozenges in the market look like hypodermic tablets."

"If I can be of any aid," I said, warming, "the two bottles of—er——"

"Tartrate of antimony and potash, and tartrate of soda and potash."

"Shall henceforth sit side by side," I concluded firmly.

"Now, there's another thing," said Mr. Bolder. "For an excipient in manipulating a pill mass which do you prefer—the magnesia carbonate or the pulverized glycerrhiza radix?"

"The—er—magnesia," I said. It was easier to say than the other word.

Mr. Bolder glanced at me distrustfully through his spectacles.

"Give me the glycerrhiza," said he. "Magnesia cakes."

"Here's another one of these fake aphasia cases," he said, presently, handing me his newspaper, and laying his finger upon an article. "I don't believe in 'em. I put nine out of ten of 'em down as frauds. A man gets sick of his business and his folks and wants to have a good time. He skips out somewhere, and when they find him he pretends to have lost his memory—don't know his own name, and won't even recognize the strawberry mark on his wife's left shoulder. Aphasia! Tut! Why can't they stay at home and forget?"

I took the paper and read, after the pungent headlines, the following:

DENVER, June 12.—Elwyn C. Bellford, a prominent lawyer is mysteriously missing from his home since three days ago, and all efforts to locate him have been in vain. Mr. Bellford is a well-known citizen of the highest standing, and has enjoyed a large and lucrative law practice. He is married and owns a fine home and the most extensive private library in the State. On the day of his disappearance, he drew quite a large sum of money from his bank. No one can be found who saw him after he left the bank. Mr. Bellford was a man of singularly quiet and domestic tastes, and seemed to find his happiness in his home and profession. If any clue at all exists to his strange disappearance, it may be found in the fact that for some months he had been deeply absorbed in an important law case in connection with the Q. Y. and Z. Railroad Company. It is feared that overwork may have affected his mind. Every effort is being made to discover the whereabouts of the missing man.

"It seems to me you are not altogether uncynical, Mr. Bolder," I said, after I had read the despatch. "This has the sound, to me, of a genuine case. Why should this man, prosperous, happily married and respected, choose suddenly to abandon everything? I know that these lapses of memory do occur, and that men do find themselves adrift without a name, a history or a home."

"Oh, gammon and jalap!" said Mr. Bolder. "It's larks they're after. There's too much education nowadays. Men know about aphasia, and they use it for an excuse. The women are wise, too. When it's all over they look you in the eye, as scientific as you please, and say: 'He hypnotized me.'"

Thus Mr. Bolder diverted, but did not aid me with his comments and philosophy.

We arrived in New York about ten at night. I rode in a cab to an hotel, and I wrote my name "Edward Pinkhammer" in the register. As I did so I felt pervade me a splendid, wild, intoxicating buoyancy—a sense of unlimited freedom, of newly attained possibilities. I was just born into the world. The old fetters—whatever they had been—were stricken from my hands and feet. The future lay before me a clear road such as an infant enters, and I could set out upon it equipped with a man's learning and experience.

I thought the hotel clerk looked at me five seconds too long. I had no baggage.

"The Druggists' Convention," I said. "My trunk has somehow failed to arrive." I drew out a roll of money.

"Ah!" said he, showing an auriferous tooth, "we have quite a number of the Western delegates stopping here." He struck a bell for the boy.

I endeavoured to give colour to my rôle.

"There is an important movement on foot among us Westerners," I said, "in regard to a recommendation to the convention that the bottles containing the tartrate of antimony and potash, and the tartrate of sodium and potash, be kept in a contiguous position on the shelf."

"Gentleman to three-fourteen," said the clerk hastily. I was whisked away to my room.

The next day I bought a trunk and clothing, and began to live the life of Edward Pinkhammer. I did not tax my brain with endeavours to solve problems of the past.

It was a piquant and sparkling cup that the great island city held up to my lips. I drank of it gratefully. The keys of

Manhattan belong to him who is able to bear them. You must be either the city's guest or its victim.

The following few days were as gold and silver. Edward Pinkhammer, yet counting back to his birth by hours only, knew the rare joy of having come upon so diverting a world full-fledged and unrestrained. I sat entranced on the magic carpets provided in theatres and roof-gardens, that transported one into strange and delightful lands full of frolic-some music, pretty girls and grotesque, drolly extravagant parodies upon humankind. I went here and there at my own dear will, bound by no limits of space, time or comportment. I dined in weird cabarets, at weirder tables d'hôte to the sound of Hungarian music and the wild shouts of mercurial artists and sculptors. Or, again, where the night life quivers in the electric glare like a kinetoscopic picture, and the millinery of the world, and its jewels, and the ones whom they adorn, and the men who make all three possible are met for good cheer and the spectacular effect. And among all these scenes that I have mentioned I learned one thing that I never knew before. And that is that the key to liberty is not in the hands of Licence, but Convention holds it. Comity has a toll-gate at which you must pay, or you may not enter the land of Freedom. In all the glitter, the seeming disorder, the parade, the abandon, I saw this law, unobtrusive, yet like iron, prevail. Therefore, in Manhattan you must obey these unwritten laws, and then you will be freest of the free. If you decline to be bound by them, you put on shackles.

Sometimes, as my mood urged me, I would seek the stately, softly murmuring palm-rooms, redolent with high-born life and delicate restraint, in which to dine. Again I would go down to the waterways in steamers packed with vociferous, bedecked, unchecked, love-making clerks and shop-girls to their crude pleasures on the island shores. And there was always Broadway—glistening, opulent, wily, varying, desirable Broadway—growing upon one like an opium habit.

One afternoon as I entered my hotel a stout man with a big nose and a black moustache blocked my way in the corridor. When I would have passed around him, he greeted me with offensive familiarity.

"Hallo, Bellford!" he cried loudly. "What the deuce are you doing in New York? Didn't know anything could drag you away from that old book den of yours. Is Mrs. B. along or is this a little business run alone, eh?"

"You have made a mistake, sir," I said coldly, releasing my hand from his grasp. "My name is Pinkhammer. You will excuse me."

The man dropped to one side, apparently astonished. As I walked to the clerk's desk I heard him call to a bell-boy and say something about telegraph blanks.

"You will give me my bill," I said to the clerk, "and have my baggage brought down in half an hour. I do not care to remain where I am annoyed by confidence men."

I moved that afternoon to another hotel, a sedate, old-fashioned one on lower Fifth Avenue.

There was a restaurant a little way off Broadway where one could be served almost *al fresco* in a tropic array of screening flora. Quiet and luxury and a perfect service made it an ideal place in which to take luncheon or refreshment. One afternoon I was there picking my way to a table among the ferns when I felt my sleeve caught.

"Mr. Bellford!" exclaimed an amazingly sweet voice.

I turned quickly to see a lady seated alone—a lady of about thirty, with exceedingly handsome eyes, who looked at me as though I had been her very dear friend.

"You were about to pass me," she said accusingly. "Don't tell me you did not know me. Why should we not shake hands—at least once in fifteen years?"

I shook hands with her at once. I took a chair opposite her at the table. I summoned with my eyebrows a hovering waiter. The lady was philandering with an orange ice. I ordered a *crème de menthe*. Her hair was reddish bronze. You could not look at it, because you could not look away from her eyes. But you were conscious of it as you are conscious of sunset while you look into the profundities of a wood at twilight.

"Are you sure you know me?" I asked.

"No," she said, smiling, "I was never sure of that."

"What would you think," I said, a little anxiously, "if I

were to tell you that my name is Edward Pinkhammer, from Cornopolis, Kansas."

"What would I think?" she repeated, with a merry glance. "Why, that you had not brought Mrs. Bellford to New York with you, of course. I do wish you had. I would have liked to see Marian." Her voice lowered slightly—"You haven't changed much, Elwyn."

I felt her wonderful eyes searching mine and my face more closely.

"Yes, you have," she amended, and there was a soft, exultant note in her latest tones; "I see it now. You haven't forgotten. You haven't forgotten for a year or a day or an hour. I told you you never could."

I poked my straw anxiously in the *crème de menthe.*

"I'm sure I beg your pardon," I said, a little uneasy at her gaze. "But that is just the trouble. I have forgotten. I've forgotten everything."

She flouted my denial. She laughed deliciously at something she seemed to see in my face.

"I've heard of you at times," she went on. "You're quite a big lawyer out West—Denver, isn't it, or Los Angeles? Marian must be very proud of you. You knew, I suppose, that I married six months after you did. You may have seen it in the papers. The flowers alone cost two thousand dollars."

She had mentioned fifteen years. Fifteen years is a long time.

"Would it be too late," I asked somewhat timorously, "to offer you congratulations?"

"Not if you dare do it," she answered, with such fine intrepidity that I was silent, and began to crease patterns on the cloth with my thumb-nail.

"Tell me one thing," she said, leaning toward me rather eagerly—"a thing I have wanted to know for many years—just from a woman's curiosity, of course—have you ever dared since that night to touch, smell or look at white roses—at white roses wet with rain and dew?"

I took a sip of *crème de menthe.*

"It would be useless, I suppose," I said, with a sigh, "for me to repeat that I have no recollection at all about these things. My memory is completely at fault. I need not say how much I regret it."

The lady rested her arms upon the table, and again her eyes disdained my words and went travelling by their own route direct to my soul. She laughed softly, with a strange quality in the sound—it was a laugh of happiness—yes, and of content—and of misery. I tried to look away from her.

"You lie, Elwyn Bellford," she breathed blissfully. "Oh, I know you lie!"

I gazed dully into the ferns.

"My name is Edward Pinkhammer," I said. "I came with the delegates to the Druggists' National Convention. There is a movement on foot for arranging a new position for the bottles of tartrate of antimony and tartrate of potash, in which, very likely, you would take little interest."

A shining landau stopped before the entrance. The lady rose. I took her hand, and bowed.

"I am deeply sorry," I said to her, "that I cannot remember. I could explain, but fear you would not understand. You will not concede Pinkhammer; and I really cannot at all conceive of the—the roses and other things."

"Good-bye, Mr. Bellford," she said, with her happy, sorrowful smile, as she stepped into her carriage.

I attended the theatre that night. When I returned to my hotel, a quiet man in dark clothes, who seemed interested in rubbing his finger-nails with a silk handkerchief, appeared, magically, at my side.

"Mr. Pinkhammer," he said casually, giving the bulk of his attention to his forefinger, "may I request you to step aside with me for a little conversation? There is a room here."

"Certainly," I answered.

He conducted me into a small, private parlour. A lady and a gentleman were there. The lady, I surmised, would have been unusually good-looking had her features not been clouded by an expression of keen worry and fatigue. She was of a style of figure and possessed colouring and features that were agreeable to my fancy. She was in a travelling-dress; she fixed upon me an earnest look of extreme anxiety, and pressed an unsteady hand to her bosom. I think she would have started forward, but the gentleman arrested her movement with an authoritative motion of his hand. He then came, himself, to meet me. He was a man of forty, a little grey about the temples, and with a strong, thoughtful face.

"Bellford, old man," he said cordially, "I'm glad to see you again. Of course we know everything is all right. I warned you, you know, that you were overdoing it. Now, you'll go back with us, and be yourself again in no time."

I smiled ironically.

"I have been 'Bellforded' so often," I said, "that it has lost its edge. Still, in the end, it may grow wearisome. Would you be willing at all to entertain the hypothesis that my name is Edward Pinkhammer, and that I never saw you before in my life?"

Before the man could reply a wailing cry came from the woman. She sprang past his detaining arm. "Elwyn!" she sobbed, and cast herself upon me, and clung tight. "Elwyn," she cried again, "don't break my heart. I am your wife—call my name once—just once! I could see you dead rather than this way."

I unwound her arms respectfully, but firmly.

"Madam," I said severely, "pardon me if I suggest that you accept a resemblance too precipitately. It is a pity," I went on, with an amused laugh, as the thought occurred to me, "that this Bellford and I could not be kept side by side upon the same shelf like tartrates of sodium and antimony for purposes of identification. In order to understand the allusion," I concluded airily, "it may be necessary for you to keep an eye on the proceedings of the Druggists' National Convention."

The lady turned to her companion, and grasped his arm.

"What is it, Doctor Volney? Oh, what is it?" she moaned.

He led her to the door.

"Go to your room for a while," I heard him say. "I will remain and talk with him. His mind? No, I think not—only a portion of the brain. Yes, I am sure he will recover. Go to your room and leave me with him."

The lady disappeared. The man in dark clothes also went

outside, still manicuring himself in a thoughtful way. I think he waited in the hall.

"I would like to talk with you a while, Mr. Pinkhammer, if I may," said the gentleman who remained.

"Very well, if you care to," I replied, "and will excuse me if I take it comfortably; I am rather tired." I stretched myself upon a couch by a window and lit a cigar. He drew a chair near by.

"Let us speak to the point," he said soothingly. "Your name is not Pinkhammer."

"I know that as well as you do," I said coolly. "But a man must have a name of some sort. I can assure you that I do not extravagantly admire the name of Pinkhammer. But when one christens one's self, suddenly the fine names do not seem to suggest themselves. But suppose it had been Scheringhausen or Scroggins! I think I did very well with Pinkhammer."

"Your name," said the other man seriously, "is Elwyn C. Bellford. You are one of the first lawyers in Denver. You are suffering from an attack of aphasia, which has caused you to forget your identity. The cause of it was over-application to your profession, and, perhaps, a life too bare of natural recreation and pleasures. The lady who has just left the room is your wife."

"She is what I would call a fine-looking woman," I said, after a judicial pause. "I particularly admire the shade of brown in her hair."

"She is a wife to be proud of. Since your disappearance, nearly two weeks ago, she has scarcely closed her eyes. We learned that you were in New York through a telegram sent by Isidore Newman, a travelling man from Denver. He said that he had met you in an hotel here, and that you did not recognize him."

"I think I remember the occasion," I said. "The fellow called me 'Bellford,' if I am not mistaken. But don't you think it about time, now, for you to introduce yourself?"

"I am Robert Volney—Doctor Volney. I have been your close friend for twenty years, and your physician for fifteen.

I came with Mrs. Bellford to trace you as soon as we got the telegram. Try, Elwyn, old man—try to remember!"

"What's the use to try!" I asked, with a little frown. "You say you are a physician. Is aphasia curable? When a man loses his memory, does it return slowly, or suddenly?"

"Sometimes gradually and imperfectly; sometimes as suddenly as it went."

"Will you undertake the treatment of my case, Doctor Volney?" I asked.

"Old friend," said he, "I'll do everything in my power, and will have done everything that science can do to cure you."

"Very well," said I. "Then you will consider that I am your patient. Everything is in confidence now—professional confidence."

"Of course," said Doctor Volney.

I got up from the couch. Someone had set a vase of white roses on the centre table—a cluster of white roses freshly sprinkled and fragrant. I threw them far out of the window, and then I laid myself upon the couch again.

"It will be best, Bobby," I said, "to have this cure happen suddenly. I'm rather tired of it all, anyway. You may go now and bring Marian in. But, oh, Doc," I said, with a sigh, as I kicked him on the shin—"good old Doc—it was glorious!"

14

Past One at Rooney's

ONLY on the lower East Side of New York do the Houses of Capulet and Montague survive. There they do not fight by the book of arithmetic. If you but bite your thumb at an upholder of your opposing house you have work cut out for your steel. On Broadway you may drag your man along a dozen blocks by his nose, and he will only bawl for the watch; but in the domain of the East Side Tybalts and Mercutios you must observe the niceties of deportment to the wink of an eyelash and to an inch of elbow-room at the bar when its patrons include foes of your house and kin.

So, when Eddie McManus, known to the Capulets as Cork McManus, drifted into Dutch Mike's for a stein of beer, and came upon a bunch of Montagues making merry with the suds, he began to observe the strictest parliamentary rules. Courtesy forbade his leaving the saloon with his thirst unslaked; caution steered him to a place at the bar where the mirror supplied the cognizance of the enemy's movements that his indifferent gaze seemed to disdain; experience whispered to him that the finger of trouble would be busy among the chattering steins at Dutch Mike's that night. Close by his side drew Brick Cleary, his Mercutio, companion of his perambulations. Thus they stood, four of the Mulberry Hill Gang and two of the Dry Dock Gang, minding their P's and Q's so solicitously that Dutch Mike kept one eye on his customers and the other on an open space beneath his bar in which it was his custom to seek safety whenever the ominous politeness of the rival associations congealed into the shapes of bullets and cold steel.

But we have not to do with the wars of the Mulberry Hills and the Dry Docks. We must to Rooney's, where, on the most blighted dead branch of the tree of life, a little pale orchid shall bloom.

Overstrained etiquette at last gave way. It is not known who first overstepped the bounds of punctilio; but the consequences were immediate. Buck Malone, of the Mulberry Hills, with a Dewey-like swiftness, got an eight-inch gun swung round from his hurricane deck. But McManus's simile must be the torpedo. He glided in under the guns and slipped a scant three inches of knife-blade between the ribs of the Mulberry Hill cruiser. Meanwhile Brick Cleary, a devotee to strategy, had skimmed across the lunch-counter and thrown the switch of the electrics, leaving the combat to be waged by the light of gunfire alone. Dutch Mike crawled from his haven and ran into the street crying for the watch instead of for a Shakespeare to immortalize the Cimmerian shindy.

The cop came, and found a prostrate, bleeding Montague supported by three distrait and reticent followers of the House. Faithful to the ethics of the gangs, no one knew whence the hurt came. There was no Capulet to be seen.

"Raus mit der interrogatories," said Buck Malone to the officer. "Sure I know who done it. I always manages to get a bird's-eye view of any guy that comes up an' makes a showcase for a hardware store out of me. No. I'm not telling you his name. I'll settle with um meself. Wow—ouch! Easy, boys! Yes, I'll attend to his case meself. I'm not making any complaint."

At midnight McManus strolled around a pile of lumber near an East Side dock, and lingered in the vicinity of a certain water-plug. Brick Cleary drifted casually to the trysting-place ten minutes later. "He'll maybe not croak," said Brick; "and he won't tell, of course. But Dutch Mike did. He told the police he was tired of having his place shot up. It's unhandy just now, because Tim Corrigan's in Europe for a week's end with Kings. He'll be back on the *Kaiser Williams* next Friday. You'll have to duck out of sight till then. Tim'll fix it up all right for us when he comes back."

This goes to explain why Cork McManus went into Rooney's one night and there looked upon the bright, stranger face of Romance for the first time in his precarious career.

Until Tim Corrigan should return from his jaunt among Kings and Princes and hold up his big white finger in private offices, it was unsafe for Cork in any of the old haunts of his gang. So he lay, perdu, in the high rear room of a Capulet, reading pink sporting sheets and cursing the slow paddle-wheels of the *Kaiser Wilhelm*.

It was on Thursday evening that Cork's seclusion became intolerable to him. Never a hart panted for water fountain as he did for the cool touch of a drifting stein, for the firm security of a foot-rail in the hollow of his shoe and the quiet, hearty challenges of friendship and repartee along and across the shining bars. But he must avoid the district where he was known. The cops were looking for him everywhere, for news was scarce, and the newspapers were harping again on the failure of the police to suppress the gangs. If they got him before Corrigan came back, the big white finger could not be uplifted; it would be too late then. But Corrigan would be home the next day, so he felt sure there would be small danger in a little excursion that night among the crass pleasures that represented life to him.

At half-past twelve McManus stood in a darkish cross-town street looking up at the name "Rooney's", picked out by incandescent lights against a signboard over a second-storey window. He had heard of the place as a tough "hang-out"; with its frequenters and its locality he was unfamiliar. Guided by certain unerring indications common to all such resorts, he ascended the stairs and entered the large room over the café.

Here were some twenty or thirty tables, at this time about half filled with Rooney's guests. Waiters served drinks. At one end a human pianola with drugged eyes hammered the keys with automatic and furious unprecision. At merciful intervals a waiter would roar or squeak a song—songs full of "Mr. Johnsons" and "babes" and "coons"—historical word guarantees of the genuineness of African melodies composed by red-waistcoated young gentlemen, natives of the cotton fields and rice swamps of West Twenty-eighth Street.

For one brief moment you must admire Rooney with me as he receives, seats, manipulates, and chaffs his guests. He is twenty-nine. He has Wellington's nose, Dante's chin, the cheek-bones of an Iroquois, the smile of Talleyrand, Corbett's footwork, and the poise of an eleven-year-old East Side Central Park Queen of the May. He is assisted by a lieutenant known as Frank, a pudgy, easy chap, swell-dressed, who goes among the tables seeing that dull care does not intrude. Now, what is there about Rooney's to inspire all this pother? It is more than respectable by daylight; stout ladies with children and mittens and bundles and unpedigreed dogs drop up of afternoons for a stein and a chat. Even by gaslight the diversions are melancholy i' the mouth—drink and ragtime, and an occasional surprise when the waiter swabs the suds from under your sticky glass. There is an answer. Transmigration! The soul of Sir Walter Raleigh has travelled from beneath his slashed doublet to a kindred home under Rooney's visible plaid waistcoat. Rooney's is twenty years ahead of the times. Rooney has removed the embargo. Rooney has spread his cloak upon the soggy crossing of public opinion, and any Elizabeth who treads upon it is as much a queen as another. Attend to the revelation of the secret. In Rooney's ladies may smoke!

McManus sat down at a vacant table. He paid for the glass of beer that he ordered, tilted his narrow-brimmed derby to the back of his brick-dust head, twined his feet among the rungs of his chair, and heaved a sigh of contentment from the breathing spaces of his innermost soul; for this mud honey was clarified sweetness to his taste. The sham gaiety, the hectic glow of counterfeit hospitality, the self-conscious, joyless laughter, the wine-born warmth, the loud music retrieving the hour from frequent whiles of awful and corroding silence, the presence of well-clothed and frank-eyed beneficiaries of Rooney's removal of the restrictions laid upon the weed, the familiar blended odours of soaked lemon-peel, flat beer, and *peau d'Espagne*—all these were manna to Cork McManus, hungry from his week in the desert of the Capulet's high rear room.

A girl, alone, entered Rooney's, glanced around with leisurely swiftness, and sat opposite McManus at his table. Her eyes rested upon him for two seconds in the look with which woman reconnoitres all men whom she for the first time confronts. In that space of time she will decide upon one of two things—either to scream for the police, or that she may marry him later on.

Her brief inspection concluded, the girl laid on the table a worn red morocco shopping-bag with the inevitable top-gallant sail of frayed lace handkerchief flying from a corner of it. After she had ordered a small beer from the immediate waiter she took from her bag a box of cigarettes and lighted one with slightly exaggerated ease of manner. Then she looked again in the eyes of Cork McManus and smiled.

Instantly the doom of each was sealed.

The unqualified desire of a man to buy clothes and build fires for a woman for a whole lifetime at first sight of her is not uncommon among that humble portion of humanity that does not care for Bradstreet or coats-of-arms or Shaw's plays. Love at first sight has occurred a time or two in high life; but, as a rule, the extempore mania is to be found among unsophisticated creatures such as the dove, the blue-tailed dingbat, and the ten-dollar-a-week clerk. Poets, subscribers to all fiction magazines, and schatchens, take notice.

With the exchange of the mysterious magnetic current came to each of them the instant desire to lie, pretend, dazzle, deceive, which is the worst thing about the hypocritical disorder known as love.

"Have another beer?" suggested Cork. In his circle the phrase was considered to be a card, accompanied by a letter of introduction and references.

"No, thanks," said the girl, raising her eyebrows and choosing her conventional words carefully. "I—merely dropped in for—a slight refreshment." The cigarette between her fingers seemed to require explanation. "My aunt is a Russian lady," she concluded, "and we often have a post perannual cigarette after dinner at home."

"Cheese it!" said Cork, whom society airs oppressed. "Your fingers are as yellow as mine."

"Say," said the girl, blazing upon him with low-voiced indignation, "what do you think I am? Say, who do you think you are talking to? What?"

She was pretty to look at. Her eyes were big, brown, intrepid and bright. Under her flat sailor hat, planted jauntily on one side, her crinkly, tawny hair parted and was drawn back, low and massy, in a thick, pendant knot behind. The roundness of girlhood still lingered in her chin and neck, but her cheeks and fingers were thinning slightly. She looked upon the world with defiance, suspicion, and sullen wonder. Her smart, short tan coat was soiled and expensive. Two inches below her black dress dropped the lowest flounce of a heliotrope silk underskirt.

"Beg your pardon," said Cork, looking at her admiringly. "I didn't mean anything. Sure, it's no harm to smoke, Maudy."

"Rooney's," said the girl, softened at once by his amends, "is the only place I know where a lady can smoke. Maybe it ain't a nice habit, but aunty lets us at home. And my name ain't Maudy, if you please; it's Ruby Delamere."

"That's a swell handle," said Cork approvingly. "Mine's McManus—Cor—er—Eddie McManus."

"Oh, you can't help that," laughed Ruby. "Don't apologize."

Cork looked seriously at the big clock on Rooney's wall. The girl's ubiquitous eyes took in the movement.

"I know it's late," she said, reaching for her bag; "but you know how you want a smoke when you want one. Ain't Rooney's all right? I never saw anything wrong here. This is twice I've been in. I work in a bookbindery on Third Avenue. A lot of us girls have been working overtime three nights a week. They won't let you smoke there, of course. I just dropped in here on my way home for a puff. Ain't it all right in here? If it ain't, I won't come any more."

"It's a little bit late for you to be out alone anywhere," said Cork. "I'm not wise to this particular joint; but anyhow you don't want to have your picture taken in it for a present to your Sunday-school teacher. Have one more beer, and then say I take you home."

"But I don't know you," said the girl, with fine scrupulosity. "I don't accept the company of gentlemen I ain't acquainted with. My aunt never would allow that."

"Why," said Cork McManus, pulling his ear, "I'm the latest thing in suitings with side vents and bell skirt when it comes to escortin' a lady. You bet you'll find me all right, Ruby. And I'll give you a tip as to who I am. My governor is one of the hottest cross-buns of the Wall Street push. Morgan's cab-horse casts a shoe every time the old man sticks his head out of the window. Me! Well, I'm in trainin' down the Street. The old man's goin' to put a seat on the Stock Exchange in my stockin' my next birthday. But it all sounds like a lemon to me. What I like is golf and yachtin' and—er—well, say a corkin' fast ten-round bout between welter-weights with walkin' gloves."

"I guess you can walk to the door with me," said the girl hesitatingly, but with a certain pleased flutter. "Still I never heard anything extra good about Wall Street brokers, or sports who go to prize-fights, either. Ain't you got any other recommendations?"

"I think you're the swellest looker I've had my lamps on in old New York," said Cork impressively.

"That'll be about enough of that, now. Ain't you the kidder!" She modified her chiding words by a deep, long, beaming, smile-embellished look at her cavalier. "We'll drink our beer before we go, ha?"

A waiter sang. The tobacco smoke grew denser, drifting and rising in spirals, waves, tilted layers, cumulus clouds, cataracts and suspended fogs like some fifth element created from the ribs of the ancient four. Laughter and chat grew louder, stimulated by Rooney's liquids and Rooney's gallant hospitality to Lady Nicotine.

One o'clock struck. Downstairs there was a sound of closing and locking doors. Frank pulled down the green shades of the front windows carefully. Rooney went below in the dark hall and stood at the front door, his cigarette cached in the hollow of his hand. Thenceforth whoever might seek admittance must present a countenance familiar to Rooney's hawk's eye —the countenance of a true sport.

Cork McManus and the bookbindery girl conversed absorbedly, with their elbows on the table. Their glasses of beer were pushed to one side, scarcely touched, with the foam on them sunken to a thin, white scum. Since the stroke of one the stale pleasures of Rooney's had become renovated and spiced; not by any addition to the list of distractions, but because from that moment the sweets became stolen ones. The flattest glass of beer acquired the tang of illegality; the mildest claret punch struck a knock-out blow at law and order; the harmless and genial company became outlaws, defying authority and rule. For after the stroke of one in such places as Rooney's, where neither bed nor board is to be had, drink may not be set before the thirsty of the city of the four million. It is the law.

"Say," said Cork McManus, almost covering the table with his eloquent chest and elbows, "was that dead straight about you workin' in a bookbindery and livin' at home—and just happenin' in here—and—and all that spiel you gave me?"

"Sure it was," answered the girl with spirit. "Why, what do you think? Do you suppose I'd lie to you? Go down to the shop and ask 'em. I handed it to you on the level."

"On the dead level?" said Cork. "That's the way I want it; because——"

"Because what?"

"I throw up my hands," said Cork. "You've got me goin'. You're the girl I've been lookin' for. Will you keep company with me, Ruby?"

"Would you like me to—Eddie?"

"Surest thing. But I wanted a straight story about—about yourself, you know. When a fellow has a girl—a steady girl—she's got to be all right, you know. She's got to be straight goods."

"You'll find I'll be straight goods, Eddie."

"Of course you will. I believe what you told me. But you can't blame me for wantin' to find out. You don't see many girls smokin' cigarettes in a place like Rooney's after midnight that are like you."

The girl flushed a little and lowered her eyes. "I see that now," she said meekly. "I didn't know how bad it looked. But I won't do it any more. And I'll go straight home every ıght and stay there. And I'll give up cigarettes if you say so, ꜀ddie—I'll cut 'em out from this minute on."

Cork's air became judicial, proprietary, condemnatory, yet sympathetic. "A lady can smoke," he decided slowly, "at times and places. Why? Because it's being a lady that helps her to pull it off."

"I'm going to quit. There's nothing to it," said the girl. She flicked the stub of her cigarette to the floor.

"At times and places," repeated Cork. "When I call round for you of evenin's we'll hunt out a dark bench in Stuyvesant Square and have a puff or two. But no more Rooney's at one o'clock—see?"

"Eddie, do you really like me?" The girl searched his hard but frank features eagerly with anxious eyes.

"On the dead level."

"When are you coming to see me—where I live?"

"Thursday—day after to-morrow evenin'. That suit you?"

"Fine. I'll be ready for you. Come about seven. Walk to the door with me to-night and I'll show you where I live. Don't forget, now. And don't you go to see any other girls before then, mister! I bet you will, though."

"On the dead level," said Cork, "you make 'em all look like rag-dolls to me. Honest, you do. I know when I'm suited. On the dead level, I do."

Against the front door downstairs repeated heavy blows were delivered. The loud crashes resounded in the room above. Only a trip-hammer or a policeman's boot could have been the author of those sounds. Rooney jumped like a bull-frog to a corner of the room, turned off the electric lights and hurried swiftly below. The room was left utterly dark except for the winking, red glow of cigars and cigarettes. A second volley of crashes came up from the assaulted door. A little, rustling, murmuring panic moved among the besieged guests. Frank, cool, smooth, reassuring, could be seen in the rosy glow of the burning tobacco, going from table to table.

"All keep still!" was his caution. "Don't talk or make any noise! Everything will be all right. Now, don't feel the slightest alarm. We'll take care of you all."

Ruby felt across the table until Cork's firm hand closed

upon hers. "Are you afraid, Eddie?" she whispered. "Are you afraid you'll get a free ride?"

"Nothin' doin' in the teeth-chatterin' line," said Cork. "I guess Rooney's been slow with his envelope. Don't you worry, girly; I'll look out for you all right."

Yet Mr. McManus's ease was only skin and muscle-deep. With the police looking everywhere for Buck Malone's assailant, and with Corrigan still on the ocean wave, he felt that to be caught in a police raid would mean an ended career for him. And just when he had met Ruby, too! He wished he had remained in the high rear room of the true Capulet reading the pink extras.

Rooney seemed to have opened the front door below and engaged the police in conference in the dark hall. The wordless, low growl of their voices came up the stairway. Frank made a wireless news station of himself at the upper door. Suddenly he closed the door, hurried to the extreme rear of the room and lighted a dim gas-jet.

"This way, everybody," he called sharply. "In a hurry, but no noise, please!"

The guests crowded in confusion to the rear. Rooney's lieutenant swung open a panel in the wall, overlooking the back yard, revealing a ladder placed already for the escape.

"Down and out, everybody!" he commanded. "Ladies first! Less talking, please! Don't crowd. There's no danger."

Among the last, Cork and Ruby waited their turn at the open panel. Suddenly she swept him aside and clung to his arm fiercely.

"Before we go out," she whispered in his ear—"before anything happens, tell me again, Eddie, do you—do you really like me?"

"On the dead level," said Cork, holding her close with one arm, "when it comes to you, I'm all in."

When they turned they found they were lost and in darkness. The last of the fleeing customers had descended. Halfway across the yard they bore the ladder, stumbling, giggling, hurrying to place it against an adjoining low building over the roof of which lay their only route to safety.

"We may as well sit down," said Cork grimly. "Maybe Rooney will stand the cops off, anyhow."

They sat at a table; and their hands came together again.

A number of men then entered the dark room, feeling their way about. One of them, Rooney himself, found the switch and turned on the electric light. The other man was a cop of the old régime—a big cop, a thick cop, a fuming abrupt cop—not a pretty cop. He went up to the pair at the table and sneered familiarly at the girl.

"What are youse doin' in here?" he asked.

"Dropped in for a smoke," said Cork mildly.

"Had any drinks?"

"Not later than one o'clock."

"Get out—quick!" ordered the cop. Then, "Sit down!" he countermanded.

He took off Cork's hat roughly and scrutinized him shrewdly. "Your name's McManus."

"Bad guess," said Cork. "It's Peterson."

"Cork McManus, or something like that," said the cop. "You put a knife into a man in Dutch Mike's saloon a week ago."

"Aw, forget it!" said Cork, who perceived a shade of doubt in the officer's tones. "You've got my mug mixed with somebody else's."

"Have I? Well, you'll come to the station with me, anyhow, and be looked over. The description fits you all right." The cop twisted his fingers under Cork's collar. "Come on!" he ordered roughly.

Cork glanced at Ruby. She was pale, and her thin nostrils quivered. Her quick eye glanced from one man's face to the other's as they spoke or moved. What hard luck! Cork was thinking—Corrigan on the briny; and Ruby met and lost almost within an hour! Somebody at the police-station would recognize him, without a doubt. Hard luck!

But suddenly the girl sprang up and hurled herself with both arms extended against the cop. His hold on Cork's collar was loosened and he stumbled back two or three paces.

"Don't go so fast, Maguire!" she cried in shrill fury. "Keep your hands off my man! You know me, and you know I'm givin' you good advice. Don't you touch him again! He's not the guy you are lookin' for—I'll stand for that."

"See here, Fanny," said the cop, red and angry, "I'll take you, too, if you don't look out! How do you know this ain't the man I want? What are you doing in here with him?"

"How do I know?" said the girl, flaming red and white by turns. "Because I've known him a year. He's mine. Oughtn't I to know? And what am I doin' here with him? That's easy."

She stooped low and reached down somewhere into a swirl of flirted draperies, heliotrope and black. An elastic snapped, she threw on the table toward Cork a folded wad of bills. The money slowly straightened itself with little leisurely jerks.

"Take that, Jimmy, and let's go," said the girl. "I'm declaring the usual dividends, Maguire," she said to the officer. "You had your usual five-dollar graft at the usual corner at ten."

"A lie!" said the cop, turning purple. "You go on my beat again and I'll arrest you every time I see you."

"No you won't," said the girl. "And I'll tell you why. Witnesses saw me give you the money to-night, and last week, too. I've been getting fixed for you."

Cork put the wad of money carefully into his pocket, and said: "Come on, Fanny; let's have some chop suey before we go home."

"Clear out, quick, both of you, or I'll——"

The cop's bluster trailed away into inconsequentiality.

At the corner of the street the two halted. Cork handed back the money without a word. The girl took it and slipped it slowly into her hand-bag. Her expression was the same she had worn when she entered Rooney's that night—she looked upon the world with defiance, suspicion and sullen wonder.

"I guess I might as well say good-bye here," she said dully. "You won't want to see me again, of course. Will you—shake hands—Mr. McManus?"

"I mightn't have got wise if you hadn't give the snap away," said Cork. "Why did you do it?"

"You'd have been pinched if I hadn't. That's why. Ain't that reason enough?" Then she began to cry. "Honest, Eddie,

I was goin' to be the best girl in the world. I hated to be what I am; I hated men: I was ready almost to die when I saw you. And you seemed different from everybody else. And when I found you liked me, too, why, I thought I'd make you believe I was good, and I was goin' to be good. When you asked to come to my house and see me, why, I'd have died rather than do anything wrong after that. But what's the use of talking about it? I'll say good-bye, if you will, Mr. McManus."

Cork was pulling at his ear. "I knifed Malone," said he. "I was the one the cop wanted."

"Oh, that's all right," said the girl listlessly. "It didn't make any difference about that."

"That was all hot air about Wall Street. I don't do nothin' but hang out with a tough gang on the East Side."

"That was all right, too," repeated the girl. "It didn't make any difference."

Cork straightened himself, and pulled his hat down low. "I could get a job at O'Brien's," he said aloud, but to himself.

"Good-bye," said the girl.

"Come on," said Cork, taking her arm. "I know a place."

Two blocks away he turned with her up the steps of a red-brick house facing a little park.

"What house is this?" she asked, drawing back. "Why are you going in there?"

A street lamp shone brightly in front. There was a brass name-plate on one side of the closed front doors. Cork drew her firmly up the steps. "Read that," said he.

She looked at the name on the plate, and gave a cry between a moan and a scream. "No, no, no, Eddie! Oh, my God, no! I won't let you do that—not now! Let me go! You shan't do that! You can't—you mustn't! Not after you know! No, no! Come away quick! Oh, my God! Please, Eddie, come!"

Half fainting, she reeled, and was caught in the bend of his arm. Cork's right hand felt for the electric button and pressed it long.

Another cop—how quickly they scent trouble when trouble is on the wing!—came along, saw them, and ran up the steps.

"Here! What are you doing with that girl?" he called gruffly.

"She'll be all right in a minute," said Cork. "It's a straight deal."

"Reverend Jeremiah Jones," read the cop from the doorplate with true detective cunning.

"Correct," said Cork. "On the dead level, we're going to get married."

15

The Indian Summer of Dry Valley Johnson

Dry valley johnson shook the bottle. You have to shake the bottle before using; for sulphur will not dissolve. Then Dry Valley saturated a small sponge with the liquid and rubbed it carefully into the roots of his hair. Besides sulphur there was sugar of lead in it and tincture of nux vomica and bay rum. Dry Valley found the recipe in a Sunday newspaper. You must next be told why a strong man came to fall a victim to a Beauty Hint.

Dry Valley had been a sheepman. His real name was Hector, but he had been rechristened after his range to distinguish him from "Elm Creek" Johnson, who ran sheep farther down the Frio.

Many years of living face to face with sheep on their own terms wearied Dry Valley Johnson. So, he sold his ranch for eighteen thousand dollars and moved to Santa Rosa to live a life of gentlemanly ease. Being a silent and melancholy person of thirty-five—or perhaps thirty-eight—he soon became that cursed and earth-cumbering thing—an elderlyish bachelor with a hobby. Some one gave him his first strawberry to eat, and he was done for.

Dry Valley bought a four-room cottage in the village, and a library on strawberry culture. Behind the cottage was a garden of which he made a strawberry patch. In his old grey woollen shirt, his brown duck trousers, and high-heeled boots he sprawled all day on a canvas cot under a live oak tree at his back door studying the history of the seductive scarlet berry.

The school teacher, Miss De Witt, spoke of him as "a fine, presentable man, for all his middle age". But, the focus of

Dry Valley's eyes embraced no women. They were merely beings who flew skirts as a signal for him to lift awkwardly his heavy, round-crowned, broad-brimmed felt Stetson whenever he met them, and then hurry past to get back to his beloved berries.

And all this recitative by the chorus is only to bring us to the point where you may be told why Dry Valley shook up the insoluble sulphur in the bottle. So long-drawn and inconsequential a thing is history—the anamorphous shadow of a milestone reaching down the road between us and the setting sun.

When his strawberries were beginning to ripen Dry Valley bought the heaviest buggy whip in the Santa Rosa store. He sat for many hours under the live oak tree plaiting and weaving in an extension to its lash. When it was done he could snip a leaf from a bush twenty feet away with the cracker. For the bright, predatory eyes of Santa Rosa youth were watching the ripening berries, and Dry Valley was arming himself against their expected raids. No greater care had he taken of his tender lambs during his ranching days than he did of his cherished fruit, warding it from the hungry wolves that whistled and howled and shot their marbles and peered through the fence that surrounded his property.

In the house next to Dry Valley's lived a widow with a pack of children that gave the husbandman frequent anxious misgivings. In the woman there was a strain of the Spanish. She had wedded one of the name of O'Brien. Dry Valley was a connoisseur in crossed strains; and he foresaw trouble in the offspring of this union.

Between the two homesteads ran a crazy picket fence overgrown with morning glory and wild gourd vines. Often he could see little heads with mops of black hair and flashing dark eyes dodging in and out between the pickets, keeping tabs on the reddening berries.

Late one afternoon Dry Valley went to the post office. When he came back, like Mother Hubbard he found the deuce to pay. The descendants of Iberian bandits and Hibernian cattle raiders had swooped down upon his strawberry patch. To the outraged vision of Dry Valley there seemed to be a sheep corral full of them; perhaps they numbered five or six. Between the rows of green plants they were stooped, hopping about like toads, gobbling silently and voraciously his finest fruit.

Dry Valley slipped into the house, got his whip, and charged the marauders. The lash curled about the legs of the nearest—a greedy ten-year-old—before they knew they were discovered. His screech gave warning; and the flock scampered for the fence like a drove of *javelis* flushed in the chaparral. Dry Valley's whip drew a toll of two more elfin shrieks before they dived through the vine-clad fence and disappeared.

Dry Valley, less fleet, followed them nearly to the pickets. Checking his useless pursuit, he rounded a bush, dropped his whip and stood, voiceless, motionless, the capacity of his powers consumed by the act of breathing and preserving the perpendicular.

Behind the bush stood Panchita O'Brien, scorning to fly. She was nineteen, the oldest of the raiders. Her night-black hair was gathered back in a wild mass and tied with a scarlet ribbon. She stood, with reluctant feet, yet nearer the brook than to the river; for childhood had environed and detained her.

She looked at Dry Valley Johnson for a moment with magnificent insolence, and before his eyes slowly crunched a luscious berry between her white teeth. Then she turned and walked slowly to the fence with a swaying, conscious motion, such as a duchess might make use of in leading a promenade. There she turned again and grilled Dry Valley Johnson once more in the dark flame of her audacious eyes, laughed a trifle school-girlishly, and twisted herself with pantherish quickness between the pickets to the O'Brien side of the wild gourd vine.

Dry Valley picked up his whip and went into his house. He stumbled as he went up the two wooden steps. The old Mexican woman who cooked his meals and swept his house called him to supper as he went through the rooms. Dry Valley went on, stumbled down the front steps, out the gate and down the road into a mesquite thicket at the edge of town. He sat down in the grass and laboriously plucked the spines from a prickly pear, one by one. This was his attitude of thought, acquired in the days when his problems were only those of wind and wool and water.

A thing had happened to the man—a thing that, if you are eligible, you must pray may pass you by. He had become enveloped in the Indian Summer of the Soul.

Dry Valley had had no youth. Even his childhood had been one of dignity and seriousness. At six he had viewed the frivolous gambols of the lambs on his father's ranch with silent disapproval. His life as a young man had been wasted. The divine fires and impulses, the glorious exaltations and despairs, the glow and enchantment of youth had passed above his head. Never a thrill of Romeo had he known; he was but a melancholy Jacques of the forest with a ruder philosophy, lacking the bitter-sweet flavour of experience that tempered the veteran years of the rugged ranger of Arden. And now in his sere and yellow leaf one scornful look from the eyes of Panchita O'Brien had flooded the autumnal landscape with a tardy and delusive summer heat.

But a sheepman is a hardy animal. Dry Valley Johnson had weathered too many northers to turn his back on a late summer, spiritual or real. Old? He would show them.

By the next mail went an order to San Antonio for an outfit of the latest clothes, colours and styles and prices no object. The next day went the recipe for the hair restorer clipped from a newspaper; for Dry Valley's sunburned auburn hair was beginning to turn silvery above his ears.

Dry Valley kept indoors closely for a week except for frequent sallies after youthful strawberry snatchers. Then, a few days later, he suddenly emerged brilliantly radiant in the hectic glow of his belated midsummer madness.

A jay-bird-blue tennis suit covered him outwardly, almost as far as his wrists and ankles. His shirt was ox-blood; his collar winged and tall; his necktie a floating oriflamme; his shoes a venomous bright tan, pointed and shaped on penitential lasts. A little flat straw hat with a striped band desecrated his weather-beaten head. Lemon-coloured kid gloves protected his oak-tough hands from the benignant May sunshine. This sad and opticsmiting creature teetered out of its den, smiling foolishly and smoothing its gloves for men and angels to see. To such a pass had Dry Valley Johnson been brought by Cupid, who always shoots game that is out of season with an arrow from the quiver of Momus. Reconstructing mythology, he had risen, a prismatic macaw, from the ashes of the grey-brown phoenix that had folded its tired wing to roost under the trees of Santa Rosa.

Dry Valley paused in the street to allow Santa Rosans within sight of him to be stunned; and then deliberately and slowly, as his shoes required, entered Mrs. O'Brien's gate.

Not until the eleven months' drought did Santa Rosa cease talking about Dry Valley Johnson's courtship of Panchita O'Brien. It was an unclassifiable procedure; something like a combination of cake-walking, deaf-and-dumb oratory, postage-stamp flirtation and parlour charades. It lasted two weeks and then came to a sudden end.

Of course Mrs. O'Brien favoured the match as soon as Dry Valley's intentions were disclosed. Being the mother of a woman child, and therefore a charter member of the Ancient Order of the Rat-trap, she joyfully decked out Panchita for the sacrifice. The girl was temporarily dazzled by having her dresses lengthened and her hair piled up on her head, and came near forgetting that she was only a slice of cheese. It was nice, too, to have as good a match as Mr. Johnson paying you attentions and to see the other girls fluttering the curtains at their windows to see you go by with him.

Dry Valley bought a buggy with yellow wheels and a fine trotter in San Antonio. Every day he drove out with Panchita. He was never seen to speak to her when they were walking or driving. The consciousness of his clothes kept his mind busy; the knowledge that he could say nothing of interest kept him dumb; the feeling that Panchita was there kept him happy.

He took her to parties and dances, and to church. He tried —oh, no man ever tried so hard to be young as Dry Valley did. He could not dance; but he invented a smile which he wore on these joyous occasions, a smile that, in him, was as great a concession to mirth and gaiety as turning handsprings would be in another. He began to seek the company of the young men in the town—even of the boys. They accepted him as a decided damper, for his attempts at sportiveness were so forced that they might as well have essayed their games in a cathedral. Neither he nor any other could estimate what progress he had made with Panchita.

The end came suddenly in one day, as often disappears the false afterglow before a November sky and wind.

Dry Valley was to call for the girl one afternoon at six for a walk. An afternoon walk in Santa Rosa was a feature of social life that called for the pick of one's wardrobe. So Dry Valley began gorgeously to array himself; and so early that he finished early, and went over to the O'Brien cottage. As he neared the porch on the crooked walk from the gate he heard sounds of revelry within. He stopped and looked through the honeysuckle vines in the open door.

Panchita was amusing her younger brothers and sisters. She wore a man's clothes—no doubt those of the late Mr. O'Brien. On her head was the smallest brother's straw hat decorated with an ink-striped paper band. On her hands were flapping yellow cloth gloves, roughly cut out and sewn for the masquerade. The same material covered her shoes, giving them the semblance of tan leather. High collar and flowing necktie were not omitted.

Panchita was an actress. Dry Valley saw his affectedly youthful gait, his limp where the right shoe hurt him, his forced smile, his awkward simulation of a gallant air, all reproduced with startling fidelity. For the first time a mirror had been held up to him. The corroboration of one of the youngsters calling, "Mamma, come and see Pancha do like Mr. Johnson," was not needed.

As softly as the caricatured tans would permit, Dry Valley tiptoed back to the gate and home again.

Twenty minutes after the time appointed for the walk Panchita tripped demurely out her gate in a thin, trim white lawn and sailor hat. She strolled up the sidewalk and slowed her steps at Dry Valley's gate, her manner expressing wonder at his unusual delinquency.

Then out of his door and down the walk strode—not the

polychromatic victim of a lost summertime, but the sheepman, rehabilitated. He wore his old grey woollen shirt, open at the throat, his brown duck trousers stuffed into his run-over boots, and his white felt sombrero on the back of his head. Twenty years or fifty he might look; Dry Valley cared not. His light blue eyes met Panchita's dark ones with a cold flash in them. He came as far as the gate. He pointed with his long arm to her house.

"Go home," said Dry Valley. "Go home to your mother. I wonder lightnin' don't strike a fool like me. Go home and play in the sand. What business have you got cavortin' around with grown men? I reckon I was locoed to be makin' a he poll-parrot out of myself for a kid like you. Go home and don't let me see you no more. Why I done it, will somebody tell me? Go home, and let me try and forget it."

Panchita obeyed and walked slowly toward her home, saying nothing. For some distance she kept her head turned and her large eyes fixed intrepidly upon Dry Valley's. At her gate she stood for a moment looking back at him, then ran suddenly and swiftly into the house.

Old Antonia was building a fire in the kitchen stove. Dry Valley stopped at the door and laughed harshly.

"I'm a pretty looking old rhinoceros to be gettin' stuck on a kid, ain't I, 'Tonia?" said he.

"Not verree good thing," agreed Antonia sagely, "for too much old man to likee *muchacha*."

"You bet it ain't," said Dry Valley grimly. "It's dum foolishness; and, besides, it hurts."

He brought at one armful the regalia of his aberration—the blue tennis suit, shoes, hat, gloves and all, and threw them in a pile at Antonia's feet.

"Give them to your old man," said he, "to hunt antelope in."

Just as the first star presided palely over the twilight Dry Valley got his biggest strawberry book and sat on the back steps to catch the last of the reading light. He thought he saw the figure of some one in his strawberry patch. He laid aside the book, got his whip and hurried forth to see.

It was Panchita. She had slipped through the picket fence

and was half-way across the patch. She stopped when she saw him and looked at him without wavering.

A sudden rage—a humiliating flush of unreasoning wrath —came over Dry Valley. For this child he had made himself a motley to the view. He had tried to bribe Time to turn backward for himself; he had—been made a fool of. At last he had seen his folly. There was a gulf between him and youth over which he could not build a bridge even with yellow gloves to protect his hands. And the sight of his torment coming to pester him with her elfin pranks—coming to plunder his strawberry vines like a mischievous schoolboy—roused all his anger.

"I told you to keep away from here," said Dry Valley. "Go back to your home."

Panchita moved slowly toward him.

Dry Valley cracked his whip.

"Go back home," said Dry Valley savagely, "and play theatricals some more. You'd make a fine man. You've made a fine one of me."

She came a step nearer, silent, and with that strange, defiant, steady shine in her eyes that had always puzzled him. Now it stirred his wrath.

His whiplash whistled through the air. He saw a red streak suddenly come out through her white dress above her knee where it had struck.

Without flinching and with the same unchanging dark glow in her eyes, Panchita came steadily toward him through the strawberry vines. Dry Valley's trembling hand released his whip handle. When within a yard of him Panchita stretched out her arms.

"God, kid!" stammered Dry Valley, "do you mean——?"

But the seasons are versatile; and it may have been springtime after all, instead of Indian Summer, that struck Dry Valley Johnson.

16

The Badge of Policeman O'Roon

It cannot be denied that men and women have looked upon one another for the first time and become instantly enamoured. It is a risky process, this love at first sight, before she has seen him in Bradstreet or he has seen her in curl papers. But these things do happen; and one instance must form a theme for this story—though not, thank Heaven, to the over-shadowing of more vital and important subjects, such as drink, policemen, horses, and earldoms.

During a certain war a troop calling itself the Gentle Riders rode into history and one or two ambuscades. The Gentle Riders were recruited from the aristocracy of the wild men of the West, and the wild men of the aristocracy of the East. In khaki there is little telling them one from another, so they became good friends and comrades all around.

Ellsworth Remsen, whose old Knickerbocker descent atoned for his modest rating at only ten millions, ate his canned beef gaily by the camp-fires of the Gentle Riders. The war was a great lark to him, so that he scarcely regretted polo and planked shad.

One of the troopers was a well-set-up, affable, cool young man, who called himself O'Roon. To this young man Remsen took an especial liking. The two rode side by side during the famous mooted up-hill charge that was disputed so hotly at the time by the Spaniards and afterwards by the Democrats.

After the war Remsen came back to his polo and shad. One day a well-set-up, affable, cool young man disturbed him at his club, and he and O'Roon were soon pounding each other and exchanging opprobious epithets after the manner of long-lost friends. O'Roon looked seedy and out of luck and perfectly contented. But it seemed that his content was only apparent.

"Get me a job, Remsen," he said. "I've just handed a barber my last shilling."

"No trouble at all," said Remsen. "I know a lot of men who have banks and stores and things down-town. Any particular line you fancy?"

"Yes," said O'Roon, with a look of interest. "I took a walk in your Central Park this morning. I'd like to be one of those bobbies on horseback. That would be about the ticket. Besides, it's the only thing I could do. I can ride a little and the fresh air suits me. Think you could land that for me?"

Remsen was sure that he could. And in a very short time he did. And they who were not above looking at mounted policemen might have seen a well-set-up, affable, cool young man on a prancing chestnut steed attending to his duties along the driveways of the park.

And now at the extreme risk of wearying old gentlemen who carry leather fob chains, and elder ladies who—but no! grandmother herself yet thrills at foolish, immortal Romeo—there must be a hint of love at first sight.

It came just as Remsen was strolling into Fifth Avenue from his club a few doors away.

A motor-car was creeping along foot by foot, impeded by a freshet of vehicles that filled the street. In the car was a chauffeur and an old gentleman with snowy side-whiskers and a Scotch plaid cap which could not be worn while automobiling except by a personage. Not even a wine agent would dare to do it. But these two were of no consequence—except, perhaps, for the guiding of the machine and the paying for it. At the old gentleman's side sat a young lady more beautiful than pomegranate blossoms, more exquisite than the first quarter moon viewed at twilight through the tops of oleanders. Remsen saw her and knew his fate. He could have flung himself under the very wheels that conveyed her, but he knew that would be the last means of attracting the attention of those who ride in motor-cars. Slowly the auto passed, and, if we place the poets above the autoists, carried the heart of Remsen with it. Here was a large city of millions and many women who at a certain distance appear to resemble pomegranate blossoms. Yet he hoped to see her again; for each one fancies that his romance has its own tutelary guardian and divinity.

Luckily for Remsen's peace of mind there came a diversion in the guise of a reunion of the Gentle Riders of the city. There were not many of them—perhaps a score—and there was wassail, and things to eat, and speeches and the Spaniard was bearded again in recapitulation. And when daylight threatened them the survivors prepared to depart. But some remained upon the battlefield. One of these was Trooper O'Roon, who was not seasoned to potent liquids. His legs declined to fulfil the obligations they had sworn to the police department.

"I'm stewed, Remsen," said O'Roon to his friend. "Why do they build hotels that go round and round like catherine wheels? They'll take away my shield and break me. I can think and talk con-con-consec-sec-secutively, but I s-s-s-stammer with my feet. I've got to go on duty in three hours. The jig is up, Remsen. The jig is up, I tell you."

"Look at me," said Remsen, who was his smiling self, pointing to his own face; "whom do you see here?"

"Goo' fellow," said O'Roon dizzily. "Goo' old Remsen."

"Not so," said Remsen. "You see Mounted Policeman O'Roon. Look at your face—no; you can't do that without a glass—but look at mine, and think of yours. How much alike are we? As two French table d'hôte dinners. With your badge, on your horse, in your uniform, will I charm nursemaids and prevent the grass from growing under people's feet in the Park this day. I will save your badge and your honour, besides having the jolliest lark I've been blessed with since we licked Spain."

Promptly on time the counterfeit presentment of Mounted Policeman O'Roon single-footed into the Park on his chestnut steed. In a uniform two men who are unlike will look like; two who somewhat resemble each other in feature and figure will appear as twin brothers. So Remsen trotted down the bridle-paths, enjoying himself hugely, so few real pleasures do ten-millionaires have.

Along the driveway in the early morning spun a victoria drawn by a pair of fiery bays. There was something foreign about the affair, for the Park is rarely used in the morning except by unimportant people who love to be healthy, poor and wise. In the vehicle sat an old gentleman with snowy side-whiskers and Scotch plaid cap which could not be worn while driving except by a personage. At his side sat the lady of Remsen's heart—the lady who looked like pomegranate blossoms and the gibbous moon.

Remsen met them coming. At the instant of their passing her eyes looked into his, and but for the ever-coward heart of a true lover he could have sworn that she flushed a faint pink. He trotted on for twenty yards, and then wheeled his horse at the sound of runaway hoofs. The bays had bolted.

Remsen sent his chestnut after the victoria like a shot. There was work cut out for the impersonator of Policeman O'Roon. The chestnut ranged alongside the off bay thirty seconds after the chase began, rolled his eye back at Remsen, and said in the only manner open to policemen's horses:

"Well, you duffer, are you going to do your share? You're not O'Roon, but it seems to me if you'd lean to the right you could reach the reins of the foolish, slow-running bay —ah! you're all right; O'Roon couldn't have done it more neatly!"

The runaway team was tugged to an inglorious halt by Remsen's tough muscles. The driver released his hands from the wrapped reins, jumped from his seat and stood at the heads of the team. The chestnut, approving his new rider, danced and pranced, reviling equinely the subdued bays. Remsen, lingering, was dimly conscious of a vague, impossible, unnecessary old gentleman in a Scotch cap who talked incessantly about something. And he was acutely conscious of a pair of violet eyes that would have drawn Saint Pyrites from his iron pillar—or whatever the illusion is—and of the lady's smile and look—a little frightened, but a look that, with the ever-coward heart of a true lover, he could not yet construe. They were asking his name and bestowing upon him well-bred thanks for his heroic deed, and the Scotch cap was especially babbling and insistent. But the eloquent appeal was in the eyes of the lady.

A little thrill of satisfaction ran through Remsen because he had a name to give which, without undue pride, was worthy of being spoken in high places, and a small fortune which, with due pride, he could leave at his end without disgrace.

He opened his lips to speak, and closed them again.

Who was he? Mounted Policeman O'Roon. The badge and the honour of his comrade were in his hands. If Ellesworth Remsen, ten-millionaire and Knickerbocker, had just rescued pomegranate blossoms and Scotch cap from possible death, where was Policeman O'Roon? Off his beat, exposed, disgraced, discharged. Love had come, but before that there had been something that demanded precedence—the fellowship of men on battlefields fighting an alien foe.

Remsen touched his cap, looked between the chestnut's ears, and took refuge in vernacularity.

"Don't mention it," he said stolidly. "We policemen are paid to do these things. It's our duty."

And he rode away—rode away cursing *noblesse oblige*, but knowing he could never have done anything else.

At the end of the day Remsen sent the chestnut to his stable and went to O'Roon's room. The policeman was again a well-set-up, affable, cool young man who sat by the window smoking cigars.

"I wish you and the rest of the police force and all badges, horses, brass buttons and men who can't drink two glasses of *brut* without getting upset were at the devil," said Remsen feelingly.

O'Roon smiled with evident satisfaction.

"Good old Remsen," he said affably, "I know all about it. They trailed me down and cornered me here two hours ago. There was a little row at home, you know, and I cut sticks just to show them. I don't believe I told you that my governor was the Earl of Ardsley. Funny you should bob against them in the Park. If you damaged that horse of mine I'll never forgive you. I'm going to buy him and take him back with me. Oh yes, and I think my sister—Lady Angela, you know—wants particularly for you to come up to the hotel with me this evening. Didn't lose my badge, did you, Remsen? I've got to turn that in at Headquarters when I resign."

17

The Lost Blend

SINCE the bar has been blessed by the clergy, and cocktails open the dinners of the elect, one may speak of the saloon. Teetotallers need not listen, if they choose; there is always the slot restaurant, where a dime dropped into the cold bouillon aperture will bring forth a dry Martini.

Con Lantry worked on the sober side of the bar in Kenealy's café. You and I stood, one-legged like geese, on the other side and went into voluntary liquidation with our week's wages. Opposite danced Con, clean, temperate, clear-headed, polite, white-jacketed, punctual, trustworthy, young, responsible, and took our money.

The saloon (whether blessed or cursed) stood in one of those little "places" which are parallelograms instead of streets, and inhabited by laundries, decayed Knickerbocker families and Bohemians who have nothing to do with either.

Over the café lived Kenealy and his family. His daughter Katherine had eyes of dark Irish—but why should you be told? Be content with your Geraldine or your Eliza Ann. For Con dreamed of her; and when she called softly at the foot of the back stairs for the pitcher of beer for dinner, his heart went up and down like a milk punch in the shaker. Orderly and fit are the rules of Romance; and if you hurl the last shilling of your fortune upon the bar for whisky, the bartender shall take it, and marry his boss's daughter, and good will grow out of it.

But not so Con. For in the presence of woman he was tongue-tied and scarlet. He who would quell with his eye the sonorous youth whom the claret punch made loquacious, or smash with lemon squeezer the obstreperous, or hurl gutterward the cantankerous without a wrinkle coming to his white lawn tie, when he stood before woman he was voiceless, incoherent, stuttering, buried beneath a hot avalanche of bashfulness and misery. What, then, was he before Katherine? A trembler, with no word to say for himself, a stone without blarney, the dumbest lover that ever babbled of the weather in the presence of his divinity.

There came to Kenealy's two sunburned men, Riley and McQuirk. They had conference with Kenealy; and then they took possession of a back room which they filled with bottles and siphons and jugs and druggist's measuring glasses. All the appurtenances and liquids of a saloon were there, but they dispensed no drinks. All day long the two sweltered in there, pouring and mixing unknown brews and decoctions from the liquors in their store. Riley had the education, and he figured on reams of paper, reducing gallons to ounces and quarts to fluid drams. McQuirk, a morose man with a red eye, dashed each unsuccessful completed mixture into the waste pipes with curses gentle, husky and deep. They laboured heavily and untiringly to achieve some mysterious solution, like two alchemists striving to resolve gold from the elements.

Into this back room one evening when his watch was done sauntered Con. His professional curiosity had been stirred by these occult bartenders at whose bar none drank, and who daily drew upon Kenealy's store of liquors to follow their consuming and fruitless experiments.

Down the back stairs came Katherine with her smile like sunrise on Gweebarra Bay.

"Good evening, Mr. Lantry," says she. "And what is the news to-day, if you please?"

"It looks like r-rain," stammered the shy one, backing to the wall.

"It couldn't do better," said Katherine. "I'm thinking there's nothing the worse off for a little water."

In the back room Riley and McQuirk toiled like bearded witches over their strange compounds. From fifty bottles they drew liquids carefully measured after Riley's figures, and shook the whole together in a great glass vessel. Then McQuirk would dash it out, with gloomy profanity, and they would begin again.

"Sit down," said Riley to Con, "and I'll tell you.

"Last summer me and Tim concludes that an American bar in this nation of Nicaragua would pay. There was a town on the coast where there's nothing to eat but quinine and nothing to drink but rum. The natives and foreigners lay down with chills and get up with fevers; and a good mixed drink is nature's remedy for all such tropical inconveniences.

"So we lays in a fine stock of wet goods in New York, and bar fixtures and glassware, and we sails for that Santa Palma town on a line steamer. On the way me and Tim sees flying fish and plays seven-up with the captain and steward, and already begins to feel like the high-ball kings of the tropic of Capricorn.

"When we gets in five hours of the country that we was going to introduce to long drinks and short change the captain calls us over to the starboard binnacle and recollects a few things.

"'I forgot to tell you, boys,' says he, 'that Nicaragua slapped an import duty of 48 per cent. *ad valorem* on all bottled goods last month. The President took a bottle of Cincinnati hair tonic by mistake for tabasco sauce, and he's getting even. Barrelled goods is free.'

"'Sorry you didn't mention it sooner,' says we. And we bought two forty-two gallon casks from the captain, and opened every bottle we had and dumped the stuffed all together in the casks. That 48 per cent. would have ruined us; so we took the chances on making that $1,200 cocktail rather than throw the stuff away.

"Well, when we landed we tapped one of the barrels. The mixture was something heartrending. It was the colour of a plate of Bowery pea-soup, and it tasted like one of those coffee substitutes your aunt makes you take for the heart trouble you get by picking losers. We gave a nigger four fingers of it to try it, and he lay under a coco-nut tree three days beating the sand with his heels and refused to sign a testimonial.

"But the other barrel! Say, bartender, did you ever put on a straw hat with a yellow band around it and go up in a balloon with a pretty girl with $8,000,000 in your pocket all at the same time? That's what thirty drops of it would make you feel like. With two fingers of it inside you you would bury your face in your hands and cry because there wasn't anything more worth while around for you to lick than little Jim Jeffries. Yes, sir, the stuff in that second barrel was distilled elixir of battle, money and high life. It was the colour of gold and as clear as glass, and it shone after dark like the sunshine was still in it. A thousand years from now you'll get a drink like that across the bar.

"Well, we started up business with that one line of drinks, and it was enough. The piebald gentry of that country stuck to it like a hive of bees. If that barrel had lasted that country would have become the greatest on earth. When we opened up of mornings we had a line of Generals and Colonels and ex-Presidents and revolutionists a block long waiting to be served. We started in at fifty cents silver a drink. The last ten gallons went easy at $5 a gulp. It was wonderful stuff. It gave a man courage and ambition and nerve to do anything; at the same time he didn't care whether his money was tainted or fresh from the Ice Trust. When that barrel was half gone Nicaragua had repudiated the National Debt, removed the duty on cigarettes and was about to declare war on the United States and England.

"'Twas by accident we discovered this king of drinks, and 'twill be by good luck if we strike it again. For ten months we've been trying. Small lots at a time, we've mixed barrels of all the harmful ingredients known to the profession of drinking. Ye could have stocked ten bars with the whiskies, brandies, cordials, bitters, gins and wines me and Tim have wasted. A glorious drink like that to be denied to the world! 'Tis a sorrow and a loss of money. The United States as a nation would welcome a drink of the sort, and pay for it."

All the while McQuirk had been carefully measuring and pouring together small quantities of various spirits, as Riley called them, from his latest pencilled prescription. The completed mixture was of a vile, mottled chocolate colour. McQuirk tasted it, and hurled it, with appropriate epithets, into the waste sink.

"'Tis a strange story, even if true," said Con. "I'll be going now along to my supper."

"Take a drink," said Riley. "We've all kinds except the lost blend."

"I never drink," said Con, "anything stronger than water. I am just after meeting Miss Katherine by the stairs. She said a true word. 'There's not anything,' says she, 'but is better off for a little water.'"

When Con had left them Riley almost felled McQuirk by a blow on the back.

"Did ye hear that?" he shouted. "Two fools are we. The six dozen bottles of 'pollinaris we had on the ship—ye opened them yourself—which barrel did ye pour them in—which barrel, ye mudhead?"

"I mind," said McQuirk, slowly, "'twas in the second barrel we opened. I mind the blue piece of paper pasted on the side of it."

"We've got it now," cried Riley. "'Twas that we lacked. 'Tis the water that does the trick. Everything else we had right. Hurry, man, and get two bottles of 'pollinaris from the bar, while I figure out the proportionments with me pencil."

An hour later Con strolled down the sidewalk toward Kenealy's café. Thus faithful employees haunt, during their recreation hours, the vicinity where they labour, drawn by some mysterious attraction.

A police patrol wagon stood at the side door. Three able cops were half carrying, half hustling Riley and McQuirk up its rear steps. The eyes and faces of each bore the bruises and cuts of sanguinary and assiduous conflict. Yet they whooped with strange joy, and directed upon the police the feeble remnants of their pugnacious madness.

"Began fighting each other in the back room," explained Kenealy to Con. "And singing! That was worse. Smashed everything pretty much up. But they're good men. They'll pay for everything. Trying to invent some new kind of cocktail, they was. I'll see they come out all right in the morning."

Con sauntered into the back room to view the battlefield. As he went through the hall Katherine was just coming down the stairs.

"Good evening again, Mr. Lantry," said she. "And is there no news from the weather yet?"

"Still threatens r-rain," said Con, slipping past with red in his smooth, pale cheek.

Riley and McQuirk had indeed waged a great and friendly battle. Broken bottles and glasses were everywhere. The room was full of alcohol fumes; the floor was variegated with spirituous puddles.

On the table stood a 32-ounce glass graduated measure. In the bottom of it were two tablespoonfuls of liquid—a bright golden liquid that seemed to hold the sunshine a prisoner in its auriferous depths.

Con smelled it. He tasted it. He drank it.

As he returned through the hall Katherine was just going up the stairs.

"No news yet, Mr. Lantry?" she asked, with her teasing laugh.

Con lifted her clear from the floor and held her there.

"The news is," he said, "that we're to be married."

"Put me down, sir!" she cried indignantly, "or I will—— Oh, Con, where, oh, wherever did you get the nerve to say it?"

18

Count and Wedding Guest

ONE evening when Andy Donovan went to dinner at his Second Avenue boarding-house, Mrs. Scott introduced him to a new boarder, a young lady, Miss Conway. Miss Conway was small and unobtrusive. She wore a plain, snuffy-brown dress, and bestowed her interest, which seemed languid, upon her plate. She lifted her diffident eyelids and shot one perspicuous, judicial glance at Mr. Donovan, politely murmured his name, and returned to her mutton. Mr. Donovan bowed with the grace and beaming smile that was rapidly winning for him social, business and political advancement, and erased the snuffy-brown one from the tablets of his consideration.

Two weeks later Andy was sitting on the front steps enjoying his cigar. There was a soft rustle behind and above him, and Andy turned his head—and had his head turned.

Just coming out of the door was Miss Conway. She wore a night-black dress of *crêpe de—crêpe de*—oh, this thin black goods. Her hat was black, and from it drooped and fluttered an ebon veil, filmy as a spider's web. She stood on the top step and drew on black silk gloves. Not a speck of white or a spot of colour about her dress anywhere. Her rich golden hair was drawn, with scarcely a ripple, into a shining, smooth knot low on her neck. Her face was plain rather than pretty, but it was now illuminated and made almost beautiful by her large grey eyes that gazed above the houses across the street into the sky with an expression of the most appealing sadness and melancholy.

Gather the idea, girls—all black, you know, with the preference for *crêpe de*—oh, *crêpe de chine*—that's it. All black, and that sad, far-away look, and the hair shining under the black veil (you have to be a blonde, of course), and try to look as if, although your young life had been blighted just as it was about to give a hop-skip-and-a-jump over the threshold of life, a walk in the park might do you good, and be sure to happen out the door at the right moment, and—oh, it'll fetch 'em every time. But it's fierce, now, how cynical I am, ain't it?—to talk about mourning costumes this way.

Mr. Donovan suddenly reinscribed Miss Conway upon the tables of his consideration. He threw away the remaining inch-and-a-quarter of his cigar, that would have been good for eight minutes yet, and quickly shifted his centre of gravity to his low-cut patent leathers.

"It's a fine, clear evening, Miss Conway," he said; and if the Weather Bureau could have heard the confident emphasis of his tones it would have hoisted the square white signal and nailed it to the mast.

"To them that has the heart to enjoy it, it is, Mr. Donovan," said Miss Conway, with a sigh.

Mr. Donovan, in his heart, cursed fair weather. Heartless weather! It should hail and blow and snow to be consonant with the mood of Miss Conway.

"I hope none of your relatives—I hope you haven't sustained a loss?" ventured Mr. Donovan.

"Death has claimed," said Miss Conway, hesitating—"not a relative, but one who—but I will not intrude my grief upon you, Mr. Donovan."

"Intrude?" protested Mr. Donovan. "Why, say, Miss Conway, I'd be delighted, that is, I'd be sorry—I mean I'm sure nobody could sympathize with you truer than I would."

Miss Conway smiled a little smile. And oh, it was sadder than her expression in repose.

"'Laugh, and the world laughs with you; weep, and they give you the laugh,'" she quoted. "I have learned that, Mr. Donovan. I have no friends or acquaintances in this city. But you have been kind to me. I appreciate it highly."

He had passed her the pepper twice at the table.

"It's tough to be alone in New York—that's a cinch," said Mr. Donovan. "But, say—whenever this little old town does loosen up and get friendly it goes the limit. Say you took a little stroll in the park, Miss Conway—don't you think it might chase away some of your mullygrubs? And if you'd allow me——"

"Thanks, Mr. Donovan. I'd be pleased to accept of your escort if you think the company of one whose heart is filled with gloom could be anyways agreeable to you."

Through the open gates of the iron-railed, old, down-town park, where the elect once took the air, they strolled, and found a quiet bench.

There is this difference between the grief of youth and that of old age; youth's burden is lightened by as much of it as another shares; old age may give and give, but the sorrow remains the same.

"He was my fiancé," confided Miss Conway, at the end of an hour. "We were going to be married next spring. I don't want you to think that I am stringing you, Mr. Donovan, but he was a real Count. He had an estate and a castle in Italy. Count Fernando Mazzini was his name. I never saw the beat of him for elegance. Papa objected, of course, and once we eloped, but papa overtook us, and took us back. I thought sure papa and Fernando would fight a duel. Papa has a livery business—in P'kipsee, you know.

"Finally, papa came round, all right, and said we might be married next spring. Fernando showed him proofs of his title and wealth, and then went over to Italy to get the castle fixed up for us. Papa's very proud, and when Fernando wanted to give me several thousand dollars for my trousseau he called him down something awful. He wouldn't even let me take a ring or any presents from him. And when Fernando sailed I came to the city and got a position as cashier in a candy store.

"Three days ago I got a letter from Italy, forwarded from P'kipsee, saying that Fernando had been killed in a gondola accident.

"That is why I am in mourning. My heart, Mr. Donovan, will remain for ever in his grave. I guess I am poor company, Mr. Donovan, but I cannot take any interest in no one. I should not care to keep you from gaiety and your friends who can smile and entertain you. Perhaps you would prefer to walk back to the house?"

Now, girls, if you want to observe a young man hustle out after a pick and shovel, just tell him that your heart is in some other fellow's grave. Young men are grave-robbers by nature. Ask any widow. Something must be done to restore that missing organ to weeping angels in *crêpe de chine*. Dead men certainly got the worst of it from all sides.

"I'm awfully sorry," said Mr. Donovan gently. "No, we won't walk back to the house just yet. And don't say you haven't no friends in this city, Miss Conway. I'm awful sorry, and I want you to believe I'm your friend, and that I'm awful sorry."

"I've got his picture here in my locket," said Miss Conway, after wiping her eyes with her handkerchief. "I never showed it to anybody; but I will to you, Mr. Donovan, because I believe you to be a true friend."

Mr. Donovan gazed long and with much interest at the photograph in the locket that Miss Conway opened for him. The face of Count Mazzini was one to command interest. It was a smooth, intelligent, bright, almost a handsome face—the face of a strong, cheerful man who might well be a leader among his fellows.

"I have a larger one, framed, in my room," said Miss Conway. "When we return I will show you that. They are all I have to remind me of Fernando. But he ever will be present in my heart, that's a sure thing."

A subtle task confronted Mr. Donovan—that of supplanting the unfortunate Count in the heart of Miss Conway. This his admiration for her determined him to do. But the magnitude of the undertaking did not seem to weigh upon his spirits. The sympathetic but cheerful friend was the rôle he essayed; and he played it so successfully that the next half-hour found them conversing pensively across two plates of ice-cream, though yet there was no diminution of the sadness in Miss Conway's large grey eyes.

Before they parted in the hall that evening she ran upstairs and brought down the framed photograph wrapped lovingly in a white silk scarf. Mr. Donovan surveyed it with inscrutable eyes.

"He gave me this the night he left for Italy," said Miss Conway. "I had the one for the locket made from this."

"A fine-looking man," said Mr. Donovan heartily. "How would it suit you, Miss Conway, to give me pleasure of your company to Coney next Sunday afternoon?"

A month later they announced their engagement to Mrs. Scott and the other boarders. Miss Conway continued to wear black.

A week after the announcement the two sat on the same bench in the down-town park, while the fluttering leaves of the trees made a dim kinetoscopic picture of them in the moonlight. But Donovan had worn a look of abstracted gloom all day. He was so silent to-night that love's lips could not keep back any longer the questions that love's heart propounded.

"What's the matter, Andy, you are so solemn and grouchy to-night?"

"Nothing, Maggie."

"I know better. Can't I tell? You never acted this way before. What is it?"

"It's nothing much, Maggie."

"Yes, it is; and I want to know. I'll bet it's some other girl you are thinking about. All right. Why don't you go get her if you want her. Take your arm away, if you please."

"I'll tell you, then," said Andy wisely, "but I guess you won't understand it exactly. You've heard of Mike Sullivan, haven't you? 'Big Mike' Sullivan, everybody calls him."

"No, I haven't," said Maggie. "And I don't want to, if he makes you act like this. Who is he?"

"He's the biggest man in New York," said Andy, almost reverently. "He can about do anything he wants to with Tammany or any other old thing in the political line. He's a mile high and as broad as East River. You say anything against Big Mike, and you'll have a million men on your collarbone in about two seconds. Why, he made a visit over to the old country a while back, and the kings took to their holes like rabbits.

"Well, Big Mike's a friend of mine. I ain't more than deuce high in the district as far as influence goes, but Mike's as good a friend to a little man, or a poor man, as he is to a big one. I met him to-day on the Bowery, and what do you think he does? Comes up and shakes hands. 'Andy,' says he. 'I've been keeping cases on you. You've been putting in some good licks over on your side of the street, and I'm proud of you. What'll you take to drink?' He takes a cigar, and I take a highball. I told him I was going to get married in two weeks. 'Andy,' says he, 'send me an invitation, so I'll keep in mind of it, and I'll come to the wedding.' That's what Big Mike says to me; and he always does what he says.

"You don't understand it, Maggie, but I'd have one of my hands cut off to have Big Mike Sullivan at our wedding. It would be the proudest day of my life. When he goes to a man's wedding, there's a guy being married that's made for life. Now, that's why I'm maybe looking sore to-night."

"Why don't you invite him, then, if he's so much to the mustard?" said Maggie lightly.

"There's a reason why I can't," said Andy sadly. "There's a reason why he mustn't be there. Don't ask me what it is, for I can't tell you."

"Oh, I don't care," said Maggie. "It's something about politics, of course. But it's no reason why you can't smile at me."

"Maggie," said Andy presently, "do you think as much of me as you did of your—as you did of the Count Mazzini?"

He waited a long time, but Maggie did not reply. And then, suddenly she leaned against his shoulder and began to cry—to cry and shake with sobs, holding his arm tightly, and wetting the *crêpe de chine* with tears.

"There, there, there!" soothed Andy, putting aside his own trouble. "And what is it, now?"

"Andy," sobbed Maggie, "I've lied to you, and you'll never marry me, or love me any more. But I feel that I've got to tell. Andy, there never was so much as the little finger of a count. I never had a beau in my life. But all the other girls had; and they talked about 'em; and that seemed to make the fellows like 'em more. And, Andy, I look swell in black—you know I do. So I went out to a photograph store and bought that picture, and had a little one made for my locket, and made up all that story about the Count, and about his being killed, so I could wear black. And nobody can love a liar, and you'll shake me, Andy, and I'll die for shame. Oh, there never was anybody I liked but you—and that's all."

But instead of being pushed away, she found Andy's arm folding her closer. She looked up and saw his face cleared and smiling.

"Could you—could you forgive me, Andy?"

"Sure," said Andy. "It's all right about that. Back to the cemetery for the Count. You've straightened everything out, Maggie. I was in hopes you would before the wedding-day. Bully girl!"

"Andy," said Maggie, with a somewhat shy smile, after she had been thoroughly assured of forgiveness, "did you believe all that story about the Count?"

"Well, not to any large extent," said Andy, reaching for his cigar case; "because it's Big Mike Sullivan's picture you've got in that locket of yours."

19

Thimble, Thimble

THESE are the directions for finding the office of Carteret & Carteret, Mill Supplies and Leather Belting:

You follow the Broadway trail down until you pass the Crosstown Line, the Bread Line, and the Dead Line, and come to the Big Canons of the Moneygrubber Tribe. Then you turn to the left, to the right, dodge a push-cart and the tongue of a two-ton four-horse dray, and hop, skip, and jump to a granite ledge on the side of a twenty-one storey synthetic mountain of stone and iron. In the twelfth storey is the office of Carteret & Carteret. The factory where they make the mill supplies and leather belting is in Brooklyn. Those commodities —to say nothing of Brooklyn—not being of interest to you, let us hold the incidents within the confines of a one-act, one-scene play, thereby lessening the toil of the reader and the expenditure of the publisher. So, if you have the courage to face four pages of type and Carteret & Carteret's office boy, Percival, you shall sit on a varnished chair in the inner office and peep at the little comedy of the Old Nigger Man, the Hunting-Case Watch, and the Open-faced Question—mostly borrowed from the late Mr. Frank Stockton, as you will conclude.

First, biography (but pared to the quick) must intervene. I am for the inverted sugar-coated quinine pill—the bitter on the outside.

The Carterets were, or was (Columbia College professors please rule), an old Virginia family. Long time ago the gentlemen of the family had worn lace ruffles and carried tinless foils and owned plantations and had slaves to burn. But the war had greatly reduced their holdings. (Of course you can perceive at once that this flavour has been shoplifted from Mr. F. Hopkinson Smith, in spite of the "et" after "Carter".) Well, anyhow:

In digging up the Carteret history I shall not take you farther back than the year 1620. The two original American Carterets came over in that year, but by different means of transportation. One brother, named John, came in the *Mayflower* and became a Pilgrim Father. You've seen his picture on the covers of the Thanksgiving magazines, hunting turkeys in the deep snow with a blunderbuss. Blandford Carteret, the other brother, crossed the pond in his own brigantine, landed on the Virginia coast, and became an F. F. V. John became distinguished for piety and shrewdness in business; Blandford for his pride, juleps, marksmanship and vast slave-cultivated plantations.

Then came the Civil War. (I must condense this historical interpolation.) Stonewall Jackson was shot; Lee surrendered; Grant toured the world; cotton went to nine cents; Old Crow whisky and Jim Crown cars were invented; the Seventy-ninth Massachusetts Volunteers returned to the Ninety-seventh Alabama Zouaves the battle flag of Lundy's Lane which they bought at a second-hand store in Chelsea, kept by a man named Skzchnzski; Georgia sent the President a sixty-pound watermelon—and that brings us up to the time when the story begins. My! but that was sparring for an opening! I really must brush up on my Aristotle.

The Yankee Carterets went into business in New York long before the war. Their house, as far as Leather Belting and Mill Supplies was concerned, was as musty and arrogant and solid as one of those old East India tea-importing concerns that you read about in Dickens. There were some rumours of a war behind its counters, but not enough to affect the business.

During and after the war, Blandford Carteret, F.F.V., lost his plantations, juleps, marksmanship and life. He bequeathed little more than his pride to his surviving family. So it came to pass that Blandford Carteret, the Fifth, aged fifteen, was invited by the leather-and-mill-supplies branch of that name to come North and learn business instead of hunting foxes and boasting of the glory of his fathers on the reduced acres of his impoverished family. The boy jumped at the chance, and, at the age of twenty-five, sat in the office of the firm equal partner with John, the Fifth, of the blunderbuss-and-turkey branch. Here the story begins again.

The young men were about the same age, smooth of face, alert, easy of manner, and with an air that promised mental and physical quickness. They were razored, blue-serged, straw-hatted, and pearl stick-pinned like other young New Yorkers who might be millionaires or bill clerks.

One afternoon at four o'clock, in the private office of the firm, Blandford Carteret opened a letter that a clerk had just brought to his desk. After reading it, he chuckled audibly for nearly a minute. John looked around from his desk inquiringly.

"It's from mother," said Blandford; "I'll read you the funny part of it. She tells me all the neighbourhood news first, of course, and then cautions me against getting my feet wet and musical comedies. After that come vital statistics about calves and pigs and an estimate of the wheat crop. And now I'll quote some:

"'And what do you think! Old Uncle Jake, who was seventy-six last Wednesday, must go travelling. Nothing would do but he must go to New York and see his "young Marster Blandford". Old as he is, he has a deal of common sense, so I've let him go. I couldn't refuse him—he seemed to have concentrated all his hopes and desires into this one adventure into the wide world. You know he was born on the plantation, and has never been ten miles away from it in his life. And he was your father's body servant during the war, and has been always a faithful vassal and servant of the family. He has often seen the gold watch—the watch that was your father's and your father's father's. I told him it was to be yours, and he begged me to allow him to take it to you and to put it into your hands himself.

"'So he has it, carefully enclosed in a buckskin case, and is bringing it to you with all the pride and importance of a king's messenger. I gave him money for the round trip and for a two weeks' stay in the city. I wish you would see to it that he gets comfortable quarters—Jake won't need much looking after—he's able to take care of himself. But I have read in the papers that African bishops and coloured potentates generally have much trouble in obtaining food and lodging in the Yankee metropolis. That maybe all right; but I don't see why the best hotel there shouldn't take Jake in. Still, I suppose it's a rule.

"'I gave him full directions about finding you, and packed his valise myself. You won't have to bother with him; but I do hope you'll see that he is made comfortable. Take the watch that he brings you—it's almost a decoration. It has been worn by true Carterets, and there isn't a stain upon it nor a false movement of the wheels. Bringing it to you is the crowning joy of old Jake's life. I wanted him to have that little outing and that happiness before it is too late. You have often heard us talk about how Jake, pretty badly wounded himself, crawled through the reddened grass at Chancellorsville to where your father lay with the bullet in his dear heart, and took the watch from his pocket to keep it from the "Yanks".

"'So my son, when the old man comes consider him as a frail but worthy messenger from the old-time life and home.

"'You have been so long away from home, and so long among the people that we have always regarded as aliens, that I'm not sure that Jake will know you when he sees you. But Jake has a keen perception, and I rather believe that he will know a Virginia Carteret at sight. I can't conceive that even ten years in Yankeeland could change a boy of mine. Anyway, I'm sure you will know Jake. I put eighteen collars in his valise. If he should have to buy others, he wears a number 15½. Please see that he gets the right ones. He will be no trouble to you at all.

"'If you are not too busy, I'd like for you to find him a place to board where they have whitemeal corn-bread, and try to keep him from taking his shoes off in your office or on the street. His right foot swells a little, and he likes to be comfortable.

"'If you can spare the time, count his handkerchiefs when they come back from the wash. I bought him a dozen new ones before he left. He should be there about the time this letter reaches you. I told him to go straight to your office when he arrives.'"

As soon as Blandford had finished the reading of this, something happened (as there should happen in stories and must happen on the stage).

Percival, the office boy, with his air of despising the world's output of mill supplies and leather belting, came in to announce that a coloured gentleman was outside to see Mr. Blandford Carteret.

"Bring him in," said Blandford, rising.

John Carteret swung around in his chair and said to Percival: "Ask him to wait a few minutes outside. We'll let you know when to bring him in."

Then he turned to his cousin with one of those broad slow smiles that was an inheritance of all the Carterets, and said:

"Bland, I've always had a consuming curiosity to understand the differences that you haughty Southerners believe to exist between 'you all' and the people of the North. Of course, I know that you consider yourselves made out of finer clay and look upon Adam as only a collateral branch of your ancestry; but I don't know why. I never could understand the differences between us."

"Well, John," said Blandford, laughing, "what you don't understand about it is just the difference, of course. I suppose it was the feudal way in which we lived that gave us our lordly baronial airs and feeling of superiority."

"But you are not feudal, now," went on John. "Since we licked you and stole your cotton and mules you've had to go to work just as we 'dam-yankees', as you call us, have always been doing. And you're just as proud and exclusive and upper-classy as you were before the war. So it wasn't your money that caused it."

"Maybe it was the climate," said Blandford, lightly, "or maybe our negroes spoiled us. I'll call old Jake in now. I'll be glad to see the old villain again."

"Wait just a moment," said John. "I've got a little theory I want to test. You and I are pretty much alike in our general appearance. Old Jake hasn't seen you since you were fifteen. Let's have him in and play fair and see which of us gets the watch. The old darky surely ought to be able to pick out his 'young marster' without any trouble. The alleged aristocratic superiority of a 'reb' ought to be visible to him at once. He couldn't make the mistake of handing over the timepiece to a Yankee, of course. The loser buys the dinner this evening and two dozen 15½ collars for Jake. Is it a go?"

Blandford agreed heartily. Percival was summoned, and told to usher the "coloured gentleman" in.

Uncle Jake stepped inside the private office cautiously. He was a little old man, as black as soot, wrinkled and bald except for a fringe of white wool, cut decorously short, that ran over his ears and around his head. There was nothing of the stage "uncle" about him: his black suit nearly fitted him; his shoes shone, and his straw hat was banded with a gaudy ribbon. In his right hand he carried something carefully concealed by his closed fingers.

Uncle Jake stopped a few steps from the door. Two young men sat in their revolving desk-chairs ten feet apart and looked at him in friendly silence. His gaze slowly shifted many times from one to the other. He felt sure that he was in the presence of one, at least, of the revered family among whose fortunes his life had begun and was to end.

One had the pleasing but haughty Carteret air; the other had the unmistakable straight, long family nose. Both had the keen black eyes, horizontal brows, and thin, smiling lips that had distinguished both the Carteret of the *Mayflower* and him of the brigantine. Old Jake had thought that he could have picked out his young master instantly from a thousand Northerners; but he found himself in difficulties. The best he could do was to use strategy.

"Howdy, Marse Blandford—howdy, suh?" he said, looking midway between the two young men.

"Howdy, Uncle Jake?" they both answered pleasantly and in unison. "Sit down. Have you brought the watch?"

Uncle Jake chose a hard-bottom chair at a respectful distance, sat on the edge of it, and laid his hat carefully on the floor. The watch in its buckskin case he gripped tightly. He had not risked his life on the battlefield to rescue that watch from his "old marster's" foes to hand it over to the enemy again without a struggle.

"Yes, suh; I got in my hand, suh. I'm gwine give it to you right away in jus' a minute. Old Missus told me to put it in young Marse Blandford's hand and tell him to wear it for the family pride and honour. It was a mighty longsome trip for an old nigger man to make—ten thousand miles, it must be, back to Old Vi'ginia, suh. You've growed mightily, young marster. I wouldn't have recognized you but for yo' powerful resemblance to the old marster."

With admirable diplomacy the old man kept his eyes roaming in the space between the two men. His words might have been addressed to either. Though neither wicked nor perverse, he was seeking for a sign.

Blandford and John exchanged winks.

"I reckon you done got you ma's letter," went on Uncle Jake. "She said she was gwine to write to you 'bout my comin' along up this er-way."

"Yes, yes, Uncle Jake," said John briskly. "My cousin and I have just been notified to expect you. We are both Carterets, you know."

"Although one of us," said Blandford, "was born and raised in the North."

"So if you will hand over the watch——" said John.

"My cousin and I——" said Blandford.

"Will then see to it——" said John.

"That comfortable quarters are found for you," said Blandford.

With credible ingenuity, old Jake set up a cackling high-pitched, protracted laugh. He beat his knee, picked, up his hat and bent the brim in an apparent paroxysm of humorous appreciation. The seizure afforded him a mask behind which he could roll his eye impartially between, above, and beyond his two tormentors.

"I sees what!" he chuckled, after a while. "You gen'lemen is tryin' to have fun with the po' old nigger. But you can't fool old Jake. I knowed you, Marse Blandford, the minute I set eyes on you. You was a po' skimpy little boy no mo' than about fo-teen when you lef' home to come No'th; but I knowed you the minute I sot eyes on you. You is the mawtal image of old marster. The other genl'emen resembles you mightily, suh; but you can't fool old Jake on a member of the Old Vi'ginia family. No, suh."

At exactly the same time both Carterets smiled and extended a hand for the watch.

Uncle Jake's wrinkled, black face lost the expression of amusement into which he had vainly twisted it. He knew that he was being teased, and that it made little real difference, as far as its safety went, into which of those outstretched hands he placed the family treasure. But it seemed to him that not only his own pride and loyalty but much of the Virginia Carterets' was at stake. He had heard down South during the war about that other branch of the family that lived in the North and fought on "the yuther side", and it had always grieved him. He had followed his "old marster's" fortunes from stately luxury through war to almost poverty. And now, with the last relic and reminder of him, blessed by "old missus", and entrusted implicitly to his care, he had come ten thousand miles (as it seemed) to deliver it into the hands of the one who was to wear it and wind it and cherish it and listen to it tick off the unsullied hours that marked the lives of the Carterets—of Virginia.

His experience and conception of the Yankees had been an impression of tyrants—"low-down, common trash"—in blue, laying waste with fire and sword. He had seen the smoke of many burning homesteads almost as grand as Carteret Hall ascending to the drowsy Southern skies. And now he was face to face with one of them—and he could not distinguish him from his "young marster" whom he had come to find and bestow upon him the emblem of his kingship—even as the arm "clothed in white samite, mystic, wonderful" laid Excalibur in the right hand of Arthur. He saw before him two young men, easy, kind, courteous, welcoming, either of whom might have been the one he sought. Troubled, bewildered, sorely grieved at his weakness of judgment, old Jake abandoned his loyal subterfuges. His right hand sweated against the buckskin cover of the watch. He was deeply humiliated and chastened. Seriously, now, his prominent, yellow-white eyes closely scanned the two young men. At the end of his scrutiny he was conscious of but one difference between them. One wore a narrow black tie with a white pearl stick-pin. The other's "four-hand" was a narrow blue one pinned with a black pearl.

And then, to old Jake's relief, there came a sudden distraction. Drama knocked at the door with imperious knuckles, and forced Comedy to the wings, and Drama peeped with a smiling but set face over the footlights.

Percival, the hater of mill supplies, brought in a card, which he handed, with the manner of one bearing a cartel, to Blue-Tie.

"'Olivia De Ormond'," read Blue-Tie from the card. He looked inquiringly at his cousin.

"Why not have her in," said Black-Tie, "and bring matters to a conclusion?"

"Uncle Jake," said one of the young men, "would you mind taking that chair over there in the corner for a while? A lady is coming in—on some business. We'll take up your case afterward."

The lady whom Percival ushered in was young and petulantly, decidedly, freshly, consciously, and intentionally pretty. She was dressed with such expensive plainness that she made you consider lace and ruffles as mere tatters and rags. But one great ostrich plume that she wore would have marked her anywhere in the army of beauty as the wearer of the merry helmet of Navarre.

Miss De Ormond accepted the swivel chair at Blue-Tie's desk. Then the gentlemen drew leather-upholstered seats conveniently near, and spoke of the weather.

"Yes," said she, "I noticed it was warmer. But I mustn't take up too much of your time during business hours. That is," she continued, "unless we talk business."

She addressed her words to Blue-Tie, with a charming smile.

"Very well," said he. "You don't mind my cousin being present, do you? We are generally rather confidential with each other—especially in business matters."

"Oh, no," carolled Miss De Ormond. "I'd rather he did

hear. He knows all about it, anyhow. In fact, he's quite a material witness because he was present when you—when it happened. I thought you might want to talk things over before—well, before any action is taken, as I believe the lawyers say."

"Have you anything in the way of a proposition to make?" asked Blue-Tie.

Miss De Ormond looked reflectively at the neat toe of one of her dull kid pumps.

"I had a proposal made to me," she said. "If the proposal sticks it cuts out the proposition. Let's have that settled first."

"Well, as far as——" began Blue-Tie.

"Excuse me, cousin," interrupted Black-Tie, "if you don't mind my cutting in." And then he turned, with a good-natured air, toward the lady.

"Now, let's recapitulate a bit," he said cheerfully. "All three of us, besides other mutual acquaintances, have been out on a good many larks together."

"I'm afraid I'll have to call the birds by another name," said Miss De Ormond.

"All right," responded Black-Tie, with unimpaired cheerfulness; "suppose we say 'squabs' when we talk about the 'proposal' and 'larks' when we discuss the 'proposition'. You have a quick mind, Miss De Ormond. Two months ago, some half-dozen of us went in a motor-car for a day's run into the country. We stopped at a road-house for dinner. My cousin proposed marriage to you then and there. He was influenced to do so, of course, by the beauty and charm which no one can deny that you possess."

"I wish I had you for a press agent, Mr. Carteret," said the beauty, with a dazzling smile.

"You are on the stage, Miss De Ormond," went on Black-Tie. "You have had, doubtless, many admirers, and perhaps other proposals. You must remember, too, that we were a party of merry-makers on that occasion. There were a good many corks pulled. That the proposal of marriage was made to you by my cousin we cannot deny. But hasn't it been your experience that, by common consent, such things lose their seriousness when viewed in the next day's sunlight? Isn't there something of a 'code' among good 'sports'—I use the word in its best sense—that wipes out each day the follies of the evening previous?"

"Oh, yes," said Miss De Ormond. "I know that very well. And I've always played up to it. But as you seem to be conducting the case—with the silent consent of the defendant—I'll tell you something more. I've got letters from him repeating the proposal. And they're signed, too."

"I understand," said Black-Tie, gravely. "What's your price for the letters?"

"I'm not a cheap one," said Miss De Ormond. "But I had decided to make you a rate. You both belong to a swell family. Well, if I *am* on the stage nobody can say a word against me truthfully. And the money is only a secondary consideration. It isn't the money I was after. I—I believed him—and—and I liked him."

She cast a soft, entrancing glance at Blue-Tie from under her long eyelashes.

"And the price?" went on Black-Tie, inexorably.

"Ten thousand dollars," said the lady, sweetly.

"Or——"

"Or the fulfilment of the engagement to marry."

"I think it is time," interrupted Blue-Tie, "for me to be allowed to say a word or two. You and I, cousin, belong to a family that has held its head pretty high. You have been brought up in a section of the country very different from the one where our branch of the family lived. Yet both of us are Carterets, even if some of our ways and theories differ. You remember it is a tradition of the family that no Carteret ever failed in chivalry to a lady or failed to keep his word when it was given."

Then Blue-Tie, with frank decision showing on his countenance, turned to Miss De Ormond.

"Olivia," said he, "on what date will you marry me?"

Before she could answer, Black-Tie again interposed.

"It is a long journey," said he, "from Plymouth Rock to Norfolk Bay. Between the two points we find the changes that nearly three centuries have brought. In that time the old order has changed. We no longer burn witches or torture slaves. And to-day we neither spread our cloaks on the mud for ladies to walk over nor treat them to the ducking-stool. It is the age of common sense, adjustment, and proportion. All of us—ladies, gentlemen, women, men, Northerners, Southerners, lords, caitiffs, actors, hardware-drummers, senators, hod-carriers and politicians—are coming to a better understanding. Chivalry is one of our words that changes its meaning every day. Family pride is a thing of many constructions—it may show itself by maintaining a moth-eaten arrogance in a cobwebbed Colonial mansion or by the prompt paying of one's debts.

"Now, I suppose you've had enough of my monologue. I've learned something of business and a little of life; and I somehow believe, cousin, that our great-great-grandfathers, the original Carterets, would endorse my view of this matter."

Black-Tie wheeled around to his desk, wrote in a cheque-book and tore out the cheque, the sharp rasp of the perforated leaf making the only sound in the room. He laid the cheque within easy reach of Miss De Ormond's hand.

"Business is business," said he. "We live in a business age. There is my personal cheque for $10,000. What do you say, Miss De Ormond—will it be orange blossoms or cash?"

Miss De Ormond picked up the cheque carelessly, folded it indifferently, and stuffed it into her glove.

"Oh, this'll do," she said, calmly. "I just thought I'd call and put it up to you. I guess you people are all right. But a girl has feelings, you know. I've heard one of you was a Southerner—I wonder which one of you it is?"

She arose, smiled sweetly, and walked to the door. There, with a flash of white teeth and a dip of the heavy plume, she disappeared.

Both of the cousins had forgotten Uncle Jake for the time. But now they heard the shuffling of his shoes as he came across the rug toward them from his seat in the corner.

"Young marster," he said, "take yo' watch."

And without hesitation he laid the ancient time-piece in the hand of its rightful owner.

20

The Head-hunter

When the war between Spain and George Dewey was over, I went to the Philippine Islands. There I remained as bush-whacker correspondent for my paper until its managing editor notified me that an eight-hundred-word cablegram describing the grief of a pet carabao over the death of an infant Moro was not considered by the office to be war news. So I resigned, and came home.

On board the trading-vessel that brought me back I pondered much upon the strange things I had sensed in the weird archipelago of the yellow-brown people. The manoeuvres and skirmishings of the petty war interested me not: I was spell-bound by the outlandish and unreadable countenance of that race that had turned its expressionless gaze upon us out of an unguessable past.

Particularly during my stay in Mindanao had I been fascinated and attracted by that delightfully original tribe of heathen known as the head-hunters. Those grim, flinty, relentless little men, never seen, but chilling the warmest noonday by the subtle terror of their concealed presence, paralleling the trail of their prey through unmapped forests, across perilous mountain-tops, adown bottomless chasms, into uninhabitable jungles, always near with the invisible hand of death uplifted, betraying their pursuit only by such signs as a beast or a bird or a gliding serpent might make—a twig crackling in the awful sweat-soaked night, a drench of dew showering from the screening foliage of a giant tree, a whisper at even from the rushes of a water-level—a hint of death for every mile and every hour—they amused me greatly those little fellows of one idea.

When you think of it, their method is beautifully and almost hilariously effective and simple.

You have your hut in which you live and carry out the destiny that was decreed for you. Spiked to the jamb of your bamboo doorway is a basket made of green withies, plaited. From time to time as vanity or ennui or love or jealousy or ambition may move you, you creep forth with your snicker-snee and take up the silent trail. Back from it you come, triumphant, bearing the severed, gory head of your victim, which you deposit with pardonable pride in the basket at the side of your door. It may be the head of your enemy, your friend, or a stranger, according as competition, jealousy, or simple sportiveness has been our incentive to labour.

In any case, your reward is certain. The village men, in passing, stop to congratulate you, as your neighbour on weaker planes of life stops to admire and praise the begonias in your front yard. Your particular brown maid lingers, with fluttering bosom, casting soft tiger's eyes at the evidence of your love for her. You chew betel-nut and listen, content, to the intermittent soft drip from the ends of the severed neck arteries. And you show your teeth and grunt like a water-buffalo—which is as near as you can come to laughing—at that the cold, acephalous body of your door ornament is being spotted by wheeling vultures in the Mindanaoan wilds.

Truly, the life of the merry head-hunter captivated me. He had reduced art and philosophy to a simple code. To take your adversary's head, to basket it at the portal of your castle, to see it lying there, a dead thing, with its cunning and stratagems and power gone—— Is there a better way to foil his plots, to refute his arguments, to establish your superiority over his skill and wisdom?

The ship that brought me home was captained by an erratic Swede, who changed his course and deposited me, with genuine compassion, in a small town on the Pacific coast of one of the Central American republics, a few hundred miles south of the port to which he had engaged to convey me. But I was wearied of movement and exotic fancies; so I leaped contentedly upon the firm sands of the village of Mojada, telling myself I should be sure to find there the rest that I craved. After all, far better to linger there (I thought), lulled by the sedative splash of the waves and the rustling of palm-fronds, than to sit upon the horsehair sofa of my parental home in the East, and there, cast down by currant wine and cake, and scourged by fatuous relatives, drivel into the ears of gaping neighbours sad stories of the death of colonial governors.

* * *

When I first saw Chloe Greene she was standing, all in white, in the doorway of her father's tile-roofed dobe house. She was polishing a silver cup with a cloth, and she looked like a pearl laid against black velvet. She turned on me a flatteringly protracted but a wiltingly disapproving gaze, and then went inside, humming a light song to indicate the value she placed upon my existence.

Small wonder: for Dr. Stamford (the most disreputable professional man between Juneau and Valparaiso) and I were zigzagging along the turfy street, tunelessly singing the words of "Auld Lang Syne" to the air of "Muzzer's Little Coal-Black Coon". We had come from the ice factory, which was Mojada's palace of wickedness, where we had been playing billiards and opening black bottles, white with frost, that we dragged with strings out of old Sandoval's ice-cold vats.

I turned in sudden rage to Dr. Stamford, as sober as the verger of a cathedral. In a moment I had become aware that we were swine cast before a pearl.

"You beast," I said, "this is half your doing. And the other half is the fault of this cursed country. I'd better have gone back to Sleepytown and died in a wild orgy of currant wine and buns than to have had this happen."

Stamford filled the empty street with his roaring laughter.

"You, too!" he cried. "And all as quick as the popping of a cork. Well, she does seem to strike agreeably upon the retina. But don't burn your fingers. All Mojada will tell you that Louis Devoe is the man."

"We will see about that," said I. "And, perhaps, whether he is *a* man as well as *the* man."

I lost no time in meeting Louis Devoe. That was easily accomplished, for the foreign colony in Mojada numbered scarce a dozen; and they gathered daily at a half decent hotel kept by a Turk, where they managed to patch together the fluttering rags of country and civilization that were left them. I sought Devoe before I did my pearl of the doorway, because I had learned a little of the game of war, and knew better than to strike for a prize before testing the strength of the enemy.

A sort of cold dismay—something akin to fear—filled me when I had estimated him. I found a man so perfectly poised, so charming, so deeply learned in the world's rituals, so full of tact, courtesy, and hospitality, so endowed with grace and ease and a kind of careless, haughty power that I almost overstepped the bounds in probing him, in turning him on the spit to find the weak point that I so craved for him to have. But I left him whole—I had to make bitter acknowledgment to myself that Louis Devoe was a gentleman worthy of my best blows; and I swore to give him them. He was a great merchant of the country, a wealthy importer and exporter. All day he sat in a fastidiously appointed office surrounded by works of art and evidences of his high culture, directing through glass doors and windows the affairs of his house.

In person he was slender and hardly tall. His small, well-shaped head was covered with thick brown hair, trimmed short, and he wore a thick brown beard also cut close and to a fine point. His manners were a pattern.

Before long I had become a regular and a welcome visitor at the Greene home. I shook my wild habits from me like a worn-out cloak. I trained for the conflict with the care of a prizefighter and the self-denial of a Brahmin.

As for Chloe Greene, I shall weary you with no sonnets to her eyebrow. She was a splendidly feminine girl, as wholesome as a November pippin, and no more mysterious than a window-pane. She had whimsical little theories that she had deduced from life, and that fitted the maxims of Epictetus like princess gowns. I wonder, after all, if that old duffer wasn't rather wise!

Chloe had a father, the Reverend Homer Greene, and an intermittent mother, who sometimes palely presided over a twilight teapot. The Reverend Homer was a burr-like man with a life-work. He was writing a concordance to the Scriptures, and had arrived as far as Kings. Being, presumably, a suitor for his daughter's hand, I was timber for his literary outpourings. I had the family tree of Israel drilled into my head until I used to cry aloud in my sleep: "And Aminadab begat Jay Eye See," and so forth, until he had tackled another book. I once made a calculation that the Reverend Homer's concordance would be worked up as far as the Seven Vials mentioned in Revelations about the third day after they were opened.

Louis Devoe, as well as I, was a visitor and an intimate friend of the Greenes. It was there I met him the oftenest, and a more agreeable man or a more accomplished I have never hated in my life.

Luckily or unfortunately, I came to be accepted as a Boy. My appearance was youthful, and I suppose I had that pleading and homeless air that always draws the motherliness that is in women and the cursed theories and hobbies of paterfamilias.

Chloe called me "Tommy," and made sisterly fun of my attempts to woo her. With Devoe she was vastly more reserved. He was the man of romance, one to stir her imagination and deepest feelings had her fancy leaned toward him. I was closer to her, but standing in no glamour; I had the task before me of winning her in what seems to me the American way of fighting—with cleanness and pluck and everyday devotion to break away the barriers of friendship that divided us, and to take her, if I could, between sunrise and dark, abetted by neither moonlight nor music nor foreign wiles.

Chloe gave no sign of bestowing her blithe affections upon either of us. But one day she let out to me an inkling of what she preferred in a man. It was tremendously interesting to me, but not illuminating as to its application. I had been tormenting her for the dozenth time with the statement and catalogue of my sentiments toward her.

"Tommy," said she, "I don't want a man to show his love for me by leading an army against another country and blowing people off the earth with cannons."

"If you mean that the opposite way," I answered, "as they say women do, I'll see what I can do. The papers are full of this diplomatic row in Russia. My people know some big people in Washington who are right next to the army people, and I could get an artillery commission and——"

"I'm not that way," interrupted Chloe. "I mean what I say. It isn't the big things that are done in the world, Tommy, that count with a woman. When the knights were riding abroad in their armour to slay dragons, many a stay-at-home page won a lonesome lady's hand by being on the spot to pick up her glove and be quick with her cloak when the wind blew. The man I am to like best, whoever he shall be, must show his love in little ways. He must never forget, after hearing it once, that I do not like to have anyone walk at my left side; that I detest bright-coloured neckties; that I prefer to sit with my back to a light; that I like candied violets; that I must not be talked to when I am looking at the moonlight shining on water, and that I very, very often long for dates with English walnuts."

"Frivolity," I said, with a frown. "Any well-trained servant would be equal to such details."

"And he must remember," went on Chloe, "to remind me of what I want when I do not know, myself, what I want."

"You're rising in the scale," I said. "What you seem to need is a first-class clairvoyant."

"And if I say that I am dying to hear a Beethoven sonata, and stamp my foot when I say it, he must know by that that what my soul craves is salted almonds; and he will have them ready in his pocket."

"Now," said I, "I am at a loss. I do not know whether your soul's affinity is to be an impresario or a fancy grocer."

Chloe turned her pearly smile upon me.

"Take less than half of what I said as a jest," she went on. "And don't think too lightly of the little things, Boy. Be a paladin if you must, but don't let it show on you. Most women are only very big children, and most men are only very little ones. Please us; don't try to overpower us. When we want a hero we can make one out of even a plain grocer the third time he catches our handkerchief before it falls to the ground."

That evening I was taken down with pernicious fever. That is a kind of coast fever with improvements and high-geared attachments. Your temperature goes up among the threes and fours and remains there, laughing scornfully and feverishly at the cinchona trees and the coal-tar derivatives. Pernicious fever is a case for a simple mathematician instead of a doctor. It is merely this formula: Vitality + the desire to live — the duration of the fever = the result.

I took to my bed in the two-roomed thatched hut where I had been comfortably established, and sent for a gallon of rum. That was not for myself. Drunk, Stamford was the best doctor between the Andes and the Pacific. He came, sat at my bedside, and drank himself into condition.

"My boy," said he, "my lily-white and reformed Romeo, medicine will do you no good. But I will give you quinine, which, being bitter, will arouse in you hatred and anger— two stimulants that will add ten per cent. to your chances. You are as strong as a caribou calf, and you will get well if the fever doesn't get in a knockout blow when you're off your guard."

For two weeks I lay on my back feeling like a Hindu widow on a burning ghat. Old Atasca, an untrained Indian nurse, sat near the door like a petrified statue of What's-the-Use, attending to her duties, which were, mainly, to see that time went by without slipping a cog. Sometimes I would fancy myself back in the Philippines, or, at worse times, sliding off the horsehair sofa in Sleepy-town.

One afternoon I ordered Atasca to vamose, and got up and dressed carefully. I took my temperature, which I was pleased to find 104. I paid almost dainty attention to my dress, choosing solicitously a necktie of a dull and subdued hue. The mirror showed that I was looking little the worse from my illness. The fever gave brightness to my eyes and colour to my face. And while I looked at my reflection my colour went and came again as I thought of Chloe Greene and the millions of eons that had passed since I'd seen her, and of Louis Devoe and the time he had gained on me.

I went straight to her house. I seemed to float rather than walk; I hardly felt the ground under my feet; I thought pernicious fever must be a great boon to make one feel so strong.

I found Chloe and Louis Devoe sitting under the awning in front of the house. She jumped up and met me with a double handshake.

"I'm glad, glad, glad to see you out again!" she cried, every word a pearl strung on the string of her sentence. "You are well, Tommy—or better, of course. I wanted to come to see you, but they wouldn't let me."

"Oh, yes," said I, carelessly, "it was nothing. Merely a little fever. I am out again, as you see."

We three sat there and talked for half an hour or so. Then Chloe looked out yearningly and almost piteously across the ocean. I could see in her sea-blue eyes some deep and intense desire. Devoe, curse him! saw it too.

"What is it?" we asked in unison.

"Coconut pudding," said Chloe, pathetically. "I've wanted some—oh, so badly, for two days. It's got beyond a wish; it's an obsession."

"The coconut season is over," said Devoe, in that voice of his that gave thrilling interest to his most commonplace words. "I hardly think one could be found in Mojada. The natives never use them except when they are green and the milk is fresh. They sell all the ripe ones to the fruiterers.'

"Wouldn't a broiled lobster or a Welsh rabbit do as well?" I remarked, with the engaging idiocy of a pernicious-fever convalescent.

Chloe came as near pouting as a sweet disposition and a perfect profile would allow her to come.

The Reverend Homer poked his ermine-lined face through the doorway and added a concordance to the conversation.

"Sometimes," said he, "Old Campos keeps the dried nuts in his little store on the hill. But it would be far better, my daughter, to restrain unusual desires, and partake thankfully of the daily dishes that the Lord has set before us."

"Stuff!" said I.

"How was that?" asked the Reverend Homer, sharply.

"I say it's tough," said I, "to drop into the vernacular, that

Miss Greene should be deprived of the food she desires—a simple thing like kalso-mine-pudding. Perhaps," I continued, solicitously, "some pickled walnuts or a fricassee of Hungarian butternuts would do as well."

Every one looked at me with a slight exhibition of curiosity.

Louis Devoe arose and made his adieus. I watched him until he had sauntered slowly and grandiosely to the corner, around which he turned to reach his great warehouse and store. Chloe made her excuses, and went inside for a few minutes to attend to some detail affecting the seven o'clock dinner. She was a past mistress in housekeeping. I had tasted her puddings and bread with beatitude.

When all had gone, I turned casually and saw a basket made of plaited green withes hanging by a nail outside the door-jamb. With a rush that made my hot temples throb there came vividly to my mind recollections of the head-hunters—*those grim, flinty, relentless little men, never seen, but chilling the warmest noonday by the subtle terror of their concealed presence. . . . From time to time, as vanity or ennui or love or jealousy or ambition may move him, one creeps forth with his snickersnee and takes up the silent trail. . . . Back he comes, triumphant, bearing the severed, gory head of his victim. . . . His particular brown or white maid lingers, with fluttering bosom, casting soft tiger's eyes at the evidence of his love for her.*

I stole softly from the house and returned to my hut. From its supporting nails in the wall I took a machete as heavy as a butcher's cleaver and sharper than a safety-razor. And then I chuckled softly to myself, and set out to the fastidiously appointed private office of Monsieur Louis Devoe, usurper to the hand of the Pearl of the Pacific.

He was never slow at thinking; he gave one look at my face and another at the weapon in my hand as I entered his door, and then he seemed to fade from my sight. I ran to the back door, kicked it open, and saw him running like a deer up the road toward the wood that began two hundred yards away. I was after him with a shout. I remember hearing children and women screaming, and seeing them flying from the road.

He was fleet, but I was stronger. A mile, and I had almost come up with him. He doubled cunningly and dashed into a brake that extended into a small cañon. I crashed through this after him, and in five minutes had him cornered in an angle of insurmountable cliffs. There his instinct of self-preservation steadied him, as it will steady even animals at bay. He turned to me, quite calm, with a ghastly smile.

"Oh, Rayburn!" he said, with such an awful effort at ease that I was impolite enough to laugh rudely in his face. "Oh, Rayburn!" said he, "come, let's have done with this nonsense! Of course, I know it's the fever and you're not yourself; but collect yourself, man—give me that ridiculous weapon, and let's go back and talk it over."

"I will go back," said I, "carrying your head with me. We will see how charmingly it can discourse when it lies in the basket at her door."

"Come," said he, persuasively, "I think better of you than to suppose that you try this sort of thing as a joke. But even the vagaries of a fever-crazed lunatic come some time to a limit. What is this talk about heads and baskets? Get yourself together and throw away that absurd cane-chopper. What would Miss Greene think of you?" he ended, with the silky cajolery that one would use towards a fretful child.

"Listen," said I. "At last you have struck upon the right note. What would she think of me? Listen," I repeated.

"There are women," I said, "who look upon horsehair sofas and currant wine as dross. To them even the calculated modulation of your well-trimmed talk sounds like the dropping of rotten plums from a tree in the night. They are the maidens who walk back and forth in the villages, scorning the emptiness of the baskets at the doors of the young men who would win them. One, such as they," I said, "is waiting. Only a fool would try to win a woman by drooling like a braggart in her doorway or by waiting upon her whims like a footman. They are all daughters of Herodias, and to gain their hearts one must lay the heads of his enemies before them with his own hands. Now, bend your neck, Louis Devoe. Do not be a coward as well as a chatterer at a lady's tea-table."

"There, there!" said Devoe, falteringly. "You know me, don't you, Rayburn?"

"Oh, yes," I said, "I know you. I know you. I know you. But the basket is empty. The old men of the village and the young men, and both the dark maidens and the ones who are as fair as pearls, walk back and forth and see its emptiness. Will you kneel now, or must we have a scuffle? It is not like you to make things go roughly and with bad form. But the basket is waiting for your head."

With that he went to pieces. I had to catch him as he tried to scamper past me like a scared rabbit. I stretched him out and got a foot on his chest, but he squirmed like a worm, although I appealed repeatedly to his sense of propriety and the duty he owed to himself as a gentleman not to make a row.

But at last he gave me the chance, and I swung the machete.

It was not hard work. He flopped like a chicken during the six or seven blows that it took to sever his head; but finally he lay still, and I tied his head in my handkerchief. The eyes opened and shut thrice while I walked a hundred yards. I was red to my feet with the drip, but what did that matter? With delight I felt under my hands the crisp touch of his short, thick, brown hair and close-trimmed beard.

I reached the house of the Greenes and dumped the head of Louis Devoe into the basket that still hung by the nail in the door-jamb. I sat in a chair under the awning and waited. The sun was within two hours of setting. Chloe came out and looked surprised.

"Where have you been, Tommy?" she asked. "You were gone when I came out."

"Look in the basket," I said, rising to my feet. She looked and gave a little scream—of delight, I was pleased to note.

"Oh, Tommy!" she said. "It was just what I wanted you to do. It's leaking a little, but that doesn't matter. Wasn't I telling you? It's the little things that count. And you remembered."

Little things! She held the ensanguined head of Louis Devoe in her white apron. Tiny streams of red widened on her apron and dripped on the floor. Her face was bright and tender.

"Little things, indeed!" I thought again. "The head-hunters are right. These are the things that women like you to do for them."

Chloe came close to me. There was no one in sight. She looked up at me with sea-blue eyes that said things they had never said before.

"You think of me," she said. "You are the man I was describing. You think of the little things, and they are what make the world worth living in. The man for me must consider my little wishes, and make me happy in small ways. He must bring me little red peaches in December if I wish for them, and then I will love him till June. I will have no knight in armour slaying his rival or killing dragons for me. You please me very well, Tommy."

I stooped and kissed her. Then a moisture broke out on my forehead, and I began to feel weak. I saw the red stains vanish from Chloe's apron, and the head of Louis Devoe turn to a brown, dried coconut.

"There will be coconut pudding for dinner, Tommy, boy," said Chloe gaily, "and you must come. I must go in for a little while."

She vanished in a delightful flutter.

Dr. Stamford tramped up hurriedly. He seized my pulse as though it were his own property that I had escaped with.

"You are the biggest fool outside of any aslyum!" he said, angrily. "Why did you leave your bed? And the idiotic things you've been doing!—and no wonder, with your pulse going like a sledge-hammer."

"Name some of them," said I.

"Devoe sent for me," said Stamford. "He saw you from his window go to old Campos' store, chase him up the hill with his own yardstick, and then come back and make off with his biggest coconut."

"It's the little things that count, after all," said I.

"It's your little bed that counts with you just now," said the doctor. "You come with me at once, or I'll throw up the case. You're as loony as a loon."

So I got no coconut pudding that evening, but I conceived a distrust as to the value of the method of the head-hunters. Perhaps for many centuries the maidens of the villages may have been looking wistfully at the heads in the baskets at the doorways, longing for other and lesser trophies.

21

The Last of the Troubadours

INEXORABLY Sam Galloway saddled his pony. He was going away from the Rancho Altito at the end of a three-months' visit. It is not to be expected that a guest should put up with wheat coffee and biscuits yellow-streaked with saleratus for longer than that. Nick Napoleon, the big negro man cook, had never been able to make good biscuits. Once before, when Nick was cooking at the Willow Ranch, Sam had been forced to fly from his *cuisine*, after only a six-weeks' sojourn.

On Sam's face was an expression of sorrow, deepened with regret and slightly tempered by the patient forgiveness of a connoisseur who cannot be understood. But very firmly and inexorably he buckled his saddle-cinches, looped his stake-rope and hung it to his saddle-horn, tied his slicker and coat on the cantle, and looped his quirt on his right wrist. The Merrydews (householders of the Rancho Altito), men, women, children, and servants, vassals, visitors, employés, dogs, and casual callers were grouped in the "gallery" of the ranch-house, all with faces set to the tune of melancholy and grief. For, as the coming of Sam Galloway to any ranch, camp, or cabin between the rivers Frio and Bravo del Norte aroused joy, so his departure caused mourning and distress.

And then, during absolute silence, except for the bumping of a hind elbow of a hound dog as he pursued a wicked flea, Sam tenderly and carefully tied his guitar across his saddle on top of his slicker and coat. The guitar was in a green duck bag; and if you catch the significance of it, it explains Sam.

Sam Galloway was the Last of the Troubadours. Of course you know about the troubadours. The encyclopaedia says they flourished between the eleventh and the thirteenth centuries. What they flourished doesn't seem clear—you may be pretty sure it wasn't a sword: maybe it was a fiddle-bow, or a forkful of spaghetti, or a lady's scarf. Anyhow, Sam Galloway was one of 'em.

Sam put on a martyred expression as he mounted his pony. But the expression on his face was hilarious compared with the one on his pony's. You see, a pony gets to know his rider mighty well, and it is not unlikely that cow ponies in pastures and at hitching racks had often guyed Sam's pony for being ridden by a guitar player instead of by a rollicking, cussing, all-wool cowboy. No man is a hero to his saddle-horse. And even an escalator in a department store might be excused for tripping up a troubadour.

Oh, I know I'm one; and so are you. You remember the stories you memorize and the card tricks you study and that little piece on the piano—how does it go—ti-tum-te-tum-ti-tum—those little Arabian Ten Minute Entertainments that you furnish when you go up to call on your rich Aunt Jane. You should know that *omnae personae in tres partes divisae sunt* Namely: Barons, Troubadours, and Workers. Barons have no inclination to read such folderol as this; and Workers have no time: so I know you must be a Troubadour, and that you will understand Sam Galloway. Whether we sing, act, dance, write, lecture, or paint, we are only troubadours; so let us make the worst of it.

The pony with the Dante Alighieri face, guided by the pressure of Sam's knees, bore that wandering minstrel sixteen miles south-eastward. Nature was in her most benignant mood. League after league of delicate, sweet flowerets made fragrant the gently undulating prairie. The east wind tempered the spring warmth; wool-white clouds flying in from the Mexican Gulf hindered the direct rays of the April sun. Sam sang songs as he rode. Under his pony's bridle he had tucked some sprigs of chaparral to keep away the deer flies. Thus crowned, the long-faced quadruped looked more Dantesque than before, and, judging by his countenance seemed to think of Beatrice.

Straight as topography permitted, Sam rode to the sheep ranch of old man Ellison. A visit to a sheep ranch seemed to him desirable just then. There had been too many people, too much noise, argument, competition, confusion at Rancho Altito. He had never conferred upon old man Ellison the favour of sojourning at his ranch; but he knew he would be welcome. The troubadour is his own passport everywhere. The Workers in the castle let down the drawbridge to him, and the Baron sets him at his left hand at table in the banquet hall. There ladies smile upon him and applaud his songs and stories, while the Workers bring boars' heads and flagons. If the Baron nods once or twice in his carved oaken chair, he does not do it maliciously.

Old man Ellison welcomed the troubadour flatteringly. He had often heard praises of Sam Galloway from other ranchmen who had been complimented by his visits, but had never aspired to such an honour for his own humble barony. I say barony because old man Ellison was the Last of the Barons. Of course, Bulwer-Lytton lived too early to know him, or he wouldn't have conferred that sobriquet upon Warwick. In life it is the duty and the function of the Baron to provide work for the Workers and lodging and shelter for the Troubadours.

Old man Ellison was a shrunken old man, with a short, yellow-white beard and a face lined and seamed by past-and-gone smiles. His ranch was a little two-room box house in a grove of hackberry trees in the lonesomest part of the sheep country. His household consisted of a Kiowa Indian man cook, four hounds, a pet sheep, and a half-tamed coyote chained to a fence-post. He owned 3,000 sheep, which he ran on two sections of leased land and many thousands of acres neither leased nor owned. Three or four times a year someone who spoke his language would ride up to his gate and exchange a few bald ideas with him. Those were red-letter days to old man Ellison. Then in what illuminated, embossed, and gorgeously decorated capitals must have been written the day on which a troubadour—a troubadour who, according to the encyclopaedia, should have flourished between the eleventh and the thirteenth centuries—drew rein at the gates of his baronial castle!

Old man Ellison's smiles came back and filled his wrinkles when he saw Sam. He hurried out of the house in his shuffling, limping way to greet him.

"Hallo, Mr. Ellison," said Sam cheerfully. "Thought I'd drop over and see you a while. Notice you've had fine rains on your range. They ought to make good grazing for your spring lambs."

"Well, well, well," said old man Ellison. "I'm mighty glad to see you, Sam. I never thought you'd take the trouble to ride over to as out-of-the-way an old ranch as this. But you're mighty welcome. 'Light. I've got a sack of new oats in the kitchen—shall I bring out a feed for your hoss?"

"Oats for him?" said Sam derisively. "No, sir-ee. He's as fat as a pig now on grass. He don't get rode enough to keep him in condition. I'll just turn him in the horse pasture with a drag rope on if you don't mind."

I am positive that never during the eleventh and thirteenth centuries did Baron, Troubadour, and Worker amalgamate as harmoniously as their parallels did that evening at old man Ellison's sheep ranch. The Kiowa's biscuits were light and tasty and his coffee strong. Ineradicable hospitality and appreciation glowed on old man Ellison's weather-tanned face. As for the troubadour, he said to himself that he had stumbled upon pleasant places indeed. A well-cooked, abundant meal, a host whom his lightest attempt to entertain seemed to delight far beyond the merits of the exertion, and the reposeful atmosphere that his sensitive soul at that time craved united to confer upon him a satisfaction and luxurious ease that he had seldom found on his tours of the ranches.

After the delectable supper, Sam untied the green duck bag and took out his guitar. Not by way of payment, mind you—neither Sam Galloway nor any other of the true troubadours are lineal descendants of the late Tommy Tucker. You have read of Tommy Tucker in the works of the esteemed but often obscure Mother Goose. Tommy Tucker sang for his supper. No true troubadour would do that. He would have his supper, and then sing for Art's sake.

Sam Galloway's repertoire comprised about fifty funny stories and between thirty and forty songs. He by no means stopped there. He could talk through twenty cigarettes on any topic that you brought up. And he never sat up when he could lie down; and never stood when he could sit. I am strongly disposed to linger with him, for I am drawing a portrait as well as a blunt pencil and a tattered thesaurus will allow.

I wish you could have seen him: he was small and tough and inactive beyond the power of imagination to conceive. He wore an ultramarine-blue woollen shirt laced down the front with a pearl-grey, exaggerated sort of shoe-string, indestructible brown duck clothes, inevitable high-heeled boots with Mexican spurs, and a Mexican straw sombrero.

That evening Sam and old man Ellison dragged their chairs out under the hackberry trees. They lighted cigarettes, and the troubadour gaily touched his guitar. Many of the songs he sang were the weird, melancholy, minor-keyed *canciones* that he had learned from the Mexican sheep herders and *vaqueros*. One, in particular, charmed and soothed the soul of the lonely baron. It was a favourite song of the sheep herders, beginning "*Huile, huile, palomita*," which being translated means, "Fly, fly, little dove." Sam sang it for old man Ellison many times that evening.

The troubadour stayed on at the old man's ranch. There was peace and quiet and appreciation there such as he had not found in the noisy camps of the cattle kings. No audience in the world could have crowned the work of poet, musician, or artist with more worshipful and unflagging approval than that bestowed upon his efforts by old man Ellison. No visit by a royal personage to a humble wood-chopper or peasant could have been received with more flattering thankfulness and joy.

On a cool, canvas-covered cot in the shade of the hackberry trees, Sam Galloway passed the greater part of his time. There he rolled his brown-paper cigarettes, read such tedious literature as the ranch afforded, and added to his repertoire of improvisations that he played so expertly on his guitar. To him, as a slave ministering to a great lord, the Kiowa brought cool water from the red jar hanging under the brush shelter, and food when he called for it. The prairie zephyrs fanned him mildly; mocking-birds at morn and eve competed with, but scarce equalled, the sweet melodies of his lyre; a perfumed stillness seemed to fill all his world. While old man

Ellison was pottering among his flocks of sheep on his mile-an-hour pony, and while the Kiowa took his siesta in the burning sunshine at the end of the kitchen, Sam would lie on his cot thinking what a happy world he lived in, and how kind it is to the ones whose mission in life it is to give entertainment and pleasure. Here he had food and lodging as good as he had ever longed for; absolute immunity from care or exertion or strife; an endless welcome, and a host whose delight at the sixteenth repetition of a song or a story was as keen as at its initial giving. Was there ever a troubadour of old who struck upon as royal a castle in his wanderings? While he lay thus, meditating upon his blessings, little brown cottontails would shyly frolic through the yard; a covey of white-topknotted blue quail would run past, in single file, twenty yards away; a *paisano* bird, out hunting for tarantulas, would hop upon the fence and salute him with sweeping flourishes of its long tail. In the eighty-acre horse pasture the pony with the Dantesque face grew fat and almost smiling. The troubadour was at the end of his wanderings.

Old man Ellison was his own *vaciero*. That means that he supplied his sheep camps with wood, water, and rations by his own labours instead of hiring a *vaciero*. On small ranches it is often done.

One morning he started for the camp of Incarnación Felipe de la Cruz y Monte Piedras (one of his sheep herders) with the week's usual rations of brown beans, coffee, meal, and sugar. Two miles away on the trail from old Fort Ewing, he met, face to face, a terrible being called King James mounted on a fiery, prancing, Kentucky-bred horse.

King James's real name was James King; but people reversed it because it seemed to fit him better, and also because it seemed to please his majesty. King James was the biggest cattleman between the Alamo plaza in San Antone and Bill Hopper's saloon in Brownsville. Also he was the loudest and most offensive bully and braggart and bad man in southwest Texas. And he always made good whenever he bragged; and the more noise he made the more dangerous he was. In the story papers it is always the quiet, mild-mannered man with light-blue eyes and a low voice who turned out to be really dangerous; but in real life and in this story such is not the case. Give me my choice between assaulting a large, loudmouthed rough-houser and an inoffensive stranger with blue eyes sitting quietly in a corner, and you will see something doing in the corner every time.

King James, as I intended to say earlier, was a fierce, two-hundred-pound, sunburned, blond man, as pink as an October strawberry, and with two horizontal slits under shaggy red eyebrows for eyes. On that day he wore a flannel shirt that was tan-coloured, with the exception of certain large areas which were darkened by transudations due to the summer sun. There seemed to be other clothing and garnishings about him, such as brown duck trousers stuffed into immense boots, and red handkerchiefs and revolvers; and a shot-gun laid across his saddle and a leather belt with millions of cartridges shining in it—but your mind skidded off such accessories; what held your gaze was just the two little horizontal slits that he used for eyes.

This was the man that old man Ellison met on the trail; and when you count up in the baron's favour that he was sixty-five and weighed ninety-eight pounds and had heard of King James's record and that he (the baron) had a hankering for the *vita simplex* and had no gun with him and wouldn't have used it if he had, you can't censure him if I tell you that the smiles with which the troubadour had filled his wrinkles went out of them and left them plain wrinkles again. But he was not the kind of baron that flies from danger. He reined in the mile-an-hour pony (no difficult feat), and saluted the formidable monarch.

King James expressed himself with royal directness.

"You're that old snoozer that's running sheep on this range, ain't you?" said he. "What right have you got to do it? Do you own any land, or lease any?"

"I have two sections leased from the state," said old man Ellison mildly.

"Not by no means you haven't," said King James. "Your lease expired yesterday; and I had a man at the land office on the minute to take it up. You don't control a foot of grass in Texas. You sheep men have got to git. Your time's up. It's a cattle country, and there ain't any room in it for snoozers. This range you've got your sheep on is mine. I'm putting up a wire fence, forty by sixty miles; and if there's a sheep inside of it when it's done it'll be a dead one. I'll give you a week to move yours away. If they ain't gone by then, I'll send six men over here with Winchesters to make mutton out of the whole lot. And if I find you here at the same time this is what you'll get."

King James patted the breech of his shot-gun warningly.

Old man Ellison rode on to the camp of Incarnación. He sighed many times, and the wrinkles in his face grew deeper. Rumours that the old order was about to change had reached him before. The end of Free Grass was in sight. Other troubles, too, had been accumulating upon his shoulders. His flocks were decreasing instead of growing; the price of wool was declining at every clip; even Bradshaw, the storekeeper at Frio City, at whose store he bought his ranch supplies, was dunning him for his last six months' bill and threatening to cut him off. And so this last greatest calamity suddenly dealt out to him by the terrible King James was a crusher.

When the old man got back to the ranch at sunset he found Sam Galloway lying on his cot, propped against a roll of blankets and wool sacks, fingering his guitar.

"Hallo, Uncle Ben," the troubadour called cheerfully. "You rolled in early this evening. I been trying a new twist on the Spanish Fandango to-day. I just about got it. Here's how she goes—listen."

"That's fine, that's mighty fine," said old man Ellison, sitting on the kitchen step and rubbing his white Scotch-terrier whiskers. "I reckon you've got all the musicians beat east and west, Sam, as far as the roads are cut out."

"Oh, I don't know," said Sam reflectively. "But I certainly do get there on variations. I guess I can handle anything in five flats about as well as any of 'em. But you look kind of fagged out, Uncle Ben—ain't you feeling right well this evening?"

"Little tired; that's all, Sam. If you ain't played yourself out, let's have that Mexican piece that starts off with '*Huile, huile, palomita*'. It seems that that song always kind of soothes and comforts me after I've been riding far or anything bothers me."

"Why, *seguramente, señor,*" said Sam. "I'll hit her up for you as often as you like. And before I forget about it, Uncle Ben, you want to jerk Bradshaw up about them last hams he sent us. They're just a little bit strong."

A man sixty-five years old, living on a sheep ranch and beset by a complication of disasters, cannot successfully and continuously dissemble. Moreover, a troubadour has eyes quick to see unhappiness in others around him—because it disturbs his own ease. So, on the next day, Sam again questioned the old man about his air of sadness and abstraction. Then old man Ellison told him the story of King James's threats and orders and that pale melancholy and red ruin appeared to have marked him for their own. The troubadour took the news thoughtfully. He had heard much about King James.

On the third day of the seven days of grace allowed him by the autocrat of the range, old man Ellison drove his buckboard to Frio City to fetch some necessary supplies for the ranch. Bradshaw was hard but not implacable. He divided the old man's order by two, and let him have a little more time. One article secured was a new, fine ham for the pleasure of the troubadour.

Five miles out of Frio City on his way home the old man met King James riding into town. His majesty could never look anything but fierce and menacing, but to-day his slits of eyes appeared to be a little wider than they usually were.

"Good day," said the king gruffly. "I've been wanting to see you. I hear it said by a cowman from Sandy yesterday that you was from Jackson County, Mississippi, originally. I want to know if that's a fact."

"Born there," said old man Ellison, "and raised there till I was twenty-one."

"This man says," went on King James, "that he thinks you was related to the Jackson County Reeveses. Was he right?"

"Aunt Caroline Reeves," said the old man, "was my half-sister."

"She was my aunt," said King James. "I run away from

home when I was sixteen. Now, let's re-talk over some things that we discussed a few days ago. They call me a bad man; and they're only half right. There's plenty of room in my pasture for your bunch of sheep and their increase for a long time to come. Aunt Caroline used to cut out sheep in cake dough and bake 'em for me. You keep your sheep where they are, and use all the range you want. How's your finances?"

The old man related his woes in detail, dignifiedly, with restraint and candour.

"She used to smuggle extra grub into my school basket—I'm speaking of Aunt Caroline," said King James. "I'm going over to Frio City to-day, and I'll ride back by your ranch to-morrow. I'll draw $2,000 out of the bank there and bring it over to you; and I'll tell Bradshaw to let you have everything you want on credit. You are bound to have heard the old saying at home that the Jackson County Reeveses and Kings would stick closer by each other than chestnut burrs. Well, I'm a King yet whenever I run across a Reeves. So you look out for me along about sundown to-morrow, and don't worry about nothing. Shouldn't wonder if the dry spell don't kill out the young grass."

Old man Ellison drove happily ranchward. Once more the smiles filled out his wrinkles. Very suddenly, by the magic of kinship and the good that lies somewhere in all hearts, his troubles had been removed.

On reaching the ranch he found that Sam Galloway was not there. His guitar hung by its buckskin string to a hackberry limb, moaning as the gulf breeze blew across its masterless strings.

The Kiowa endeavoured to explain.

"Sam, he catch pony," said he, "and say he ride to Frio City. What for no can damn sabe. Say he come back to-night. Maybe so. That all."

As the first stars came out the troubadour rode back to his haven. He pastured his pony and went into the house, his spurs jingling martially.

Old man Ellison sat at the kitchen table, having a tin cup of before-supper coffee. He looked contented and pleased.

"Hallo, Sam," said he, "I'm darned glad to see ye back. I

don't know how I managed to get along on this ranch, anyhow, before ye dropped in to cheer things up. I'll bet ye've been skylarking around with some of them Frio City gals now, that's kept ye so late."

And then old man Ellison took another look at Sam's face and saw that the minstrel had changed to the man of action.

And while Sam is unbuckling from his waist old man Ellison's six-shooter, that the latter had left behind when he drove to town, we may well pause to remark that anywhere and whenever a troubadour lays down the guitar and takes up the sword trouble is sure to follow. It is not the expert thrust of Athos nor the cold skill of Aramis nor the iron wrist of Porthos that we have to fear—it is the Gascon's fury—the wild and unacademic attack of the troubadour—the sword of D'Artagnan.

"I done it," said Sam. "I went over to Frio City to do it. I couldn't let him put the skibunk on you, Uncle Ben. I met him in Summers's saloon. I knowed what to do. I said a few things to him that nobody else heard. He reached for his gun first—half a dozen fellows saw him do it—but I got mine unlimbered first. Three doses I gave him—right around the lungs, and a saucer could have covered up all of 'em. He won't bother you no more."

"This—is—King—James—you speak—of?" asked old man Ellison, while he sipped his coffee.

"You bet it was. And they took me before the county judge; and the witnesses what saw him draw his gun first was all there. Well, of course, they put me under $300 bond to appear before the court, but there was four or five boys on the spot ready to sign the bail. He won't bother you no more, Uncle Ben. You ought to have seen how close them bullet holes was together. I reckon playing a guitar as much as I do must kind of limber a fellow's trigger finger up a little, don't you think, Uncle Ben?"

Then there was a little silence in the castle, except for the spluttering of a venison steak that the Kiowa was cooking.

"Sam," said old man Ellison, stroking his white whiskers with a tremulous hand, "would you mind getting the guitar and playing that '*Huile, huile, palomita*' piece once or twice?

It always seems to be kind of soothing and comforting when a man's tired and fagged out."

There is no more to be said, except that the title of the story is wrong. It should have been called *The Last of the Barons.* There never will be an end to the troubadours; and now and then it does seem that the jingle of their guitars will drown the sound of the muffled blows of the pickaxes and trip-hammers of all the Workers in the world.

22

The Sleuths

In the Big City a man will disappear with the suddenness and completeness of the flame of a candle that is blown out. All the agencies of inquisition—the hounds of the trail, the sleuths of the city's labyrinths, the closet detectives of theory and induction—will be invoked to the search. Most of the man's face will be seen no more. Sometimes he will reappear in Sheboygan or in the wilds of Terre Haute,* calling himself one of the synonyms of "Smith", and without memory of events up to a certain time, including his grocer's bill. Sometimes it will be found, after dragging the rivers, and polling the restaurants to see if he may be waiting for a well-done sirloin, that he has moved next door.

This snuffing out of a human being like the erasure of a chalk man from a blackboard, is one of the most impressive themes in dramaturgy.

The case of Mary Snyder, in point, should not be without interest.

A man of middle age, of the name of Meeks, came from the West to New York to find his sister, Mrs. Mary Snyder, a widow, aged fifty-two, who had been living for a year in a tenement house in a crowded neighbourhood.

At her address he was told that Mary Snyder had moved away longer than a month before. No one could tell him her new address.

On coming out Mr. Meeks addressed a policeman who was standing on the corner, and explained his dilemma.

"My sister is very poor," he said, "and I am anxious to find her. I have recently made quite a lot of money in a lead mine, and I want her to share my prosperity. There is no use in advertising her, because she cannot read."

The policeman pulled his moustache and looked so thoughtful and mighty that Meeks could almost feel the joyful tears of his sister Mary dropping upon his bright blue tie.

"You go down in the Canal Street neighbourhood," said the policeman, "and get a job drivin' the biggest dray you can find. There's old women always gettin' knocked over by drays down there. You might see 'er among 'em. If you don't want to do that you better go 'round to head-quarters and get 'em to put a fly cop on to the dame."

At police head-quarters Meeks received ready assistance. A general alarm was sent out, and copies of a photograph of Mary Snyder that her brother had were distributed among the stations. In Mulberry Street the chief assigned Detective Mullins to the case.

The detective took Meeks aside and said:

"This is not a very difficult case to unravel. Shave off your whiskers, fill your pockets with good cigars, and meet me in the café of the Waldorf at three o'clock this afternoon."

Meeks obeyed. He found Mullins there. They had a bottle of wine, while the detective asked questions concerning the missing woman.

"Now," said Mullins, "New York is a big city, but we've got the detective business systematized. There are two ways we can go about finding your sister. We will try one of 'em first. You say she's fifty-two?"

"A little past," said Meeks.

The detective conducted the Westerner to a branch advertising office of one of the largest dailies. There he wrote the following "ad" and submitted it to Meeks.

"Wanted, at once—one hundred attractive chorus girls for a new musical comedy. Apply all day at No. —— Broadway."

Meeks was indignant.

"My sister," said he, "is a poor, hard-working, elderly woman. I do not see what aid an advertisement of this kind would be toward finding her."

"All right," said the detective. "I guess you don't know New York. But if you've got a grouch against this scheme we'll try the other one. It's a sure thing. But it'll cost you more."

"Never mind the expense," said Meeks; "we'll try it."

The sleuth led him back to the Waldorf. "Engage a couple of bedrooms and a parlour," he advised, "and let's go up."

This was done, and the two were shown to a superb suite on the fourth floor. Meeks looked puzzled. The detective sank into a velvet armchair, and pulled out his cigar case.

"I forgot to suggest, old man," he said, "that you should have taken the rooms by the month. They wouldn't have stuck you so much for 'em."

"By the month!" exclaimed Meeks. "What do you mean?"

"Oh, it'll take time to work the game this way. I told you it would cost you more. We'll have to wait till spring. There'll be a new city directory out then. Very likely your sister's name and address will be in it."

Meeks rid himself of the city detective at once. On the next day someone advised him to consult Shamrock Jolnes, New York's famous private detective, who demanded fabulous fees, but performed miracles in the way of solving mysteries and crimes.

After waiting for two hours in the ante-room of the great detective's apartment, Meeks was shown into his presence. Jolnes sat in a purple dressing-gown at an inlaid ivory chess table, with a magazine before him, trying to solve the mystery of "They". The famous sleuth's thin, intellectual face, piercing eyes, and rate per word are too well known to need description.

Meeks set forth his errand. "My fee, if successful will be $500," said Shamrock Jolnes.

Meeks bowed his agreement to the price.

"I will undertake your case, Mr. Meeks," said Jolnes finally. "The disappearance of people in this city has always been an interesting problem to me. I remember a case that I brought to a successful outcome a year ago. A family bearing the name of Clark disappeared suddenly from a small flat in which they were living. I watched the flat building for two months for a clue. One day it struck me that a certain milkman and a grocer's boy always walked backward when they carried their wares upstairs. Following out by induction the idea that this observation gave me, I at once located the missing family. They had moved into the flat across the hall and changed their name to Kralc."

Shamrock Jolnes and his client went to the tenement house where Mary Snyder had lived, and the detective demanded to be shown the room in which she had lived. It had been occupied by no tenant since her disappearance.

The room was small, dingy, and poorly furnished. Meeks seated himself dejectedly on a broken chair, while the great detective searched the walls and floor and the few sticks of old, rickety furniture for a clue.

At the end of half an hour Jolnes had collected a few seemingly unintelligible articles—a cheap black hat-pin, a piece torn off a theatre programme, and the end of a small torn card on which was the word "left" and the characters "C 12".

Shamrock Jolnes leaned against the mantel for ten minutes, with his head resting upon his hand, and an absorbed look upon his intellectual face. At the end of that time he exclaimed, with animation:

"Come, Mr. Meeks; the problem is solved. I can take you directly to the house where your sister is living. And you may have no fears concerning her welfare, for she is amply provided with funds—for the present at least."

Meeks felt joy and wonder in equal proportions.

"How did you manage it?" he asked, with admiration in his tones.

Perhaps Jolnes's only weakness was a professional pride in his wonderful achievements in induction. He was ever ready to astound and charm his listeners by describing his methods.

"By elimination," said Jolnes, spreading his clues upon a little table, "I got rid of certain parts of the city to which Mrs. Snyder might have removed. You see this hat-pin? That eliminates Brooklyn. No woman attempts to board a car at the Brooklyn Bridge without being sure that she carries a hat-pin with which to fight her way into a seat. And now I will demonstrate to you that she could not have gone to Harlem. Behind this door are two hooks in the wall. Upon one of these Mrs. Snyder has hung her bonnet, and upon the other her shawl. You will observe that the bottom of the hanging shawl has gradually made a soiled streak against the plastered wall. The mark is clean-cut, proving that there is no fringe on the shawl. Now, was there ever a case where a middle-aged woman, wearing a shawl, boarded a Harlem train without there being a fringe on the shawl to catch in the gate and delay the passengers behind her? So we eliminate Harlem.

"Therefore I conclude that Mrs. Snyder has not moved very far away. On this torn piece of card you see the word 'left', the letter 'C', and the number '12'. Now, I happen to know that No. 12 Avenue C is a first-class boarding-house, far beyond your sister's means—as we suppose. But then I find this piece of a theatre programme, crumpled into an odd shape. What meaning does it convey? None to you, very likely, Mr. Meeks; but it is eloquent to one whose habits and training take cognizance of the smallest things.

"You have told me that your sister was a scrub woman. She scrubbed the floors of offices and hallways. Let us assume that she procured such work to perform in a theatre. Where is valuable jewellery lost the oftenest, Mr. Meeks? In the theatres, of course. Look at that piece of programme, Mr. Meeks. Observe the round impression on it. It has been wrapped around a ring—perhaps a ring of great value. Mrs Snyder found the ring while at work in the theatre. She hastily tore off a piece of a programme, wrapped the ring carefully, and thrust it into her bosom. The next day she disposed of it, and, with her increased means, looked about her for a more comfortable place in which to live. When I reach thus far in the chain I see nothing impossible about No. 12 Avenue C. It is there we will find your sister, Mr. Meeks."

Shamrock Jolnes concluded his convincing speech with the smile of a successful artist. Meeks's admiration was too great for words. Together they went to No. 12 Avenue C. It was an old-fashioned, brown-stone house in a prosperous and respectable neighbourhood.

They rang the bell, and on inquiring were told that no Mrs. Snyder was known there, and that not within six months had a new occupant come to the house.

When they reached the sidewalk again, Meeks examined

the clues which he had brought away from his sister's old room.

"I am no detective," he remarked to Jolnes as he raised the piece of theatre programme to his nose, "but it seems to me that instead of a ring having been wrapped in this paper, it was one of those round peppermint drops. And this piece with the address on it looks to me like the end of a seat coupon—No. 12, row C, left aisle."

Shamrock Jolnes had a far-away look in his eyes.

"I think you would do well to consult Juggins," said he.

"Who is Juggins?" asked Meeks.

"He is the leader," said Jolnes, "of a new modern school of detectives. Their methods are different from ours, but it is said that Juggins has solved some extremely puzzling cases. I will take you to him."

They found the greater Juggins in his office. He was a small man with light hair, deeply absorbed in reading one of the bourgeois works of Nathaniel Hawthorne.

The two great detectives of different schools shook hands with ceremony, and Meeks was introduced.

"State the facts," said Juggins, going on with his reading.

When Meeks ceased, the greater one closed his book and said:

"Do I understand that your sister is fifty-two years of age, with a large mole on the side of her nose, and that she is a very poor widow, making a scanty living by scrubbing, and with a very homely face and figure?"

"That describes her exactly," admitted Meeks. Juggins rose and put on his hat.

"In fifteen minutes," he said, "I will return, bringing you her present address."

Shamrock Jolnes turned pale, but forced a smile.

Within the specified time Juggins returned and consulted a little slip of paper held in his hand.

"Your sister, Mary Snyder," he announced calmly, "will be found at No. 162 Chilton Street. She is living in the back hall-bedroom, five flights up. The house is only four blocks from here," he continued, addressing Meeks. "Suppose you go and verify the statement and then return here. Mr. Jolnes will await you, I dare say."

Meeks hurried away. In twenty minutes he was back again, with a beaming face.

"She is there and well!" he cried. "Name your fee!"

"Two dollars," said Juggins.

When Meeks had settled his bill and departed, Shamrock Jolnes stood with his hat in his hand before Juggins.

"If it would not be asking too much," he stammered—"if you would favour me so far—would you object to——"

"Certainly not," said Juggins pleasantly. "I will tell you how I did it. You remember the description of Mrs. Snyder? Did you ever know a woman like that who wasn't paying weekly instalments on an enlarged crayon portrait of herself? The biggest factory of that kind in the country is just around the corner. I went there and got her address off the books. That's all."

23

The Whirligig of Life

JUSTICE-OF-THE-PEACE BENAJA WIDDUP sat in the door of his office smoking his elder-stem pipe. Half-way to the zenith the Cumberland range rose blue-grey in the afternoon haze. A speckled hen swaggered down the main street of the "settlement", cackling foolishly.

Up the road came a sound of creaking axles, and then a slow cloud of dust, and then a bull-cart bearing Ransie Bilbro and his wife. The cart stopped at the Justice's door, and the two climbed down. Ransie was a narrow six feet of sallow brown skin and yellow hair. The imperturbability of the mountains hung upon him like a suit of armour. The woman was calicoed, angled, snuff-brushed, and weary with unknown desires. Through it all gleamed a faint protest of cheated youth unconscious of its loss.

The Justice of the Peace slipped his feet into his shoes, for the sake of dignity, and moved to let them enter.

"We-all," said the woman, in a voice like the wind blowing through pine boughs, "wants a divo'ce." She looked at Ransie to see if he noted any flaw or ambiguity or evasion or partiality or selfpartisanship in her statement of their business.

"A divo'ce," repeated Ransie, with a solemn nod. "We-all can't git along together nohow. It's lonesome enough fur to live in the mount'ins when a man and a woman keers fur one another. But when she's a-spittin' like a wildcat or a-sullenin' like a hoot-owl in the cabin, a man ain't got no call to live with her."

"When he's a no-'count varmint," said the woman, without any especial warmth, "a-traipsin' along of scalawags and moonshiners and a-layin' on his back pizen 'ith co'n whisky, and a-pesterin' folks with a pack o' hungry, triflin' houn's to feed!"

"When she keeps a-throwin' skillet lids," came Ransie's antiphony, "and slings b'ilin' water on the best coon-dog in the Cumberlands, and sets herself agin' cookin' a man's victuals, and keeps him awake o' nights accusin' him of a sight of doin's!"

"When he's al'ays a-fightin' the revenues, and gits a hard name in the mount'ins fur a mean man, who's gwine to be able fur to sleep o' nights?"

The Justice of the Peace stirred deliberately to his duties. He placed his one chair and a wooden stool for his petitioners. He opened his book of statutes on the table and scanned the index. Presently he wiped his spectacles and shifted his inkstand.

"The law and the statutes," said he, "air silent on the subjeck of divo'ce as fur as the jurisdiction of this co't air concerned. But, accordin' to equity and the Constitution and the golden rule, it's a bad barg'in that can't run both ways. If a justice of the peace can marry a couple, it's plain that he is bound to be able to divo'ce 'em. This here office will issue a decree of divo'ce and abide by the decision of the Supreme Co't to hold it good."

Ransie Bilbro drew a small tobacco-bag from his trousers pocket. Out of this he shook upon the table a five-dollar note. "Sold a b'arskin and two foxes fur that," he remarked. "It's all the money we got."

"The regular price of a divo'ce in this co't," said the Justice, "air five dollars." He stuffed the bill into the pocket of his homespun vest with a deceptive air of indifference. With much bodily toil and mental travail he wrote the decree upon half a sheet of foolscap, and then copied it upon the other. Ransie Bilbro and his wife listened to his reading of the document that was to give them freedom:

"Know all men by these presents that Ransie Bilbro and his wife, Ariela Bilbro, this day personally appeared before me and promises that hereinafter they will neither love, honour, nor obey each other, neither for better nor worse, being of sound mind and body, and accept summons for divorce according to the peace and dignity of the State. Herein fail not, so help you God. Benaja Widdup, justice of the peace in and for the county of Piedmont, State of Tennessee."

The Justice was about to hand one of the documents to Ransie. The voice of Ariela delayed the transfer. Both men looked at her. Their dull masculinity was confronted by something sudden and unexpected in the woman.

"Judge, don't you give him that air paper yit. 'Tain't all settled, nohow. I got to have my rights first. I got to have my ali-money. 'Tain't no kind of a way to do fur a man to divo'ce his wife' 'thout her havin' a cent fur to do with. I'm a-layin' off to be a-goin' up to brother Ed's up on Hogback Mount'n. I'm bound fur to hev a pa'r of shoes and some snuff and things besides. Ef Ranse kin affo'd a divo'ce, let him pay me ali-money."

Ransie Bilbro was stricken to dumb perplexity. There had been no previous hint of alimony. Women were always bringing up startling and unlooked-for issues.

Justice Benaja Widdup felt that the point demanded judicial decision. The authorities were also silent on the subject of alimony. But the woman's feet were bare. The trail to Hogback Mountain was steep and flinty.

"Ariela Bilbro," he asked, in official tones, "how much did you 'low would be good and sufficient ali-money in the case befo' the co't."

"I 'lowed," she answered, "fur the shoes and all, to say five dollars. That ain't much fur ali-money, but I reckon that'll git me up to brother Ed's."

"The amount," said the Justice, "air not onreasonable. Ransie Bilbro, you air ordered by the co't to pay the plaintiff the sum of five dollars befo' the decree of divo'ce air issued."

"I hain't no mo' money," breathed Ransie heavily. "I done paid you all I had."

"Otherwise," said the Justice, looking severely over his spectacles, "you air in contempt of co't."

"I reckon if you gimme till to-morrow," pleaded the husband, "I mout be able to rake or scrape it up somewhars. I never looked for to be a-payin' no ail-money."

"The case air adjourned," said Benaja Widdup, "till to-morrow, when you-all will present yo'selves and obey the order of the co't. Followin' of which the decrees of divo'ce will be delivered." He sat down in the door and began to loosen a shoestring.

"We mout as well go down to Uncle Ziah's," decided Ransie, "and spend the night." He climbed into the car on one side, and Ariela climbed in on the other. Obeying the flap of his rope, the little red bull slowly came around on a track, and the cart crawled away in the nimbus arising from its wheels.

Justice-of-the-Peace Benaja Widdup smoked his elder-stem pipe. Late in the afternoon he got his weekly paper and read it until the twilight dimmed its lines. Then he lit the tallow candle on his table, and read until the moon rose, marking the time for supper. He lived in the double log cabin on the slope near the girdled poplar. Going home to supper he crossed a little branch darkened by a laurel thicket. The dark figure of a man stepped from the laurels and pointed a rifle at his breast. His hat was pulled down low, and something covered most of his face.

"I want yo' money," said the figure, "'thout any talk. I'm gettin' nervous, and my finger's a-wabblin' on this here trigger."

"I've only got f-f-five dollars," said the Justice, producing it from his vest pocket.

"Roll it up," came the order, "and stick it in the end of this here gun-bar'l."

The bill was crisp and new. Even fingers that were clumsy and trembling found little difficulty in making a spill of it and inserting it (this with less ease) into the muzzle of the rifle.

"Now I reckon you kin be goin' along," said the robber.

The Justice lingered not on his way.

* * *

The next day came the little red bull, drawing the cart to the office door. Justice Benaja Widdup had his shoes on, for he was expecting the visit. In his presence Ransie Bilbro handed to his wife a five-dollar bill. The official's eye sharply viewed it. It seemed to curl up as though it had been rolled and inserted into the end of a gun-barrel. But the Justice refrained from comment. It is true that other bills might be inclined to curl. He handed each one a decree of divorce. Each stood awkwardly silent, slowly folding the guarantee of freedom. The woman cast a shy glance full of constraint at Ransie.

"I reckon you'll be goin' back up to the cabin," she said, "along 'ith the bull-cart. There's bread in the tin box settin' on the shelf. I put the bacon in the b'ilin'-pot to keep the hounds from gittin' it. Don't forget to wind the clock to-night."

"You air a-goin' to your brother Ed's?" asked Ransie, with fine unconcern.

"I was 'lowin' to get along up thar afore night. I ain't sayin' as they'll pester theyselves any to make me welcome, but I hain't nowhar else fur to go. It's a right smart ways, and I reckon I better be goin'. I'll be a-sayin' good-bye, Ranse—that is, if you keer fur to say so."

"I don't know as anybody's a hound dog," said Ransie, in a martyr's voice, "fur to not want to say good-bye—'less you air so anxious to git away that you don't want me to say it."

Ariela was silent. She folded the five-dollar bill and her decree carefully, and placed them in the bosom of her dress. Benaja Widdup watched the money disappear with mournful eyes behind his spectacles.

And then with his next words he achieved rank (as his thoughts ran) with either the great crowd of the world's sympathizers or the little crowd of its great financiers.

"Be kind o'lonesome in the old cabin to-night, Ranse," he said.

Ransie Bilbro stared out at the Cumberlands, clear blue now in the sunlight. He did not look at Ariela.

"I 'low it might be lonesome," he said; "but when folks gits mad and wants a divo'ce, you can't make folks stay."

"There's others wanted a divo'ce," said Ariela, speaking to the wooden stool. "Besides, nobody don't want nobody to stay."

"Nobody never said they didn't."

"Nobody never said they did. I reckon I better start on now to brother Ed's."

"Nobody can't wind that old clock."

"Want me to go back along 'ith you in the cart and wind it fur you, Ranse?"

The mountaineer's countenance was proof against emotion. But he reached out a big hand and enclosed Ariela's thin brown one. Her soul peeped out once through her impassive face, hallowing it.

"Them hounds shan't pester you no more," said Ransie. "I reckon I been mean and low down. You wind that clock, Ariela."

"My heart hit's in that cabin, Ranse," she whispered, "along 'ith you. I ain't a-goin' to git mad no more. Le's be startin', Ranse, so's we kin git home by sundown."

Justice-of-the-Peace Benaja Widdup interposed as they started for the door, forgetting his presence.

"In the name of the State of Tennessee," he said, "I forbid you-all to be a-defyin' of its laws and statutes. This co't is mo' than willin' and full of joy to see the clouds of discord and misunderstandin' rollin' away from two lovin' hearts, but it air the duty of the co't to p'eserve the morals and integrity of the State. The co't reminds you that you air no longer man and wife, but air divo'ced by regular decree, and as such air not entitled to the benefits and 'purtenances of the mattermonal estate."

Ariela caught Ransie's arm. Did those words mean that she must lose him now when they had just learned the lesson of life?

"But the co't air prepared," went on the Justice, "fur to remove the disabilities set up by the decree of divo'ce. The co't air on hand to perform the solemn ceremony of marri'ge, thus fixin' things up and enablin' the parties in the case to resume the honour'ble and elevatin' state of mattermony which they desires. The fee fur performin' said ceremony will be, in this case, to wit, five dollars."

Ariela caught the gleam of promise in his words. Swiftly her hand went to her bosom. Freely as an alighting dove the bill fluttered to the Justice's table. Her sallow cheek coloured as she stood hand in hand with Ransie and listened to the reuniting words.

Ransie helped her into the cart, and climbed in beside her. The little red bull turned once more, and they set out, hand-clasped, for the mountains.

Justice-of-the-Peace Benaja Widdup sat in his door and took off his shoes. Once again he fingered the bill tucked down in his vest pocket. Once again he smoked his elder-stem pipe. Once again the speckled hen swaggered down the main street of the "settlement", cackling foolishly.

24

A Madison Square Arabian Night

To Carson Chalmers, in his apartment near the square, Phillips brought the evening mail. Besides the routine correspondence there were two items bearing the same foreign postmark.

One of the incoming parcels contained a photograph of a woman. The other contained an interminable letter, over which Chalmers hung, absorbed, for a long time. The letter was from another woman; and it contained poisoned barbs, sweetly dipped in honey, and feathered with innuendoes concerning the photographed woman.

Chalmers tore this letter into a thousand bits and began to wear out his expensive rug by striding back and forth upon it. Thus an animal from the jungle acts when it is caged, and thus a caged man acts when he is housed in a jungle of doubt.

By and by the restless mood was overcome. The rug was not an enchanted one. For sixteen feet he could travel along it; three thousand miles was beyond its power to aid.

Phillips appeared. He never entered; he invariably appeared, like a well-oiled genie.

"Will you dine here, sir, or out?" he asked.

"Here," said Chalmers, "and in half an hour." He listened glumly to the January blasts making an aeolian trombone of the empty street.

"Wait," he said to the disappearing genie. "As I came home across the end of the square I saw many men standing there in rows. There was one mounted upon something, talking. Why do these men stand in rows, and why are they there?"

"They are homeless men, sir," said Phillips. "The man standing on the box tries to get lodging for them for the night. People come around to listen and give him money. Then he sends as many as the money will pay for to some lodging-house. That is why they stand in rows; they get sent to bed in order as they come."

"By the time dinner is served," said Chalmers, "have one of those men here. He will dine with me."

"W-w-which——" began Phillips, stammering for the first time during his service.

"Choose one at random," said Chalmers. "You might see that he is reasonably sober—and a certain amount of cleanliness will not be held against him. That is all."

It was an unusual thing for Carson Chalmers to play the Caliph. But on that night he felt the inefficacy of conventional antidotes to melancholy. Something wanton and egregious, something high-flavoured and Arabian, he must have to lighten his mood.

On the half-hour Phillips had finished his duties as slave of the lamp. The waiters from the restaurant below had whisked aloft the delectable dinner. The dining-table, laid for two, glowed cheerily in the glow of the pink-shaded candles.

And now Phillips, as though he ushered a cardinal—or held in charge a burglar—wafted in the shivering guest who had been haled from the line of mendicant lodgers.

It is a common thing to call such men wrecks; if the comparison be used here it is the specific one of a derelict come to grief through fire. Even yet some flickering combustion illuminated the drifting hulk. His face and hands had been recently washed—a rite insisted upon by Phillips as a memorial to the slaughtered conventions. In the candle-light he stood, a flaw in the decorous fitting of the apartment. His face was a sickly white, covered almost to the eyes with a stubble the shade of a red Irish setter's coat. Phillips' comb had failed to control the pale brown hair, long matted and conformed to the contour of a constantly worn hat. His eyes were full of a hopeless, tricky defiance like that seen in a cur's that is cornered by his tormentors. His shabby coat was buttoned high, but a quarter-inch of redeeming collar showed above it. His manner was singularly free from embarrassment when Chalmers rose from his chair across the round dining-table.

"If you will oblige me," said the host, "I shall be glad to have your company at dinner."

"My name is Plumer," said the highway guest, in harsh and aggressive tones. "If you're like me, you like to know the name of the party you're dining with."

"I was going to say," continued Chalmers somewhat hastily, "that mine is Chalmers. Will you sit opposite?"

Plumer, of the ruffled plumes, bent his knees for Phillips to slide the chair beneath him. He had an air of having sat at attended boards before. Phillips set out the anchovies and olives.

"Good!" barked Plumer; "going to be in courses, is it? All right my jovial ruler of Bagdad. I'm your Scheherezade all the way to the tooth-picks. You're the first Caliph with a genuine Oriental flavour I've struck. What luck! And I was forty-third in the line. I finished counting just as your welcome emissary arrived to bid me to the feast. I had about as much chance of getting a bed to-night as I have of being the next Prime Minister. How will you have the sad story of my life, Mr. Al Raschid—a chapter with each course, or the whole edition with the cigars and coffee?"

"The situation does not seem a novel one to you," said Chalmers, with a smile.

"By the chin-whiskers of the prophet—no!" answered the guest. "New York's as full of cheap Haroun al Raschids as Bagdad is of fleas. I've been held up for my story with a loaded meal pointed at my head twenty times. Catch anybody in New York giving you something for nothing! They spell curiosity and charity with the same set of building blocks. Lots of 'em will stake you to a dime and chopsuey; and a few of 'em will play Caliph to the tune of a top sirloin; but everyone of 'em will stand over you till they screw your autobiography out of you with footnotes, appendix and unpublished fragments. Oh, I know what to do when I see victuals coming toward me in little old Bagdad-on-the-Subway. I strike the asphalt three times with my forehead and get ready to spiel yarns for my supper. I claim descent from the late Tommy Tucker, who was forced to hand out vocal harmony for his predigested wheaterina and spoop-ju."

"I do not ask your story," said Chalmers. "I tell you frankly that it was a sudden whim that prompted me to send for some stranger to dine with me. I assure you you will not suffer through any curiosity of mine."

"Oh, fudge!" exclaimed the guest, enthusiastically tackling his soup; "I don't mind it a bit. I'm a regular Oriental magazine with a red cover and the leaves cut when the Caliph walks abroad. In fact, we fellows in the bed-line have a sort of union rate for things of this sort. Somebody's always stopping and wanting to know what brought us down so low in the world. For a sandwich and a glass of beer I tell 'em that drink did it. For corned beef and cabbage and a cup of coffee I give 'em the hard-hearted-landlord—six-months-in-the-hospital-lost-job story. A sirloin steak and a quarter for a bed gets the Wall Street tragedy of the swept-away fortune and the gradual descent. This is the first spread of this kind I've stumbled against. I haven't got a story to fit it. I'll tell you what, Mr. Chalmers, I'm going to tell you the truth for this, if you'll listen to it. It'll be harder for you to believe than the made-up ones."

An hour later the Arabian guest lay back with a sigh of satisfaction while Phillips brought the coffee and cigars and cleared the table.

"Did you ever hear of Sherrard Plumer?" he asked, with a strange smile.

"I remember the name," said Chalmers. "He was a painter, I think, of a good deal of prominence a few years ago."

"Five years," said the guest. "Then I went down like a chunk of lead. I'm Sherrard Plumer! I sold the last portrait I painted for $2,000. After that I couldn't have found a sitter for a gratis picture."

"What was the trouble?" Chalmers could not resist asking.

"Funny thing," answered Plumer grimly. "Never quite understood it myself. For a while I swam like a cork. I broke into the swell crowd and got commissions right and left. The newspapers called me a fashionable painter. Then the funny things began to happen. Whenever I finished a picture people would come to see it, and whisper and look queerly at one another.

"I soon found out what the trouble was. I had a knack of bringing out in the face of a portrait the hidden character of the original. I don't know how I did it—I painted what I saw—but I know it did me. Some of my sitters were fearfully enraged and refused their pictures. I painted the portrait of a very beautiful and popular society dame. When it was finished her husband looked at it with a peculiar expression on his face, and the next week he sued for divorce.

"I remember one case of a prominent banker who sat to me. While I had his portrait on exhibition in my studio an acquaintance of his came in to look at it. 'Bless me,' says he, 'does he really look like that?' I told him it was considered a faithful likeness. 'I never noticed that expression about his eyes before,' said he; 'I think I'll drop downtown and change my bank account.' He did drop down, but the bank account was gone and so was Mr Banker.

"It wasn't long till they put me out of business. People don't want their secret meannesses shown up in a picture. They can smile and twist their own faces and deceive you, but the picture can't. I couldn't get an order for another picture, and I had to give up. I worked as a newspaper artist for a while, and then for a lithographer, but my work with them got me into the same trouble. If I drew from a photograph my drawing showed up characteristics and expressions that you couldn't find in the photo, but I guess they were in the original, all right. The customers raised lively rows, especially the women, and I never could hold a job long. So I began to rest my weary head upon the breast of Old Booze for comfort. And pretty soon I was in the free-bed line and doing oral fiction for handouts among the food-bazaars. Does the truthful statement weary thee, O Caliph? I can turn on the Wall Street disaster stop if you prefer, but that requires a tear, and I'm afraid I can't hustle one up after tha good dinner."

"No, no," said Chalmers earnestly, "you interest me very much. Did all your portraits reveal some unpleasant trait, or were there some that did not suffer from the ordeal of your peculiar brush?"

"Some? Yes," said Plumer. "Children generally, a good many women and a sufficient number of men. All people aren't bad, you know. When they were all right the pictures were all right. As I said, I don't explain it, but I'm telling you facts."

On Chalmers' writing-table lay the photograph that he had received that day in the foreign mail. Ten minutes later he had Plumer at work making a sketch from it in pastels. At the end of an hour the artist rose and stretched wearily.

"It's done," he yawned. "You'll excuse me for being so long. I got interested in the job. Lord! but I'm tired. No bed last night you know. Guess it'll have to be good night now, O Commander of the Faithful!"

Chalmers went as far as the door with him and slipped some bills into his hand.

"Oh! I'll take 'em," said Plumer. "All that's included in the fall. Thanks. And for the very good dinner. I shall sleep on feathers to-night and dream of Bagdad. I hope it won't turn out to be a dream in the morning. Farewell, most excellent Caliph!"

Again Chalmers paced restlessly upon his rug. But his beat lay as far from the table whereon lay the pastel sketch as the room would permit. Twice, thrice, he tried to approach it, but failed. He could see the dun and gold and brown of the colours, but there was a wall about it built by his fears that kept him at a distance. He sat down and tried to calm himself. He sprang up and rang for Phillips.

"There is a young artist in this building," he said, "—a Mr. Reineman—do you know which is his apartment?"

"Top floor, front, sir," said Phillips.

"Go up and ask him to favour me with his presence here for a few minutes."

Reineman came at once. Chalmers introduced himself.

"Mr. Reineman," said he, "there is a little pastel sketch on yonder table. I would be glad if you will give me your opinion of it as to its artistic merits and as a picture."

The young artist advanced to the table and took up the

sketch. Chalmers half turned away, leaning upon the back of a chair.

"How—do—you—find it?" he asked slowly.

"As a drawing," said the artist, "I can't praise it enough. It's the work of a master—bold and fine and true. It puzzles me a little; I haven't seen any pastel work near as good in years."

"The face, man—the subject—the original—what would you say of that?"

"The face," said Reineman, "is the face of one of God's own angels. May I ask who——"

"My wife!" shouted Chalmers, wheeling and pouncing upon the astonished artist, gripping his hand and pounding his back. "She is travelling in Europe. Take that sketch, boy, and paint the picture of your life from it and leave the price to me."

25

The Passing of Black Eagle

FOR some months of a certain year a grim bandit infested the Texas border along the Rio Grande. Peculiarly striking to the optic nerve was this notorious marauder. His personality secured him the title of "Black Eagle, the Terror of the Border". Many fearsome tales are on record concerning the doings of him and his followers. Suddenly, in the space of a single minute, Black Eagle vanished from earth. He was never heard of again. His own band never even guessed the mystery of his disappearance. The border ranches and settlements feared he would come again to ride and ravage the mesquite flats. He never will. It is to disclose the fate of Black Eagle that this narrative is written.

The initial movement of the story is furnished by the foot of a bartender in St. Louis. His discerning eye fell upon the form of Chicken Ruggles as he pecked with avidity at the free lunch. Chicken was a "hobo". He had a long nose like the bill of a fowl, an inordinate appetite for poultry, and a habit of gratifying it without expense, which accounts for the name given him by his fellow-vagrants.

Physicians agree that the partaking of liquids at meal times is not a healthy practice. The hygiene of the saloon promulgates the opposite. Chicken had neglected to purchase a drink to accompany his meal. The bartender rounded the counter, caught the injudicious diner by the ear with a lemon squeezer, led him to the door and kicked him into the street.

Thus the mind of Chicken was brought to realize the signs of coming winter. The night was cold; the stars shone with unkindly brilliance; people were hurrying along the streets in two egotistic, jostling streams. Men had donned their overcoats, and Chicken knew to an exact percentage the increased difficulty of coaxing dimes from those buttoned-in vest pockets. The time had come for his annual exodus to the south.

A little boy, five or six years old, stood looking with covetous eyes in a confectioner's window. In one small hand he held an empty two-ounce vial; in the other he grasped tightly something flat and round, with a shining milled edge. The scene presented a field of operations commensurate to Chicken's talents and daring. After sweeping the horizon to make sure that no official tug was cruising near, he insidiously accosted his prey. The boy, having been early taught by his household to regard altruistic advances with extreme suspicion, received the overtures coldly.

Then Chicken knew that he must make one of those desperate, nerve-shattering plunges into speculation that fortune sometimes requires of those who would win her favour. Five cents was his capital, and this he must risk against the chance of winning what lay within the close grasp of the youngster's chubby hand. It was a fearful lottery, Chicken knew. But he must accomplish his end by strategy, since he had a wholesome terror of plundering infants by force. Once, in a park, driven by hunger, he had committed an onslaught upon a bottle of peptonized infant's food in the possession of an occupant of a baby carriage. The outraged infant had so promptly opened its mouth and pressed the button that communicated with the welkin that help arrived, and Chicken did his thirty days in a snug coop. Wherefore he was, as he said, "leary of kids."

Beginning artfully to question the boy concerning his choice of sweets, he gradually drew out the information he wanted. Mamma said he was to ask the drug store man for ten cents' worth of paregoric in the bottle; he was to keep his hand shut tight over the dollar; he must not stop to talk to anyone in the street; he must ask the drug store man to wrap up the change and put it in the pocket of his trousers. Indeed, they had pockets—two of them! And he liked chocolate creams best.

Chicken went into the store and turned plunger. He invested his entire capital in C.A.N.D.Y. stocks, simply to pave the way to the greater risk following.

He gave the sweets to the youngster, and had the satisfaction of perceiving that confidence was established. After that it was easy to obtain leadership of the expedition; to take the investment by the hand and lead it to a nice drug store he knew of in the same block. There Chicken, with a parental air, passed over the dollar and called for the medicine, while the boy crunched his candy, glad to be relieved of the responsibility of the purchase. And then the successful investor, searching his pockets, found an overcoat button—the extent of his winter trousseau—and, wrapping it carefully, placed the ostensible change in the pocket of confiding juvenility. Setting the youngster's face homeward and patting him benevolently on the back—for Chicken's heart was as soft as those of his feathered namesakes—the speculator quit the market with a profit of 1,700 per cent. on his invested capital.

Two hours later an Iron Mountain freight engine pulled out of the railroad yards, Texas bound, with a string of empties. In one of the cattle cars, half buried in excelsior, Chicken lay at ease. Beside him in his nest was a quart bottle of very poor whisky and a paper bag of bread and cheese. Mr. Ruggles, in his private car, was on his trip south for the winter season.

For a week that car was trundled southward, shifted, laid over, and manipulated after the manner of rolling stock, but Chicken stuck to it, leaving it only at necessary times to satisfy his hunger and thirst. He knew it must go down to the cattle country, and San Antonio, in the heart of it, was his goal. There the air was salubrious and mild; the people indulgent and long-suffering. The bartenders there would not kick him. If he should eat too long or too often at one place they would swear at him as if by rote and without heat. They swore so drawlingly, and they rarely paused short of their full vocabulary, which was copious, so that Chicken had often gulped a good meal during the process of the vituperative prohibition. The season there was always spring-like; the plazas were pleasant at night, with music and gaiety; except during the slight and infrequent cold snaps one could sleep comfortably out of doors in case the interiors should develop inhospitality.

At Texarkana his car was switched to the I. and G.N. Then still southward it trailed until, at length, it crawled across the Colorado bridge at Austin, and lined out, straight as an arrow, for the run to San Antonio.

When the freight halted at that town Chicken was fast asleep. In ten minutes the train was off again for Laredo, the end of the road. Those empty cattle cars were for distribution along the line at points from which the ranches shipped their stock.

When Chicken awoke his car was stationary. Looking out between the slats he saw it was a bright, moonlit night. Scrambling out, he saw his car with three others abandoned on a little siding in a wild and lonesome country. A cattle pen and chute stood on one side of the track. The railroad bisected a vast, dim ocean of prairie, in the midst of which Chicken, with his futile rolling stock, was as completely stranded as was Robinson with his land-locked boat.

A white post stood near the rails. Going up to it, Chicken read the letters at the top, S. A. 90. Laredo was nearly as far to the south. He was almost a hundred miles from any town. Coyotes began to yelp in the mysterious sea around him. Chicken felt lonesome. He had lived in Boston without an education, in Chicago without nerve, in Philadelphia without a sleeping-place, in New York without a pull, and in Pittsburg sober, and yet he had never felt so lonely as now.

Suddenly through the intense silence he heard the whicker of a horse. The sound came from the side of the track toward the east, and Chicken began to explore timorously in that direction. He stepped high along the mat of curly mesquite grass, for he was afraid of everything there might be in this wilderness—snakes, rats, brigands, centipedes, mirages, cowboys, fandangoes, tarantulas, tamales—he had read of them in the story-papers. Rounding a clump of prickly pear that reared high its fantastic and menacing array of rounded heads, he was struck to shivering terror by a snort and a thunderous plunge, as the horse, himself startled, bounded away some fifty yards, and then resumed his grazing. But here was the one thing in the desert that Chicken did not fear.

He had been reared on a farm; he had handled horses, understood them, and could ride.

Approaching slowly and speaking soothingly, he followed the animal, which, after its first flight, seemed gentle enough, and secured the end of the twenty-foot lariat that dragged after him in the grass. It required him but a few moments to contrive the rope into an ingenious nose-bridle, after the style of the Mexican *borsal*. In another he was upon the horse's back and off at a splendid lope, giving the animal free choice of direction. "He will take me somewhere," said Chicken to himself.

It would have been a thing of joy, that untrammelled gallop over the moonlit prairie, even to Chicken, who loathed exertion, but that his mood was not for it. His head ached; a growing thirst was upon him; the "somewhere" whither his lucky mount might convey him as full of dismal peradventure.

And now he noted that the horse moved to a definite goal. Where the prairie lay smooth he kept his course straight as an arrow's toward the east. Deflected by hill or arroyo or impracticable spinous brakes, he quickly flowed again into the current, charted by his unerring instinct. At last, upon the side of a gentle rise, he suddenly subsided to a complacent walk. A stone's cast away stood a little mott of coma trees; beneath it a *jacal* such as the Mexicans erect—a one-room house of upright poles daubed with clay and roofed with grass or tule reeds. An experienced eye would have estimated the spot as the headquarters of a small sheep ranch. In the moonlight the ground in the near-by corral showed pulverized to a level smoothness by the hoofs of the sheep. Everywhere was carelessly distributed the paraphernalia of the place—ropes, bridles, saddles, sheep pelts, wool sacks, feed troughs, and camp litter. The barrel of drinking water stood in the end of the two-horse wagon near the door. The harness was piled, promiscuous, upon the wagon tongue, soaking up the dew.

Chicken slipped to earth, and tied the horse to a tree. He halloed again and again, but the house remained quiet. The door stood open, and he entered cautiously. The light was sufficient for him to see that no one was at home. He struck a match and lighted a lamp that stood on a table. The room was that of a bachelor ranchman who was content with the necessaries of life. Chicken rummaged intelligently until he found what he had hardly dared hope for—a small, brown jug that still contained something near a quart of his desire.

Half an hour later, Chicken—now a gamecock of hostile aspect—emerged from the house with unsteady steps. He had drawn upon the absent ranchman's equipment to replace his own ragged attire. He wore a suit of coarse brown ducking, the coat being a sort of rakish bolero, jaunty to a degree. Boots he had donned, and spurs that whirled with every lurching step. Buckled around him was a belt full of cartridges with a big six-shooter in each of its two holsters.

Prowling about, he found blankets, a saddle and bridle with which he caparisoned his steed. Again mounting he rode swiftly away, singing a loud and tuneless song.

* * *

But King's band of desperadoes, outlaws and horse and cattle thieves were in camp at a secluded spot on the bank of the Frio. Their depredations in the Rio Grande country, while no bolder than usual, had been advertised more extensively, and Captain Kinney's company of rangers had been ordered down to look after them. Consequently Bud King, who was a wise general, instead of cutting out a hot trail for the upholders of the law, as his men wished to do, retired for the time to the prickly fastnesses of the Frio valley.

Though the move was a prudent one, and not incompatible with Bud's well-known courage, it raised dissension among the members of the band. In fact, while they thus lay ingloriously *perdu* in the brush, the question of Bud King's fitness for the leadership was argued, with closed doors, as it were, by his followers. Never before had Bud's skill or efficiency been brought to criticism; but his glory was waning (and such is glory's fate) in the light of a newer star. The sentiment of the band was crystallizing into the opinion that

Black Eagle could lead them with more lustre, profit and distinction.

This Black Eagle—sub-titled the "Terror of the Border"—had been a member of the gang about three months.

One night while they were in camp on the San Miguel water-hole a solitary horseman on the regulation fiery steed dashed in among them. The new-comer was of a portentous and devastating aspect. A beak-like nose with a predatory curve projected above a mass of bristling, blue-black whiskers. His eye was cavernous and fierce. He was spurred, sombreroed, booted, garnished with revolvers, abundantly drunk, and very much unafraid. Few people in the country drained by the Rio Bravo would have cared thus to invade alone the camp of Bud King. But this fell bird swooped fearlessly upon them and demanded to be fed.

Hospitality in the prairie country is not limited. Even if your enemy pass your way you must feed him before you shoot him. You must empty your larder into him before you empty your lead. So the stranger of undeclared intentions was set down to a mighty feast.

A talkative bird he was, full of most marvellous loud tales and exploits, and speaking a language at times obscure but never colourless. He was a new sensation to Bud King's men, who rarely encountered new types. They hung, delighted, upon his vainglorious boasting, the spicy strangeness of his lingo, his contemptuous familiarity with life, the world, and remote places, and the extravagant frankness with which he conveyed his sentiments.

To their guest the band of outlaws seemed to be nothing more than a congregation of country bumpkins whom he was "stringing for grub" just as he would have told his stories at the back door of a farmhouse to wheedle a meal. And, indeed, his ignorance was not without excuse, for the "bad man" of the South-west does not run to extremes. Those brigands might justly have been taken for a little party of peaceable rustics assembled for a fish-fry or pecan gathering. Gentle of manner, slouching of gait, soft-voiced, unpicturesquely clothed; not one of them presented to the eye any witness of the desperate records they had earned.

For two days the glittering stranger within the camp was feasted. Then, by common consent, he was invited to become a member of the band. He consented, presenting for enrolment the prodigious name of "Captain Montressor". This name was immediately overruled by the band, and "Piggy" substituted as a compliment to the awful and insatiate appetite of its owner.

Thus did the Texas border receive the most spectacular brigand that ever rode its chaparral.

For the next three months Bud King conducted business as usual, escaping encounters with law officers and being content with reasonable profits. The band ran off some very good companies of horses from the ranges, and a few bunches of fine cattle which they got safely across the Rio Grande and disposed of to fair advantage. Often the band would ride into the little villages and Mexican settlements, terrorizing the inhabitants and plundering for the provisions and ammunition they needed. It was during these bloodless raids that Piggy's ferocious aspect and frightful voice gained him a renown more widespread and glorious than those other gentle-voiced and sad-faced desperadoes could have acquired in a lifetime.

The Mexicans, most apt in nomenclature, first called him The Black Eagle, and used to frighten the babes by threatening them with tales of the dreadful robber who carried off little children in his great beak. Soon the name extended, and Black Eagle, the Terror of the Border, became a recognized factor in exaggerated newspaper reports and ranch gossip.

The country from the Nueces to the Rio Grande was a wild but fertile stretch, given over to the sheep and cattle ranches. Range was free; the inhabitants were few; the law was mainly a letter, and the pirates met with little opposition until the flaunting and garish Piggy gave the band undue advertisement. Then McKinney's ranger company headed for those precincts, and Bud King knew that it meant grim and sudden war or else temporary retirement. Regarding the risk to be unnecessary, he drew off his band to an almost inaccessible spot on the bank of the Frio. Wherefore, as has been said, dissatisfaction arose among the members, and impeachment proceedings against Bud were premeditated with Black Eagle in high favour for the succession. Bud King was not unaware of the sentiment, and he called aside Cactus Taylor, his trusted lieutenant, to discuss it.

"If the boys," said Bud, "ain't satisfied with me, I'm willin' to step out. They're buckin' against my way of handlin' 'em. And 'specially because I concludes to hit the brush while Sam Kinney is ridin' the line. I saves 'em from bein' shot or sent up on a state contract, and they up and says I'm no good."

"It ain't so much that," explained Cactus, "as it is they're plum locoed about Piggy. They want them whiskers and that nose of his to split the wind at the head of the column."

"There's somethin' mighty seldom about Piggy," declared Bud, musingly. "I never yet see anything on the hoof that he exactly grades up with. He can shore holler a plenty, and he straddles a hoss from where you laid the chunk. But he ain't never been smoked yet. You know, Cactus, we ain't had a row since he's been with us. Piggy's all right for skearin' the greaser kids and layin' waste a cross-roads store. I reckon he's the finest canned oyster buccaneer and cheese pirate that ever was, but how's his appetite for fightin'? I've knowed some citizens you'd think was starvin' for trouble get a bad case of dyspepsy the first dose of lead they had to take."

"He talks all spraddled out," said Cactus, "'bout the rookuses he's been in. He claims to have saw the elephant and hearn the owl."

"I know," replied Bud, using the cow-puncher's expressive phrase of scepticism, "but it sounds to me!"

This conversation was held one night in camp while the other members of the band—eight in number—were sprawling around the fire, lingering over their supper. When Bud and Cactus ceased talking they heard Piggy's formidable voice holding forth to the others as usual while he was engaged in checking, though never satisfying, his ravening appetite.

"Wat's de use," he was saying, "of chasin' little red cowses and hosses 'round for t'ousands of miles? Dere ain't nuttin' in it. Gallopin' t'rough dese bushes and briers, and gettin' a t'irst dat a brewery couldn't put out, and missin' meals! Say! You know what I'd do if I was main finger of dis bunch? I'd stick up a train. I'd blow de express car and make hard dollars where you guys gets wind. Youse makes me tired. Dis sook-cow kind of cheap sport gives me a pain."

Later on, a deputation waited on Bud. They stood on one leg, chewed mesquite twigs and circumlocuted, for they hated to hurt his feelings. Bud foresaw their business, and made it easy for them. Bigger risks and larger profits were what they wanted.

The suggestion of Piggy's about holding up a train had fired their imagination and increased their admiration for the dash and boldness of the instigator. They were such simple, artless, and custom-bound bushrangers that they had never before thought of extending their habits beyond the running off of live-stock and the shooting of such of their acquaintances as ventured to interfere.

Bud acted "on the level", agreeing to take a subordinate place in the gang until Black Eagle should have been given a trial as leader.

After a great deal of consultation, studying of time-tables, and discussion of the country's topography, the time and place for carrying out their new enterprise was decided upon. At that time there was a feedstuff famine in Mexico and a cattle famine in certain parts of the United States, and there was a brisk international trade. Much money was being shipped along the railroads that connected the two republics. It was agreed that the most promising place for the contemplated robbery was at Espina, a little station on the I. and G.N., about forty miles north of Laredo. The train stopped there one minute; the country around was wild and unsettled; the station consisted of but one house in which the agent lived.

Black Eagle's band set out, riding by night. Arriving in the vicinity of Espina, they rested their horses all day in a thicket a few miles distant.

The train was due at Espina at 10.30 p.m. They could rob the train and be well over the Mexican border with their booty by daylight the next morning.

To do Black Eagle justice, he exhibited no signs of flinching from the responsible honours that had been conferred upon him.

He assigned his men to their respective posts with discretion, and coached them carefully as to their duties. On each side of the track four of the band were to lie concealed in the chaparral. Gotch-Ear Rodgers was to stick up the station agent. Bronco Charlie was to remain with the horses, holding them in readiness. At a spot where it was calculated the engine would be when the train stopped, Bud King was to lie hidden on one side, Black Eagle himself on the other. The two would get the drop on the engineer and fireman, force them to descend and proceed to the rear. Then the express car would be looted, and the escape made. No one was to move until Black Eagle gave the signal by firing his revolver. The plan was perfect.

At ten minutes to train time every man was at his post, effectually concealed by the thick chaparral that grew almost to the rails. The night was dark and lowering, with a fine drizzle falling from the flying gulf clouds. Black Eagle crouched behind a bush within five yards of the track. Two six-shooters were belted around him. Occasionally he drew a large black bottle from his pocket and raised it to his mouth.

A star appeared far down the track which soon waxed into the headlight of the approaching train. It came on with an increasing roar; the engine bore down upon the ambushing desperadoes with a glare and a shriek like some avenging monster come to deliver them to justice. Black Eagle flattened himself upon the ground. The engine, contrary to their calculations, instead of stopping between him and Bud King's place of concealment, passed fully forty yards farther before it came to a stand.

The bandit leader rose to his feet and peered around the bush. His men all lay quiet, awaiting the signal. Immediately opposite Black Eagle was a thing that drew his attention. Instead of being a regular passenger train it was a mixed one. Before him stood a box car, the door of which, by some means, had been left slightly open. Black Eagle went up to it, and pushed the door farther open. An odour came forth—a damp, rancid, familiar, musty, intoxicating, beloved odour stirring strongly at old memories of happy days and travels. Black Eagle sniffed at the witching smell as the returned wanderer smells of the rose that twines his boyhood's cottage home. Nostalgia seized him. He put his hand inside. Excelsior —dry, springy, curly, soft, enticing, covered the floor. Outside the drizzle had turned to a chilling rain.

The train bell clanged. The bandit chief unbuckled his belt and cast it, with its revolvers, upon the ground. His spurs followed quickly, and his broad sombrero. Black Eagle was moulting. The train started with a rattling jerk. The ex-Terror of the Border scrambled into the box car and closed the door. Stretched luxuriously upon the excelsior, with the black bottle clasped closely to his breast, his eyes closed, and a foolish, happy smile upon his terrible features, Chicken Ruggles started upon his return trip.

Undisturbed, with the band of desperate bandits lying motionless, awaiting the signal to attack, the train pulled out from Espina. As its speed increased and the black masses of chaparral went whizzing past on either side, the express messenger, lighting his pipe, looked through his window and remarked, feelingly:

"What a jim-dandy place for a hold-up!"

26

At Arms with Morpheus

I NEVER could quite understand how Tom Hopkins came to make that blunder, for he had been through a whole term at a medical college—before he inherited his aunt's fortune—and had been considered strong in therapeutics.

We had been making a call together that evening, and afterwards Tom ran up to my rooms for a pipe and a chat before going on to his own luxurious apartments. I had stepped into the other room for a moment when I heard Tom sing out:

"Oh, Billy, I'm going to take about four grains of quinine, if you don't mind—I'm feeling all blue and shivery. Guess I'm taking cold."

"All right," I called back. "The bottle is on the second shelf. Take it in a spoonful of that elixir of eucalyptus. It knocks the bitter out."

After I came back we sat by the fire and got our briars going. In about eight minutes Tom sank back into a gentle collapse.

I went straight to the medicine cabinet and looked.

"You unmitigated hayseed!" I growled. "See what money will do for a man's brains!"

There stood the morphine bottle with the stopper out, just as Tom had left it.

I routed out another young M.D. who roomed on the floor above, and sent him for old Doctor Gales, two squares away. Tom Hopkins has too much money to be attended by rising young practitioners alone.

When Gales came we put Tom through as expensive a course of treatment as the resources of the profession permit. After the more drastic remedies we gave him citrate of caffeine in frequent doses and strong coffee, and walked him up and down the floor between two of us. Old Gales pinched him and slapped his face and worked hard for the big cheque he could see in the distance. The young M.D. from the next floor gave Tom a most hearty, rousing kick, and then apologized to me.

"Couldn't help it," he said. "I never kicked a millionaire before in my life. I may never have another opportunity."

"Now," said Doctor Gales, after a couple of hours, "he'll do. But keep him awake for another hour. You can do that by talking to him and shaking him up occasionally. When his pulse and respiration are normal then let him sleep. I'll leave him with you now."

I was left alone with Tom, whom we had laid on a couch. He lay very still, and his eyes were half closed. I began my work of keeping him awake.

"Well, old man," I said, "you've had a narrow squeak, but we've pulled you through. When you were attending lectures, Tom, didn't any of the professors ever casually remark that m-o-r-p-h-i-a never spells 'quinia', especially in four-grain doses? But I won't pile it up on you until you get on your feet. But you ought to have been a druggist, Tom; you're splendidly qualified to fill prescriptions."

Tom looked at me with a faint and foolish smile.

"B'ly," he murmured, "I feel jus' like a hum'n bird flyin' around a jolly lot of most 'shpensive roses. Don' bozzer me. Goin' sleep now."

And he went to sleep in two seconds. I shook him by the shoulder.

"Now, Tom," I said severely, "this won't do. The big doctor said you must stay awake for at least an hour. Open your eyes. You're not entirely safe yet, you know. Wake up."

Tom Hopkins weighs one hundred and ninety-eight. He gave me another somnolent grin, and fell into deeper slumber. I would have made him move about, but I might as well have tried to make Cleopatra's Needle waltz around the room with me. Tom's breathing became stertorous, and that, in connection with morphia poisoning, means danger.

Then I began to think. I could not rouse his body; I must

strive to excite his mind. "Make him angry", was an idea that suggested itself! Good! I thought; but how? There was not a joint in Tom's armour. Dear old fellow! He was good-nature itself, and a gallant gentleman, fine and true and clean as sunlight. He came from somewhere down South, where they still have ideals and a code. New York had charmed, but had not spoiled him. He had that old-fashioned, chivalrous reverence for women, that—— Eureka!—there was my idea! I worked the thing up for a minute or two in my imagination. I chuckled to myself at the thought of springing a thing like that on old Tom Hopkins. Then I took him by the shoulder and shook him till his ears flopped. He opened his eyes lazily. I assumed an expression of scorn and contempt, and pointed my finger within two inches of his nose.

"Listen to me, Hopkins," I said, in cutting and distinct tones, "you and I have been good friends, but I want you to understand that in the future my doors are closed against any man who acts as much like a scoundrel as you have."

Tom looked the least bit interested.

"What's the matter, Billy?" he muttered composedly. "Don't your clothes fit you?"

"If I were in your place," I went on, "which, thank God, I'm not, I think I would be afraid to close my eyes. How about that girl you left waiting for you down among those lonesome Southern pines—the girl that you've forgotten since you came into your confounded money? Oh, I know what I'm talking about. While you were a poor medical student she was good enough for you. But now, since you are a millionaire, it's different. I wonder what she thinks of the performances of that peculiar class of people which she has been taught to worship—the Southern gentlemen? I'm sorry, Hopkins, that I was forced to speak about these matters, but you've covered it up so well and played your part so nicely that I would have sworn you were above such unmanly tricks."

Poor Tom. I could scarcely keep from laughing outright to see him struggling against the effects of the opiate. He was distinctly angry, and I didn't blame him. Tom had a Southern temper. His eyes were open now, and they showed a gleam or two of fire. But the drug still clouded his mind and bound his tongue.

"C-c-confound you," he stammered, "I'll s-smash you."

He tried to rise from the couch. With all his size he was very weak now. I thrust him back with one arm. He lay there glaring like a lion in a trap.

"That will hold you for a while, you old loony," I said to myself. I got up and lit my pipe, for I was needing a smoke. I walked around a bit, congratulating myself on my brilliant idea.

I heard a snore. I looked around. Tom was asleep again. I walked over and punched him on the jaw. He looked at me as pleasant and ungrudging as an idiot. I chewed my pipe and gave it to him hard.

"I want you to recover yourself and get out of my rooms as soon as you can," I said insultingly. "I've told you what I think of you. If you have any honour or honesty left you will think twice before you attempt again to associate with gentlemen. She's a poor girl, isn't she?" I sneered. "Somewhat too plain and unfashionable for us since we got our money. Be ashamed to walk on Fifth Avenue with her, wouldn't you? Hopkins, you're forty-seven times worse than a cad. Who cares for your money? I don't. I'll bet that girl don't. Perhaps if you didn't have it you'd be more of a man. As it is you've made a cur of yourself, and"—I thought that quite dramatic—"perhaps broken a faithful heart." (Old Tom Hopkins breaking a faithful heart!) "Let me be rid of you as soon as possible."

I turned my back on Tom, and winked at myself in a mirror. I heard him moving, and I turned again quickly. I didn't want a hundred and ninety-eight pounds falling on me from the rear. But Tom had only turned partly over, and laid one arm across his face. He spoke a few words rather more distinctly than before.

"I couldn't have—talked this way—to you, Billy, even if I'd heard people—lyin' 'bout you. But jus' soon's I can s-stand up—I'll break your neck—don' f'get it."

I did feel a little ashamed then. But it was to save Tom. In the morning, when I explained it, we would have a good laugh over it together.

In about twenty minutes Tom dropped into a sound, easy slumber. I felt his pulse, listened to his respiration, and let him sleep. Everything was normal, and Tom was safe. I went into the other room and tumbled into bed.

I found Tom up and dressed when I awoke the next morning. He was entirely himself again with the exception of shaky nerves and a tongue like a white-oak chip.

"What an idiot I was," he said thoughtfully. "I remember thinking that quinine bottle looked queer while I was taking the dose. Have much trouble in bringing me round?"

I told him no. His memory seemed bad about the entire affair. I concluded that he had no recollection of my efforts to keep him awake, and decided not to enlighten him. Some other time, I thought, when he was feeling better, we would have some fun over it.

When Tom was ready to go he stopped, with the door open, and shook my hand.

"Much obliged, old fellow," he said quietly, "for taking so much trouble with me—and for what you said. I'm going down now to telegraph to the little girl."

27

A Ghost of a Chance

"ACTUALLY a *hod*!" repeated Mrs. Kinsolving pathetically.

Mrs. Bellamy Bellmore arched a sympathetic eyebrow. Thus she expressed condolence and a generous amount of apparent surprise.

"Fancy her telling everywhere," recapitulated Mrs. Kinsolving, "that she saw a ghost in the apartment she occupied here—our choicest guest-room—a ghost, carrying a hod on its shoulder—the ghost of an old man in overalls, smoking a pipe and carrying a hod! The very absurdity of the thing shows her malicious intent. There never was a Kinsolving that carried a hod. Every one knows that Mr. Kinsolving's father accumulated his money by large building contracts, but he never worked a day with his own hands. He had this house built from his own plans; but—oh, a hod! Why need she have been so cruel and malicious?"

"It is really too bad," murmured Mrs. Bellmore, with an approving glance of her fine eyes about the vast chamber done in lilac and old gold. "And it was in this room she saw it! Oh, no, I'm not afraid of ghosts. Don't have the least fear on my account. I'm glad you put me in here. I think family ghosts so interesting! But, really, the story does sound a little inconsistent. I should have expected something better from Mrs. Fischer-Suympkins. Don't they carry bricks in hods? Why should a ghost bring bricks into a villa built of marble and stone? I'm so sorry, but it makes me think that age is beginning to tell upon Mrs. Fischer-Suympkins."

"This house," continued Mrs. Kinsolving, "was built upon the site of an old one used by the family during the Revolution. There wouldn't be anything strange in its having a ghost. And there was a Captain Kinsolving who fought in General Greene's army, though we've never been able to secure any papers to vouch for it. If there is to be a family ghost, why couldn't it have been his, instead of a brick-layer's?"

"The ghost of a Revolutionary ancestor wouldn't be a bad idea," agreed Mrs. Bellmore; "but you know how arbitrary and inconsiderate ghosts can be. Maybe, like love, they are 'engendered in the eye'. One advantage of those who see ghosts is that their stories can't be disproved. By a spiteful eye, a Revolutionary knapsack might easily be construed to be a hod. Dear Mrs. Kinsolving, think no more of it. I am sure it was a knapsack."

"But she told everybody!" mourned Mrs. Kinsolving, inconsolable. "She insisted upon the details. There is the pipe. And how are you going to get out of the overalls?"

"Shan't get into them," said Mrs. Bellmore, with a prettily suppressed yawn; "too stiff and wrinkly. Is that you, Felice? Prepare my bath, please. Do you dine at seven at Clifftop, Mrs. Kinsolving? So kind of you to run in for a chat before dinner! I love those little touches of informality with a guest. They give such a home flavour to a visit. So sorry; I must be dressing. I am so indolent I always postpone it until the last moment."

Mrs. Fischer-Suympkins had been the first large plum that the Kinsolvings had drawn from the social pie. For a long time the pie itself had been out of reach on a top shelf. But the purse and the pursuit had at last lowered it. Mrs. Fischer-Suympkins was the heliograph of the smart society parading corps. The glitter of her wit and actions passed along the line, transmitting whatever was latest and most daring in the game of peep-show. Formerly, her fame and leadership had been secure enough not to need the support of such artifices as handing around live frogs for favours at a cotillon. But, now, these things were necessary to the holding of her throne. Beside, middle age had come to preside, incongruous, at her capers. The sensational papers had cut her space from a page to two columns. Her wit developed a sting; her manners became more rough and inconsiderate, as if she felt the royal necessity of establishing her autocracy by scorning the conventionalities that bound lesser potentates.

To some pressure at the command of the Kinsolvings, she had yielded so far as to honour their house by her presence, for an evening and night. She had her revenge upon her hostess by relating, with grim enjoyment and sarcastic humour, her story of the vision carrying the hod. To that lady, in raptures at having penetrated thus far toward the coveted inner circle, the result came as a crushing disappointment. Everybody either sympathized or laughed, and there was little to choose between the two modes of expression.

But, later on, Mrs. Kinsolving's hopes and spirits were revived by the capture of a second and greater prize.

Mrs. Bellamy Bellmore had accepted an invitation to visit at Clifftop, and would remain for three days. Mrs. Bellmore was one of the younger matrons, whose beauty, descent, and wealth gave her a reserved seat in the holy of holies that required no strenuous bolstering. She was generous enough thus to give Mrs. Kinsolving the accolade that was so poignantly desired; and, at the same time, she thought how much it would please Terence. Perhaps it would end by solving him.

Terence was Mrs. Kinsolving's son, aged twenty-nine, quite good-looking enough, and with two or three attractive and mysterious traits. For one, he was very devoted to his mother, and that was sufficiently odd to deserve notice. For others, he talked so little that it was irritating, and he seemed either very shy or very deep. Terence interested Mrs. Bellmore, because she was not sure which it was. She intended to study him a little longer, unless she forgot the matter. If he was only shy, she would abandon him, for shyness is a bore. If he was deep, she would also abandon him, for depth is precarious.

On the afternoon of the third day of her visit, Terence hunted up Mrs. Bellmore, and found her in a nook actually looking at an album.

"It's so good of you," said he, "to come down here and retrieve the day for us. I suppose you have heard that Mrs. Fischer-Suympkins scuttled the ship before she left. She knocked a whole plank out of the bottom with a hod. My mother is grieving herself ill about it. Can't you manage to see a ghost for us while you are here, Mrs. Bellmore—a bang-up, swell ghost, with a coronet on his head and a cheque-book under his arm?"

"That was a naughty old lady, Terence," said Mrs. Bellmore, "to tell such stories. Perhaps you gave her too much supper. Your mother doesn't really take it seriously, does she?"

"I think she does," answered Terence. "One would think every brick in the hod had dropped on her. It's a good mammy, and I don't like to see her worried. It's to be hoped that the ghost belongs to the hod-carriers' union, and will go out on a strike. If he doesn't, there will be no peace in this family."

"I'm sleeping in the ghost-chamber," said Mrs. Bellmore pensively. "But it's so nice I wouldn't change it, even if I were afraid, which I'm not. It wouldn't do for me to submit a counter story of a desirable, aristocratic shade, would it? I would do so, with pleasure, but it seems to me it would be too obviously an antidote for the other narrative to be effective."

"True," said Terence, running two fingers thoughtfully into his crisp brown hair; "that would never do. How would it work to see the same ghost again, minus the overalls, and have gold bricks in the hod? That would elevate the spectre from degrading toil to a financial plane. Don't you think that would be respectable enough?"

"There was an ancestor who fought against the Britishers, wasn't there? Your mother said something to that effect."

"I believe so; one of those old chaps in raglan vests and golf trousers. I don't care a continental for a continental, myself. But the mother has set her heart on pomp and heraldry and pyrotechnics, and I want her to be happy."

"You are a good boy, Terence," said Mrs. Bellmore, sweeping her silks close to one side of her, "not to beat your mother. Sit here by me, and let's look at the album, just as people used to do twenty years ago. Now, tell me about every one of them. Who is this tall, dignified gentleman leaning against the horizon, with one arm on the Corinthian column?

"That old chap with the big feet?" inquired Terence, craning his neck. "That's great-uncle O'Brannigan. He used to keep a rath-skeller on the Bowery."

"I asked you to sit down, Terence. If you are not going to amuse or obey me, I shall report in the morning that I saw a ghost wearing an apron and carrying schooners of beer. Now, that is better. To be shy, at your age, Terence, is a thing that you should blush to acknowledge."

At breakfast on the last morning of her visit, Mrs. Bellmore startled and entranced every one present by announcing positively that she had seen the ghost.

"Did it have a—a—a——?" Mrs. Kinsolving, in her suspense and agitation, could not bring out the word.

"No, indeed—far from it."

There was a chorus of questions from others at the table. "Weren't you frightened?" "What did it do?" "How did it look?" "How was it dressed?" "Did it say anything?" "Didn't you scream?"

"I'll try to answer everything at once," said Mrs. Bellmore heroically, "although I'm frightfully hungry. Something awakened me—I'm not sure whether it was a noise or a touch—and there stood the phantom. I never burn a light at night, so the room was quite dark, but I saw it plainly. I wasn't dreaming. It was a tall man, all misty white from head to foot. It wore the full dress of the old Colonial days—powdered hair, baggy coat skirts, lace ruffles, and a sword. It looked intangible and luminous in the dark, and moved without a sound. Yes, I was a little frightened at first—or startled, I should say. It was the first ghost I had ever seen. No, it didn't say anything. I didn't scream. I raised up on my elbow, and then it glided silently away, and disappeared when it reached the door."

Mrs. Kinsolving was in the seventh heaven. "The description is that of Captain Kinsolving, of General Greene's army, one of our ancestors," she said, in a voice that trembled with pride and relief. "I really think I must apologize for our ghostly relative, Mrs. Bellmore. I am afraid he must have badly disturbed your rest."

Terence sent a smile of pleased congratulation toward his mother. Attainment was Mrs. Kinsolving's, at last, and he loved to see her happy.

"I suppose I ought to be ashamed to confess," said Mrs. Bellmore, who was now enjoying her breakfast, "that I wasn't very much disturbed. I presume it would have been the customary thing to scream and faint and have all of you running about in picturesque costumes. But, after the first alarm was over, I really couldn't work myself up to a panic. The ghost retired from the stage quietly and peacefully, after doing its little turn, and I went to sleep again."

Nearly all listened, and politely accepted Mrs. Bellmore's story as a made-up affair, charitably offered as an offset to the unkind vision seen by Mrs. Fischer-Suympkins. But one or two present perceived that her assertions bore the genuine stamp of her own convictions. Truth and candour seemed to attend upon every word. Even a scoffer at ghosts—if he were very observant—would have been forced to admit that she had, at least in a very vivid dream, been honestly aware of the weird visitor.

Soon Mrs. Bellmore's maid was packing. In two hours the auto would come to convey her to the station. As Terence was strolling upon the east piazza, Mrs. Bellmore came up to him, with a confidential sparkle in her eye.

"I didn't wish to tell the others all of it," she said, "but I will tell you. In a way, I think you should be held responsible. Can you guess in what manner the ghost awakened me last night?"

"Rattled chains," suggested Terence, after some thought, "or groaned? They usually do one or the other."

"Do you happen to know," continued Mrs. Bellmore with sudden irrelevancy, "if I resemble any one of the female relatives of your restless ancestor, Captain Kinsolving?"

"Don't think so," said Terence with an extremely puzzled air. "Never heard of any of them being noted beauties."

"Then, why," said Mrs. Bellmore, looking the young man

gravely in the eye, "should that ghost have kissed me, as I'm sure it did?"

"Heavens!" exclaimed Terence, in wide-eyed amazement; "you don't mean that, Mrs. Bellmore! Did he actually kiss you?"

"I said *it*," corrected Mrs. Bellmore. "I hope the impersonal pronoun is correctly used."

"But why did you say I was responsible?"

"Because you are the only living male relative of the ghost."

"I see. 'Unto the third and fourth generation. But, seriously, did he—did it—how do you——?"

"Know? How does anyone know? I was asleep, and that is what awakened me, I'm almost certain."

"Almost?"

"Well, I awoke just as—oh, can't you understand what I mean? When anything arouses you suddenly, you are not positive whether you dreamed, or—and yet you know that —— Dear me, Terence, must I dissect the most elementary sensations in order to accommodate your extremely practical intelligence?"

"But about kissing ghosts, you know," said Terence humbly, "I require the most primary instruction. I never kissed a ghost. Is it—is it——?"

"The sensation," said Mrs. Bellmore, with deliberate, but slightly smiling emphasis, "since you are seeking instruction, is a mingling of the material and the spiritual."

"Of course," said Terence, suddenly growing serious, "it was a dream or some kind of an hallucination. Nobody believes in spirits, these days. If you told the tale out of kindness of heart, Mrs. Bellmore, I can't express how grateful I am to you. It has made my mother supremely happy. That Revolutionary ancestor was a stunning idea."

Mrs. Bellmore sighed. "The usual fate of ghostseers is mine," she said resignedly. "My privileged encounter with a spirit is attributed to lobster salad or mendacity. Well, I have, at least, one memory left from the wreck—a kiss from the unseen world. Was Captain Kinsolving a very brave man, do you know, Terence?"

"He was licked at Yorktown, I believe," said Terence, reflecting. "They say he skedaddled with his company, after the first battle there."

"I thought he must have been timid," said Mrs. Bellmore absently. "He might have had another."

"Another battle?" asked Terence dully.

"What else could I mean? I must go and get ready now; the auto will be here in an hour. I've enjoyed Clifftop immensely. Such a lovely morning, isn't it, Terence?"

On her way to the station, Mrs. Bellmore took from her bag a silk handkerchief, and looked at it with a little peculiar smile. Then she tied it in several very hard knots, and threw it, at a convenient moment, over the edge of the cliff along which the road ran.

In his room, Terence was giving some directions to his man, Brooks. "Have this stuff done up in a parcel," he said, "and ship it to the address on that card."

The card was that of a New York costumer. The "stuff" was a gentleman's costume of the days of '76, made of white satin, with silver buckles, white silk stockings, and white kid shoes. A powdered wig and a sword completed the dress.

"And look about, Brooks," added Terence a little anxiously, "for a silk handkerchief with my initials in one corner. I must have dropped it somewhere."

It was a month later when Mrs. Bellmore and one or two others of the smart crowd were making up a list of names for a coaching trip through the Catskills. Mrs. Bellmore looked over the list for a final censoring. The name of Terence Kinsolving was there. Mrs. Bellmore ran her prohibitive pencil lightly through the name.

"Too shy!" she murmured sweetly, in explanation.

28

The Door of Unrest

I SAT an hour by sun, in the editor's room of the Montopolis *Weekly Bugle*. I was the editor.

The saffron rays of the declining sunlight filtered through the cornstalks in Micajah Widdup's garden-patch, and cast an amber glory upon my paste-pot. I sat at the editorial desk in my non-rotary revolving chair, and prepared my editorial against the oligarchies. The room, with its one window, was already a prey to the twilight. One by one, with my trenchant sentences, I lopped off the heads of the political hydra, while I listened, full of kindly peace, to the home-coming cow-bells and wondered what Mrs. Flanagan was going to have for supper.

Then in from the dusky, quiet street there drifted and perched himself upon a corner of my desk old Father Time's younger brother. His face was beardless and as gnarled as an English walnut. I never saw clothes such as he wore. They would have reduced Joseph's coat to a monochrome. But the colours were not the dyer's. Stains and patches and the work of sun and rust were responsible for the diversity. On his coarse shoes was the dust, conceivably, of a thousand leagues. I can describe him no further, except to say that he was little and weird and old—old I began to estimate in centuries when I saw him. Yes, and I remember that there was an odour, a faint odour like aloes, or possibly like myrrh or leather; and I thought of museums.

And then I reached for a pad and pencil, for a business is business, and visits of the oldest inhabitants are sacred and honourable, requiring to be chronicled.

"I am glad to see you, sir," I said. "I would offer you a chair, but—you see, sir," I went on, "I have lived in Montopolis only three weeks, and I have not met many of our citizens." I turned a doubtful eye upon his dust-stained shoes, and concluded with a newspaper phrase, "I suppose that you reside in our midst?"

My visitor fumbled in his raiment, drew forth a soiled card, and handed it to me. Upon it was written, in plain but unsteadily formed characters, the name "Michob Ader".

"I am glad you called, Mr. Ader," I said. "As one of our older citizens, you must view with pride the recent growth and enterprise of Montopolis. Among other improvements, I think I can promise that the town will now be provided with a live, enterprising newspa——"

"Do ye know the name on that card?" asked my caller, interrupting me.

"It is not a familiar one to me," I said.

Again he visited the depths of his ancient vestments. This time he brought out a torn leaf of some book or journal, brown and flimsy with age. The heading of the page was the *Turkish Spy* in old-style type; the printing upon it was this:

There is a man come to Paris in this year 1643 who pretends to have lived these sixteen hundred years. He says of himself that he was a shoemaker in Jerusalem at the time of the Crucifixion; that his name is Michob Ader; and that when Jesus, the Christian Messias, was condemned by Pontius Pilate, the Roman president, he paused to rest while bearing his cross to the place of crucifixion before the door of Michob Ader. The shoemaker struck Jesus with his fist, saying, "Go; why tarriest thou?" The Messias answered him: "I indeed am going; but thou shalt tarry until I come"; thereby condemning him to live until the day of judgment. He lives for ever, but at the end of every hundred years he falls into a fit or trance, on recovering from which he finds himself in the same state of youth in which he was when Jesus suffered, being then about thirty years of age.

Such is the story of the Wandering Jew, as told by Michob Ader, who relates——

Here the printing ended.

I must have muttered aloud something to myself about the

Wandering Jew, for the old man spake up, bitterly and loudly.

"'Tis a lie," said he, "like nine-tenths of what ye call history. 'Tis a Gentile I am, and no Jew. I am after footing it out of Jerusalem, my son; but if that makes me a Jew, then everything that comes out of a bottle is babies' milk. Ye have my name on the card ye hold; and ye have read the bit of paper they call the *Turkish Spy* that printed the news when I stepped into their office on the 12th day of June, in the year 1643, just as I have called upon ye to-day."

I laid down my pencil and pad. Clearly it would not do. Here was an item for the local column of the *Bugle* that—but it would not do. Still, fragments of the impossible "personal" began to flit through my conventionalized brain. "Uncle Michob is as spry on his legs as a young chap of only a thousand or so." "Our venerable caller relates with pride that George Wash—— no, Ptolemy the Great—once dandled him on his knee at his father's house." "Uncle Michob says that our wet spring was nothing in comparison with the dampness that ruined the crops around Mount Ararat when he was a boy——" But no, no—it would not do.

I was trying to think of some conversational subject with which to interest my visitor, and was hesitating between walking matches and the Pliocene Age, when the old man suddenly began to weep poignantly and distressfully.

"Cheer up, Mr. Ader," I said a little awkwardly; "this matter may blow over in a few hundred years more. There has already been a decided reaction in favour of Judas Iscariot and Colonel Burr and the celebrated violinist, Signor Nero. This is the age of whitewash. You must not allow yourself to become downhearted."

Unknowingly, I had struck a chord. The old man blinked belligerently through his senile tears.

"'Tis time," he said, "that the liars be doin' justice to somebody. Yer historians are no more than a pack of old women gabblin' at a wake. A finer man than the Imperor Nero niver wore sandals. Man, I was at the burnin' of Rome. I knowed the Imperor well, for in them days I was a well-known character. In thim days they had rayspect for a man that lived for ever.

"But 'twas of the Imperor Nero I was goin' to tell ye. I struck into Rome, up the Appian Way, on the night of July the 16th, the year 64. I had just stepped down by way of Siberia and Afghanistan; and one foot of me had a frost-bite, and the other a blister burned by the sand of the desert; and I was feelin' a bit blue from doin' patrol duty from the North Pole down to the Last Chance corner in Patagonia, and bein' miscalled a Jew into the bargain. Well, I'm tellin' ye I was passin' the Circus Maximus, and it was dark as pitch over the way, and then I heard somebody sing out, 'Is that you, Michob?'

"Over ag'inst the wall, hid out amongst a pile of barrels and old dry-goods boxes, was the Imperor Nero wid his togy wrapped around his toes, smokin' a long, black cigar.

"'Have one, Michob?' says he.

"'None of the weeds for me,' says I—'nayther pipe nor cigar. What's the use,' says I, 'of smokin' when ye've not got the ghost of a chance of killin' yeself by doin' it?'

"'True for ye, Michob Ader, my perpetual Jew,' says the Imperor; 'ye're not always wandering. Sure, 'tis danger gives the spice of our pleasures—next to their bein' forbidden.'

"'And for what,' says I, 'do ye smoke be night in dark places widout even a cinturion in plain clothes to attend ye?'

"'Have ye ever heard, Michob,' says the Imperor, 'of predestinarianism?'

"'I've had the cousin of it,' says I. 'I've been on the trot with pedestrianism for many a year, and more to come, as ye well know.'

"'The longer word,' says me friend Nero, 'is the tachin' of this new sect of people they call the Christians. 'Tis them that's raysponsible for me smokin' be night in holes and corners of the dark.'

"And then I sets down and takes off a shoe and rubs me foot that is frosted, and the Imperor tells me about it. It seems that since I passed that way before, the Imperor had mandamused the Impress wid a divorce suit, and Misses Poppaea, a cilibrated lady, was ingaged, widout riferences, as housekeeper at the palace. 'All in one day,' says the Imperor, 'she puts up new lace windy-curtains in the palace and joins the anti-tobacco society, and whin I feels the need of a smoke I must be after sneakin' out to these piles of lumber in the dark.' So there in the dark me and the Imperor sat, and I told him of me travels. And when they say the Imperor was an incindiary, they lie. 'Twas that night the fire started that burnt the city. 'Tis my opinion that it began from a stump of cigar that he threw down among the boxes. And 'tis a lie that he fiddled. He did all he could for six days to stop it, sir."

And now I detected a new flavour to Mr. Michob Ader. It had not been myrrh or balm or hyssop that I had smelled. The emanation was the odour of bad whisky—and worse still, of low comedy—the sort that small humorists manufacture by clothing the grave and reverend things of legend and history in the vulgar, topical frippery that passes for a certain kind of wit. Michob Ader as an impostor, claiming nineteen hundred years, and playing his part with the decency of respectable lunacy, I could ensure; but as a tedious wag, cheapening his egregious story with song-book levity, his importance as an entertainer grew less.

And then, as if he suspected my thoughts, he suddenly shifted his key.

"You'll excuse me, sir," he whined, "but sometimes I get a little mixed in my head. I am a very old man; and it is hard to remember everything."

I knew that he was right, and that I should not try to reconcile him with Roman history; so I asked for news concerning other ancients with whom he had walked familiar.

Above my desk hung an engraving of Raphael's cherubs. You could yet make out their forms, though the dust blurred their outlines strangely.

"Ye calls them 'cher-rubs'," cackled the old man. "Babes, ye fancy they are, with wings. And there's one wid legs and a bow and arrow that ye call Cupid—I know where they was found. The great-great-great-grandfather of thim all was a billy-goat. Bein' an editor, sir, do ye happen to know where Solomon's Temple stood?"

I fancied that it was in—in Persia? Well, I did not know.

"'Tis not in history nor in the Bible where it was. But I saw it, meself. The first pictures of cher-rubs and cupids was sculptured upon thim walls and pillars. Two of the biggest, sir, stood in the adytum to form the baldachin over the Ark. But the wings of thim sculptures intindid for horns. And the faces was the faces of goats. Ten thousand goats there was in and about the temple. And your cher-rubs was billy-goats in the days of King Solomon, but the painters misconstrued the horns into wings.

"And I knew Tamerlane, the lame Timour, sir, very well. I saw him at Keghut and at Zaranj. He was a little man no larger than yerself, with hair the colour of an amber pipe-stem. They buried him at Samarkand. I was at the wake, sir. Oh, he was a fine-built man in his coffin, six feet long, with black whiskers to his face. And I see 'em throw turnips at the Imperor Vispacian in Africa. All over the world I have tramped, sir, without the body of me findin' any rest. 'Twas so commanded. I saw Jerusalem destroyed, and Pompeii go up in the fireworks; and I was at the coronation of Charlemagne and the lynchin' of Joan of Arc. And everywhere I go there comes storms and revolutions and plagues and fires. 'Twas so commanded. Ye have heard of the Wandering Jew. 'Tis all so, except that divil a bit am I a Jew. But history lies, as I have told ye. Are ye quite sure, sir, that ye haven't a drop of whisky convenient? Ye well know that I have many miles of walking before me."

"I have none," said I, "and, if you please, I am about to leave for my supper."

I pushed my chair back creakingly. This ancient land-lubber was becoming as great an affliction as any cross-bowed mariner. He shook a musty effluvium from his piebald clothes, overturned my inkstand, and went on with his insufferable nonsense.

"I wouldn't mind it so much," he complained, "if it wasn't for the work I must do on Good Fridays. Ye know about Pontius Pilate, sir, of course. His body, whin he killed himself, was pitched into a lake on the Alps mountains. Now, listen to the job that 'tis mine to perform on the night of ivery Good Friday. The ould divil goes down in the pool and drags up Pontius, and the water is bilin' and spewin' like a wash pot. And the ould divil sets the body on top of a throne on the rocks, and thin comes me share of the job. Oh, sir, ye would pity me thin—ye would pray for the poor Wandering Jew that niver was a Jew if ye could see the horror of the thing that I must do. 'Tis I that must fetch a bowl of water and kneel down before it till it washes its hands. I declare to ye that Pontius Pilate, a man dead two hundred years, dragged up with the lake slime coverin' him and fishes wrigglin' inside of him widout eyes, and in the discomposition of the body, sits there, sir, and washes his hands in the bowl I hold for him on Good Fridays. 'Twas so commanded."

Clearly, the matter had progressed far beyond the scope of the *Bugle*'s local column. There might have been employment here for the alienist or for those who circulate the pledge; but I had had enough of it. I got up, and repeated that I must go.

At this he seized my coat, grovelled upon my desk, and burst again into distressful weeping. Whatever it was about, I said to myself that his grief was genuine.

"Come now, Mr. Ader," I said soothingly; "what is the matter?"

The answer came brokenly through his racking sobs: "Because I would not . . . let the poor Christ . . . rest . . . upon the step."

His hallucination seemed beyond all reasonable answer; yet the effect of it upon him scarcely merited disrespect. But I knew nothing that might assuage it; and I told him once more that both of us should be leaving the office at once.

Obedient at last, he raised himself from my dishevelled desk, and permitted me to half lift him to the floor. The gale of his grief had blown away his words; his freshet of tears had soaked away the crust of his grief. Reminiscence died in him —at least, the coherent part of it.

"'Twas me that did it," he muttered, as I led him toward the door—"me, the shoemaker of Jerusalem."

I got him to the sidewalk, and in the augmented light I saw that his face was seared and lined and warped by a sadness almost incredibly the product of a single lifetime.

And then high up in the firmamental darkness we heard the clamant cries of some great, passing birds. My Wandering Jew lifted his hand, with side-tilted head.

"The Seven Whistlers!" he said, as one introduces well-known friends.

"Wild geese," said I; "but I confess that their number is beyond me."

"They follow me everywhere," he said. "'Twas so commanded. What ye hear is the souls of the seven Jews that helped with the Crucifixion. Sometimes they're plovers and sometimes geese, but ye'll find them always flyin' where I go."

I stood, uncertain how to take my leave. I looked down the street, shuffled my feet, looked back again—and felt my hair rise. The old man had disappeared.

And then my capillaries relaxed, for I dimly saw him footing it away through the darkness. But he walked so swiftly and silently and contrary to the gait promised by his age that my composure was not all restored, though I knew not why.

That night I was foolish enough to take down some dust-covered volumes from my modest shelves. I searched *Hermippus Redivivus* and *Salathiel* and the *Pepys Collection* in vain. And then, in a book called *The Citizen of the World*, and in one or two centuries old, I came upon what I desired. Michob Ader had indeed come to Paris in the year 1643, and related to the *Turkish Spy* an extraordinary story. He claimed to be the Wandering Jew, and that——

But here I fell asleep, for my editorial duties had not been light that day.

Judge Hoover was the *Bugle*'s candidate for congress. Having to confer with him, I sought his home early the next morning; and we walked together down town through a little street with which I was unfamiliar.

"Did you ever hear of Michob Ader?" I asked him, smiling.

"Why, yes," said the judge. "And that reminds me of my shoes he has for mending. Here is his shop now."

Judge Hoover stepped into a dingy, small shop. I looked

up at the sign, and saw "Mike O'Bader, Boot and Shoe maker," on it. Some wild geese passed above, honking clearly. I scratched my ear and frowned, and then trailed into the shop.

There sat my Wandering Jew on his shoemaker's bench, trimming a half-sole. He was drabbled with dew, grass-stained, unkempt, and miserable; and on his face was still the unexplained wretchedness, the problematic sorrow, the esoteric woe, that had been written there by nothing less, it seemed, than the stylus of the centuries.

Judge Hoover inquired kindly concerning his shoes. The old shoemaker looked up, and spoke sanely enough. He had been ill, he said, for a few days. The next day the shoes would be ready. He looked at me, and I could see that I had no place in his memory. So out we went, and on our way.

"Old Mike," remarked the candidate, "has been on one of his sprees. He gets crazy drunk regularly once a month. But he's a good shoemaker."

"What is his history?" I inquired.

"Whisky," epitomized Judge Hoover. "That explains him."

I was silent, but I did not accept the explanation. And so, when I had the chance, I asked old man Sellers, who browsed daily on my exchanges.

"Mike O'Bader," said he, "was makin' shoes in Montopolis when I come here goin' on fifteen year ago. I guess whisky's his trouble. Once a month he gets off the track, and stays so a week. He's got a rigmarole somethin' about his bein' a Jew pedler that he tells ev'rybody. Nobody won't listen to him any more. When he's sober he ain't sich a fool—he's got a sight of books in the back room of his shop that he reads. I guess you can lay all his trouble to whisky."

But again I would not. Not yet was my Wandering Jew rightly construed for me. I trust that woman may not be allowed a title to all the curiosity in the world. So when Montopolis's oldest inhabitant (some ninety score years younger than Michob Ader) dropped in to acquire promulgation in print, I siphoned his perpetual trickle of reminiscence in the direction of the uninterpreted maker of shoes.

Uncle Abner was the Complete History of Montopolis bound in butternut.

"O'Bader," he quavered, "come here in '69. He was the first shoemaker in the place. Folks generally considers him crazy at times now. But he don't harm nobody. I s'pose drinkin' upset his mind—yes, drinkin' very likely done it. It's a powerful bad thing, drinkin'. I'm an old, old man, sir, and I never see no good in drinkin'."

I felt disappointment. I was willing to admit drink in the case of my shoemaker, but I preferred it as a recourse instead of a cause. Why had he pitched upon his perpetual, strange note of the Wandering Jew? Why his unutterable grief during his aberration? I could not yet accept whisky as an explanation.

"Did Mike O'Bader ever have a great loss or trouble of any kind?" I asked.

"Lemme see! About thirty year ago there was somethin' of the kind, I recollect. Montopolis, sir, in them days used to be a mighty strict place.

"Well, Mike O'Bader had a daughter then—a right pretty girl. She was too gay a sort for Montopolis, so one day she slips off to another town and runs away with a circus. It was two years before she comes back, all fixed up in fine clothes and rings and jewellery, to see Mike. He wouldn't have nothin' to do with her, so she stays around town, a while, anyway. I reckon the men folks wouldn't have raised no objections, but the women egged 'em on to order her to leave town. But she had plenty of spunk, and told 'em to mind their own business.

"So one night they decided to run her away. A crowd of men and women drove her out of her house, and chased her with sticks and stones. She run to her father's door, callin' for help. Mike opens it, and when he sees who it is he hits her with his fist and knocks her down and shuts the door.

"And then the crowd kept on chunkin' her till she run clear out of town. And the next day they finds her drowned dead in Hunter's mill pond. I mind it all now. That was thirty year ago."

I leaned back in my non-rotary revolving chair and nodded gently, like a mandarin, at my paste-pot.

"When old Mike has a spell," went on Uncle Abner, tepidly garrulous, "he thinks he's the Wanderin' Jew."

"He is," said I, nodding away.

And Uncle Abner cackled insinuatingly at the editor's remark, for he was expecting at least a "stickful" in the "Personal Notes" of the *Bugle*.

29

Transformation of Martin Burney

IN behalf of Sir Walter's soothing plant let us look into the case of Martin Burney.

They were constructing the Speedway along the west bank of the Harlem River. The grub-boat of Dennis Corrigan, sub-contractor, was moored to a tree on the bank. Twenty-two men belonging to the little green island toiled there at the sinew-cracking labour. One among them, who wrought in the kitchen of the grub-boat, was of the race of the Goths. Over them all stood the exorbitant Corrigan, harrying them like the captain of a galley crew. He paid them so little that most of the gang, work as they might, earned little more than food and tobacco; many of them were in debt to him. Corrigan boarded them all in the grub-boat, and gave them good grub, for he got it back in work.

Martin Burney was farthest behind of all. He was a little man, all muscles and hands and feet, with a grey-red, stubbly beard. He was too light for the work, which would have glutted the capacity of a steam shovel.

The work was hard. Besides that, the banks of the river were humming with mosquitoes. As a child in a dark room fixes his regard on the pale light of a comforting window, these toilers watched the sun that brought around the one hour of the day that tasted less bitter. After the sundown supper they would huddle together on the river bank, and send the mosquitoes whining and eddying back from the malignant puffs of twenty-three reeking pipes. Thus socially banded against the foe, they wrenched out of the hour a few well-smoked drops from the cup of joy.

Each week Burney grew deeper in debt. Corrigan kept a small stock of goods on the boat, which he sold to the men at prices that brought him no loss. Burney was a good customer at the tobacco counter. One sack when he went to work in the morning and one when he came in at night, so much was his account swelled daily. Burney was something of a smoker. Yet it was not true that he ate his meals with a pipe in his mouth, which had been said of him. The little man was not discontented. He had plenty to eat, plenty of tobacco, and a tyrant to curse; so why should not he, an Irishman, be well satisfied?

One morning as he was starting with the others for work he stopped at the pine counter for his usual sack of tobacco.

"There's no more for ye," said Corrigan. "Your account's closed. Ye are a losing investment. No, not even tobaccy, my son. No more tobaccy on account. If ye want to work on and eat, do so, but the smoke of ye has all ascended. 'Tis my advice that ye hunt a new job."

"I have no tobaccy to smoke in my pipe this day, Mr. Corrigan," said Burney, not quite understanding that such a thing could happen to him.

"Earn it," said Corrigan, "and then buy it."

Burney stayed on. He knew of no other job. At first he did not realize that tobacco had got to be his father and mother, his confessor and sweetheart, and wife and child.

For three days he managed to fill his pipe from the other men's sacks, and then they shut him off, one and all. They told him, rough but friendly, that of all things in the world tobacco must be quickest forthcoming to a fellow-man desiring it, but that beyond the immediate temporary need requisition upon the store of a comrade is pressed with great danger to friendship.

Then the blackness of the pit arose and filled the heart of Burney. Sucking the corpse of his deceased dudheen, he staggered through his duties with his barrowful of stones and dirt, feeling for the first time that the curse of Adam was upon him. Other men bereft of a pleasure might have recourse to other delights, but Burney had only two comforts in life. One was his pipe, the other was an ecstatic hope that there would be no Speedways to build on the other side of Jordan.

At meal times he would let the other men go first into the grub-boat, and then he would go down on his hands and knees, grovelling fiercely upon the ground where they had been sitting, trying to find some stray crumbs of tobacco. Once he sneaked down the river bank and filled his pipe with dead willow leaves. At the first whiff of the smoke he spat in the direction of the boat and put the finest curse he knew on Corrigan—one that began with the first Corrigans born on earth and ended with the Corrigans that shall hear the trumpet of Gabriel blow. He began to hate Corrigan with all his shaking nerves and soul. Even murder occurred to him in a vague sort of way. Five days he went without the taste of tobacco—he who had smoked all day and thought the night misspent in which he had not awakened for a pipeful or two under the bedclothes.

One day a man stopped at the boat to say that there was work to be had in the Bronx Park, where a large number of labourers were required in making some improvements.

After dinner Burney walked thirty yards down the river bank away from the maddening smell of the others' pipes. He sat down upon a stone. He was thinking he would set out for the Bronx. At least he could earn tobacco there. What if the books did say he owed Corrigan? Any man's work was worth his keep. But then he hated to go without getting even with the hard-hearted screw who had put his pipe out. Was there any way to do it?

Softly stepping among the clods came Tony, he of the race of Goths, who worked in the kitchen. He grinned at Burney's elbow, and that unhappy man, full of race animosity and holding urbanity in contempt, growled at him: "What d'ye want, ye—— Dago?"

Tony also contained a grievance—and a plot. He, too, was a Corrigan hater, and had been primed to see it in others.

"How you like-a Mr. Corrigan?" he asked. "You think-a him a nice-a man?"

"To hell with 'm," he said. "May his liver turn to water, and the bones of him crack in the cold of his heart. May dog fennel grow upon his ancestors' graves, and the grandsons of his children be born without eyes. May whisky turn to clabber in his mouth, and every time he sneezes may he blister the soles of his feet. And the smoke of his pipe—may it make his eyes water, and the drops fall on the grass that his cows eat and poison the butter that he spreads on his bread."

Though Tony remained a stranger to the beauties of this imagery, he gathered from it the conviction that it was sufficiently anti-Corrigan in its tendency. So, with the confidence of a fellow-conspirator, he sat by Burney upon the stone and unfolded his plot.

It was very simple in design. Every day after dinner it was Corrigan's habit to sleep for an hour in his bunk. At such times it was the duty of the cook and his helper, Tony, to leave the boat so that no noise might disturb the autocrat. The cook always spent this hour in walking exercise. Tony's plan was this: After Corrigan should be asleep he (Tony) and Burney would cut the mooring ropes that held the boat to the shore. Tony lacked the nerve to do the deed alone. Then the awkward boat would swing out into a swift current and surely overturn against a rock there was below.

"Come on and do it," said Burney. "If the back of ye aches from the lick he give ye as the pit of me stomach does for the taste of a bit of smoke, we can't cut the ropes too quick."

"All a-right," said Tony. "But better wait 'bout-a ten minute more. Give-a Corrigan plenty time get good-a sleep."

They waited, sitting upon the stone. The rest of the men were at work out of sight around a bend in the road. Everything would have gone well—except, perhaps, with Corrigan, had not Tony been moved to decorate the plot with its conventional accompaniment. He was of dramatic blood, and perhaps he intuitively divined the appendage to villainous machinations as prescribed by the stage. He pulled from his shirt bosom a long, black, beautiful, venomous cigar, and handed it to Burney.

"You like-a smoke while we wait?" he asked.

Burney clutched it and snapped off the end as a terrier bites at a rat. He laid it to his lips like a long-lost sweetheart. When the smoke began to draw, he gave a long, deep sigh, and the bristles of his grey-red moustache curled down over the cigar like the talons of an eagle. Slowly the red faded from the whites of his eyes. He fixed his gaze dreamily upon the hills across the river. The minutes came and went.

"'Bout time to go now," said Tony. "That damn-a Corrigan he be in the reever very quick."

Burney started out of his trance with a grunt. He turned his head and gazed with a surprised and pained severity at his accomplice. He took the cigar partly from his mouth, but sucked it back again immediately, chewed it lovingly once or twice, and spoke, in virulent puffs, from the corner of his mouth:

"What is it, ye yaller haythen? Would ye lay contrivances against the enlightened races of the earth, ye instigator of illegal crimes? Would ye seek to persuade Martin Burney into the dirty tricks of an indecent Dago? Would ye be for murderin' your benefactor, the good man that gives ye food and work? Take that, ye punkin-coloured assassin!"

The torrent of Burney's indignation carried with it bodily assault. The toe of his shoe sent the would-be cutter of ropes tumbling from his seat.

Tony arose and fled. His vendetta he again relegated to the files of things that might have been. Beyond the boat he fled and away-away; he was afraid to remain.

Burney, with expanded chest, watched his late co-plotter disappear. Then he, too, departed, setting his face in the direction of the Bronx.

In his wake was a rank and pernicious trail of noisome smoke that brought peace to his heart and drove the birds from the roadside into the deepest thickets.

30

The Guardian of the Accolade

NOT the least important of the force of the Weymouth Bank was Uncle Bushrod. Sixty years had Uncle Bushrod given of faithful service to the house of Weymouth as chattel, servitor, and friend. Of the colour of the mahogany bank furniture was Uncle Bushrod—thus dark was he externally; white as the uninked pages of the bank ledgers was his soul. Eminently pleasing to Uncle Bushrod would the comparison have been; for to him the only institution in existence worth considering was the Weymouth Bank, of which he was something between porter and generalissimo-in-charge.

Weymouthville lay, dreamy and umbrageous, among the low foothills along the brow of a Southern Valley. Three banks there were in Weymouthville. Two were hopeless, misguided enterprises, lacking the presence and prestige of a Weymouth to give them glory. The third was The Bank, managed by the Weymouths—and Uncle Bushrod. In the old Weymouth homestead—the red brick, white-porticoed mansion, the first to your right as you crossed Elder Creek, coming into town—lived Mr. Robert Weymouth (the president of the bank), his widowed daughter, Mrs. Vesey—called "Miss Letty" by every one—and her two children, Nan and Guy. There, also, in a cottage on the grounds resided Uncle Bushrod and Aunt Malindy, his wife. Mr. William Weymouth (the cashier of the bank) lived in a modern, fine house on the principal avenue.

Mr. Robert was a large, stout man, sixty-two years of age, with a smooth plump face, long iron-grey hair and fiery blue eyes. He was hightempered, kind, and generous, with a youthful smile and a formidable, stern voice that did not always mean what it sounded like. Mr. William was a milder man, correct in deportment and absorbed in business. The

Weymouths formed The Family of Weymouthville, and were looked up to, as was their right of heritage.

Uncle Bushrod was the bank's trusted porter, messenger, vassal and guardian. He carried a key to the vault, just as Mr. Robert and Mr. William did. Sometimes there was ten, fifteen, or twenty thousand dollars in sacked silver stacked on the vault floor. It was safe with Uncle Bushrod. He was a Weymouth in heart, honesty and pride.

Of late Uncle Bushrod had not been without worry. It was on account of Marse Robert. For nearly a year Mr. Robert had been known to indulge in too much drink. Not enough, understand, to become tipsy, but the habit was getting a hold upon him, and every one was beginning to notice it. Half a dozen times a day he would leave the bank and step around to the Merchants and Planters' Hotel to take a drink. Mr. Robert's usual keen judgment and business capacity became a little impaired. Mr. William, a Weymouth, but not so rich in experience, tried to dam the inevitable backflow of the tide, but with incomplete success. The deposits in the Weymouth Bank dropped from six figures to five. Past-due paper began to accumulate, owing to injudicious loans. No one cared to address Mr. Robert on the subject of temperance. Many of his friends said that the cause of it had been the death of his wife some two years before. Others hesitated on account of Mr. Robert's quick temper, which was extremely apt to resent personal interference of such a nature. Miss Letty and the children noticed the change and grieved about it. Uncle Bushrod also worried, but he was one of those who would not have dared to remonstrate, although he and Marse Robert had been raised almost as companions. But there was a heavier shock coming to Uncle Bushrod than that caused by the bank president's toddies and juleps.

Mr. Robert had a passion for fishing, which he usually indulged whenever the season and business permitted. One day, when reports had been coming in relating to the bass and perch, he announced his intention of making a two or three days' visit to the lakes. He was going down, he said, to Reedy Lake with Judge Archinard, an old friend.

Now, Uncle Bushrod was treasurer of the Sons and

Daughters of the Burning Bush. Every association he belonged to made him treasurer without hesitation. He stood AA1 in coloured circles. He was understood among them to be Mr. Bushrod Weymouth, of the Weymouth Bank.

The night following the day on which Mr. Robert mentioned his intended fishing-trip the old man woke up and rose from his bed at twelve o'clock, declaring he must go down to the bank and fetch the pass-book of the Sons and Daughters, which he had forgotten to bring home. The bookkeeper had balanced it for him that day, put the cancelled cheques in it, and snapped two elastic bands around it. He put but one band around other pass-books.

Aunt Malindy objected to the mission at so late an hour, denouncing it as foolish and unnecessary, but Uncle Bushrod was not to be deflected from a duty.

"I done told Sister Adaline Hoskins," he said, "to come by here for dat book to-morrer mawnin' at sebin o'clock, for to kyar' it to de meetin' of de bo'd of 'rangements, and dat book gwine to be here when she come."

So Uncle Bushrod put on his old brown suit, got his thick hickory stick, and meandered through the almost deserted streets of Weymouthville. He entered the bank, unlocking the side door, and found the pass-book where he had left it, in the little back room used for private consultations, where he always hung his coat. Looking about casually, he saw that everything was as he had left it, and was about to start for home when he was brought to a standstill by the sudden rattle of a key in the front door. Someone came quickly in, closed the door softly, and entered the counting-room through the door in the iron railing.

That division of the bank's space was connected with the back room by a narrow passage-way, now in deep darkness.

Uncle Bushrod, firmly gripping his hickory stick, tip-toed gently up this passage until he could see the midnight intruder into the sacred precincts of the Weymouth Bank. One dim gas-jet burned there, but even in its nebulous light he perceived at once that the prowler was the bank's president.

Wondering, fearful, undecided what to do, the old coloured

man stood motionless in the gloomy strip of hall-way, and waited developments.

The vault, with its big iron door, was opposite him. Inside that was the safe, holding the papers of value, the gold and currency of the bank. On the floor of the vault was, perhaps, eighteen thousand dollars in silver.

The president took his key from his pocket, opened the vault and went inside, nearly closing the door behind him. Uncle Bushrod saw, through the narrow aperture, the flicker of a candle. In a minute or two—it seemed an hour to the watcher—Mr. Robert came out, bringing with him a large hand-satchel, as if fearful that he might be observed. With one hand he closed and locked the vault door.

With a reluctant theory forming itself beneath his wool, Uncle Bushrod waited and watched, shaking in his concealing shadow.

Mr. Robert set the satchel softly upon a desk, and turned his coat collar up about his neck and ears. He was dressed in a rough suit of grey, as if for travelling. He glanced with frowning intentness at the big office clock above the burning gas-jet, and then looked lingeringly about the bank—lingeringly and fondly, Uncle Bushrod thought, as one who bids farewell to dear and familiar scenes.

Now he caught up his burden again and moved promptly and softly out of the bank by the way he had come, locking the front door behind him.

For a minute or longer Uncle Bushrod was as stone in his tracks. Had that midnight rifler of safes and vaults been any other on earth than the man he was, the old retainer would have rushed upon him and struck to save the Weymouth property. But now the watcher's soul was tortured by the poignant dread of something worse than mere robbery. He was seized by an accusing terror that said the Weymouth name and the Weymouth honour were about to be lost. Marse Robert robbing the bank! What else could it mean? The hour of the night, the stealthy visit to the vault, the satchel brought forth full and with expedition and silence, the prowler's rough dress, his solicitous reading of the clock, and noiseless departure—what else could it mean?

And then to the turmoil of Uncle Bushrod's thoughts came the corroborating recollection of preceding events—Mr. Robert's increasing intemperance and consequent many moods of royal high spirits and stern tempers; the casual talk he had heard in the bank of the decrease in business and difficulty in collecting loans. What else could it all mean but that Mr. Robert Weymouth was an absconder—was about to fly with the bank's remaining funds, leaving Mr. William, Miss Letty, little Nan, Guy and Uncle Bushrod to bear the disgrace?

During one minute Uncle Bushrod considered these things, and then he awoke to sudden determination and action.

"Lawd! Lawd!" he moaned aloud, as he hobbled hastily toward the side door. "Sech a come-off after all dese here years of big doin's an fine doin's. Scan'lous sights upon de yearth when de Weymouth fambly done turn out robbers and 'bezzlers! Time for Uncle Bushrod to clean out somebody's chicken-coop and eben matters up. Oh, Lawd! Marse Robert you ain't gwine do dat. 'N Miss Letty an' dem chillun so proud and talkin' 'Weymouth, Weymouth', all de time! I'm gwine to stop you ef I can. 'Spec you shoot Mr. Nigger's head off he fool wid you, but I'm gwine stop you ef I can."

Uncle Bushrod, aided by his hickory stick, impeded by his rheumatism, hurried down the street toward the railroad station, where the two lines touching Weymouthville met. As he had expected and feared, he saw there Mr. Robert, standing in the shadow of the building, waiting for the train. He held the satchel in his hand.

When Uncle Bushrod came within twenty yards of the bank president, standing like a huge, grey ghost by the station wall, sudden perturbation seized him. The rashness and audacity of the thing he had come to do struck him fully. He would have been happy could he have turned and fled from the possibilities of the famous Weymouth wrath. But again he saw, in his fancy, the white, reproachful face of Miss Letty, and the distressed looks of Nan and Guy, should he fail in his duty and they question him as to his stewardship.

Braced by the thought, he approached in a straight line, clearing his throat and pounding with his stick so that he might be early recognized. Thus he might avoid the likely danger of too suddenly surprising the sometimes hasty Mr. Robert.

"Is that you, Bushrod?" called the clamant, clear voice of the grey ghost.

"Yes, suh, Marse Robert."

"What the devil are you doing out at this time of night?"

For the first time in his life, Uncle Bushrod told Marse Robert a falsehood. He could not repress it. He would have to circumlocute a little. His nerve was not equal to a direct attack.

"I done been down, suh, to see ol' Aunt M'ria Patterson. She taken sick in de night, and I kyar'ed her a bottle of M'lindy's medercine. Yes, suh."

"Humph!" said Robert. "You better get home out of the night air. It's damp. You'll hardly be worth killing to-morrow on account of your rheumatism. Think it'll be a clear day, Bushrod?"

"I 'low it will, suh. De sun sot red las' night."

Mr. Robert lit a cigar in the shadow, and the smoke looked like his grey ghost expanding and escaping into the night air. Somehow, Uncle Bushrod could barely force his reluctant tongue to the dreadful subject. He stood, awkward, shambling, with his feet upon the gravel and fumbling with his stick. But then, afar off—three miles away, at the Jimtown switch—he heard the faint whistle of the coming train, the one that was to transport the Weymouth name into the regions of dishonour and shame. All fear left him. He took off his hat and faced the chief of the clan he served, the great, royal, kind, lofty, terrible Weymouth—he bearded him there at the brink of the awful thing that was about to happen.

"Marse Robert," he began, his voice quavering a little with the stress of his feelings, "you 'member de day dey all rode de tunnament at Oak Lawn? De day, suh, dat you win in de ridin', and you crown Miss Lucy de queen?"

"Tournament?" said Mr. Robert, taking his cigar from his mouth. "Yes, I remember very well the——but what the deuce are you talking about tournaments here at midnight for? Go 'long home, Bushrod. I believe you're sleep-walking."

"Miss Lucy tetch you on de shoulder," continued the old man, never heeding, "wid a s'ord, and say: 'I mek you a knight, Suh Robert—rise up, pure and fearless and widout reproach.' Dat what Miss Lucy say. Dat's been a long time ago, but me nor you ain't forgot it. And den dar's another time we ain't forgot—de time when Miss Lucy lay on her las' bed. She sent for Uncle Bushrod, and she say: 'Uncle Bushrod, when I die, I want you to take good care of Mr. Robert. Seem like'—so Miss Lucy say—'he listen to you mo' dan to anybody else. He apt to be mighty fractious sometimes, and maybe he cuss you when you try to 'suade him, but he need somebody what understand him to be 'round wid him. He am like a little child sometimes'—so Miss Lucy say, wid her eyes shinin' in her po', thin face—'but he always been—'dem was her words—'my knight, pure and fearless and widout reproach.'"

Mr. Robert began to mask, as was his habit, a tendency to soft-heartedness with a spurious anger.

"You—you old windbag!" he growled, through a cloud of swirling cigar smoke. "I believe you are crazy. I told you to go home, Bushrod. Miss Lucy said that, did she? Well, we haven't kept the scutcheon very clear. Two years ago last week, wasn't it, Bushrod, when she died? Confound it! Are you going to stand there all night gabbing like a coffee-coloured gander?"

The train whistled again. Now it was at the water tank, a mile away.

"Marse Robert," said Uncle Bushrod, laying his hand on the satchel that the banker held, "for Gawd's sake, don' take dis wid you. I knows what's in it. I knows where you got it in de bank. Don' kyar' it wid you. Dey's big trouble in dat valise for Miss Lucy and Miss Lucy's child's chillun. Hit's bound to destroy de name of Weymouth and bow down dem dat own it wid shame and triberlation. Marse Robert, you can kill dis ole nigger ef you will, but don't take away dis 'er' valise. If I ever crosses over the Jordan, what I gwine to say to Miss

Lucy when she ax me: Uncle Bushrod, wharfo' didn' you take good care of Mr. Robert?"

Mr. Robert Weymouth threw away his cigar and shook free one arm with that peculiar gesture that always preceded his outbursts of irascibility. Uncle Bushrod bowed his head to the expected storm, but he did not flinch. If the house of Weymouth was to fall, he would fall with it. The banker spoke, and Uncle Bushrod blinked with surprise. The storm was there, but it was suppressed to the quietness of a summer breeze.

"Bushrod," said Mr. Robert, in a lower voice than he usually employed, "you have overstepped all bounds. You have presumed upon the leniency with which you have been treated to meddle unpardonably. So you know what is in this satchel! Your long and faithful service is some excuse, but—go home, Bushrod—not another word!"

But Bushrod grasped the satchel with a firmer hand. The headlights of the train was now lightening the shadows about the station. The roar was increasing, and folks were stirring about at the track side.

"Marse Robert, gimme dis 'er' valise. I got a right, suh, to talk to you dis 'er' way. I slaved for you and 'tended to you from a child up. I went th'ough de war as yo' body-servant tell we whipped de Yankees and sent 'em back to de No'th. I was at yo' weddin', and I wasn' fur away when yo' Miss Letty was bawn. And Miss Letty's chillun, dey watches to-day for Uncle Bushrod when he come home ever' evenin'. I been a Weymouth, all 'cept in colour and entitlements. Both of us is old, Marse Robert. 'Tain't goin' to be long tell we gwine to see Miss Lucy and has to give an account of our doin's. De ole nigger man won't be 'spected to say much mo' dan he done all he could by de fambly dat owned him. But de Weymouths, dey must say dey been livin' pure and fearless and widout reproach. Gimme dis valise, Marse Robert—I'm gwine to hab it. I'm gwine to take it back to de bank and lock it up in de vault. I'm gwine to do Miss Lucy's biddin'. Turn 'er loose, Marse Robert."

The train was standing at the station. Some men were pushing trucks along the side. Two or three sleepy passengers got off and wandered away into the night. The conductor stepped to the gravel, swung his lantern and called: "Hello, Frank!" at someone invisible. The bell clanged, the brakes hissed, the conductor drawled, "All aboard!"

Mr. Robert released his hold on the satchel. Uncle Bushrod hugged it to his breast with both arms, as a lover clasps his first beloved.

"Take it back with you, Bushrod," said Mr. Robert, thrusting his hands into his pockets. "And let the subject drop—now mind! You've said quite enough. I'm going to take this train. Tell Mr. William I will be back on Saturday. Good night."

The banker climbed the steps of the moving train and disappeared in a coach. Uncle Bushrod stood motionless, still embracing the precious satchel. His eyes were closed and his lips were moving in thanks to the Master above for the salvation of the Weymouth honour. He knew Mr. Robert would return when he said he would. The Weymouths never lied. Nor now, thank the Lord! could it be said that they embezzled the money in banks.

Then, awake to the necessity for further guardianship of Weymouth trust funds, the old man started for the bank with the redeemed satchel.

* * *

Three hours from Weymouthville, in the grey dawn, Mr. Robert alighted from the train at a lonely flag-station. Dimly he could see the figure of a man waiting on the platform, and the shape of a spring-waggon, team and driver. Half a dozen lengthy fishing-poles projected from the waggon's rear.

"You're here, Bob," said Judge Archinard, Mr. Robert's old friend and schoolmate. "It's going to be a royal day for fishing. I thought you said—why, didn't you bring along the stuff?"

The president of the Weymouth Bank took off his hat and rumpled his grey locks.

"Well, Ben, to tell you the truth, there's an infernally presumptuous old nigger belonging in my family that broke up the arrangement. He came down the depot and vetoed the whole proceeding. He means all right, and—well, I reckon he *is* right. Somehow, he had found out what I had along—though I hid it in the bank vault and sneaked it out at midnight. I reckon he has noticed that I've been indulging a little more than a gentleman should, and he laid for me with some reaching arguments.

"I'm going to quit drinking," Mr. Robert concluded. "I've come to the conclusion that a man can't keep it up and be quite what he'd like to be—'pure and fearless and without reproach'—that's the way old Bushrod quoted it."

"Well, I'll have to admit," said the judge, thoughtfully, as they climbed into the waggon, "that the old darky's argument can't conscientiously be overruled."

"Still," said Mr. Robert, with a ghost of a sigh, "there was two quarts of the finest old silk-velvet Bourbon in that satchel you ever wet your lips with."

31

One Thousand Dollars

"ONE thousand dollars," repeated Lawyer Tolman solemnly and severely, "and here is the money."

Young Gillian gave a decidedly amused laugh as he fingered the thin package of new fifty-dollar notes.

"It's such a confoundedly awkward amount," he explained genially, to the lawyer. "If it had been ten thousand a fellow might wind up with a lot of fireworks and do himself credit. Even fifty dollars would have been less trouble."

"You heard the reading of your uncle's will," continued Lawyer Tolman, professionally dry in his tones. "I do not know if you paid much attention to its details. I must remind you of one. You are required to render to us an account of the manner of expenditure of this $1,000 as soon as you have disposed of it. The will stipulates that. I trust that you will so far comply with the late Mr. Gillian's wishes."

"You may depend upon it," said the young man politely, "in spite of the extra expense it will entail. I may have to engage a secretary. I was never good at accounts."

Gillian went to his club. There he hunted out one whom he called Old Bryson.

Old Bryson was calm and forty and sequestered. He was in a corner reading a book, and when he saw Gillian approaching he sighed, laid down his book and took off his glasses.

"Old Bryson, wake up," said Gillian. "I've a funny story to tell you."

"I wish you would tell it to someone in the billiard-room," said Old Bryson. "You know how I hate your stories."

"This is a better one than usual," said Gillian, rolling a cigarette, "and I'm glad to tell it to you. It's too sad and funny to go with the rattling of billiard balls. I've just come from my late uncle's firm of legal corsairs. He leaves me an even thousand dollars. Now, what can a man possibly do with a thousand dollars?"

"I thought," said Old Bryson, showing as much interest as a bee shows in a vinegar cruet, "that the late Septimus Gillian was worth something like half a million."

"He was," assented Gillian joyously, "and that's where the joke comes in. He's left his whole cargo of doubloons to a microbe. That is, part of it goes to the man who invents a new bacillus, and the rest to establish a hospital for doing away with it again. There are one or two trifling bequests on the side. The butler and the housekeeper get a seal and $10 each. His nephew gets $1,000."

"You've always had plenty of money to spend," observed Old Bryson.

"Tons," said Gillian. "Uncle was the fairy godmother as far as an allowance was concerned."

"Any other heirs?" asked Old Bryson.

"None." Gillian frowned at his cigarette and kicked the upholstered leather of a divan uneasily. "There is a Miss Hayden, a ward of my uncle, who lived in his house. She's a quiet thing—musical—the daughter of somebody who was unlucky enough to be his friend. I forgot to say that she was in on the seal ring and $10 joke, too. I wish I had been. Then I could have had two bottles of brut, tipped the waiter with the ring, and had the whole business off my hands. Don't be superior and insulting, Old Bryson—tell me what a fellow can do with a thousand dollars."

Old Bryson rubbed his glasses and smiled. And when Old Bryson smiled, Gillian knew that he intended to be more offensive than ever.

"A thousand dollars," he said, "means much or little. One man may buy a happy home with it and laugh at Rockefeller. Another could send his wife South with it and save her life. A thousand dollars would buy pure milk for one hundred babies during June, July, and August, and save fifty of their lives. You could count upon a half-hour's diverversion with it at faro in one of the fortified art galleries. It would furnish an education to an ambitious boy. I am told that a genuine Corot was secured for that amount in an auction room yesterday. You could move to a New Hampshire town and live respectably two years on it. You could rent Madison Square Garden for one evening with it, and lecture your audience, if you should have one, on the precariousness of the profession of heir-presumptive."

"People might like you, Old Bryson," said Gillian, always unruffled, "if you wouldn't moralize. I asked you to tell me what I could do with a thousand dollars."

"You?" said Bryson, with a gentle laugh. "Why, Bobby Gillian, there's only one logical thing you could do. You can go buy Miss Lotta Lauriere a diamond pendant with the money, and then take yourself off to Idaho and inflict your presence upon a ranch. I advise a sheep ranch, as I have a particular dislike for sheep."

"Thanks," said Gillian, rising, "I thought I could depend upon you, Old Bryson. You've hit on the very scheme. I wanted to chuck the money in a lump, for I've got to turn in an account for it, and I hate itemizing."

Gillian phoned for a cab and said to the driver:

"The stage entrance of the Columbine Theatre."

Miss Lotta Lauriere was assisting Nature with a powder puff, almost ready for her call at a crowded matinée, when her dresser mentioned the name of Mr. Gillian.

"Let it in," said Miss Lauriere. "Now, what is it, Bobby? I'm going on in two minutes."

"Rabbit-foot your right ear a little," suggested Gillian critically. "That's better. It won't take two minutes for me. What do you say to a little thing in the pendant line? I can stand three ciphers with a figure one in front of 'em."

"Oh, just as you say," carolled Miss Lauriere. "My right glove, Adams. Say, Bobby, did you see that necklace Della Stacey had on the other night? Twenty-two hundred dollars it cost at Tiffany's. But of course—pull my sash a little to the left, Adams."

"Miss Lauriere for the opening chorus!" cried the call-boy without.

Gillian strolled out to where his cab was waiting.

"What would you do with a thousand dollars if you had it?" he asked the driver.

"Open a s'loon," said the cabby promptly and huskily. "I know a place I could take money in with both hands. It's a four-storey brick on a corner. I've got it figured out. Second storey—Chinks and chop suey; third floor—manicures and foreign missions; fourth floor—poolroom. If you was thinking of putting up the cap——"

"Oh, no," said Gillian, "I merely asked from curiosity. I take you by the hour. Drive till I tell you to stop."

Eight blocks down Broadway Gillian poked up the trap with his cane and got out. A blind man sat upon a stool on the sidewalk selling pencils. Gillian went out and stood before him.

"Excuse me," he said, "but would you mind telling me what you would do if you had a thousand dollars?"

"You got out of that cab that just drove up, didn't you?" asked the blind man.

"I did," said Gillian.

"I guess you are all right," said the pencil dealer, "to ride in a cab by daylight. Take a look at that, if you like."

He drew a small book from his coat-pocket and held it out. Gillian opened it, and saw that it was a bank deposit book. It showed a balance of $1,785 to the blind man's credit.

Gillian returned the book and got into the cab.

"I forgot something," he said. "You may drive to the law offices of Tolman & Sharp, at —— Broadway."

Lawyer Tolman looked at him hostilely and inquiringly through his gold-rimmed glasses.

"I beg your pardon," said Gillian cheerfully, "but may I ask you a question? It is not an impertinent one, I hope. Was Miss Hayden left anything by my uncle's will besides the ring and the $10?"

"Nothing," said Mr. Tolman.

"I thank you very much, sir," said Gillian, and out he went to his cab. He gave the driver the address of his late uncle's home.

Miss Hayden was writing letters in the library. She was small and slender and clothed in black. But you would have noticed her eyes. Gillian drifted in with his air of regarding the world as inconsequent.

"I've just come from old Tolman's," he explained. "They've been going over the papers down there. They found a"—Gillian searched his memory for a legal term—"they found an amendment or a postscript or something to the will. It seemed that the old boy loosened up a little on second thoughts and willed you a thousand dollars. I was driving up this way, and Tolman asked me to bring you the money. Here it is. You'd better count it to see if it's right." Gillian laid the money beside her hand on the desk.

Miss Hayden turned white. "Oh!" she said, and again "Oh!"

Gillian half turned and looked out the window.

"I suppose, of course," he said, in a low voice, "that you know I love you."

"I am sorry," said Miss Hayden, taking up her money.

"There is no use?" asked Gillian, almost lightheartedly.

"I am sorry," she said again.

"May I write a note?" asked Gillian, with a smile. He seated himself at the big library table. She supplied him with paper and pen, and then went back to her secretaire.

Gillian made out his account of his expenditure of the thousand dollars in these words:

"Paid by the black sheep, Robert Gillian, $1,000 on account of the eternal happiness, owed by Heaven to the best and dearest woman on earth."

Gillian slipped his writing into an envelope, bowed, and went his way.

His cab stopped again at the offices of Tolman & Sharp.

"I have expended the thousand dollars," he said, cheerily, to Tolman of the gold glasses, "and I have come to render account of it as I agreed. There is quite a feeling of summer in the air—do you not think so, Mr. Tolman?" He tossed a white envelope on the lawyer's table. "You will find there a memorandum, sir, of the *modus operandi* of the vanishing of the dollars."

Without touching the envelope, Mr. Tolman went to a door and called his partner, Sharp. Together they explored the caverns of an immense safe. Forth they dragged as trophy of their search a big envelope sealed with wax. This they forcibly invaded, and wagged their venerable heads together over its contents. Then Tolman became spokesman.

"Mr. Gillian," he said formally, "there was a codicil to your uncle's will. It was intrusted to us privately, with instructions that it be not opened until you had furnished us with a full account of your handling of the $1,000 bequest in the will. As you have fulfilled the conditions, my partner and I have read the codicil. I do not wish to encumber your understanding with its legal phraseology, but I will acquaint you with the spirit of its contents.

"In the event that your disposition of the $1,000 demonstrates that you possess any of the qualifications that deserve reward, much benefit will accrue to you. Mr. Sharp and I are named as the judges, and I assure you that we will do our duty strictly according to justice—with liberality. We are not at all unfavourably disposed toward you, Mr. Gillian. But let us return to the letter of the codicil. If your disposal of the money in question has been prudent, wise, or unselfish, it is in our power to hand you over bonds to the value of $50,000, which have been placed in our hands for that purpose. But if —as our client, the late Mr. Gillian, explicitly provides—you have used this money as you have used money in the past—I quote the late Mr. Gillian—in reprehensible dissipation among disreputable associates—the $50,000 is to be paid to Miriam Hayden, ward of the late Mr. Gillian, without delay. Now, Mr. Gillian, Mr. Sharp and I will examine your account in regard to the $1,000. You submit it in writing, I believe. I hope you will repose confidence in our decision."

Mr. Tolman reached for the envelope. Gillian was a little the quicker in taking it up. He tore the account and its cover leisurely into strips and dropped them into his pocket.

"It's all right," he said smilingly. "There isn't a bit of need to bother you with this. I don't suppose you'd understand these itemized bets, anyway. I lost the thousand dollars on the races. Good day to you, gentlemen."

Tolman & Sharp shook their heads mournfully at each other when Gillian left, for they heard him whistling gaily in the hallway as he waited for the elevator.

32

The Memento

MISS LYNETTE D'ARMANDE turned her back on Broadway. This was but tit for tat, because Broadway had often done the same thing to Miss D'Armande. Still, the "tats" seemed to have it, for the ex-leading lady of the "Reaping the Whirlwind" Company had everything to ask of Broadway, while there was no vice versa.

So Miss Lynette D'Armande turned the back of her chair to her window that overlooked Broadway, and sat down to stitch in time the lisle-thread heel of a black silk stocking. The tumult and glitter of the roaring Broadway beneath her window had no charm for her; what she greatly desired was the stifling air of a dressing-room on that fairyland street and the roar of an audience gathered in that capricious quarter. In the meantime, those stockings must not be neglected. Silk does wear out so, but—after all, isn't it just the only goods there is?

The Hotel Thalia looks on Broadway as Marathon looks on the sea. It stands like a gloomy cliff above the whirlpool where the tides of two great thoroughfares clash. Here the player-bands gather at the end of their wanderings, to loosen the buskin and dust the sock. Thick in the streets around it are booking-offices, theatres, agents, schools, and the lobster-palaces to which those thorny paths lead.

Wandering through the eccentric halls of the dim and fusty Thalia, you seem to have found yourself in some great ark or caravan about to sail, or fly, or roll away on wheels. About the house lingers a sense of unrest, of expectation, of transientness, even of anxiety and apprehension. The halls are a labyrinth. Without a guide you wander like a lost soul in a Sam Loyd puzzle.

Turning any corner, a dressing-sack or a *cul-de-sac* may

bring you up short. You meet alarming tragedians stalking in bath-robes in search of rumoured bath-rooms. From hundreds of rooms come the buzz of talk, scraps of new and old songs, and the ready laughter of the convened players.

Summer has come; their companies have disbanded, and they take their rest in their favourite caravansary, while they besiege the managers for engagements for the coming season.

At this hour of the afternoon the day's work of tramping the rounds of the agents' offices is over. Past you, as you ramble distractedly through the mossy halls, flit audible visions of houris, with veiled, starry eyes, flying tag-ends of things, and a swish of silk, bequeathing to the dull hallways an odour of gaiety and a memory of *frangipanni*. Serious young comedians, with versatile Adam's apples, gather in doorways and talk of Booth. Far-reaching from somewhere comes the smell of ham and red cabbage, and the crash of dishes on the American plan.

The indeterminate hum of life in the Thalia is enlivened by the discreet popping—at reasonable and salubrious intervals—of beer-bottle corks. Thus punctuated, life in the genial hostel scans easily—the comma being the favourite mark, semicolons frowned upon, and periods barred.

Miss D'Armande's room was a small one. There was room for her rocker between the dresser and the wash-stand if it were placed longitudinally. On the dresser were its usual accoutrements, plus the ex-leading lady's collected souvenirs of road engagements and photographs of her dearest and best professional friends.

At one of these photographs she looked twice or thrice as she darned, and smiled friendlily.

"I'd like to know where Lee is just this minute," she said, half-aloud.

If you had been privileged to view the photograph thus flattered, you would have thought at the first glance that you saw the picture of a many-petalled, white flower, blown through the air by a storm. But the floral kingdom was not responsible for that swirl of petalous whiteness.

You saw the filmy, brief skirt of Miss Rosalie Ray as she made a complete heels-over-head turn in her wistaria-entwined swing, far out from the stage, high above the heads of the audience. You saw the camera's inadequate representation of the graceful, strong kick, with which she, at this exciting moment, sent flying, high and far, the yellow silk garter that each evening spun from her agile limb and descended upon the delighted audience below.

You saw, too, amid the black-clothed, mainly masculine patrons of select vaudeville a hundred hands raised with the hope of staying the flight of the brilliant aerial token.

Forty weeks of the best circuits this act had brought Miss Rosalie Ray for each of two years. She did other things during her twelve minutes—a song and dance, imitations of two or three actors who are but imitations of themselves, and a balancing feat with a step-ladder and feather-duster; but when the blossom-decked swing was let down from the flies, and Miss Rosalie sprang smiling into the seat, with the golden circlet conspicuous in the place whence it was soon to slide and become a soaring and coveted guerdon—then it was that the audience rose in its seat as a single man—or presumably so—and endorsed the speciality that made Miss Ray's name a favourite in the booking-offices.

At the end of the two years Miss Ray suddenly announced to her dear friend, Miss D'Armande, that she was going to spend the summer at an antediluvian village on the north shore of Long Island, and that the stage would see her no more.

Seventeen minutes after Miss Lynnette D'Armande had expressed her wish to know the whereabouts of her old chum, there were sharp raps at her door.

Doubt not that it was Rosalie Ray. At the shrill command to enter she did so, with something of a tired flutter, and dropped a heavy handbag on the floor. Upon my word, it was Rosalie, in a loose, travel-stained automobileless coat, closely tied brown veil with yard-long flying ends, grey walking-suit and tan Oxfords with lavender over-gaiters.

When she threw off her veil and hat, you saw a pretty enough face, now flushed and disturbed by some unusual emotion, and restless, large eyes with discontent marring their brightness. A heavy pile of dull auburn hair, hastily put up, was escaping in crinkling waving strands and curling small locks from the confining combs and pins.

The meeting of the two was not marked by the effusion vocal, gymnastical, osculatory, and catechetical that distinguishes the greetings of their unprofessional sisters in society. There was a brief clinch, two simultaneous labial dabs, and they stood on the same footing of the old days. Very much like the short salutations of soldiers or of travellers in foreign wilds are the welcomes between the strollers at the corners of their criss-cross roads.

"I've got the hall-room two flights up above yours," said Rosalie, "but I came straight to see you before going up. I didn't know you were here till they told me."

"I've been in since the last of April," said Lynnette. "And I'm going on the road with a 'Fatal Inheritance' Company. We open next week in Elizabath. I thought you'd quit the stage, Lee. Tell me about yourself."

Rosalie settled herself with a skilful wriggle on the top of Miss D'Armande's wardrobe trunk, and leaned her head against the papered wall. From long habit, thus can peripatetic leading ladies and their sisters make themselves as comfortable as though the deepest arm-chairs embraced them.

"I'm going to tell you, Lynn," she said, with a strangely sardonic and yet carelessly resigned look on her youthful face. "And then to-morrow I'll strike the old Broadway trail again, and wear some more paint off the chairs in the agents' offices. If anybody had told me any time in the last three months up to four o'clock this afternoon that I'd ever listen to that 'Leave-your-name-and-address' rot of the booking bunch again, I'd have given 'em the real Mrs. Fiske laugh. Loan me a handkerchief, Lynn. Gee! but those Long Island trains are fierce. I've got enough soft coal cinders on my face to go on and play *Topsy* without using the cork. And, speaking of corks—got anything to drink, Lynn?"

Miss D'Armande opened a door of the washstand and took out a bottle.

"There's nearly a pint of Manhattan. There's a cluster of carnations in the drinking-glass, but——"

"Oh, pass the bottle. Save the glass for company. Thanks! That hits the spot. The same to you. My first drink in three months!"

"Yes, Lynn, I quit the stage at the end of last season. I quit it because I was sick of the life. And especially because my heart and soul were sick of men—of the kind of men we stage people have to be up against. You know what the game is to us—it's a fight against 'em all the way down the line, from the manager who wants us to try his new motor-car to the bill-posters who want to call us by our front names.

"And the men we have to meet after the show are the worst of all. The stage-door kind, and the manager's friends who take us to supper, and show their diamonds, and talk about seeing 'Dan' and 'Dave' and 'Charlie' for us. They're beasts, and I hate 'em.

"I tell you, Lynn, it's the girls like us on the stage that ought to be pitied. It's girls from good homes that are honestly ambitious and work hard to rise in the profession, but never do get there. You hear a lot of sympathy sloshed around on chorus girls and their fifteen dollars a week. Piffle! There ain't a sorrow in the chorus that a lobster cannot heal.

"If there's any tears to shed, let 'em fall for the actress that gets a salary of from thirty to forty-five dollars a week for taking a leading part in a bum show. She knows she'll never do any better; but she hangs on for years, hoping for the 'chance' that never comes.

"And the fool plays we have to work in! Having another girl roll you around the stage by the hind legs in a 'Wheel-barrow Chorus' in a musical comedy is dignified drama compared with the idiotic things I've had to do in the thirty-centers.

"But what I hated most was the men—the men leering and blathering at you across tables, trying to buy you with Würzburger or Extra Dry, according to their estimate of your price. And the men in the audiences, clapping, yelling, snarling, crowding, writhing, gloating—like a lot of wild beasts, with their eyes fixed on you, ready to eat you up if you come in reach of their claws. Oh, how I hate 'em!

"Well, I'm not telling you much about myself, am I, Lynn?

"I had two hundred dollars saved up, and I cut the stage the first of the summer. I went over on Long Island, and found the sweetest little village that ever was, called Soundport, right on the water. I was going to spend the summer there, and study up on elocution, and try to get a class in the fall. There was an old widow lady with a cottage near the beach who sometimes rented a room or two just for company, and she took me in. She had another boarder, too—the Reverend Arthur Lyle.

"Yes, he was the head-liner. You're on, Lynn. I'll tell you all of it in a minute. It's only a one-act play.

"The first time he walked on, Lynn, I felt myself going; the first lines he spoke, he had me. He was different from the men in audiences. He was tall and slim, and you never heard him come in the room, but you *felt* him. He had a face like a picture of a knight—like one of that Round Table bunch—and a voice like a 'cello solo. And his manners!

"Lynn, if you'd take John Drew in his best drawing-room scene and compare the two you'd have John arrested for disturbing the peace.

"I'll spare you the particulars; but in less than a month Arthur and I were engaged. He preached at a little one-night stand of a Methodist church. There was to be a parsonage the size of a lunchwagon, and hens and honeysuckles when we were married. Arthur used to preach to me a good deal about Heaven, but he never could get my mind quite off those honeysuckles and hens.

"No; I didn't tell him I'd been on the stage. I hated the business and all that went with it; I'd cut it out for ever, and I didn't see any use of stirring things up. I was a good girl, and I didn't have anything to confess, except being an elocutionist, and that was about all the strain my conscience would stand.

"Oh, I tell you, Lynn, I was happy. I sang in the choir and attended the sewing society, and recited that 'Annie Laurie' thing with the whistling stunt in it, 'in a manner bordering upon the professional', as the weekly village paper reported it.

And Arthur and I went rowing, and walking in the woods, and clamming, and that poky little village seemed to me the best place in the world. I'd have been happy to live there always, too, if——

"But one morning old Mrs. Gurley, the widow lady, got gossipy while I was helping her string beans on the back porch, and began to gush information, as folks who rent out their rooms usually do. Mr. Lyle was her idea of a saint on earth—as he was mine, too. She went over all his virtues and graces, and wound up by telling me that Arthur had had an extremely romantic love-affair, not long before, that had ended unhappily. She didn't seem to be on to the details, but she knew that he had been hit pretty hard. He was paler and thinner, she said, and he had some kind of a remembrance or keepsake of the lady in a little rosewood box that he kept locked in his desk drawer in his study.

"'Several times,' says she, 'I've seen him gloomerin' over that box of evenings, and he always locks it up, right away if anybody comes into the room.'

"Well, you can imagine how long it was before I got Arthur by the wrist and led him down stage and hissed in his ear.

"That same afternoon we were lazying around in a boat among the water-lilies at the edge of the bay.

"'Arthur,' says I, 'you never told me you'd had another love-affair. But Mrs. Gurley did,' I went on, to let him know I knew. I hate to hear a man lie.

"'Before you came,' says he, looking me frankly in the eye, 'there was a previous affection—a strong one. Since you know of it, I will be perfectly candid with you.'

"'I am waiting,' says I.

"'My dear Ida,' says Arthur—of course, I went by my real name while I was in Soundport—'this former affection was a spiritual one, in fact. Although the lady aroused my deepest sentiments, and was, as I thought, my ideal woman, I never met her, and never spoke to her. It was an ideal love. My love for you, while no less ideal, is different. You wouldn't let that come between us."

"'Was she pretty?' I asked.

"'She was very beautiful,' said Arthur.

"'Did you see her often?' I asked.

"'Something like a dozen times,' says he.

"'Always from a distance?' says I.

"'Always from quite a distance,' says he.

"'And you loved her?' I asked.

"'She seemed my ideal of beauty and grace—and soul,' says Arthur.

"'And this keepsake that you keep under lock and key, and moon over at times, is that a remembrance from her?"

"'A memento,' says Arthur, 'that I have treasured.'

"'Did she send it to you?'

"'It came to me from her,' says he.

"'In a roundabout way?" I asked.

"'Somewhat roundabout,' says he, 'and yet rather direct.'

"'Why didn't you ever meet her?' I asked. 'Were your positions in life so different?'

"'She was far above me,' says Arthur. 'Now, Ida,' he goes on, 'this is all of the past. You're not going to be jealous, are you?'

"'Jealous!' says I. 'Why, man, what are you talking about? It makes me think ten times as much of you as I did before I knew about it.'

"And it did, Lynn—if you can understand it. That ideal love was a new one on me, but it struck me as being the most beautiful and glorious thing I'd ever heard of. Think of a man loving a woman he'd never even spoken to, and being faithful just to what his mind and heart pictured her. Oh, it sounded great to me. The men I'd always known come at you with either diamonds, knock-out-drops or a raise of salary—and their ideals!—well, we'll say no more.

"Yes, it made me think more of Arthur than I did before. I couldn't be jealous of that far-away divinity that he used to worship, for I was going to have him myself. And I began to look upon him as a saint on earth, just as old lady Gurley did.

"About four o'clock this afternoon a man came to the house for Arthur to go and see somebody that was sick among his church bunch. Old lady Gurley was taking her afternoon snore on a couch, so that left me pretty much alone.

"In passing by Arthur's study I looked in, and saw his bunch of keys hanging in the drawer of his desk, where he'd forgotten 'em. Well, I guess we're all to the Mrs. Bluebeard now and then, ain't we, Lynn? I made up my mind I'd have a look at that memento he kept so secret. Not that I cared where it was—it was just curiosity.

"While I was opening the drawer I imagined one or two things it might be. I thought it might be a dried rosebud she'd dropped down to him from a balcony, or maybe a picture of her he'd cut out of a magazine, she being so high up in the world.

"I opened the drawer, and there was the rosewood casket about the size of a gent's collar box. I found the little key in the bunch that fitted it and unlocked it and raised the lid.

"I took one look at that memento, and then I went to my room and packed my trunk. I threw a few things into my grip, gave my hair a flirt or two with a side-comb, put on my hat, and went in and gave the old lady's foot a kick. I'd tried awfully hard to use proper and correct language while I was there for Arthur's sake, and I had the habit down pat, but it left me then.

"'Stop sawing gourds,' says I, 'and sit up and take notice. The ghost's about to walk. I'm going away from here, and I owe you eight dollars. The expressman will call for my trunk.'

"I handed her the money.

"'Dear me, Miss Crosby!' says she. 'Is anything wrong? I thought you were pleased here. Dear me, young women are so hard to understand, and so different from what you expect 'em to be.'

"'You're damn right,' says I. 'Some of 'em are. But you can't say that about men. *When you know the one man you know 'em all!* That settles the human-race question.'

"And then I caught the four-thirty-eight, soft-coal unlimited; and here I am."

"You didn't tell me what was in the box, Lee," said Miss D'Armande anxiously.

"One of those yellow silk garters that I used to kick off my leg into the audience during that old vaudeville swing act of mine. Is there any of the cocktail left, Lynn!"

33

Calloway's Code

THE New York *Enterprise* sent H. B. Calloway as special correspondent to the Russo–Japanese–Portsmouth war.

For two months Calloway hung about Yokohama and Tokio, shaking dice with the other correspondents for drinks of 'rickshaws—oh, no, that's something to ride in; anyhow, he wasn't earning the salary that his paper was paying him. But that was not Calloway's fault. The little brown men who held the strings of Fate between their fingers were not ready for the readers of the *Enterprise* to season their breakfast bacon and eggs with the battles of the descendants of the gods.

But soon the column of correspondents that were to go out with the First Army tightened their field-glass belts and went down to the Yalu with Kuroki. Calloway was one of these.

Now, this is no history of the battle of the Yalu River. That has been told in detail by the correspondents who gazed at the shrapnel smoke rings from a distance of three miles. But, for justice's sake, let it be understood that the Japanese commander prohibited a nearer view.

Calloway's feat was accomplished before the battle. What he did was to furnish the *Enterprise* with the biggest beat of the war. That paper published exclusively and in detail the news of the attack on the lines of the Russian General Zassulitch on the same day that it was made. No other paper printed a word about it for two days afterward, except a London paper, whose account was absolutely incorrect and untrue.

Calloway did this in face of the fact that General Kuroki was making his moves and laying his plans with the profoundest secrecy as far as the world outside his camps was concerned. The correspondents were forbidden to send out any news whatever of his plans; and every message that was allowed on the wires was censored with rigid severity.

The correspondent for the London paper handed in a cablegram describing Kuroki's plans; but as it was wrong from beginning to end the censor grinned and let it go through.

So, there they were—Kuroki on one side of the Yalu with forty-two thousand infantry, five thousand cavalry, and one hundred and twenty-four guns. On the other side, Zassulitch waited for him with only twenty-three thousand men, and with a long stretch of river to guard. And Calloway had got hold of some important inside information that he knew would bring the *Enterprise* staff around a cablegram as thick as flies around a Park Row lemonade stand. If he could only get that message past the censor—the new censor who had arrived and taken his post that day.

Calloway did the obviously proper thing. He lit his pipe and sat down on a gun carriage to think it over. And there we must leave him; for the rest of the story belongs to Vesey, a sixteen-dollar-a-week reporter on the *Enterprise*.

* * *

Calloway's cablegram was handed to the managing editor at four o'clock in the afternoon. He read it three times; and then drew a pocket mirror from a pigeon-hole in his desk, and looked at his reflection carefully. Then he went over to the desk of Boyd, his assistant (he usually called Boyd when he wanted him), and laid the cablegram before him.

"It's from Calloway," he said. "See what you make of it."

The message was dated at Wi-ju, and these were the words of it:

Foregone preconcerted rash witching goes muffled rumour mine dark silent unfortunate richmond existing great hotly brute select mooted parlous beggars ye angel incontrovertible.

Boyd read it twice.

"It's either a cipher or a sunstroke," said he.

"Ever hear of anything like a code in the office—a secret code?" asked the m. e., who had held his desk for only two years. Managing editors come and go.

"None except the vernacular that the lady specials write in," said Boyd. "Couldn't be an acrostic, could it?"

"I thought of that," said the m. e., "but the beginning letters contain only four vowels. It must be a code of some sort."

"Try 'em in groups," suggested Boyd. "Let's see—'Rash witching goes'—not with me it doesn't. 'Muffled rumour mine'—must have an underground wire. 'Dark silent unfortunate richmond'—no reason why he should knock that town so hard. 'Existing great hotly'—no, it doesn't pan out. I'll call Scott."

The city editor came in a hurry, and tried his luck. A city editor must know something about everything; so Scott knew a little about cipher-writing.

"It may be what is called an inverted alphabet cipher," said he. "I'll try that. 'R' seems to be the oftenest used initial letter, with the exception of 'm.' Assuming 'r' to mean 'e,' the most frequently used vowel, we transpose the letters—so."

Scott worked rapidly with his pencil for two minutes; and then showed the first word according to his reading—the word "Scejtzez."

"Great!" cried Boyd. "It's a charade. My first is a Russian general. Go on, Scott."

"No, that won't work," said the city editor. "It's undoubtedly a code. It's impossible to read it without the key. Has the office ever used a cipher code?"

"Just what I was asking," said the m. e. "Hustle everybody up that ought to know. We must get at it some way. Calloway has evidently got hold of something big, and the censor has put the screws on, or he wouldn't have cabled in a lot of chop suey like this."

Throughout the office of the *Enterprise* a drag-net was sent, hauling in such members of the staff as would be likely to know of a code, past or present, by reason of their wisdom, information, natural intelligence, or length of servitude. They got together in a group in the city room, with the m. e. in the centre. No one had heard of a code. All began to explain to the head investigator that newspapers never use a code, anyhow—that is, a cipher code. Of course the Associated Press stuff is a sort of code—an abbreviation, rather—but——

The m. e. knew all that, and said so. He asked each man how long he had worked on the paper. Not one of them had drawn pay from an *Enterprise* envelope for longer than six years.

Calloway had been on the paper twelve years.

"Try old Heffelbauer," said the m. e. "He was here when Park Row was a potato patch."

Heffelbauer was an institution. He was half janitor, half handy-man about the office, and half watchman—thus becoming the peer of thirteen and one-half tailors. Sent for, he came, radiating his nationality.

"Heffelbauer," said the m. e., "did you ever hear of a code belonging to the office a long time ago—a private code? You know what a code is, don't you?"

"Yah," said Heffelbauer. "Sure I know vat a code is. Yah, apout dwelf or fifteen year ago der office had a code. Der reborters in der city-room haf it here."

"Ah!" said the m. e. "We're getting on the trail now. Where was it kept, Heffelbauer? What do you know about it?"

"Somedimes," said the retainer, "dey keep it in der little room behind der library room."

"Can you find it?" asked the m. e. eagerly. "Do you know where it is?"

"Mein Gott!" said Heffelbauer. "How long you dink a code live? Der reborters call him a maskeet. But von day he butt mit his head der editor, und——"

"Oh, he's talking about a goat," said Boyd. "Get out, Heffelbauer."

Again discomfited, the concerted wit and resource of the *Enterprise* huddled around Calloway's puzzle, considering its mysterious words in vain.

Then Vesey came in.

Vesey was the youngest reporter. He had a thirty-two-inch chest and wore a number fourteen collar; but his bright

Scotch plaid suit gave him presence and conferred no obscurity upon his whereabouts. He wore his hat in such a position that people followed him about to see him take it off, convinced that it must be hung upon a peg driven into the back of his head. He was never without an immense, knotted, hard-wood cane with a German-silver tip on its crooked handle. Vesey was the best photograph hustler in the office. Scott said it was because no living human being could resist the personal triumph it was to hand his picture over to Vesey. Vesey always wrote his own news stories, except the big ones, which were sent to the re-write men. Add to this fact that among all the inhabitants, temples, and groves of the earth nothing existed that could abash Vesey, and his dim sketch is concluded.

Vesey butted into the circle of cipher readers very much as Heffelbauer's "code" would have done, and asked what was up. Someone explained, with the touch of half-familiar condescension that they always used toward him. Vesey reached out and took the cablegram from the m. e.'s hand. Under the protection of some special Providence, he was always doing appalling things like that, and coming off unscathed.

"It's a code," said Vesey. "Anybody got the key?"

"The office has no code," said Boyd, reaching for the message. Vesey held to it.

"Then old Calloway expects us to read it, anyhow," said he. "He's up a tree, or something, and he's made this up so as to get it by the censor. It's up to us. Gee! I wish they had sent me, too. Say—we can't afford to fall down on our end of it. 'Foregone, preconcerted rash, witching'—h'm."

Vesey sat down on a table corner and began to whistle softly, frowning at the cablegram.

"Let's have it, please," said the m. e. "We've got to get to work on it."

"I believe I've got a line on it," said Vesey. "Give me ten minutes."

He walked to his desk, threw his hat into a waste-basket, spread out flat on his chest like a gorgeous lizard, and started his pencil going. The wit and wisdom of the *Enterprise* remained in a loose group, and smiled at one another, nodding their heads toward Vesey. Then they began to exchange their theories about the cipher.

It took Vesey exactly fifteen minutes. He brought to the m. e. a pad with the code-key written on it.

"I felt the swing of it as soon as I saw it," said Vesey. "Hurrah for old Calloway! He's done the Japs and every paper in town that prints literature instead of news. Take a look at that."

Thus had Vesey set forth the reading of the code:

Foregone—conclusion
Preconcerted—arrangement
Rash—act
Witching—hour of midnight
Goes—without saying
Muffled—report
Rumour—hath it
Mine—host
Dark—horse
Silent—majority
Unfortunate—pedestrians[1]
Richmond—in the field
Existing—conditions
Great—White Way
Hotly—contested
Brute—force
Select—few
Mooted—question
Parlours—times
Beggars—description
Ye—correspondent
Angel—unawares
Incontrovertible—fact

"It's simply newspaper English," explained Vesey. "I've been reporting on the *Enterprise* long enough to know it by

[1] Mr. Vesey afterwards explained that the logical journalistic complement of the word "unfortunate" was once the word "victim". But, since the automobile became so popular, the correct following word is now "pedestrian". Of course, in Galloway's code it meant infantry.

heart. Old Calloway gives us the cue word, and we use the word that naturally follows it just as we use 'em in the paper. Read it over, and you'll see how pat they drop into their places. Now, here's the message he intended us to get."

Vesey handed out another sheet of paper.

Concluded arrangement to act at hour of midnight without saying. Report hath it that a large body of cavalry and an overwhelming force of infantry will be thrown into the field. Conditions white. Way contested by only a small force. Question *The Times* description. Its correspondent is unaware of the facts.

"Great stuff!" cried Boyd excitedly. "Kuroki crosses the Yalu to-night and attacks. Oh, we won't do a thing to the sheets that make up with Addison's essays, real estate transfers, and bowling scores!"

"Mr. Vesey," said the m.e., with his jollying-which-you-should-regard-as-a-favour manner, "you have cast a serious reflection upon the literary standards of the paper that employs you. You have also assisted materially in giving us the biggest 'beat' of the year. I will let you know in a day or two whether you are to be discharged or retained at a larger salary. Somebody send Ames to me."

Ames was the king-pin, the snowy-petalled marguerite, the star-bright looloo of the rewrite men. He saw attempted murder in the pains of green-apple colic, cyclones in the summer zephyr, lost children in every top-spinning urchin, an uprising of the down-trodden masses in every hurling of a derelict potato at a passing automobile. When not rewriting, Ames sat on the porch of his Brooklyn villa playing checkers with his ten-year-old son.

Ames and the "war editor" shut themselves in a room. There was a map in there stuck full of little pins that represented armies and divisions. Their fingers had been itching for days to move those pins along the crooked line of the Yalu. They did so now; and in words of fire Ames translated Calloway's brief message into a front-page masterpiece that set the world talking. He told of the secret councils of the Japanese officers; gave Kuroki's flaming speeches in full; counted the cavalry and infantry to a man and a horse; described the quick and silent building of the bridge at Suikauchen, across which the Mikado's legions were hurled upon the surprised Zassulitch, whose troops were widely scattered along the river. And the battle!—well, you know what Ames can do with a battle if you give him just one smell of smoke for a foundation. And in the same story, with seemingly supernatural knowledge, he gleefully scored the most profound and ponderous paper in England for the false and misleading account of the intended movements of the Japanese First Army printed in its issue of *the same date*.

Only one error was made; and that was the fault of the cable operator at Wi-ju. Calloway pointed it out after he came back. The word "great" in his code should have been "gauge", and its complemental words "of battle". But it went to Ames "conditions white", and of course he took that to mean snow. His description of the Japanese army struggling through the snow-storm, blinded by the whirling flakes, was thrillingly vivid. The artists turned out some effective illustrations that made a hit as pictures of the artillery dragging their guns through the drifts. But, as the attack was made on the first day of May, the "conditions white" excited some amusement. But it made no difference to the *Enterprise*, anyway.

It was wonderful. And Calloway was wonderful in having made the new censor believe that his jargon of words meant no more than a complaint of the dearth of news and a petition for more expense money. And Vesey was wonderful. And most wonderful of all are words, and how they make friends one with another, being oft associated, until not even obituary notices them do part.

* * *

On the second day following, the city editor halted at Vesey's desk where the reporter was writing the story of a man who had broken his leg by falling into a coal-hole—Ames having failed to find a murder motive in it.

"The old man says your salary is to be raised to twenty a week," said Scott.

"All right," said Vesey. "Every little helps. Say—Mr. Scott, which would you say—'We can state without fear of successful contradiction', or 'On the whole it can be safely asserted'?"

34

Phoebe

"You are a man of many novel adventures and varied enterprises," I said to Captain Patricio Maloné. "Do you believe that the possible element of good luck or bad luck—if there is such a thing as luck—has influenced your career or persisted for or against you to such an extent that you were forced to attribute results to the operation of the aforesaid good luck or bad luck?"

This question (of almost the dull insolence of legal phraseology) was put while we sat in Rousselin's little red-tiled café near Congo Square in New Orleans.

Brown-faced, white-hatted, finger-ringed captains of adventure came often to Rousselin's for the cognac. They came from sea and land, and were chary of relating the things they had seen—not because they were more wonderful than the fantasies of the Ananiases of print, but because they were so different. And I was a perpetual wedding-guest, always striving to cast my buttonhole over the finger of one of these mariners of fortune. This Captain Maloné was a Hiberno-Iberian Creole who had gone to and fro in the earth and walked up and down in it. He looked like any other well-dressed man of thirty-five whom you might meet, except that he was hopelessly weather-tanned and wore on his chain an ancient ivory-and-gold Peruvian charm against evil, which has nothing at all to do with his story.

"My answer to your question," said the Captain, smiling, "will be to tell you the story of Bad-Luck Kearny. That is, if you don't mind hearing it."

My reply was to pound on the table for Rousselin.

* * *

"Strolling along Tchoupitous Street one night," began Captain Maloné, "I noticed, without especially taxing my interest, a small man walking rapidly toward me. He stepped upon a wooden cellar door, crashed through it and disappeared. I rescued him from a heap of soft coal below. He dusted himself briskly, swearing fluently in a mechanical tone, as an underpaid actor recites the gipsy's curse. Gratitude and the dust in his throat seemed to call for fluids to clear them away. His desire for liquidation was expressed so heartily that I went with him to a café down the street where we had some vile vermouth and bitters.

"Looking across that little table I had my first clear sight of Francis Kearny. He was about five feet seven, but as tough as a cypress knee. His hair was darkest red, his mouth such a mere slit that you wondered how the flood of his words came rushing from it. His eyes were the brightest and lightest blue and the hopefullest that I ever saw. He gave the double impression that he was at bay and that you had better not crowd him further.

"'Just in from a gold-hunting expedition on the coast of Costa Rica,' he explained. 'Second mate of a banana steamer told me the natives were panning out enough from the beach sands to buy all the rum, red calico, and parlour melodeons in the world. The day I got there a syndicate named Incorporated Jones gets a government concession to all minerals from a given point. For a next choice I take coast fever and count green and blue lizards for six weeks in a grass hut. I had to be notified when I was well, for the reptiles were actually there. Then I shipped back as third cook on a Norwegian tramp that blew up her boiler two miles below Quarantine. I was due to bust through that cellar door here to-night, so I hurried the rest of the way up the river, roustabouting on a lower coast packet that made a landing for every fisherman that wanted a plug of tobacco. And now I'm here for what comes next. And it'll be along, it'll be along,' said this queer Mr. Kearny; 'it'll be along on the beams of my bright but not very particular star.'

"From the first the personality of Kearny charmed me. I saw in him the bold heart, the restless nature, and the valiant front against the buffets of fate that make his countrymen such valuable comrades in risk and adventure. And just then I was wanting such men. Moored at a fruit company's pier I had a 500-ton steamer ready to sail the next day with a cargo of sugar, lumber, and corrugated iron for a port in—well, let us call the country Esperando—it has not been long ago, and the name of Patricio Maloné is still spoken there when its unsettled politics are discussed. Beneath the sugar and iron were packed a thousand Winchester rifles. In Aguas Frias, the capital, Don Rafael Valdevia, Minister of War, Esperando's greatest-hearted and most able patriot, awaited my coming. No doubt you have heard, with a smile, of the insignificant wars and uprisings in those little tropic republics. They make but a faint clamour against the din of great nations' battles; but down there, under all the ridiculous uniforms and petty diplomacy and senseless countermarchings and intrigue, are to be found statesmen and patriots. Don Rafael Valdevia was one. His great ambition was to raise Esperando into peace and honest prosperity and the respect of the serious nations. So he waited for my rifles in Aguas Frias. But one would think I am trying to win a recruit in you! No; it was Francis Kearny I wanted. And so I told him, speaking long over our execrable vermouth, breathing the stifling odour from garlic and tarpaulins, which, as you know, is the distinctive flavour of cafés in the lower slant of our city. I spoke of the tyrant President Cruz and the burdens that his greed and insolent cruelty laid upon the people. And at that Kearny's tears flowed. And then I dried them with a picture of the fat rewards that would be ours when the oppressor should be overthrown and the wise and generous Valdevia in his seat. Then Kearney leaped to his feet and wrung my hand with the strength of a roustabout. He was mine, he said, till the last minion of the hated despot was hurled from the highest peaks of the Cordilleras into the sea.

"I paid the score and we went out. Near the door Kearny's elbow overturned an upright glass showcase, smashing it into little bits. I paid the storekeeper the price he asked.

"'Come to my hotel for the night,' I said to Kearny. 'We sail to-morrow at noon.'

"He agreed; but on the sidewalk he fell to cursing again in

the dull, monotonous, glib way that he had done when I pulled him out of the coal cellar.

"'Captain,' said he, 'before we go any further, it's no more than fair to tell you that I'm known from Baffin's Bay to Terra del Fuego as "Bad-Luck" Kearny. And I'm It. Everything I get into goes up in the air except a balloon. Every bet I ever made I lost except when I coppered it. Every boat I ever sailed on sank except the submarines. Everything I was ever interested in went to pieces except a patent bombshell that I invented. Everything I ever took hold of and tried to run I ran into the ground except when I tried to plough. And that's why they call me Bad-Luck Kearny. I thought I'd tell you.'

"'Bad luck,' said I, 'or what goes by the name, may now and then tangle the affairs of any man. But if it persist beyond the estimate of what we may call the "averages" there must be a cause for it.'

"'There is,' said Kearny emphatically, 'and when we walk another square I will show it to you.'

"Surprised, I kept by his side until we came to Canal Street and out into the middle of its great width.

"Kearny seized me by the arm and pointed a tragic forefinger at a rather brilliant star that shone steadily about thirty degrees above the horizon.

"'That's Saturn,' said he, 'the star that presides over bad luck and evil and disappointment and nothing doing and trouble. I was born under that star. Every move I make, up bobs Saturn and blocks it. He's the hoodoo planet of the heavens. They say he's 73,000 miles in diameter and no solider of body than split-pea soup, and he's got as many disreputable and malignant rings as Chicago. Now, what kind of a star is that to be born under?'

"I asked Kearny where he had obtained all this astonishing knowledge.

"'From Azrath, the great astrologer of Cleveland, Ohio,' said he. 'That man looked at a glass ball and told me my name before I'd taken a chair. He prophesied the date of my birth and death before I'd said a word. And then he cast my horoscope, and the sidereal system socked me in the solar plexus. It was bad luck for Francis Kearny from A to Izard and for his friends that were implicated with him. For that I gave up ten dollars. This Azrath was sorry, but he respected his profession too much to read the heavens wrong for any man. It was night time, and he took me out on a balcony and gave me a free view of the sky. And he showed me which Saturn was, and how to find it in different balconies and longitudes.

"'But Saturn wasn't all. He was only the man higher up. He furnishes so much bad luck that they allow him a gang of deputy sparklers to help hand it out. They're circulating and revolving and hanging around the main supply all the time, each one throwing the hoodoo on his own particular district.

"'You see that ugly little red star about eight inches above and to the right of Saturn?' Kearny asked me. 'Well, that's her. That's Phoebe. She's got me in charge. "By the day of your birth," said Azrath to me, "your life is subjected to the influence of Saturn. By the hour and minute of it you must dwell under the sway and direct authority of Phoebe, the ninth satellite." So said this Azrath.' Kearny shook his fist viciously skyward. 'Curse her, she's done her work well,' said he. 'Ever since I was astrologized, bad luck has followed me like my shadow, as I told you. And for many years before. Now, Captain, I've told you my handicap as a man should. If you're afraid this evil star of mine might cripple your scheme, leave me out of it.'

"I reassured Kearny as well as I could. I told him that for the time we would banish astrology and astronomy from our heads. The manifest valour and enthusiasm of the man drew me. 'Let us see what a little courage and diligence will do against bad luck,' I said. 'We will sail to-morrow for Esperando.'

"Fifty miles down the Mississippi our steamer broke her rudder. We sent for a tug to tow us back and lost three days. When we struck the blue waters of the Gulf, all the storm clouds of the Atlantic seemed to have concentrated above us. We thought surely to sweeten those leaping waves with our sugar, and to stack our arms and lumber on the floor of the Mexican Gulf.

"Kearny did not seek to cast off one iota of the burden of our danger from the shoulders of his fatal horoscope. He weathered every storm on deck, smoking a black pipe, to keep which alight rain and sea-water seemed but as oil. And he shook his fist at the black clouds behind which his baleful star winked its unseen eye. When the skies cleared one evening, he reviled his malignant guardian with grim humour.

"'On watch, aren't you, you red-headed vixen? Out making it hot for little Francis Kearny and his friends, according to Hoyle. Twinkle, twinkle, little devil! You're a lady, aren't you?—dogging a man with bad luck just because he happened to be born while your boss was floorwalker. Get busy and sink the ship, you one-eyed banshee. Phoebe! H'm! Sounds as mild as a milkmaid. You can't judge a woman by her name. Why couldn't I have had a man star? I can't make the remarks to Phoebe that I could to a man. Oh, Phoebe, you be—blasted!'

"For eight days gales and squalls and waterspouts beat us from our course. Five days only should have landed us in Esperando. Our Jonah swallowed the bad credit of it with appealing frankness; but that scarcely lessened the hardships our cause was made to suffer.

"At last one afternoon we steamed into the calm estuary of the little Rio Escondido. Three miles up this we crept, feeling for the shallow channel between the low banks that were crowded to the edge with gigantic trees and riotous vegetation. Then our whistle gave a little toot, and in five minutes we heard a shout, and Carlos—my brave Carlos Quintana—crashed through the tangled vines waving his cap madly for joy.

"A hundred yards away was his camp, where three hundred chosen patriots of Esperando were awaiting our coming. For a month Carlos had been drilling them there in the tactics of war, and filling them with the spirit of revolution and liberty.

"'My Captain—*compadre mio*!' shouted Carlos, while yet my boat was being lowered. 'You should see them in the drill by *companias*—in the column wheel—in the march by fours—they are superb! Also in the manual of arms—but, alas! performed only with sticks of bamboo. The guns, *capitan*—say that you have brought the guns!'

"'A thousand Winchesters, Carlos,' I called to him. 'And two Gatlings.'

"'*Valgame Dios!*' he cried, throwing his cap in the air. 'We shall sweep the world!'

"At that moment Kearny tumbled from the steamer's side into the river. He could not swim, so the crew threw him a rope and drew him back aboard. I caught his eye and his look of pathetic but still bright and undaunted consciousness of his guilty luck. I told myself that although he might be a man to shun, he was also one to be admired.

"I gave orders to the sailing-master that the arms, ammunition, and provisions were to be landed at once. That was easy in the steamer's boats, except for the two Gatling guns. For their transportation ashore we carried a stout flatboat, brought for the purpose in the steamer's hold.

"In the meantime I walked with Carlos to the camp and made the soldiers a little speech in Spanish, which they received with enthusiasm; and then I had some wine and a cigarette in Carlos's tent. Later we walked back to the river to see how the unloading was being conducted.

"The small arms and provisions were already ashore, and the petty officers and squads of men conveying them to camp. One Gatling had been safely landed; the other was just being hoisted over the side of the vessel as we arrived. I noticed Kearny darting about on board, seeming to have the ambition of ten men, and to be doing the work of five. I think his zeal bubbled over when he saw Carlos and me. A rope's end was swinging loose from some part of the tackle. Kearny leaped impetuously and caught it. There was a crackle and a hiss and a smoke of scorching hemp, and the Gatling dropped straight as a plummet through the bottom of the flatboat and buried itself in twenty feet of water and five feet of river mud.

"I turned my back on the scene. I heard Carlos's loud cries as if from some extreme grief too poignant for words. I heard the complaining murmur of the crew and the maledictions of Torres, the sailing-master—I could not bear to look.

"By night some degree of order had been restored in camp. Military rules were not drawn strictly, and the men were grouped about the fires of their several messes, playing games of chance, singing their native songs, or discussing with voluble animation the contingencies of our march upon the capital.

"To my tent, which had been pitched for me close to that of my chief lieutenant, came Kearny, indomitable, smiling, bright-eyed, bearing no traces of the buffets of his evil star. Rather was his aspect that of a heroic martyr whose tribulations were so high-sourced and glorious that he even took a splendour and a prestige from them.

"'Well, Captain,' he said, 'I guess you realize that Bad-Luck Kearny is still on deck. It was a shame, now, about that gun. She only needed to be slewed two inches to clear the rail; and that's why I grabbed that rope's end. Who'd have thought that a sailor—even a Sicilian lubber on a banana coaster—would have fastened a line in a bow-knot? Don't think I'm trying to dodge the responsibility, Captain. It's my luck.'

"'There are men, Kearny,' said I gravely, 'who pass through life blaming upon luck and chance the mistakes that result from their own faults and incompetency. I do not say that you are such a man. But if all your mishaps are traceable to that tiny star, the sooner we endow our colleges with chairs of moral astronomy, the better.'

"'It isn't the size of the star that counts,' said Kearny; 'it's the quality. Just the way it is with women. That's why they gave the biggest planets masculine names, and the little stars feminine ones—to even things up when it comes to getting their work in. Suppose they had called my star Agamemnon or Bill McCarty or something like that instead of Phoebe. Every time one of those old boys touched their calamity button and sent me down one of their wireless pieces of bad luck, I could talk back and tell 'em what I thought of 'em in suitable terms. But you can't address such remarks to a Phoebe.'

"'It pleases you to make a joke of it, Kearny,' said I, without smiling. 'But it is no joke to me to think of my Gatling mired in the river ooze.'

"'As to that,' said Kearny, abandoning his light mood at once, 'I have already done what I could. I have had some experience in hoisting stone in quarries. Torres and I have already spliced three hawsers and stretched them from the steamer's stern to a tree on shore. We will rig a tackle and have the gun on terra firma before noon to-morrow.'

"One could not remain long at outs with Bad-Luck Kearny.

"'Once more,' said I to him, 'we will waive this question of luck. Have you ever had experience in drilling raw troops?'

"'I was first sergeant and drill-master,' said Kearny, 'in the Chilean army for one year. And captain of artillery for another.'

"'What became of your command?' I asked.

"'Shot down to a man,' said Kearny, 'during the revolutions against Balmaceda.'

"Somehow the misfortunes of the evil-starred one seemed to turn to me their comedy side; I lay back upon my goat's-hide cot and laughed until the woods echoed. Kearny grinned. 'I told you how it was,' he said.

"'To-morrow,' I said, 'I shall detail one hundred men under your command for manual-of-arms drill and company evolutions. You will rank as lieutenant. Now, for God's sake, Kearny,' I urged him, 'try to combat this superstition, if it is one. Bad luck may be like any other visitor—preferring to stop where it is expected. Get your mind off stars. Look upon Esperando as your planet of good fortune.'

"'I thank you, Captain,' said Kearny quietly. 'I will try to make it the best handicap I ever ran.'

"By noon the next day the submerged Gatling was rescued, as Kearny had promised. Then Carlos and Manuel Ortiz and Kearny (my lieutenants) distributed Winchesters among the troops and put them through an incessant rifle drill. We fired no shots, blank or solid, for of all coasts Esperando is the stillest; and we had no desire to sound any warnings in the ear of that corrupt government until they should carry with them the message of Liberty and the downfall of Oppression.

"In the afternoon came a mule-rider bearing a written message to me from Don Rafael Valdevia in the capital, Aguas Frias.

"Whenever that man's name comes to my lips, words of tribute to his greatness, his noble simplicity, and his conspicuous genius follow irrepressibly. He was a traveller, a student of peoples and governments, a master of sciences, a poet, an orator, a leader, a soldier, a critic of the world's campaigns and the idol of the people of Esperando. I had been honoured by his friendship for years. It was I who first turned his mind to the thought that he should leave for his monument a new Esperando—a country freed from the rule of unscrupulous tyrants, and a people made happy and prosperous by wise and impartial legislation. When he had consented he threw himself into the cause with the undivided zeal with which he endowed all of his acts. The coffers of his great fortune were opened to those of us to whom were entrusted the secret moves of the game. His popularity was already so great that he had practically forced President Cruz to offer him the portfolio of Minister of War.

"The time, Don Rafael said in his letter, was ripe. Success, he prophesied, was certain. The people were beginning to clamour publicly against Cruz's misrule. Bands of citizens in the capital were even going about of nights hurling stones at public buildings and expressing their dissatisfaction. A bronze statue of President Cruz in the Botanical Gardens had been lassoed about the neck and overthrown. It only remained for me to arrive with my force and my thousand rifles, and for himself to come forward and proclaim himself the people's saviour, to overthrow Cruz in a single day. There would be but a half-hearted resistance from the six hundred Government troops stationed in the capital. The country was ours. He presumed that by this time my steamer had arrived at Quintana's camp. He proposed the eighteenth of July for the attack. That would give us six days in which to strike camp and march to Aguas Frias. In the meantime Don Rafael remained my good friend and *compadre en la causa de la libertad.*

"On the morning of the fourteenth we began our march toward the sea-following range of mountains, over the sixty-mile trail to the capital. Our small arms and provisions were laden on pack mules. Twenty men harnessed to each Gatling gun rolled them smoothly along the flat, alluvial lowlands. Our troops, well-shod and well-fed, moved with alacrity and heartiness. I and my three lieutenants were mounted on the tough mountain ponies of the country.

"A mile out of camp one of the pack mules, becoming stubborn, broke away from the train, and plunged from the path into the thicket. The alert Kearny spurred quickly after it and intercepted its flight. Rising in his stirrups, he released one foot and bestowed upon the mutinous animal a hearty kick. The mule tottered and fell with a crash broadside upon the ground. As we gathered around it, it walled its great eyes almost humanly toward Kearny and expired. That was bad; but worse, to our minds, was the concomitant disaster. Part of the mule's burden had been one hundred pounds of the finest coffee to be had in the tropics. The bag burst and spilled the priceless brown mass of the ground berries among the dense vines and weeds of the swampy land. *Mala suerte!* When you take away from an Esperandan his coffee, you abstract his patriotism and 50 per cent. of his value as a soldier. The men began to rake up the precious stuff; but I beckoned Kearny back along the trail where they would not hear. The limit had been reached.

"I took from my pocket a wallet of money and drew out some bills.

"'Mr. Kearny,' said I, 'here are some funds belonging to Don Rafael Valdevia, which I am expending in his cause. I know of no better service it can buy for him than this. Here is one hundred dollars. Luck or no luck, we part company here. Star or no star, calamity seems to travel by your side. You will return to the steamer. She touches at Amotapa to discharge her lumber and iron, and then puts back to New Orleans. Hand this note to the sailing-master, who will give you passage.' I wrote on a leaf torn from my book, and placed it and the money in Kearny's hand.

"'Good-bye,' I said, extending my own. 'It is not that I am

displeased with you; but there is no place in this expedition for—let us say, the Señorita Phoebe.' I said this with a smile, trying to smooth the thing for him. 'May you have better luck, *companero*.'

"Kearny took the money and the paper.

"'It was just a little touch,' said he, 'just a little lift with the toe of my boot—but what's the odds?—that blamed mule would have died if I had only dusted his ribs with a powder puff. It was my luck. Well, Captain, I would have liked to be in that little fight with you over in Aguas Frias. Success to the cause. *Adios!*'

"He turned around and set off down the trail without looking back. The unfortunate mule's pack-saddle was transferred to Kearny's pony, and we again took up the march.

"Four days we journeyed over the foot-hills and mountains, fording icy torrents, winding around the crumbling brows of ragged peaks, creeping along rocky flanges that overlooked awful precipices, crawling breathlessly over tottering bridges that crossed bottomless chasms.

"On the evening of the seventeenth we camped by a little stream on the bare hills five miles from Aguas Frias. At daybreak we were to take up the march again.

"At midnight I was standing outside my tent inhaling the fresh cold air. The stars were shining bright in the cloudless sky, giving the heavens their proper aspect of illimitable depth and distance when viewed from the vague darkness of the blotted earth. Almost at its zenith was the planet Saturn; and with a half-smile I observed the sinister red sparkle of his malignant attendant—the demon star of Kearny's ill luck. And then my thoughts strayed across the hills to the scene of our coming triumph, where the heroic and noble Don Rafael awaited our coming to set a new and shining star in the firmament of nations.

"I heard a slight rustling in the deep grass to my right. I turned and saw Kearny coming toward me. He was ragged and dew-drenched and limping. His hat and one boot were gone. About one foot he had tied some makeshift of cloth and grass. But his manner as he approached was that of a man who knows his own virtues well enough to be superior to rebuffs.

"'Well, sir,' I said, staring at him coldly, 'if there is anything in persistence, I see no reason why you should not succeed in wrecking and ruining us yet.'

"'I kept half a day's journey behind,' said Kearny, fishing out a stone from the covering of his lame foot, 'so the bad luck wouldn't touch you. I couldn't help it, Captain; I wanted to be in on this game. It was a pretty tough trip, especially in the department of the commissary. In the low grounds there were always bananas and oranges. Higher up it was worse; but your men left a good deal of goat meat hanging on the bushes in the camps. Here's your hundred dollars. You're nearly there now, Captain. Let me in on the scrapping to-morrow.'

"'Not for a hundred times a hundred would I have the tiniest thing go wrong with my plans now,' I said, 'whether caused by evil planets or the blunders of mere man. But yonder is Aguas Frias, five miles away, and a clear road. I am of the mind to defy Saturn and all his satellites to spoil our success now. At any rate, I will not turn away to-night as weary a traveller and as good a soldier as you are, Lieutenant Kearny. Manuel Ortiz's tent is there by the brightest fire. Rout him out and tell him to supply you with food and blankets and clothes. We march again at daybreak.'

"Kearny thanked me briefly but feelingly and moved away.

"He had gone scarcely a dozen steps when a sudden flash of bright light illumined the surrounding hills; a sinister, growling, hissing sound like escaping steam filled my ears. Then followed a roar as of distant thunder, which grew louder every instant. This terrifying noise culminated in a tremendous explosion, which seemed to rock the hills as an earthquake would; the illumination waxed to a glare so fierce that I clapped my hands to my eyes to save them. I thought the end of the world had come. I could think of no natural phenomenon that would explain it. My wits were staggering. The deafening explosion trailed off into the rumbling roar that had preceded it; and through this I heard the frightened shouts of my troops as they stumbled from their resting-places and rushed wildly about. Also I heard the harsh tones of Kearny's voice crying: 'They'll blame it on me, of course, and what the devil it is, it's not Francis Kearny that can give you an answer.'

"I opened my eyes. The hills were still there, dark and solid. It had not been, then, a volcano or an earthquake. I looked up at the sky and saw a comet-like trail crossing the zenith and extending westward—a fiery trail waning fainter and narrower each moment.

"'A meteor!' I called aloud. 'A meteor has fallen. There is no danger.'

"And then all other sounds were drowned by a great shout from Kearny's throat. He had raised both hands above his head and was standing tiptoe.

"'PHOEBE'S GONE!' he cried, with all his lungs. 'She's busted and gone to hell. Look, Captain, the little red-headed hoodoo has blown herself to smithereens. She found Kearny too tough to handle, and she puffed up with spite and meanness till her boiler blew up. It'll be Bad-Luck Kearny no more. Oh, let us be joyful!

"Humpy Dumpy sat on a wall;
Humpy busted, and that'll be all!"

"I looked up, wondering, and picked out Saturn in his place. But the small red twinkling luminary in his vicinity, which Kearny had pointed out to me as his evil star, had vanished. I had seen it there but half an hour before; there was no doubt that one of those awful and mysterious spasms of nature had hurled it from the heavens.

"I clapped Kearny on the shoulder.

"'Little man,' said I, 'let this clear the way for you. It appears that astrology has failed to subdue you. Your horoscope must be cast anew with pluck and loyalty for controlling stars. I play you to win. Now, get to your tent, and sleep. Daybreak is the word.'

"At nine o'clock on the morning of the eighteenth of July I rode into Aguas Frias with Kearny at my side. In his clean linen suit and with his military poise and keen eye he was a model of a fighting adventurer. I had visions of him riding as commander of President Valdevia's body-guard when the plums of the new republic should begin to fall.

"Carlos followed with the troops and supplies. He was to halt in a wood outside the town and remain concealed there until he received the word to advance.

"Kearny and I rode down the Calle Ancha toward the *residencia* of Don Rafael at the other side of the town. As we passed the superb white buildings of the University of Esperando, I saw at an open window the gleaming spectacles and bald head of Herr Bergowitz, professor of the natural sciences and friend of Don Rafael and of me and of the cause. He waved his hand to me, with his broad, bland smile.

"There was no excitement apparent in Aguas Frias. The people went about leisurely as at all times; the market was thronged with bare-headed women buying fruit and *carne*; we heard the twang and tinkle of string bands in the patios of the *cantinas*. We could see that it was a waiting game that Don Rafael was playing.

"His *residencia* was a large but low building around a great courtyard in grounds crowded with ornamental trees and tropic shrubs. At his door an old woman who came informed us that Don Rafael had not yet arisen.

"'Tell him,' said I, 'that Captain Maloné and a friend wish to see him at once. Perhaps he has overslept.'

"She came back looking frightened.

"'I have called,' she said, 'and rung his bell many times, but he does not answer.'

"I knew where his sleeping-room was. Kearny and I pushed by her and went to it. I put my shoulder against the thin door and forced it open.

"In an arm-chair by a great table covered with maps and books sat Don Rafael with his eyes closed. I touched his hand. He had been dead many hours. On his head above one ear was a wound caused by a heavy blow. It had ceased to bleed long before.

"I made the old woman call a *mozo*, and dispatched him in haste to fetch Herr Bergowitz.

"He came, and we stood about as if we were half stunned

by the awful shock. Thus can the letting of a few drops of blood from one man's veins drain the life of a nation.

"Presently Herr Bergowitz stooped and picked up a darkish stone the size of an orange which he saw under the table. He examined it closely through his great glasses with the eye of science.

"'A fragment,' said he, 'of a detonating meteor. The most remarkable one in twenty years exploded above this city a little after midnight this morning.'

"The professor looked quickly up at the ceiling. We saw the blue sky through a hole the size of an orange nearly above Don Rafael's chair.

"I heard a familiar sound, and turned. Kearny had thrown himself on the floor and was babbling his compendium of bitter, blood-freezing curses against the star of his evil luck.

"Undoubtedly Phoebe had been feminine. Even when hurtling on her way to fiery dissolution and everlasting doom, the last word had been hers."

* * *

Captain Maloné was not unskilled in narrative. He knew the point where a story should end. I sat revelling in his effective conclusion, when he aroused me by continuing:

"Of course," said he, "our schemes were at an end. There was no one to take Don Rafael's place. Our little army melted away like dew before the sun.

"One day after I had returned to New Orleans I related this story to a friend who holds a professorship in Tulane University.

"When I had finished he laughed and asked whether I had any knowledge of Kearny's luck afterwards. I told him no, that I had seen him no more; but that when he left me, he had expressed confidence that his future would be successful now that his unlucky star had been overthown.

"'No doubt,' said the professor, 'he is happier not to know one fact. If he derived his bad luck from Phoebe, the ninth satellite of Saturn, that malicious lady is still engaged in overlooking his career. The star close to Saturn that he imagined to be her was near that planet simply by the chance of its orbit—probably at different times he has regarded many other stars that happened to be in Saturn's neighbourhood as his evil one. The real Phoebe is visible only through a very good telescope.'

"About a year afterward," continued Captain Maloné, "I was walking down a street that crossed the Poydras Market. An immensely stout, pink-faced lady in black satin crowded me from the narrow sidewalk with a frown. Behind her trailed a little man laden to the gunwales with bundles and bags of goods and vegetables.

"It was Kearny—but changed. I stopped and shook one of his hands, which still clung to a bag of garlic and red peppers.

"'How is the luck, old *companero*?' I asked him. I had not the heart to tell him the truth about his star.

"'Well,' said he, 'I am married, as you may guess.'

"'Francis!' called the big lady, in deep tones, 'are you going to stop in the street talking all day?'

"'I am coming, Phoebe dear,' said Kearny, hastening after her."

* * *

Captain Maloné ceased again.

"After all, do you believe in luck?" I asked.

"Do you?" answered the Captain, with his ambiguous smile shaded by the brim of his soft straw hat.

35

The Pint Flask

A PROMINENT Houston colonel, who is also a leading church member, started for church last Sunday morning with his family, as was his custom. He was serene and solid-looking, and his black frock coat and light grey trousers fitted him snugly and stylishly. They passed along Main Street on the way to church, and the colonel happened to think of a letter on his desk that he wanted, so he told his family to wait at the door a moment while he stopped in his office to get it. He went in and got the letter, and, to his surprise, there was a disreputable-looking pint whisky flask with about an ounce of whisky left in it standing on his desk. The colonel abominates whisky and never touches a drop of anything strong. He supposed that someone, knowing this, had passed his desk, and set the flask there by way of a mild joke.

He looked about for a place to throw the bottle, but the back door was locked, and he tried unsuccessfully to raise the window that overlooked the alley. The colonel's wife, wondering why he was so long in coming, opened the door and surprised him, so that scarcely thinking what he was doing he thrust the flask under his coat tail into his hip pocket.

"Why don't you come on?" asked his wife. "Didn't you find the letter?"

He couldn't do anything but go with her. He should have produced the bottle right there, and explained the situation, but he neglected his opportunity. He went on down Main Street with his family, with the pint flask feeling as big as a keg in his pocket. He was afraid some of them would notice it bulging under his coat, so he lagged somewhat in the rear. When he entered his pew at church and sat down there was a sharp crack, and the odour of mean whisky began to work its way around the church. The colonel saw several people elevate their noses and look inquiringly around and he turned as red as a beet. He heard a female voice in the pew behind him whisper loudly:

"Old Colonel J—— is drunk again. They say he is hardly ever sober now, and some people say he beats his wife nearly every day."

The colonel recognized the voice of one of the most notorious female gossipers in Houston. He turned around and glared at her. She then whispered a little louder:

"Look at him. He really looks dangerous. And to come to church that way, too!"

* * *

The colonel knew that the bottle had cracked and he was afraid to move, but a piece of it fell out on the floor. He usually knelt during prayer, but today he sat bolt upright on the seat. His wife noticed his unusual behaviour and whispered:

"James, you don't know how you pain me. You don't pray any more. I knew what the result would be when I let you go to hear Ingersoll lecture. You are an infidel. And—what is that I smell? Oh, James, you have been drinking, and on Sunday, too!"

The colonel's wife put her handkerchief to her eyes, and he ground his teeth in rage.

After the services were over, and they had reached home, his wife took her seat on the back porch and began to cap some strawberries for dinner. This prevented his going out in the back yard and throwing the bottle over the fence, as he had intended. His two little boys hung close around him, as they always did on Sunday, and he found it impossible to get rid of it. He took them out for a stroll in the front yard. Finally, he sent them both in the house on some pretext, and drawing out the bottle hurled it into the street. The crack in it had been only a slight one, and as it struck a soft heap of trash when it fell, it did not break.

The colonel felt immediately relieved, but just as the little boys ran back he heard a voice in the street say:

"See here, sir, law's against throwing glass in the street. I saw you do it, but take it back, and it'll be all right this time."

The colonel turned and saw a big policeman handing the terrible bottle toward him over the fence. He took it and thrust it back into his pocket with a low but expressive remark. His little boys ran up and shouted:

"Oh, papa, what was that the policeman gave you? Let's see it!"

They clutched at his coat tails, and grabbed for his pockets, and the colonel backed against the fence.

"Go away from here, you little devils," he yelled. "Go in the house or I'll thrash you both."

* * *

The colonel went into the house and put on his hat. He resolved to get rid of the bottle if he had to walk a mile to do it.

"Where are you going?" asked his wife in astonishment. "Dinner is almost ready. Why don't you pull off your coat and cool off, James, as you usually do?"

She gazed at him with the deepest suspicion, and that irritated him.

"Confound the dinner," he said, angrily. "I'm hungry—no, I mean I'm sick; I don't want any dinner—I'm going to take a walk."

"Papa, please show us what the policeman gave you," said one of his little boys.

"Policeman!" echoed the colonel's wife. "Oh, James, to think that you would act this way! I know you haven't been drinking, but what is the matter with you? Come in and lie down. Let me pull off your coat."

She tried to pull off the colonel's Prince Albert, as she generally did, but he got furiously angry and danced away from her.

"Take your hands off me, woman," he cried. "I've got a headache, and I'm going for a walk. I'll throw the blamed thing away if I have to go to the North Pole to do it."

The colonel's wife shook her head as he went out the gate.

"He's working too hard," she said. "Maybe a walk will do him good."

The colonel went down several blocks watching for opportunity to dispose of the flask. There were a good many people on the streets, and there seemed to be always somebody looking at him.

Two or three of the colonel's friends met him, and stared at him curiously. His face was much flushed, his hat was on the back of his head and there was a wild glare in his eyes. Some of them passed without speaking, and the colonel laughed bitterly. He was getting desperate. Whenever he would get to a vacant lot, he would stop and gaze searchingly in every direction to see if the coast was clear, so that he could pull out the flask and drop it. People began to watch him from windows, and two or three little boys began to follow him. The colonel turned around and spoke sharply to them, and they replied:

"Look at the old guy with a jag on lookin' for a place to lie down. W'y don't yer go to de calaboose and snooze it off, mister?"

* * *

The colonel finally dodged the boys, and his spirits rose as he saw before him a vacant square covered with weeds, in some places as high as his head.

Here was a place where he could get rid of the bottle. The minister of his church lived on the opposite side of the vacant square, but the weeds were so high that the house was completely hidden.

The colonel looked guiltily around and seeing no one, plunged into a path that led through the weeds. When he reached the centre, where they were highest, he stopped and drew the whisky flask from his pocket. He looked at it a moment; smiled grimly, and said aloud:

"Well, you've given me lots of trouble that nobody knows anything about but me."

He was about to drop the flask when he heard a noise, and looking up he saw his minister standing in the path before him, gazing at him with horrified eyes.

"My dear Colonel J——," said the good man. "You distress me beyond measure. I never knew that you drank. I am indeed deeply grieved to see you here in this condition."

The colonel was infuriated beyond control. "Don't give a d—— if you are," he shouted. "I'm drunk as a biled owl, and I don't care who knows it. I'm always drunk. I've drunk 15,000 gallons of whisky in the last two weeks. I'm a bad man about this time every Sunday. Here goes the bottle once more for luck."

He hurled the flask at the minister and it struck him on the ear and broke into twenty pieces. The minister let out a yell and turned and ran back to his house.

The colonel gathered a pile of stones and hid among the tall weeds, resolved to fight the whole town as long as his ammunition held out. His hard luck had made him desperate. An hour later three mounted policemen got into the weeds, and the colonel surrendered. He had cooled off by that time enough to explain matters, and as he was well known to be a perfectly sober and temperate citizen, he was allowed to go home.

But you can't get him to pick up a bottle now, empty or full.

36

The Mirage on the Frio

THE sheep man rejected the offer of a match, and lit his pipe from a burning brand. We were down on Buffalo Bayou fishing, and had cooked and eaten supper. Fried fresh fish, coffee, corn bread, potatoes, and just enough crisp bacon to flavour gave us a supper at which none murmured.

We reclined at ease and worshipped the goddess Nicotine. The moon made a glory in the eastern sky and spread a white shimmering glamour upon the black water of the bayou. A phantom tug crept down stream, leaving a ghostly, wavering silver wake, and a mysterious lapping and washing along the unseen shores. Mosquitoes hummed angrily about the borders of the hanging cloud of tobacco smoke. A dank fresh smell arose from bursting buds and wild flowers. We five sat in the chiaroscuro of the live oaks and cypresses, and babbled as most men and all women will when Night, the tongue loosener, succeeds the discrete Day.

Night should be held responsible for poets, breach of promise suits, betrayed secrets and dull stories. The man who will not tell more than he knows in the moonlight of a spring night is a rarity. Four of us were more or less hardened to moonlight and roses; one among us was young enough to note the soft effect of Luna's kiss upon the dim tree tops, the aerial perspective of the drifting gulf clouds, and the dim white eyes of the dogwood blossoms peering out of the wooded darkness. He noted and spake his thoughts without stint of adjectives, while we world-worn passengers grunted in reply; puffed at our cigars and pipes, and refused to commit ourselves on such trifling matters.

"Isn't it beautiful?" asked the young man. "The sky like the dome of some dream temple, the woods dark with mystery and the silence broken only by the faint breathing of nature."

"It's nice, and no mistake," answered the insurance agent, "but let me tell you, I've known men to plant the seeds of incurable disease along this old bayou. Feel that dampness rising every minute? A fellow never knows what is going to happen. Especially a man with a family dependent on him should——"

"Shut up," snapped the druggist. "For talking shop, recommend me to a man in your line. This is a pleasure trip we are on, and I have to have it spoiled by ringing in business. Talk about your malaria, why, two bottles of my——"

"There you go, just as bad," said the lawyer. "You fellows have run in the same old rut so long you can't get your minds on anything else. Put me on the witness stand, and I'll swear that I never mention my own business outside of my office; if I don't, kick me clean out of court."

"This night," said the sheep man, "reminds me of the night I was lost in the brush along the Frio. That was the night before the morning I seen the mi-ridge."

"The—ah—oh! the mirage?" said the young man.

"No," said the sheep man, "it wasn't no mi-rosh; this was a mi-ridge, and the plainest one I ever seen. They happened somethin' queer about this one, too, and I don't often tell it, after seein' that incredoolity generally waits upon the relatin' of it."

* * *

"Light up," said the druggist, reaching for the tobacco sack, "and let us have your yarn. There are very few things a man can't believe now-a-days."

"It was in the fall of '80," said the sheep man, "when I was runnin' sheep in La Salle County. There came a norther that scattered my flock of 1,500 muttons to thunderation. The shepherd couldn't hold 'em and they split up right and left, through the chaparral. I got on my hoss and hunted all one day, and I rounded up the biggest part of 'em during the afternoon. I seen a Mexican ridin' along what told me they was a big 'tajo of 'em down near the Palo Blanco crossin' of the Frio. I rode over that way, and when sundown come I was down in a big mesquite flat, where I couldn't see fifty yards before me any ways. Well, I got lost. For some four or five hours my pony stumbled around in the sacuista grass, windin' about this way and that, without knowin' any more than I did where he was at. 'Bout twelve o'clock I give it up, staked my pony and laid down under my saddle blanket to wait till mornin'. I was awful worried about my wife and the kid, who was by themselves on the ranch, for I knew they'd be scared half to death. There wasn't much to be afraid of, but you know how women folks are when night comes, 'specially when they wasn't any neighbour in ten miles of 'em.

* * *

"I was up at daylight, and soon as I'd got my bearin's I knowed just where I was. Right where I was I seen the Fort Ewell road, and a big dead elm on one side that I knew. I was just eighteen miles from my ranch. I jumped in the saddle, when all at once, looking across the Frio towards home, I seen this mi-ridge. These mi-ridges are sure wonderful. I never seen but three or four. It was a kind of misty mornin', with woolly gulf clouds a-flyin' across, and the hollows was all hazy. I seen my ranch-house, shearin' pen, the fences with saddles hangin' on 'em, the wood pile, with the axe stickin' in a log, and everything about the yard as plain as if they was only 200 yards away, and I was lookin' at 'em on a foggy mornin'. Everything looked somewhat ghostly like, and a little taller and bigger than it really was, but I could see even the white curtains at the windows and the pet sheep grazin' 'round the corral. It made me feel funny to see everything so close, when I knew I was eighteen miles away.

"All to once I seen the door open, and wife come out with the kid in her arms. It was all I could do to keep from hollerin' at her. You bet, I was glad to see her anyhow, and know they was all safe. Just then I seen somethin' big and black a-movin', and it growed plainer, like it had kinder come into focus, and it was a Mexican with a broad-brimmed sombrero, on a hoss, what rode up to the fence. He stopped there a minute and then I seen my wife run into the house and shut the door. I seen the Mexican jump off his hoss, try the door, and then go and get the axe at the wood pile. He came back and commenced to split down the door. The miridge commenced to get dimmer and faint like. I don't know what made me do such a fool thing, but I couldn't help it. I jerked my Winchester out'n its scabbard, drawed a bead on the darned scoundrel and fired. Then I cussed myself for an idiot, for tryin' to shoot somethin' eighteen miles away, jabbed my Winchester back in the scabbard, stuck my spurs in my broncho, and split through the brush like a roadrunner after a rattlesnake.

* * *

"I made that eighteen miles in eighty minutes. I never took the road, but crashed through the chaparral, jumped prickly pear and arroyo just as they come. When I got to the ranch I fell off my pony, and he leaned up against the fence streamin' wet and lookin' at me mighty reproachful. I never breathed in jumpin' from the fence to the back door. I clattered up the steps and yelled for Sallie, but my voice sounded to me like somebody's else's, 'way off. The door opened and out tumbled the wife and the kid, all right, but scared as wild ducks. 'Oh, Jim,' says the wife, 'where, oh where have you been? A drunken Mexican attacked the house this morning and tried to cut down the door with an axe.' I tried to ask some questions, but I couldn't. 'Look,' says Sallie.

"The other door was busted all to pieces and the axe was lyin' on the step, and the Mexican was lyin' on the ground and a Winchester ball had passed clear through his head."

"Who shot him?" asked the lawyer.

"I've told you all I know," said the sheep man. "Sallie said the man dropped all of a sudden while he was choppin' at the door, and she never heard no gun shoot. I don't pretend to explain nothin', I'm telling you what happened. You might say somebody in the brush seen him breakin' in the door and shot him, usin' noiseless powder, and then slipped away wit-out leavin' his card, or you might say you don't know nothin' at all about it, as I do."

"Do you think——" began the young man.

"No, I don't think," said the sheep man, rather shortly. "I said I'd tell you about the mi-ridge I seen, and I told you just as it happened. Is they any coffee left in that pot?"

37

A Houston Romance

About two years ago one of the most popular young society men in Houston mysteriously disappeared. He had been the glass of fashion and the mould of form of the Magnolia City for several years. Especially was he noted for his exquisite and fashionable dress, and he was regarded as the leader in bringing out the latest and correct styles of clothing. No one in Houston ever saw a wrinkle in his elegantly fitting clothes, or a spot upon his snowy linen. He possessed sufficient means to enable him to devote his whole time to society and the art of dress and his whole bearing and manners was well nigh equal to the famous Beau Brummell.

About a year ago it was noticed that he was beginning to grow preoccupied and reserved. His gay and gallant manner was as Chesterfieldian as ever, but he was becoming more silent and moody, and there seemed to be something weighing upon his mind. Suddenly, without a word of farewell, he disappeared, and no traces of him could be discovered. He left a good balance in the bank to his credit, and society racked its brains to conjecture some reason for his mysterious disappearance. He had no relatives in Houston, and with proverbial fickleness his acquaintances and butterfly friends soon allowed him to pass from their minds.

* * *

The mystery has at length been cleared up. A young Houston merchant who was an intimate associate with the young society man took a trip to Europe in September.

While in Italy he had a desire to visit one of the old monasteries among the Alps; so one day he ascended the Passo di San Giacomo, a road little wider than a bridle path that led up for 7,000 feet among the glaciers of the Leopontine Alps. Far up, perched upon a snow-covered crag, he could see the monastery of the Franciscan monks—the Minorite Friars of the Cismontana group of the Franciscans.

He picked his cautious way up the narrow way, pausing now and then to admire the rainbow hues that flashed from frozen glaciers, or the vast drifts of snow packed among the crevasses high above his head.

After six hours' arduous toil he stood before the massive iron gates of the monastery. He rang the bell, and a grim warden bade him enter and partake of the hospitality of the brothers. He was ushered into a vast dim hall, with walls and floors of cold grey stone. The monk who admitted him bade him wait, as the brothers were about to pass through on their way to their cells from evening prayer. A deep-toned bell clanged once; a great door softly opened, and a procession of shaved monks filed slowly and noiselessly past. Their heads were bowed and, as they told their beads, their lips moved in silent prayer.

As they came past the visitor he was astounded to see among the devout monks the form of the man who had once been the curled darling and pattern of elegance in Houston.

* * *

He called his name and the monk, startled by his voice, raised his head and stepped from the ranks of his brother penitents. The others continued their silent march until another great door had closed behind them.

The Houston man gazed at the friar in wonder.

He wore a long black robe, slightly confined at the waist by a hempen cord, that hung to his feet in classic, shapely folds. The crown of his head was shaven and his face was as smooth as a maiden's. But the most noticeable thing was the expression of absolute peace and serene happiness that shone from his features. There was no trace of the worried and absent look that his friends had noticed before he disappeared.

A calm and holy beatitude beamed from his face like a benison.

"In heaven's name," said his friend, "what brought you

here to bury yourself forever from the world; why did you leave your friends and pleasures to pass your days in this dreary place?"

"Listen," said the monk, "and I will tell you. I am now supremely and ecstatically happy. I have attained the goal of my desires. Look at this robe." He glanced proudly at the dark, severe robe that swept downward from his waist in graceful folds.

"I am one man," he continued, "who has arrived at the fruition of his dearest earthly hopes. I have got something on at least that will not bag at the knees."

38

The Marquis and Miss Sally

WITHOUT knowing it, Old Bill Bascom had the honour of being overtaken by fate the same day with the Marquis of Borodale.

The Marquis lived in Regent Square, London. Old Bill lived on Limping Doe Creek, Hardeman County, Texas. The cataclysm that engulfed the Marquis took the form of a bursting bubble known as the Central and South American Mahogany and Caoutchouc Monopoly. Old Bill's Nemesis was in the no less perilous shape of a band of civilized Indian cattle thieves from the Territory who ran off his entire herd of four hundred head, and shot Old Bill dead as he trailed after them. To even up the consequences of the two catastrophes, the Marquis, as soon as he found that all he possessed would pay only fifteen shillings in the pound of his indebtedness shot himself.

Old Bill left a family of six motherless sons and daughters, who found themselves without even a red steer left to eat, or a red cent to buy one with.

The Marquis left one son, a young man who had come to the States and established a large and well-stocked ranch in the Panhandle of Texas. When this young man learned the news he mounted his pony and rode to town. There he placed everything he owned except his horse, saddle, Winchester, and fifteen dollars in his pockets, in the hands of his lawyers, with instructions to sell and forward the proceeds to London to be applied to the payment of his father's debts. Then he mounted his pony and rode southward.

One day, arriving about the same time, but by different trails, two young chaps rode up to the Diamond-Cross ranch, on the Little Piedra, and asked for work. Both were dressed neatly and sprucely in cowboy costume. One was a straight-set fellow, with delicate handsome features, short brown hair, and smooth face, sunburned to a golden brown. The other applicant was stouter and broad-shouldered, with fresh red complexion, somewhat freckled, reddish curling hair, and a rather plain face, made attractive by laughing eyes and a pleasant mouth.

The superintendent of the Diamond-Cross was of the opinion that he could give them work. In fact, word had reached him that morning that the camp cook—a most important member of the outfit—had straddled his broncho and departed, being unable to withstand the fire of fun and practical jokes of which he was, ex-officio, the legitimate target.

"Can either of you cook?" asked the superintendent.

"I can," said the reddish-haired fellow, promptly. "I've cooked in camp quite a lot. I'm willing to take the job until you've got something else to offer."

"Now, that's the way I like to hear a man talk," said the superintendent, approvingly. "I'll give you a note to Saunders, and he'll put you to work."

Thus the names of John Bascom and Charles Norwood were added to the pay-roll of the Diamond-Cross. The two left for the round-up camp immediately after dinner. Their directions were simple, but sufficient: "Keep down the arroyo for fifteen miles till you get there." Both being strangers from afar, young, spirited, and thus thrown together by chance for a long ride, it is likely that the comradeship that afterward existed so strongly between them began that afternoon as they meandered along the little valley of the Canada Verda.

They reached their destination just after sunset. The main camp of the round-up was comfortably located on the bank of a long water-hole, under a fine mott of timber. A number of small A tents pitched upon grassy spots and the big wall tent for provisions showed that the camp was intended to be occupied for a considerable length of time.

The round-up had ridden in but a few moments before, hungry and tired, to a supperless camp. The boys were engaged in an emulous display of anathemas supposed to fit the case of the absconding cook. While they were unsaddling and hobbling their ponies, the new-comers rode in and inquired for Pink Saunders. The boss of the round-up came forth and was given the superintendent's note.

Pink Saunders, though a boss during working hours, was a humorist in camp, where everybody, from cook to superintendent, is equal. After reading the note he waved his hand toward the camp and shouted, ceremoniously, at the top of his voice: "Gentlemen, allow me to present to you the Marquis and Miss Sally."

At the words both the new arrivals betrayed confusion. The newly employed cook started, with a surprised look on his face, but, immediately recollecting that "Miss Sally" is the generic name for the male cook in every west Texas cow camp, he recovered his composure with a grin at his own expense.

His companion showed little less discomposure, even turning angrily, with a bitten lip, and reaching for his saddle pommel, as if to remount his pony; but "Miss Sally" touched his arm and said, laughing, "Come now, Marquis; that was quite a compliment from Saunders. It's that distinguished air of yours and aristocratic nose that made him call you that."

He began to unsaddle, and the Marquis, restored to equanimity, followed his example. Rolling up his sleeves, Miss Sally sprang for the grub wagon, shouting:

"I'm the new cook, b'thunder! Some of you chaps rustle a little wood for a fire, and I'll guarantee you a hot square meal inside of thirty minutes." Miss Sally's energy and good-humour, as he ransacked the grub wagon for coffee, flour, and bacon, won the good opinion of the camp instantly.

And also, in days following, the Marquis, after becoming better acquainted, proved to be a cheerful, pleasant fellow, always a little reserved, and taking no part in the rough camp frolics; but the boys gradually came to respect this reserve—which fitted the title Saunders had given him—and even to like him for it. Saunders had assigned him to a place holding the herd during the cuttings. He proved to be a skilful rider and as good with the lariat or in the branding pen as most of them.

The Marquis and Miss Sally grew to be quite close comrades. After supper was over, and everything cleaned up, you would generally find them together, Miss Sally smoking his brier-root pipe, and the Marquis plaiting a quirt or scraping rawhide for a new pair of hobbles.

The superintendent did not forget his promise to keep an eye on the cook. Several times, when visiting the camp, he held long talks with him. He seemed to have taken a fancy to Miss Sally. One afternoon he rode up, on his way back to the ranch from a tour of the camps, and said to him:

"There'll be a man here in the morning to take your place. As soon as he shows up you come to the ranch. I want you to take charge of the ranch accounts and correspondence. I want somebody that I can depend upon to keep things straight when I'm away. The wages'll be all right. The Diamond-Cross'll hold its end up with a man who'll look after its interests."

"All right," said Miss Sally, as quietly as if he had expected the notice all along. "Any objections to my bringing my wife down to the ranch?"

"You married?" said the superintendent, frowning a little. "You didn't mention it when we were talking."

"Because I'm not," said the cook. "But I'd like to be. Thought I'd wait till I got a job under roof. I couldn't ask her to live in a cow camp."

"Right," agreed the superintendent. "A camp isn't quite the place for a married man—but—well, there's plenty of room at the house, and if you suit us as well as I think you will you can afford it. You write to her to come on."

"All right," said Miss Sally again, "I'll ride in as soon as I am relieved to-morrow."

It was a rather chilly night, and after supper the cow-punchers were lounging about a big fire of dried mesquite chunks.

Their usual exchanges of jokes and repartee had dwindled almost to silence, but silence in a cow camp generally betokens the brewing of mischief.

Miss Sally and the Marquis were seated upon a log, discussing the relative merits of the lengthened or shortened stirrup in long-distance riding. The Marquis arose presently and went to a tree near by to examine some strips of rawhide he was seasoning for making a lariat. Just as he left a little puff of wind blew some scraps of tobacco from a cigarette that Dry-Creek Smithers was rolling, into Miss Sally's eyes. While the cook was rubbing at them, with tears flowing, "Phonograph" Davis—so called on account of his strident voice—arose and began a speech.

"Fellers and citizens! I desire to perpound a interrogatory. What is the most grievious spectacle what the human mind can contemplate?"

A volley of answers responded to his question.

"A busted flush!"

"A Maverick when you ain't got your branding-iron!"

"Yourself!"

"The hole in the end of some other feller's gun!"

"Shet up, you ignoramuses," said old Taller, the fat cow-puncher. "Phony knows what it is. He's waitin' for to tell us."

"No, fellers and citizens," continued Phonograph.

"Them spectacles you've e-numerated air shore grievious, and way up yonder close to the so-lution, but they ain't it. The most grievious spectacle air that"—he pointed to Miss Sally, who was still rubbing his streaming eyes—"a trustin' and a inveegled female a-weepin' tears on account of her heart bein' busted by a false deceiver. Air we men or air we catamounts to gaze upon the blightin' of our Miss Sally's affections by a a-risto-crat, which has come among us with his superior beauty and his glitterin' title to give the weeps to the lovely critter we air bound to pertect? Air we goin' to act like men, or air we goin' to keep on eatin' soggy chuck from her cryin' so plentiful over the breadpan?"

"It's a gallopin' shame," said Dry-Creek, with a sniffle. "It ain't human. I've noticed the varmint a-palaverin' round her frequent. And him a Marquis! Ain't that a title, Phony?"

"It's somethin' like a king," the Brushy Creek Kid hastened to explain, "only lower in the deck. Guess it comes in between the Jack and the ten-spot."

"Don't misconstruct me," went on Phonograph, "as undervaluatin' the a-ristocrats. Some of 'em air proper people and can travel right along with the Watson boys. I've herded some with 'em myself. I've viewed the elephant with the Mayor of Fort Worth, and I've listened to the owl with the gen'ral passenger agent of the Katy, and they can keep up with the percession from where you laid the chunk. But when a Marquis monkeys with the innocent affections of a cook-lady, may I inquire what the case seems to call for?"

"The leathers," shouted Dry-Creek Smithers.

"You hearn 'er, Charity!" was the Kid's form of corroboration.

"We've got your company," assented the cowpunchers, in chorus.

Before the Marquis realized their intention, two of them seized him by each arm and led him up to the log. Phonograph Davis, self-appointed to carry out the sentence, stood ready, with a pair of stout leather leggings in his hands.

It was the first time they had ever laid hands on the Marquis during their somewhat rude sports.

"What are you up to?" he asked, indignantly, with flashing eyes.

"Go easy, Marquis," whispered Rube Fellows, one of the boys that held him. "It's all in fun. Take it good-natured and they'll let you off light. They're only goin' to stretch you over the log an tan you eight or ten times with the leggin's. 'Twont hurt much."

The Marquis, with an exclamation of anger, his white teeth gleaming, suddenly exhibited a surprising strength. He wrenched with his arms so violently that the four men were swayed and dragged many yards from the log. A cry of anger escaped him, and then Miss Sally, his eyes cleared of the tobacco, saw, and he immediately mixed with the struggling group.

But at that moment a loud "Hallo!" rang in their ears, and a buckboard drawn by a team of galloping mustangs spun into the camp-fire's circle of light. Every man turned to look, and what they saw drove from their minds all thoughts of carrying out Phonograph Davis's rather time-worn contribution to the evening's amusement. Bigger game than the Marquis was at hand, and his captors released him and stood staring at the approaching victim.

The buckboard and team belonged to Sam Holly, a cattleman from the Big Muddy. Sam was driving, and with him was a stout smooth-faced man, wearing a frock coat and a high silk hat. That was the county judge, Mr. Dave Hackett, candidate for re-election. Sam was escorting him about the county, among the camps, to shake up the sovereign voters.

The men got out, hitched the team to a mesquite, and walked toward the fire.

Instantly every man in camp, except the Marquis, Miss Sally, and Pink Saunders, who had to play host, uttered a frightful yell of assumed terror and fled on all sides into the darkness.

"Heavens alive!" exclaimed Hackett, "are we as ugly as that? How do you do, Mr. Saunders? Glad to see you again. What are you doing to my hat, Holly?"

"I was afraid of this hat," said Sam Holly, meditatively. He had taken the hat from Hackett's head and was holding it in his hand, looking dubiously around at the shadows beyond the firelight where now absolute stillness reigned. "What do you think, Saunders?"

Pink grinned.

"Better elevate it some," he said, in the tone of one giving disinterested advice. "The light ain't none too good. I wouldn't want it on my head."

Holly stepped upon the hub of a hind wheel of the grub wagon, and hung the hat upon a limb of a live oak. Scarcely had his foot touched the ground when the crash of a dozen six-shooters split the air, and the hat fell to the ground riddled with bullets.

A hissing noise was heard as if from a score of rattlesnakes, and now the cow-punchers emerged on all sides from the darkness, stepping high, with ludicrously exaggerated caution and "hist"-ing to one another to observe the utmost prudence in approaching. They formed a solemn wide circle about the hat, gazing at it in manifest alarm, and seized every few moments by little stampedes of panicky flight.

"It's the varmint," said one in awed tones, "that flits up and down in the low grounds at night, saying, 'Willie-Wallo!'"

"It's the venomous Kypootum," proclaimed another. "It stings after it's dead, and hollers after it's buried."

"It's the chief of the hairy tribe," said Phonograph Davis "But it's stone dead, now, boys."

"Don't you believe it," demurred Dry-Creek. "It's only 'possumin''. It's the dreaded High-gollacum fantod from the forest. There's only one way to destroy its life."

He led forward Old Taller, the 240-pound cowpuncher. Old Taller placed the hat upright on the ground and solemnly sat upon it, crushing it as flat as a pancake.

Hackett had viewed these proceedings with wide-open eyes. Sam Holly saw that his anger was rising, and said to him:

"Here's where you win or lose, Judge. There are sixty votes on the Diamond Cross. The boys are trying your mettle. Take it as a joke, and I don't think you'll regret it." And Hackett saw the point and rose to the occasion.

Advancing to where the slayers of the wild beast were standing above its remains and declaring it to be at last defunct, he said, with deep earnestness:

"Boys, I must thank you for this gallant rescue. While driving through the arroyo that cruel monster that you have so fearlessly and repeatedly slaughtered sprang upon us from the tree tops. To you I shall consider that I owe my life, and also, I hope, re-election to the office for which I am again a candidate. Allow me to hand you my card."

The cow-punchers, always so sober-faced while engaged in their monkey-shines, relaxed into a grin of approval.

But Phonograph Davis, his appetite for fun not yet appeased, had something more up his sleeve.

"Pardner," he said, addressing Hackett with grave severity, "many a camp would be down on you for turnin' loose a pernicious varmint like that in it; but, bein' as we all escaped without loss of life, we'll overlook it. You can play square with us if you'll do it."

"How's that?" asked Hackett suspiciously.

"You're authorized to perform the sacred rights and lefts of mattermony, air you not?"

"Well, yes," replied Hackett. "A marriage ceremony conducted by me would be legal."

"A wrong air to be righted in this here camp," said Phonograph, virtuously. "A aristocrat have slighted a 'umble but beautchoos female wat's pinin' for his affections. It's the jooty of the camp to drag forth the haughty descendant of a hundred—or maybe a hundred and twenty-five—earls, even so at the p'int of a lariat, and jine him to the weepin' lady. Fellows! round up Miss Sally and the Marquis, there's goin' to be a weddin'."

This whim of Phonograph's was received with whoops of appreciation. The cow-punchers started to apprehend the principles of the proposed ceremony.

"Kindly prompt me," said Hackett, wiping his forehead, though the night was cool, "how far this thing is to be carried. And might I expect any further portions of my raiment to be mistaken for wild animals and killed?"

"The boys are livelier than usual to-night," said Saunders. "The boys they are talking about marrying are two of the boys—a herd rider and the cook. It's another joke. You and Sam will have to sleep here to-night anyway; p'rhaps you'd better see 'em through with it. Maybe they'll quiet down after that."

The matchmakers found Miss Sally seated on the tongue of the grub wagon, calmly smoking his pipe. The Marquis leaning idly against one of the trees under which the supply tent was pitched.

Into this tent they were both hustled, and Phonograph, as master of ceremonies, gave orders for the preparations.

"You, Dry-Creek and Jimmy, and Ben and Taller—hump yourselves to the wildwood and rustle flowers for the blow-out—mesquite'll do—and get that Spanish dagger blossom at the corner of the horse corral for the bride to pack. You, Limpy, get out that red and yaller blanket of your'n for Miss Sally's skyirt. Marquis, you'll do 'thout fixin'; nobody don' ever look at the groom."

During their absurd preparation, the two principals were

left alone for a few moments in the tent. The Marquis suddenly showed wild perturbation.

"This foolishness must not go on," he said, turning to Miss Sally a face white in the light of the lantern hanging to the ridge-pole.

"Why not?" said the cook, with an amused smile. "It's fun for the boys; and they've always let you off pretty light in their frolics. I don't mind it."

"But you don't understand," persisted the Marquis, pleadingly. "That man is county judge, and his acts are binding. I can't—oh, you don't know——"

The cook stepped forward and took the Marquis's hands.

"Sally Bascom," he said, "I KNOW!"

"You know!" faltered the Marquis, trembling. "And you want to——"

"More than I ever wanted anything. Will you—here come the boys!"

The cow-punchers crowded in, laden with armfuls of decorations.

"Perfidous coyote!" said Phonograph, sternly, addressing the Marquis. "Air you willing to patch up the damage you've did this ere slab-sided but trustin' bunch o' calico by single-footin' easy to the altar, or will we have to rope ye, and drag you thar?"

The Marquis pushed back his hat, and leaned jauntily against some high-piled sacks of beans. His cheeks were flushed, and his eyes were shining.

"Go on with the rat killin'," said he.

A little while after a procession approached the tree under which Hackett, Holly, and Saunders were sitting smoking.

Limpy Walker was in the lead, extracting a doleful tune from his concertina. Next came the bride and groom. The cook wore the gorgeous Navajo blanket tied around his waist and carried in one hand the waxen-white Spanish dagger blossom as large a peck-measure and weighing fifteen pounds. His hat was ornamented with mesquite branches and yellow ratama blooms. A resurrected mosquito bar served as a veil. After them stumbled Phonograph Davis, in the character of the bride's father, weeping into a saddle blanket with sobs that could be heard a mile away. The cow-punchers followed by twos, loudly commenting upon the bride's appearance in a supposed imitation of the audiences at fashionable weddings.

Hackett rose as the procession halted before him, and after a little lecture upon matrimony, asked:

"What are your names?"

"Sally and Charles," answered the cook.

"Join hands, Charles and Sally."

Perhaps there never was a stranger wedding. For, wedding it was, though only two of those present knew it.

When the ceremony was over, the cow-punchers gave one yell of congratulation and immediately abandoned their foolery for the night. Blankets were unrolled, and sleep became the paramount question

The cook (divested of his decorations) and the Marquis lingered for a moment in the shadow of the grub wagon. The Marquis leaned her head against his shoulder.

"I didn't know what else to do," she was saying. "Father was gone, and we kids had to rustle. I had helped him so much with the cattle that I thought I'd turn cowboy. There wasn't anything else I could make a living at. I wasn't much stuck on it though, after I got here, and I'd have left only——"

"Only what?"

"You know. Tell me something. When did you first—what made you——"

"Oh, it was as soon as we struck the camp, when Saunders bawled out 'The Marquis and Miss Sally!' I saw how rattled you got at the name, and I had my sus——"

"Cheeky!" whispered the Marquis. "And why should you think that I thought he was calling me 'Miss Sally'?"

"Because," answered the cook, calmly, "I was the Marquis. My father was the Marquis of Borodale. But you'll excuse that, won't you, Sally? It really isn't my fault, you know."

39

Helping the Other Fellow

But can thim that helps others help thimselves?

—*Mulvaney.*

I

THIS is the story that William Trotter told me on the beach at Aguas Frescas while I waited for the gig of the captain of the fruit steamer *Andador*, which was to take me aboard. Reluctantly I was leaving the Land of Always Afternoon. William was remaining, and he favoured me with a condensed oral autobiography as we sat on the sands in the shade cast by the Bodega Naçional.

As usual, I became aware that the Man from Bombay had already written the story; but as he had compressed it to an eight-word sentence, I have become an expansionist, and have quoted his phrase above, with apologies to him and best regards to *Terence*.

II

"Don't you ever have a desire to go back to the land of derby hats and starched collars?" I asked him. "You seem to be a handy man and a man of action," I continued, "and I am sure I could find you a comfortable job somewhere in the States."

Ragged, shiftless, barefooted, a confirmed eater of the lotos, William Trotter had pleased me much, and I hated to see him gobbled up by the tropics.

"I've no doubt you could," he said, idly splitting the bark from a section of sugar-cane. "I've no doubt you could do much for me. If every man could do as much for himself as he can for others, every country in the world would be holding millenniums instead of centennials."

There seemed to be pabulum in W. T.'s words. And then another idea came to me.

I had a brother in Chicopee Falls who owned manufactories—cotton, or sugar, or A.A. sheetings, or something in the commercial line. He was vulgarly rich, and therefore reverenced art. The artistic temperament of the family was monopolized at my birth. I knew that Brother James would honour my slightest wish. I would demand from him a position in cotton, sugar, or sheetings for William Trotter—something, say, at two hundred a month or thereabouts. I confided my beliefs and made my large propositions to William. He had pleased me much, and he was ragged.

While we were talking, there was a sound of firing guns—four or five, rattlingly, as if by a squad. The cheerful noise came from the direction of the cuartel, which is a kind of makeshift barracks for the soldiers of the republic.

"Hear that?" said William Trotter. "Let me tell you about it.

"A year ago I landed on this coast with one solitary dollar. I have the same sum in my pocket to-day. I was second cook on a tramp fruiter; and they marooned me here early one morning, without benefit of clergy, just because I poulticed the face of the first mate with cheese omelette at dinner. The fellow had kicked because I'd put horseradish in it instead of cheese.

"When they threw me out of the yawl into three feet of surf, I waded ashore and sat down under a palm-tree. By and by a fine-looking white man with a red face and white clothes, genteel as possible, but somewhat under the influence, came and sat down beside me.

"I had noticed there was a kind of a village back of the beach, and enough scenery to outfit a dozen moving-picture shows. But I thought, of course, it was a cannibal suburb, and I was wondering whether I was to be served with carrots or mushrooms. And, as I say, this dressed-up man sits beside me, and we become friends in the space of a minute or two. For an hour we talked, and he told me all about it.

"It seems that he was a man of parts, conscientiousness, and plausibility, besides being educated and a wreck to his appetites. He told me all about it. Colleges had turned him out, and distilleries had taken him in. Did I tell you his name? It was Clifford Wainwright. I didn't exactly catch the cause of his being cast away on that particular stretch of South America; but I reckon it was his own business. I asked him if he'd ever been second cook on a tramp fruiter, and he said no; so that concluded my line of surmises. But he talked like the encyclopedia from 'A—Berlin' to 'Trilo—Zyria'. And he carried a watch—a silver arrangement with works, and up to date within twenty-four hours, anyhow.

"'I'm pleased to have met you,' says Wainwright. 'I'm a devotee to the great joss Booze; but my ruminating facilities are unrepaired,' says he—or words to that effect. 'And I hate,' says he, 'to see fools trying to run the world.'

"'I never touch a drop,' says I, 'and there are many kinds of fools; and the world runs on its own apex, according to science, with no meddling from me.'

"'I was referring,' says he, 'to the president of this republic. His country is in a desperate condition. Its treasury is empty, it's on the verge of war with Nicamala, and if it wasn't for the hot weather the people would be starting revolutions in every town. Here is a nation,' goes on Wainwright, 'on the brink of destruction. A man of intelligence could rescue it from its impending doom in one day by issuing the necessary edicts and orders. President Gomez knows nothing of statesmanship or policy. Do you know Adam Smith?'

"'Lemme see,' says I. 'There was a one-eared man named Smith in Fort Worth, Texas, but I think his first name was ——'

"'I am referring to the political economist,' says Wainwright.

"'S'mother Smith, then,' says I. 'The one I speak of never was arrested.'

"So Wainwright boils some more with indignation at the insensibility of people who are not corpulent to fill public positions; and then he tells me he is going out to the president's summer palace, which is four miles from Aguas Frescas, to instruct him in the art of running steam-heated republics.

"'Come along with me, Trotter,' says he, 'and I'll show you what brains can do.'

"'Anything in it?' I asks.

"'The satisfaction,' says he, 'of redeeming a country of two hundred thousand population from ruin back to prosperity and peace.'

"'Great,' says I. 'I'll go with you. I'd prefer to eat a live broiled lobster just now; but give me liberty as second choice if I can't be in at the death.'

"Wainwright and me permeates through the town, and he halts at a rum-dispensary.

"'Have you any money?' he asks.

"'I have,' says I, fishing out my silver dollar. 'I always go about with adequate sums of money.'

"'Then we'll drink,' says Wainwright.

"'Not me,' says I. 'Not any demon rum or any of its ramifications for mine. It's one of my non-weaknesses.'

"'It's my failing,' says he. 'What's your particular soft point?'

"'Industry,' says I, promptly. 'I'm hard-working, diligent, industrious, and energetic.'

"'My dear Mr. Trotter,' says he, 'surely I've known you long enough to tell you you are a liar. Every man must have his own particular weakness, and his own particular strength in other things. Now, you will buy me a drink of rum, and we will call on President Gomez.'"

III

"Well, sir," Trotter went on, "we walks the four miles out, through a virgin conservatory of palms and ferns and other roof-garden products, to the president's summer White House. It was blue, and reminded you of what you see on the stage in the third act, which they describe as 'same as the first,' on the programmes.

"There was more than fifty people waiting outside the iron fence that surrounded the house and grounds. There was generals and agitators and épergnes in gold-laced uniforms, and citizens in diamonds and Panama hats—all waiting to get an audience with the Royal Five-Card Draw. And in a kind of a summer-house in front of the mansion we could see a burnt-sienna man eating breakfast out of gold dishes and taking his time. I judged that the crowd outside had come out for their morning orders and requests, and was afraid to intrude.

"But C. Wainwright wasn't. The gate was open, and he walked inside and up to the president's table as confident as a man who knows the head waiter in a fifteen-cent restaurant. And I went with him, because I had only seventy-five cents, and there was nothing else to do.

"The Gomez man rises from his chair, and looks, coloured man as he was, like he was about to call out for a corporal of the guard, post number one. But Wainwright says some phrases to him in a peculiarly lubricating manner; and the first thing you know we was all three of us seated at the table, with coffee and rolls and iguana cutlets coming as fast as about ninety peons could rustle 'em.

"And then Wainwright begins to talk; but the president interrupts him.

"'You Yankees,' says he, polite, 'assuredly take the cake for assurance, I assure you'—or words to that effect. He spoke English better than you or me. 'You've had a long walk,' says he, 'but it's nicer in the cool morning to walk than to ride. May I suggest some refreshments?' says he.

"'Rum,' says Wainwright.

"'Gimme a cigar,' says I.

"Well, sir, the two talked an hour, keeping the generals and equities all in their good uniforms waiting outside the fence. And while I smoked, silent, I listened to Clifford Wainwright making a solid republic out of the wreck of one. I didn't follow his arguments with any special collocation of international intelligibility, but he had Mr. Gomez's attention glued and riveted. He takes out a pencil and marks the white linen tablecloth all over with figures and estimates and deductions. He speaks more or less disrespectfully of import and export duties and custom-house receipts and taxes and treaties and budgets and concessions and such truck that politics and government require; and when he gets through the Gomez man hops up and shakes his hand and says he's saved the country and the people.

"'You shall be rewarded,' says the president.

"'Might I suggest another—rum?' says Wainwright.

"'Cigar for me—darker brand,' says I.

"Well, sir, the president sent me and Wainwright back to the town in a victoria hitched to two flea-bitten selling-platers—but the best the country afforded.

"I found out afterwards that Wainwright was a regular beachcomber—the smartest man on the whole coast, but kept down by rum. I liked him.

"One day I inveigled him into a walk out a couple of miles from the village, where there was an old grass hut on the bank of a little river. While he was sitting on the grass, talking beautiful of the wisdom of the world that he had learned in books, I took hold of him easy and tied his hands and feet together with leather thongs that I had in my pocket.

"'Lie still,' says I, 'and meditate on the exigencies and irregularities of life till I get back.'

"I went to a shack in Aguas Frescas where a mighty wise girl named Timotea Carrizo lived with her mother. The girl was just about as nice as you ever saw. In the States she would have been called a brunette; but she was better than a brunette—I should say she was what you might term an écru shade. I knew her pretty well. I told her about my friend Wainwright. She gave me a double handful of bark—calisaya, I think it was—and some more herbs that I was to mix with it, and told me what to do. I was to make tea of it and give it to him, and keep him from rum for a certain time. And for two weeks I did it. You know, I liked Wainwright. Both of us was broke; but Timotea sent us goat-meat and plantains and tortillas every day; and at last I got the curse of drink lifted from Clifford Wainwright. He lost his taste for it. And in the cool of the evening him and me would sit on the roof of Timotea's mother's hut, eating harmless truck like toffee and rice and stewed crabs, and playing the accordion.

"About that time President Gomez found out that the

advice of C. Wainwright was the stuff he had been looking for. The country was pulling out of debt, and the treasury had enough boodle in it for him to amuse himself occasionally with the night-latch. The people were beginning to take their two-hour siestas again every day—which was the surest sign of prosperity.

"So down from the regular capital he sends for Clifford Wainwright and makes him his private secretary at twenty thousand Peru dollars a year. Yes, sir—so much. Wainwright was on the water-wagon—thanks to me and Timotea—and he was soon in clover with the government gang. Don't forget what done it—calisaya bark with them other herbs mixed—make a tea of it, and give a cupful every two hours. Try it yourself. It takes away the desire.

"As I said, a man can do a lot more for another party than he can for himself. Wainwright, with his brains, got a whole country out of trouble and on its feet; but what could he do for himself? And without any special brains, but with some nerve and common sense, I put him on his feet because I never had the weakness that he did—nothing but a cigar for mine, thanks. And——"

Trotter paused. I looked at his tattered clothes and at his deeply sunburnt, hard, thoughtful face.

"Didn't Cartwright ever offer to do anything for you?" I asked.

"Wainwright," corrected Trotter. "Yes, he offered me some pretty good jobs. But I'd have had to leave Aguas Frescas; so I didn't take any of 'em up. Say, I didn't tell you much about that girl—Timotea. We rather hit it off together. She was as good as you find 'em anywhere—Spanish, mostly, with just a twist of lemon-peel on top. What if they did live in a grass hut and went bare-armed?

"A month ago," went on Trotter, "she went away. I don't know where to. But——"

"You'd better come back to the States," I insisted. "I can promise you positively that my brother will give you a position in cotton, sugar, or sheetings—I am not certain which."

"I think she went back with her mother," said Trotter,

"to the village in the mountains that they come from. Tell me, what would this job you speak of pay?"

"Why," said I, hesitating over commerce, "I should say fifty or a hundred dollars a month—maybe two hundred."

"Ain't it funny," said Trotter, digging his toes in the sand. "what a chump a man is when it comes to paddling his own canoe? I don't know. Of course, I'm not making a living here. I'm on the bum. But—well, I wish you could have seen that Timotea. Every man has his own weak spot."

The gig from the *Andador* was coming ashore to take out the captain, purser, and myself, the lone passenger. "I'll guarantee," said I confidently, "that my brother will pay you seventy-five dollars a month."

"All right, then," said William Trotter. "I'll——"

But a soft voice called across the blazing sands. A girl, faintly lemon-tinted, stood in the Calle Real and called. She was bare-armed—but what of that?

"It's her!" said William Trotter, looking. "She's come back! I'm obliged, but I can't take the job. Thanks, just the same. Ain't it funny how we can't do nothing for ourselves, but we can do wonders for the other fellow? You was about to get me with your financial propositions; but we've all got our weak points. Timotea's mine. And, say!" Trotter had turned to leave, but he retraced the step or two that he had taken. "I like to have left you without saying good-bye," said he. "It kind of rattles you when they go away unexpected for a month and come back the same way. Shake hands. So long! Say, do you remember them gunshots we heard a while ago up at the cuartel? Well, I knew what they was, but I didn't mention it. It was Clifford Wainwright being shot by a squad of soldiers against a stone wall for giving away secrets of state to that Nicamala republic. Oh, yes, it was rum that did it. He backslided and got his. I guess we all have our weak points, and can't do much toward helping ourselves. Mine's waiting for me. I'd have liked to have that job with your brother, but—we've all got our weak points. So long!"

IV

A big black Carib carried me on his back through the surf to the ship's boat. On the way the purser handed me a letter that he had brought for me at the last moment from the post office in Aguas Frescas. It was from my brother. He requested me to meet him at the St. Charles Hotel in New Orleans and accept a position with his house—in either cotton, sugar, or sheetings, and with five thousand dollars a year as my salary.

When I arrived at the Crescent City I hurried away—far away from the St. Charles to a dim *chambre garnie* in Bienville Street. And there, looking down from my attic window from time to time at the old, yellow, absinthe house across the street, I wrote this story to buy my bread and butter.

"Can thim that helps others help thimselves?"

40

The Caliph and the Cad

SURELY there is no pastime more diverting than that of mingling, incognito, with persons of wealth and station. Where else but in those circles can one see life in its primitive, crude state, unhampered by the conventions that bind the dwellers in a lower sphere?

There was a certain Caliph of Bagdad who was accustomed to go down among the poor and lowly for the solace obtained from the relation of their tales and histories. Is it not strange that the humble and poverty-stricken have not availed themselves of the pleasure they might glean by donning diamonds and silks and playing Caliph among the haunts of the upper world?

There was one who saw the possibilities of thus turning the tables on Haroun al Raschid. His name was Corny Brannigan, and he was a truck driver for a Canal Street importing firm. And if you read further you will learn how he turned upper Broadway into Bagdad and learned something about himself that he did not know before.

Many people would have called Corny a snob—preferably by means of a telephone. His chief interest in life, his chosen amusement, and his sole diversion after working hours, was to place himself in juxtaposition—since he could not hope to mingle—with people of fashion and means.

Every evening after Corny had put up his team and dined at a lunch-counter that made immediateness a speciality, he would clothe himself in evening raiment as correct as any you will see in the palm rooms. Then he would betake himself to that ravishing, radiant roadway devoted to Thespis, Thaïs, and Bacchus.

For a time he would stroll about the lobbies of the best hotels, his soul steeped in blissful content. Beautiful women, cooing like doves, but feathered like birds of Paradise, flicked him with their robes as they passed. Courtly gentlemen attended them, gallant and assiduous. And Corny's heart within him swelled like Sir Lancelot's, for the mirror spoke to him as he passed and said: "Corny, lad, there's not a guy among 'em that looks a bit the sweller than yerself. And you drivin' of a truck and them swearin' off their taxes and playin' the red in art galleries with the best in the land!"

And the mirrors spake the truth. Mr. Corny Brannigan had acquired the outward polish, if nothing more. Long and keen observation of polite society had gained for him its manner, its genteel air, and—most difficult of acquirement—its repose and ease.

Now and then in the hotels Corny had managed conversation and temporary acquaintance with substantial, if not distinguished, guests. With many of these he had exchanged cards, and the ones he received he carefully treasured for his own use later. Leaving the hotel lobbies, Corny would stroll leisurely about, lingering at the theatre entrance, dropping into the fashionable restaurants as if seeking some friend. He rarely patronized any of these places; he was no bee come to suck honey, but a butterfly flashing his wings among the flowers whose calyces held no sweets for him. His wages were not large enough to furnish him with more than the outside garb of the gentleman. To have been one of the beings he so cunningly imitated, Corny Brannigan would have given his right hand.

One night Corny had an adventure. After absorbing the delights of an hour's lounging in the principal hotels along Broadway, he passed up into the stronghold of Thespis. Cab drivers hailed him as a likely fare, to his prideful content. Languishing eyes were turned upon him as a hopeful source of lobsters and the delectable, ascendant globules of effervescence. These overtures and unconscious compliments Corny swallowed as manna, and hoped Bill, the off horse, would be less lame in the left forefoot in the morning.

Beneath a cluster of milky globes of electric light Corny paused to admire the sheen of his low-cut patent leather shoes. The building occupying the angle was a pretentious café. Out of this came a couple, a lady in a white, cobwebby evening gown, with a lace wrap like a wreath of mist thrown over it, and a man, tall, faultless, assured—too assured. They moved to the edge of the sidewalk and halted. Corny's eye, ever alert for "pointers" in "swell" behaviour, took them in with a sidelong glance.

"The carriage is not here," said the lady. "You ordered it to wait?"

"I ordered it for nine-thirty," said the man. "It should be here now."

A familiar note in the lady's voice drew a more especial attention from Corny. It was pitched in a key well known to him. The soft electric shone upon her face. Sisters of sorrow have no quarters fixed for them. In the index to the book of breaking hearts you will find that Broadway follows very soon after the Bowery. This lady's face was sad, and her voice was attuned with it. They waited, as if for the carriage. Corny waited too, for it was out of doors, and he was never tired of accumulating and profiting by knowledge of gentlemanly conduct.

"Jack," said the lady, "don't be angry. I've done everything I could to please you this evening. Why do you act so?"

"Oh, you're an angel," said the man. "Depend upon woman to throw the blame upon a man."

"I'm not blaming you. I'm only trying to make you happy."

"You go about it in a very peculiar way."

"You have been cross with me all the evening without any cause."

"Oh, there isn't any cause except—you make me tired."

Corny took out his card case and looked over his collection. He selected one that read: "Mr. White, of Kensington, London." This card he had inveigled from a tourist at the King Edward Hotel. Corny stepped up to the man and presented it with a correctly formal air.

"May I ask why I am selected for the honour?" asked the lady's escort.

Now, Mr. Corny Brannigan had a very wise habit of saying

little during his imitations of the Caliph of Bagdad. The advice of Lord Chesterfield, "Wear a black coat and hold your tongue", he believed in without having heard. But now speech was demanded and required of him.

"No gent," said Corny, "would talk to a lady like you done. Fie upon you, Willie! Even if she happens to be your wife you ought to have more respect for your clothes than to chin her back that way. Maybe it ain't my butt-in, but it goes, anyhow—you strike me as bein' a whole lot to the wrong."

The lady's escort indulged in more elegantly expressed but fetching repartee. Corny, eschewing his truck driver's vocabulary, retorted as nearly as he could in polite phrases. Then diplomatic relations were severed; there was a brief but lively set-to with other than oral weapons, from which Corny came forth easily victor.

A carriage dashed up, driven by a tardy and solicitous coachman.

"Will you kindly open the door for me?" asked the lady. Corny assisted her to enter, and took off his hat. The escort was beginning to scramble up from the sidewalk.

"I beg your pardon, ma'am," said Corny, "if he's your man."

"He's no man of mine," said the lady. "Perhaps he—but there's no chance of his being now. Drive home, Michael. If you care to take this—with my thanks."

Three red roses were thrust through the carriage window into Corny's hand. He took them, and the hand for an instant; and then the carriage sped away.

Corny gathered his foe's hat and began to brush the dust from his clothes.

"Come along," said Corny, taking the other man by the arm.

His late opponent was yet a little dazed by the hard knocks he had received. Corny led him carefully into a saloon three doors away.

"The drinks for us," said Corny, "me and my friend."

"You're a queer feller," said the lady's late escort—"lick a man and then want to set 'em up."

"You're my best friend," said Corny exultantly. "You

don't understand? Well, listen. You just put me wise to somethin'. I been playin' gent a long time, thinkin' it was just the glad rags I had and nothin' else. Say—you're a swell, ain't you? Well, you trot in that class, I guess. I don't; but I found out one thing—I'm a gentleman, by——, and I know it now. What'll you have to drink?"

41

The Duel

THE gods, lying beside their nectar on 'Lympus and peeping over the edge of the cliff, perceive a difference in cities. Although it would seem that to their vision towns must appear as large or small ant-hills without special characteristics, yet it is not so. Studying the habits of ants from so great a height should be but a mild diversion when coupled with the soft drink that mythology tells us is their only solace. But doubtless they have amused themselves by the comparison of villages and towns; and it will be no news to them (nor, perhaps, to many mortals), that in one particularity New York stands unique among the cities of the world. This shall be the theme of a little story addressed to the man who sits smoking with his Sabbath-slippered feet on another chair, and to the woman who snatches the paper for a moment while boiling greens or a narcotized baby leaves her free. With these I love to sit upon the ground and tell sad stories of the death of Kings.

New York City is inhabited by 4,000,000 mysterious strangers; thus beating Bird Centre by three millions and half a dozen nine's. They came here in various ways and for many reasons—Hendrik Hudson, the art schools, green goods, the stork, the annual dressmakers' convention, the Pennsylvania Railroad, love of money, the stage, cheap excursion rates, brains, personal column ads., heavy walking shoes, ambition, freight trains—all these have had a hand in making up the population.

But every man Jack when he first sets foot on the stones of Manhattan has got to fight. He has got to fight at once until either he or his adversary wins. There is no resting between rounds. It is slugging from the first. It is a fight to a finish.

Your opponent is the City. You must do battle with it from

the time the ferry-boat lands you on the island until either it is yours or it has conquered you. It is the same whether you have a million in your pocket or only the price of a week's lodging.

The battle is to decide whether you shall become a New Yorker or turn the rankest outlander and Philistine. You must be one or the other. You cannot remain neutral. You must be for or against—lover or enemy—bosom friend or outcast. And, oh, the city is a general in the ring. Not only by blows does it seek to subdue you. It woos you to its heart with the subtlety of a siren. It is a combination of Delilah, green Chartreuse, Beethoven, chloral and John L. in his best days.

In other cities you may wander and abide as a stranger man as long as you please. You may live in Chicago until your hair whitens, and be a citizen and still prate of beans if Boston mothered you, and without rebuke. You may become a civic pillar in any other town but Knickerbocker's, and all the time publicly sneering at its buildings, comparing them with the architecture of Colonel Telfair's residence in Jackson, Miss., whence you hail, and you will not be set upon. But in New York you must be either a New Yorker or an invader of a modern Troy, concealed in the wooden horse of your conceited provincialism. And this dreary preamble is only to introduce to you the unimportant figures of William and Jack.

They came out of the West together, where they had been friends. They came to dig their fortunes out of the big city.

Father Knickerbocker met them at the ferry, giving one a right-hander on the nose and the other an uppercut with his left, just to let them know that the fight was on.

William was for business; Jack was for art. Both were young and ambitious; so they countered and clinched. I think they were from Nebraska or possibly Missouri or Minnesota. Anyhow, they were out for success and scraps and scads, and they tackled the city like two Lochinvars with brass knucks and a pull at the City Hall.

Four years afterward William and Jack met at luncheon. The business man blew in like a March wind, hurled his silk hat at a waiter, dropped into the chair that was pushed under him, seized the bill of fare, and had ordered as far as cheese before the artist had time to do more than nod. After the nod a humorous smile came into his eyes.

"Billy," he said, "you're done for. The city has gobbled you up. It has taken you and cut you to its pattern and stamped you with its brand. You are so nearly like ten thousand men I have seen to-day that you couldn't be picked out from them if it weren't for your laundry marks."

"Camembert," finished William. "What's that? Oh, you've still got your hammer out for New York, have you? Well, little old Noisyville-on-the-Subway is good enough for me. It's giving me mine. And, say, I used to think the West was the whole round world—only slightly flattened at the poles whenever Bryan ran. I used to yell myself hoarse about the free expense, and hang my hat on the horizon, and say cutting things in the grocery to little soap drummers from the East. But I'd never seen New York, then, Jack. Me for it from the rathskellers up. Sixth Avenue is the West to me now. Have you heard this fellow Crusoe sing? The desert isle for him, I say, but my wife made me go. Give me May Irwin or E. S. Willard any time."

"Poor Billy," said the artist, delicately fingering a cigarette. "You remember, when we were on our way to the East, how we talked about this great, wonderful city, and how we meant to conquer it and never let it get the best of us? We were going to be just the same fellows we had always been, and never let it master us. It has downed you, old man. You have changed from a maverick into a butterick."

"Don't see exactly what you are driving at," said William. "I don't wear an alpaca coat with blue trousers and a seersucker vest on dress occasions, like I used to do at home. You talk about being cut to a pattern—well, ain't the pattern all right? When you're in Rome you've got to do as the Dagoes do. This town seems to me to have other alleged metropolises skinned to flag stations. According to the railroad schedule I've got in my mind, Chicago and Saint Jo and Paris, France, are asterisk stops—which means you wave a red flag and get on every other Tuesday. I like this little suburb of Tarrytown-on-the-Hudson. There's something or somebody doing all the time. I'm clearing $8,000 a year selling automatic pumps, and I'm living like kings-up. Why, yesterday, I was introduced to John W. Gates. I took an auto ride with a wine agent's sister. I saw two men run over by a street car, and I seen Edna May play in the evening. Talk about the West, why, the other night I woke everybody up in the hotel hollering. I dreamed I was walking on a board sidewalk in Oshkosh. What have you got against this town, Jack? There's only one thing in it that I don't care for, and that's a ferry-boat."

The artist gazed dreamily at the cartridge paper on the wall. "This town," said he, "is a leech. It drains the blood of the country. Whoever comes to it accepts a challenge to a duel. Abandoning the figure of the leech, it is a juggernaut, a Moloch, a monster to which the innocence, the genius, and the beauty of the land must pay tribute. Hand to hand every newcomer must struggle with the leviathan. You've lost, Billy. It shall never conquer me. I hate it as one hates sin or pestilence or—the colour work in a ten-cent magazine. I despise its very vastness and power. It has the poorest millionaires, the littlest great men, the haughtiest beggars, the plainest beauties, the lowest skyscrapers, the dolefullest pleasures of any town I ever saw. It has caught you, old man, but I will never run beside its chariot wheels. It glosses itself as the Chinaman glosses his collars. Give me the domestic finish. I could stand a town ruled by wealth or one ruled by an aristocracy; but this is one controlled by its lowest ingredients. Claiming culture, it is the crudest; asseverating its preeminence, it is the basest; denying all outside values and virtue, it is the narrowest. Give me the pure air and the open heart of the West Country. I would go back there to-morrow if I could."

"Don't you like this *filet mignon*?" said William. "Shucks, now, what's the use to knock the town! It's the greatest ever. I couldn't sell one automatic pump between Harrisburg and Tommy O'Keefe's saloon, in Sacramento, where I sell twenty here. And have you seen Sara Bernhardt in 'Andrew Mack' yet?"

"The town's got you, Billy," said Jack.

"All right," said William. "I'm going to buy a cottage on Lake Ronkonkoma next summer."

At midnight Jack raised his window and sat close to it. He caught his breath at what he saw, though he had seen and felt it a hundred times.

Far below and around lay the city like a ragged purple dream. The irregular houses were like the broken exteriors of cliffs lining deep gulches and winding streams. Some were mountainous; some lay in long, monotonous rows like the basalt precipices hanging over desert cañons. Such was the background of the wonderful, cruel, enchanting, bewildering, fatal, great city. But into this background were cut myriads of brilliant parallelograms and circles and squares through which glowed many coloured lights. And out of the violet and purple depths ascended like the city's soul sounds and odours and thrills that make up the civic body. There arose the breath of gaiety unrestrained, of love, of hate, of all the passions that man can know. There below him lay all things, good or bad, that can be brought from the four corners of the earth to instruct, please, thrill, enrich, despoil, elevate, cast down, nurture or kill. Thus the flavour of it came up to him and went into his blood.

There was a knock on his door. A telegram had come for him. It came from the West, and these were its words:

"Come back home and the answer will be yes.

"DOLLY."

He kept the boy waiting ten minutes, and then wrote the reply: "Impossible to leave here at present." Then he sat at the window again and let the city put its cup of mandragora to his lips again.

After all it isn't a story; but I wanted to know which one of the heroes won the battle against the city. So I went to a very learned friend and laid the case before him. What he said was: "Please don't bother me; I have Christmas presents to buy."

So there it rests; and you will have to decide for yourself.

42

The Song and the Sergeant

HALF a dozen people supping at a table in one of the Upper Broadway all-night restaurants were making too much noise. Three times the manager walked past them with a politely warning glance; but their argument had waxed too warm to be quelled by a manager's gaze. It was midnight, and the restaurant was filled with patrons from the theatres of that district. Some among the dispersed audiences must have recognized among the quarrelsome sextet the faces of the players belonging to the Carroll Comedy Company.

Four of the six made up the company. Another was the author of the comedietta, "A Gay Coquette", which the quartette of players had been presenting with fair success at several vaudeville houses in the city. The sixth at the table was a person inconsequent in the realm of art, but one at whose bidding many lobsters had perished.

Loudly the six maintained their clamorous debate. No: one of the party was silent except when answers were stormed from him by the excited ones. That was the comedian of "A Gay Coquette". He was a young man with a face even too melancholy for his profession.

The oral warfare of four immoderate tongues was directed at Miss Clarice Carroll, the twinkling star of the small aggregation. Excepting the downcast comedian, all members of the party united in casting upon her with vehemence the blame of some momentous misfortune. Fifty times they told her: "It is your fault, Clarice—it is you alone who spoilt the scene. It is only of late that you have acted this way. At this rate the sketch will have to be taken off."

Miss Carroll was a match for any four. Gallic ancestry gave her a vivacity that could easily mount to fury. Her large eyes flashed a scorching denial at her accusers. Her slender, eloquent arms constantly menaced the table-ware. Her high, clear soprano voice rose to what would have been a scream had it not possessed so pure a musical quality. She hurled back at the attacking four their denunciations in tones sweet, but of too great carrying power for a Broadway restaurant.

Finally they exhausted her patience both as a woman and an artist. She sprang up like a panther, managed to smash half a dozen plates and glasses with one royal sweep of her arm, and defied her critics. They rose and wrangled more loudly. The comedian sighed and looked a trifle sadder and disinterested. The manager came tripping and suggested peace. He was told to go to the popular synonym for war so promptly that the affair might have happened at The Hague.

Thus was the manager angered. He made a sign with his hand and a waiter slipped out of the door. In twenty minutes the party of six was in a police station facing a grizzled and philosophical desk sergeant.

"Disorderly conduct in a restaurant," said the policeman who had brought the party in.

The author of "A Gay Coquette" stepped to the front. He wore nose-glasses and evening clothes, even if his shoes had been tans before they met the patent-leather-polish bottle.

"Mr. Sergeant," said he, out of his throat, like Actor Irving, "I would like to protest against this arrest. The company of actors who are performing in a little play that I have written, in company with a friend and myself, were having a little supper. We became deeply interested in the discussion as to which one of the cast is responsible for a scene in the sketch that lately has fallen so flat that the piece is about to become a failure. We may have been rather noisy and intolerant of interruption by the restaurant people; but the matter was of considerable importance to all of us. You see that we are sober and are not the kind of people who desire to raise disturbances. I hope that the case will not be pressed and that we may be allowed to go."

"Who makes the charge?" asked the sergeant.

"Me," said a white-aproned voice in the rear. "De restaurant sent me to. De gang was raisin' a rough-house and breakin' dishes."

"The dishes were paid for," said the playwright. "They were not broken purposely. In her anger because we remonstrated with her for spoiling the scene, Miss——"

"It's not true, sergeant," cried the clear voice of Miss Clarice Carroll. In a long coat of tan silk and a red-plumed hat, she bounded before the desk.

"It's not my fault," she cried indignantly. "How dare they say such a thing! I've played the title rôle ever since it was staged, and if you want to know who made it a success, ask the public—that's all."

"What Miss Carroll says is true in part," said the author. "For five months the comedietta was a drawing card in the best houses. But during the last two weeks it has lost favour. There is one scene in it in which Miss Carroll made a big hit. Now she hardly gets a hand out of it. She spoils it by acting it entirely different from her old way."

"It is not my fault," reiterated the actress.

"There are only two of you on in the scene," argued the playwright hotly, "you and Delmars, here——"

"Then it's his fault," declared Miss Carroll, with a lightning glance of scorn from her dark eyes. The comedian caught it, and gazed with increased melancholy at the panels of the sergeant's desk.

The night was a dull one in that particular police station.

The sergeant's long-blunted curiosity awoke a little.

"I've heard you," he said to the author. And then he addressed the thin-faced and ascetic-looking lady of the company who played "Aunt Turnip-top" in the little comedy.

"Who do you think spoils the scene you are fussing about?" he asked.

"I'm no knocker," said that lady, "and everybody knows it. So, when I say that Clarice falls down every time in that scene, I'm judging her art and not herself. She was great in it once. She does it something fierce now. It'll dope the show if she keeps it up."

The sergeant looked at the comedian.

"You and the lady have this scene together, I understand. I suppose there's no use asking you which one of you queers it?"

The comedian avoided the direct rays from the two fixed stars of Miss Carroll's eyes.

"I don't know," he said, looking down at his patent-leather toes.

"Are you one of the actors?" asked the sergeant of a dwarfish youth with a middle-aged face.

"Why, say!" replied the last Thespian witness, "you don't notice any tin spear in my hands, do you? You haven't heard me shout: 'See, the Emperor comes!' since I've been in here, have you? I guess I'm on the stage long enough for 'em not to start a panic by mistaking me for a thin curl of smoke rising above the footlights."

"In your opinion, if you've got one," said the sergeant, "is the frost that gathers on the scene in question the work of the lady or the gentleman who takes part in it?"

The middle-aged youth looked pained.

"I regret to say," he answered, "that Miss Carroll seems to have lost her grip on that scene. She's all right in the rest of the play, but—but I tell you, sergeant, she can do it—she has done it equal to any of 'em—and she can do it again."

Miss Carroll ran forward glowing and palpitating.

"Thank you, Jimmy, for the first good word I've had in many a day," she cried. And then she turned her eager face toward the desk.

"I'll show you, sergeant, whether I am to blame. I'll show them whether I can do that same. Come, Mr. Delmars, let us begin. You will let us, won't you, sergeant?"

"How long will it take?" asked the sergeant dubiously.

"Eight minutes," said the playwright. "The entire play consumes but thirty."

"You may go ahead," said the sergeant. "Most of you seem to side against the little lady. Maybe she had a right to crack up a saucer or two in that restaurant. We'll see how she does the turn before we take that up."

The matron of the police station had been standing near, listening to the singular argument. She came nigher and stood near the sergeant's chair. Two or three of the reserves strolled in, big and yawning.

"Before beginning the scene," said the playwright, "and

assuming that you have not seen a production of 'A Gay Coquette', I will make a brief but necessary explanation. It is a musical-farce-comedy—burlesque-comedietta. As the title implies, Miss Carroll's rôle is that of a gay, rollicking, mischievous, heartless coquette. She sustains that character throughout the entire comedy part of the production. And I have designed the extravaganza features so that she may preserve and present the same coquettish idea.

"Now, the scene in which we take exception to Miss Carroll's acting is called the 'gorilla dance'. She is costumed to represent a wood nymph, and there is a great song-and-dance scene with a gorilla—played by Mr. Delmars, the comedian. A tropical-forest stage is set.

"That used to get four and five recalls. The main thing was the acting and the dance—it was the funniest thing in New York for five months. Delmars's song, 'I'll Woo Thee to My Sylvan Home', while he and Miss Carroll were cutting hide-and-seek capers among the tropical plants, was a winner."

"What's the trouble with the scene now?" asked the sergeant.

"Miss Carroll spoils it right in the middle of it," said the playwright wrathfully.

With a wide gesture of her ever-moving arms the actress waved back the little group of spectators, leaving a space in front of the desk for the scene of her vindication or fall. Then she whipped off her long tan cloak and tossed it across the arm of the policeman who still stood officially among them.

Miss Carroll had gone to supper well cloaked, but in the costume of the tropic wood nymph. A skirt of fern leaves touched her knee; she was like a humming bird—green and golden and purple.

And then she danced a fluttering, fantastic dance, so agile and light and mazy in her steps that the other three members of the Carroll Comedy Company broke into applause at the art of it.

And at the proper time Delmars leaped out at her side, mimicking the uncouth, hideous bounds of the gorilla so funnily that the grizzled sergeant himself gave a short laugh like the closing of a padlock. They danced together the gorilla dance, and won a hand from all.

Then began the most fantastic part of the scene—the wooing of the nymph by the gorilla. It was a kind of dance itself—eccentric and prankish, with the nymph in coquettish and seductive retreat, followed by the gorilla as he sang "I'll Woo Thee to My Sylvan Home".

The song was a lyric of merit. The words were nonsense, as befitted the play, but the music was worthy of something better. Delmars struck into it in a rich tenor that owned a quality that shamed the flippant words.

During one verse of the song the wood nymph performed the grotesque evolutions designed for the scene. At the middle of the second verse she stood still, with a strange look on her face, seeming to gaze dreamily into the depths of the scenic forest. The gorilla's last leap had brought him to her feet, and there he knelt, holding her hand, until he had finished the haunting lyric that was set in the absurd comedy like a diamond in a piece of putty.

When Delmars ceased Miss Carroll started, and covered a sudden flow of tears with both hands.

"There!" cried the playwright, gesticulating with violence; "there you have it, sergeant. For two weeks she has spoiled that scene in just that manner at every performance. I have begged her to consider that it is not Ophelia or Juliet that she is playing. Do you wonder now at our impatience? Tears for the gorilla song! The play is lost!"

Out of her bewitchment, whatever it was, the wood nymph flared suddenly, and pointed a desperate finger at Delmars.

"It is you—you who have done this," she cried wildly. "You never sang that song that way until lately. It is your doing."

"I give it up," said the sergeant.

And then the grey-haired matron of the police station came forward from behind the sergeant's chair.

"Must an old woman teach you all?" she said. She went up to Miss Carroll and took her hand.

"The man's wearing his heart out for you, my dear.

Couldn't you tell it the first note you heard him sing? All of his monkey flip-flops wouldn't have kept it from me. Must you be deaf as well as blind? That's why you couldn't act your part, child. Do you love him or must he be a gorilla for the rest of his days?"

Miss Carroll whirled around and caught Delmars with a lightning glance of her eye. He came toward her, melancholy.

"Did you hear, Mr. Delmars?" she asked with a catching breath.

"I did," said the comedian. "It is true. I didn't think there was any use. I tried to let you know with the song."

"Silly!" said the matron; "why didn't you speak?"

"No, no," cried the wood nymph, "his way was the best. I didn't know, but—it was just what I wanted, Bobby."

She sprang like a green grasshopper; and the comedian opened his arms, and—smiled.

"Get out of this," roared the desk sergeant to the waiting waiter from the restaurant. "There's nothing doing here for you."

43

The Pimienta Pancakes

WHILE we were rounding up a bunch of the Triangle-O cattle in the Frio bottoms a projecting branch of a dead mesquite caught my wooden stirrup and gave my ankle a wrench that laid me up in camp for a week.

On the third day of my compulsory idleness I crawled out near the grub wagon, and reclined helpless under the conversational fire of Judson Odom, the camp cook. Jud was a monologist by nature, whom Destiny, with customary blundering, had set in a profession wherein he was bereaved, for the greater portion of his time, of an audience.

Therefore, I was manna in the desert of Jud's obmutescence.

Betimes I was stirred by invalid longings for something to eat that did not come under the caption of "grub". I had visions of the maternal pantry "deep as first love, and wild with all regret", and then I asked—

"Jud, can you make pancakes?"

Jud laid down his six-shooter, with which he was preparing to pound an antelope steak, and stood over me in what I felt to be a menacing attitude. He further endorsed my impression that his pose was resentful by fixing upon me with his light blue eyes a look of cold suspicion.

"Say you," he said, with candid, though not excessive, choler, "did you mean that straight, or was you trying to throw the gaff into me? Some of the boys been telling you about me and that pancake racket?"

"No, Jud," I said sincerely, "I meant it. It seems to me I'd swap my pony and saddle for a stack of buttered brown pancakes with some first crop, open kettle, New Orleans sweetening. Was there a story about pancakes?"

Jud was mollified at once when he saw that I had not been

dealing in allusions. He brought some mysterious bags and tin boxes from the grub wagon and set them in the shade of the hackberry where I lay reclined. I watched him as he began to arrange them leisurely and untie their many strings.

"No, not a story," said Jud, as he worked, "but just the logical disclosures in the case of me and that pink-eyed snoozer from Mired Mule Cañada and Miss Willella Learight. I don't mind telling you.

"I was punching then for old Bill Toomey, on the San Miguel. One day I gets all ensnared up in aspirations for to eat some canned grub that hasn't ever mooed or baaed or grunted or been in peck measures. So, I gets on my bronc and pushes the wind for Uncle Emsley Telfair's store at the Pimienta Crossing on the Nueces.

"About three in the afternoon I throwed my bridle rein over a mesquite limb and walked the last twenty yards into Uncle Emsley's store. I got up on the counter and told Uncle Emsley that the signs pointed to the devastation of the fruit crop of the world. In a minute I had a bag of crackers and a long-handled spoon, with an open can each of apricots and pineapples and cherries and greengages beside of me with Uncle Emsley busy chopping away with the hatchet at the yellow clings. I was feeling like Adam before the apple stampede, and was digging my spurs into the side of the counter and working with my twenty-four-inch spoon when I happened to look out of the window into the yard of Uncle Emsley's house, which was next to the store.

"There was a girl standing there—an imported girl with fixings on—philandering with a croquet maul and amusing herself by watching my style of encouraging the fruit-canning industry.

"I slid off the counter and delivered up my shovel to Uncle Emsley.

"'That's my niece,' says he; 'Miss Willella Learight, down from Palestine on a visit. Do you want that I should make you acquainted?'

"'The Holy Land,' I says to myself, my thoughts milling some as I tried to run 'em into the corral. 'Why not? There was sure angels in Pales—— Why yes, Uncle Emsley,' I says out loud, 'I'd be awful edified to meet Miss Learight.'

"So Uncle Emsley took me out in the yard and gave us each other's entitlements.

"I never was shy about women. I never could understand why some men who can break a mustang before breakfast and shave in the dark, get all left-handed and full of perspiration and excuses when they see a bolt of calico draped around what belongs in it. Inside of eight minutes me and Miss Willella was aggravating the croquet balls around as amiable as second cousins. She gave me a dig about the quantity of canned fruit I had eaten, and I got back at her, flat-footed, about how a certain lady named Eve started the fruit trouble in the first free-grass pasture—'Over in Palestine, wasn't it?' says I, as easy and pat as roping a one-year-old.

"That was how I acquired cordiality for the proximities of Miss Willella Learight; and the disposition grew larger as time passed. She was stopping at Pimienta Crossing for her health, which was very good, and for the climate, which was forty per cent. hotter than Palestine. I rode over to see her once every week for a while, and then I figured it out that if I doubled the number of trips I would see her twice as often.

"One week I slipped in a third trip, and that's where the pancakes and the pink-eyed snoozer busted into the game.

"That evening, while I set on the counter with a peach and two damsons in my mouth, I asked Uncle Emsley how Miss Willella was.

"'Why,' says Uncle Emsley, 'she's gone riding with Jackson Bird, the sheep man from over at Mired Mule Cañada.'

"I swallowed the peach seed and the two damson seeds. I guess somebody held the counter by the bridle while I got off; and then I walked out straight ahead till I butted against the mesquite where my roan was tied.

"'She's gone riding,' I whispered in my bronc's ear, 'with Birdstone Jack, the hired mule from Sheep Man's Cañada. Did you get that, old Leather-and-Gallops?'

"That bronc of mine wept, in his way. He'd been raised a cow pony and he didn't care for snoozers.

"I went back and said to Uncle Emsley: 'Did you say a sheep man?"

"'I said a sheep man,' says Uncle again. 'You must have heard tell of Jackson Bird. He's got eight sections of grazing and four thousand head of the finest Merinos south of the Arctic Circle.'

"I went out and sat on the ground in the shade of the store and leaned against a prickly pear. I sifted sand into my boots with unthinking hands while I soliloquized a quantity about this bird with the Jackson plumage to his name.

"I never had believed in harming sheep men. I see one, one day, reading a Latin grammar on hossback, and I never touched him! They never irritated me like they do most cowmen. You wouldn't go to work, now, and impair and disfigure snoozers, would you, that eat on tables and wear little shoes and speak to you on subjects? I had always let 'em pass, just as you would a jack-rabbit; with a polite word and a guess about the weather, but no stopping to swap canteens. I never thought it was worth while to be hostile with a snoozer. and because I'd been lenient, and let 'em live, here was one going around riding with Miss Willella Learight!

"An hour by sun they came loping back and stopped at Uncle Emsley's gate. The sheep person helped her off; and they stood throwing each other sentences all sprightful and sagacious for a while. And then this feathered Jackson flies up in his saddle and raises his little stewpot of a hat, and trots off in the direction of his mutton ranch. By this time I had turned the sand out of my boots and unpinned myself from the prickly pear; and by the time he gets half a mile out of Pimienta, I singlefoots up beside him on my bronc.

"I said that snoozer was pink-eyed, but he wasn't. His seeing arrangement was grey enough, but his eyelashes was pink and his hair was sandy, and that gave you the idea. Sheep man?—he wasn't more than a lamb man, anyhow—a little thing with his neck involved in a yellow silk handkerchief, and shoes tied up in bowknots.

"'Afternoon!' says I to him. 'You now ride with a equestrian who is commonly called Dead-Moral-Certainty Judson, on account of the way I shoot. When I want a stranger to know me I always introduce myself before the draw, for I never did like to shake hands with ghosts.'

"'Ah,' says he, just like that—'Ah, I'm glad to know you, Mr. Judson. I'm Jackson Bird, from over at Mired Mule Ranch.'

"Just then one of my eyes saw a roadrunner skipping down the hill with a young tarantula in his bill, and the other eye noticed a rabbit-hawk sitting on a dead limb in a water-elm. I popped over one after the other with my forty-five, just to show him. 'Two out of three,' says I. 'Birds just naturally seem to draw my fire wherever I go.'

"'Nice shooting,' says the sheep man, without a flutter. 'But don't you sometimes ever miss the third shot? Elegant fine rain that was last week for the young grass, Mr. Judson?' says he.

"'Willie,' says I, riding over close to his palfrey, 'your infatuated parents may have denounced you by the name of Jackson, but you sure moulted into a twittering Willie—let us slough off this here analysis of rain and the elements, and get down to talk that is outside the vocabulary of parrots. That is a bad habit you have got of riding with young ladies over at Pimienta. I've known birds,' says I, 'to be served on toast for less than that. Miss Willella,' says I, 'don't ever want any nest made out of sheep's wool by a tomtit of the Jacksonian branch of ornithology. Now, are you going to quit, or do you wish for to gallop up against this Dead-Moral-Certainty attachment to my name, which is good for two hyphens and at least one set of funeral obsequies?'

"Jackson Bird flushed up some, and then he laughed.

"'Why, Mr. Judson,' says he, 'you've got the wrong idea. I've called on Miss Learight a few times; but not for the purpose you imagine. My object is purely a gastronomical one.'

"I reached for my gun.

"'Any coyote,' says I, 'that would boast of dishonourable ——'

"'Wait a minute,' says this Bird, 'till I explain. What would I do with a wife? If you ever saw that ranch of mine!

I do my own cooking and mending. Eating—that's all the pleasure I get out of sheep-raising. Mr. Judson, did you ever taste the pancakes that Miss Learight makes?'

"'Me? No,' I told him. 'I never was advised that she was up to any culinary manoeuvres.'

"'They're golden sunshine,' says he; 'honey-browned by the ambrosial fires of Epicurus. I'd give two years of my life to get the recipe for making them pancakes. That's what I went to see Miss Learight for,' says Jackson Bird, 'but I haven't been able to get it from her. It's an old recipe that's been in the family for seventy-five years. They hand it down from one generation to another, but they don't give it away to outsiders. If I could get that recipe, so I could make them pancakes for myself on my ranch, I'd be a happy man,' says Bird.

"'Are you sure,' I says to him, 'that it ain't the hand that mixes the pancakes that you're after?'

"'Sure,' says Jackson. 'Miss Learight is a mighty nice girl, but I can assure you my intentions go no further than the gastro——' but he seen my hand going down to my holster and he changed his similitude—'than the desire to procure a copy of the pancake recipe,' he finishes.

"'You ain't such a bad little man,' says I, trying to be fair. 'I was thinking some of making orphans of your sheep, but I'll let you fly away this time. But you stick to pancakes,' says I, 'as close as the middle one of a stack; and don't go and mistake sentiments for syrup, or there'll be singing at your ranch, and you won't hear it.'

"'To convince you that I am sincere,' says the sheep man, 'I'll ask you to help me. Miss Learight and you being closer friends, maybe she would do for you what she wouldn't for me. If you will get me a copy of that pancake recipe, I give you my word that I'll never call upon her again.'

"'That's fair,' I says, and I shook hands with Jackson Bird. 'I'll get it for you if I can, and glad to oblige.' And he turned off down the big pear flat on the Piedra, in the direction of Mired Mule; and I steered north-west for old Bill Toomey's ranch.

"It was five days afterward when I got another chance to

ride over to Pimienta. Miss Willella and me passed a gratifying evening at Uncle Emsley's. She sang some, and exasperated the piano quite a lot with quotations from the operas. I gave imitations of a rattlesnake, and told her about Snaky McFee's new way of skinning cows, and described the trip I made to Saint Louis once. We was getting along in one another's estimations fine. Thinks I, if Jackson Bird can now be persuaded to migrate, I win. I recollect his promise about the pancake recipe, and I thinks I will persuade it from Miss Willella and give it to him; and then if I catches Birdie off of Mired Mule again, I'll make him hop the twig.

"So, along about ten o'clock, I put on a wheedling smile and says to Miss Willella: 'Now, if there's anything I do like better than the sight of a red steer on green grass it's the taste of a nice hot pancake smothered in sugar-house molasses.'

"Miss Willella gives a little jump on the piano stool, and looked at me curious.

"'Yes,' says she, 'they're real nice. What did you say was the name of that street in Saint Louis, Mr. Odom, where you lost your hat?"

"'Pancake Avenue,' says I, with a wink, to show her that I was on about the family recipe, and couldn't be side-corralled off of the subject. 'Come, now Miss Willella,' I says; 'let's hear how you make 'em. Pancakes is just whirling in my head like wagon wheels. Start her off, now—pound of flour, eight dozen eggs, and so on. How does the catalogue of constituents run?'

"'Excuse me for a moment, please,' says Miss Willella, and she gives me a quick kind of sideways look, and slides off the stool. She ambled out into the other room, and directly Uncle Emsley comes in in his shirt sleeves, with a pitcher of water. He turns around to get a glass on the table, and I see a forty-five in his hip pocket. 'Great post-holes!' thinks I, 'but here's a family thinks a heap of cooking recipes, protecting it with fire-arms. I've known outfits that wouldn't do that much by a family feud.'

"'Drink this here down,' says Uncle Emsley, handing me the glass of water. 'You've rid too far to-day, Jud, and got yourself over-excited. Try to think about something else now.'

"'Do you know how to make them pancakes, Uncle Emsley?' I asked.

"'Well, I'm not as apprised in the anatomy of them as some,' says Uncle Emsley, 'but I reckon you take a sifter of plaster of paris and a little dough and saleratus and corn meal, and mix 'em with eggs and buttermilk as usual. Is old Bill going to ship beeves to Kansas City again this spring, Jud?'

"That was all the pancake specifications I could get that night. I didn't wonder that Jackson Bird found it uphill work. So I dropped the subject and talked with Uncle Emsley a while about hollow-horn and cyclones. And then Miss Willella came and said 'Good night,' and I hit the breeze for the ranch.

"About a week afterward I met Jackson Bird riding out of Pimienta as I rode in, and we stopped in the road for a few frivolous remarks.

"'Got the bill of particulars for them flapjacks yet?' I asked him.

"'Well, no,' says Jackson. 'I don't seem to have any success in getting hold of it. Did you try?'

"'I did,' says I, 'and 'twas like trying to dig a prairie dog out of his hole with a peanut hull. That pancake recipe must be a jookalorum, the way they hold on to it.'

"'I'm most ready to give it up,' says Jackson, so discouraged in his pronunciations that I felt sorry for him; 'but I did want to know how to make them pancakes to eat on my lonely ranch,' says he. 'I lie awake of nights thinking how good they are.'

"'You keep on trying for it,' I tells him, 'and I'll do the same. One of us is bound to get a rope over its horns before long. Well, so-long, Jacksy.'

"You see, by this time we was on the peacefullest of terms. When I saw that he wasn't after Miss Willella I had more endurable contemplations of that sandy-haired snoozer. In order to help out the ambitions of his appetite I kept on trying to get that recipe from Miss Willella. But every time I would say 'pancakes,' she would get sort of remote and fidgety about the eye, and try to change the subject. If I held her to it she would slide out and round up Uncle Emsley with his pitcher of water and hip-pocket howitzer.

"One day I galloped over to the store with a fine bunch of blue verbenas that I cut out of a herd of wild flowers over on Poisoned Dog Prairie. Uncle Emsley looked at 'em with one eye shut and says—

"'Haven't ye heard the news?'

"'Cattle up?' I asks.

"'Willella and Jackson Bird was married in Palestine yesterday,' says he. 'Just got a letter this morning.'

"I dropped them flowers in a cracker-barrel, and let the news trickle in my ears and down towards my upper left-hand shirt pocket until I got to my feet.

"'Would you mind saying that over again once more, Uncle Emsley?' says I. 'Maybe my hearing has got wrong, and you only said that prime heifers was 4.80 on the hoof, or something like that.'

"'Married yesterday,' says Uncle Emsley, 'and gone to Waco and Niagara Falls on a wedding tour. Why, didn't you see none of the signs all along? Jackson Bird has been courting Willella ever since that day he took her out riding.'

"'Then,' says I, in a kind of yell, 'what was all this zizzaparoola he gives me about pancakes? Tell me *that*.'

"When I said 'pancakes', Uncle Emsley sort of dodged and stepped back.

"'Somebody's been dealing me pancakes from the bottom of the deck,' I says, 'and I'll find out. I believe you know. Talk up,' says I, 'or we'll mix a panful of batter right here.'

"I slid over the counter after Uncle Emsley. He grabbed at his gun, but it was in a drawer, and he missed it two inches. I got him by the front of his shirt and shoved him in a corner.

"'Talk pancakes,' says I, 'or be made into one. Does Miss Willella make 'em?'

"'She never made one in her life and I never saw one,' says Uncle Emsley, soothing. 'Calm down now, Jud—calm down. You've got excited, and that wound in your head is contaminating your sense of intelligence. Try not to think about pancakes.'

"'Uncle Emsley,' says I, 'I'm not wounded in the head except so far as my natural cogitative instincts run to runts. Jackson Bird told me he was calling on Miss Willella for the purpose of finding out her system of producing pancakes, and he asked me to help him get the bill of lading of the ingredients. I done so, with the result as you see. Have I been sodded down with Johnson grass by a pink-eyed snoozer, or what?'

"'Slack up your grip on my dress shirt,' says Uncle Emsley, 'and I'll tell you. Yes, it looks like Jackson Bird has gone and humbugged you some. The day after he went riding with Willella he came back and told me and her to watch out for you whenever you got to talking about pancakes. He said you was in camp once where they was cooking flapjacks, and one of the fellows cut you over the head with a frying-pan. Jackson said that whenever you got overhot or excited that wound hurt you and made you kind of crazy, and you went raving about pancakes. He told us to just get you worked off of the subject and soothed down, and you wouldn't be dangerous. So, me and Willella done the best by you we know how. Well, well,' says Uncle Emsley, 'that Jackson Bird is sure a seldom kind of a snoozer.'"

During the progress of Jud's story he had been slowly but deftly combining certain portions of the contents of his sacks and cans. Toward the close of it he set before me the finished product—a pair of red-hot, rich-hued pancakes on a tin plate. From some secret hoarding place he also brought a lump of excellent butter and a bottle of golden syrup.

"How long ago did these things happen?" I asked him.

"Three years," said Jud. "They're living on the Mired Mule Ranch now. But I haven't seen either of 'em since. They say Jackson Bird was fixing his ranch up fine with rocking-chairs and window curtains all the time he was putting me up the pancake tree. Oh, I got over it after a while. But the boys kept the racket up."

"Did you make these cakes by the famous recipe?" I asked.

"Didn't I tell you there wasn't no recipe?" said Jud. "The

boys hollered pancakes till they got pancake hungry, and I cut this recipe out of a newspaper. How does the truck taste?"

"They're delicious," I answered. "Why don't you have some, too, Jud?"

I was sure I heard a sigh.

"Me?" said Jud. "I don't never eat 'em."

44

The Legend of San Jacinto

The Hermit of the Battle Ground Relates an Ancient Tradition to a Post Man

THE battle ground of San Jacinto is a historic spot, very dear to those who make the past reputation of Texas a personal matter. A Texan who does not thrill at the mention of the locality where General Sam Houston, and other gentlemen named after the counties of Texas, captured Santa Anna and his portable bar and side arms, is a base-born slave.

A few days ago a *Post* reporter who has a friend who is a pilot on the tug boat *Hoodoo Jane* went down the bayou to the battle ground with the intention of gathering from some of the old inhabitants a few of the stories and legends that are so plentiful concerning the events that occurred on that memorable spot.

The *Hoodoo Jane* let the reporter off at the battle ground, which is on the bank of the bayou, and he wandered about under the thick grove of trees and then out upon the low flat country where the famous battle is said to have raged. Down under a little bunch of elm trees was a little cabin, and the reporter wandered thither in the hope of finding an old inhabitant.

A venerable man emerged from the cabin, apparently between 75 and 80 years of age, with long white hair and silvery beard.

"Come hither, youth," he said. "Would'st know the legend of this place? Then cross my palm with silver, and I'll tell it thee."

"Good father," said the reporter, "Gramercy, and by my

halidome, and Got wot, as you love me, ask me not for silver, but even fire away with your old legend."

"Then sit you here," said the hermit, "and I will tell you the legend of the battle ground of San Jacinto.

"A great many years ago, when these silver locks of mine were dark and my step as quick and blithe as thine, my mother told me this tale. How well I remember the day. It was twilight, and the evening shadows were growing long under the trees. She laid her hand upon my head and said:

* * *

"'My boy, I will tell you the legend of San Jacinto. It is a beautiful story, and was told to me by my father, who was one of the earliest settlers in the State. Ah! what a man he was—six feet in height, sinewy as an oaken withe, and as bold as a lion. One day, I remember, he came home after a long, hard fight with the Indians. He took me on his knee as gently as a woman would, this great strong father of mine, and said:

"'"Listen, little Sunbeam, and I will tell you the grand old story of San Jacinto. It is a legend known to few. It will make your bright eyes dance in your head with wonder. I heard it from my uncle, who was a strange man, and held in dread by all who knew him. One night when the moon was going down in the west and the big owls were hooting mournfully in the woods, he pointed out to me that great grove of trees on the bayou's bank, and taking me by the arm whispered: 'Do you see them, lad, do you see them?'

"'"It was almost dark where we stood alone in the deep grass, and the wind made strange sounds as it swept across the flat.

"'"'I have never breathed to a mortal a word of this story, lad,' said my uncle, 'but it must out. Listen; when I was a child my grandmother told me the legend of San Jacinto. The next day she died. She told it to me at midnight on this very spot. There was a storm raging, and the furious wind beat us under this old oak for shelter. My grandmother's eyes, ordinarily so dim and weak, blazed like stars. She seemed fifty years younger as she raised her trembling hand towards the old battle ground and said:

“‘“‘“Child, for the first time in many years a human tongue is about to reveal the secret that this silent spot holds in its eternal bosom. I will now tell you the legend of San Jacinto as told me by my father's half-brother. He was a silent, moody man, fond of reading and solitary walks. One day I found him weeping. When he saw me he brushed the tears away from his eyes and said gently:

* * *

“‘“‘“‘Is that you, little one? Come and I will tell you something that I have kept locked in my breast for many a year. There is a mournful legend connected with this spot that must be told. Sit by my side, and I will tell it you. I had it from my grandmother's sister, who was a well-known character in her day. How well I remember her words. She was a gentle and lovely woman, and her sweet and musical tones added interest to the quaint and beautiful legend.

“‘“‘“‘“Once upon a time,” she said, “I was riding with my uncle's step-father across this valley, when he gazed upon that grove of trees and said:

“‘“‘“‘“‘Hast ever heard the legend of San Jacinto?’

“‘“‘“‘“‘Nay,’ I said.

“‘“‘“‘“‘I will tell it thee,’ he said. ‘Many years ago when I was a lad, my father and I stopped in the shade there to rest. The sun was just setting, and he pointed to the spot and said:

“‘“‘“‘“‘“My son, I am growing old and will not be with you long. There is an old legend connected with this ground, and I feel that it should be told you. A long time ago, before you were born my grandfather one day——”’”’”’”’”

“See here, you old blatherskite,” said the *Post* reporter, “you've got this story back for about 600 years before the Pontius Pilate's time now. Don't you know a news item from an inscription on the pyramids? Our paper doesn't use plate matter. Why don't you work this gag of yours off on the syndicates?”

The aged hermit then frowned and reached under his coat tail, and the reporter ran swiftly, but in a dignified manner, to the *Hoodoo Jane* and embarked.

But there is a legend about the San Jacinto battle ground somewhere in the neighbourhood, if one could only get at it.

45

A Mystery of Many Centuries

Up to a few years ago man regarded the means of locomotion possessed by the fair sex as a sacred areanum into which it were desecration to inquire.

The bicycle costume has developed the fact that there are two—well, that there are two. Whereas man bowed down and worshipped what he could not understand nor see, when the veil of mystery was rent, his reverence departed. For generations woman has been supposed in moving from one place to another to simply get there. Whether born like Venus in an invisible car drawn by two milk-white doves, or wafted imperceptibly by the force of her own sweet will, admiring man did not pause to consider. He only knew that there was a soft rustle of unseen drapery, an entrancing frou-frou of something agitated but unknown, and the lovely beings would be standing on another spot. Whereat he wondered, adoring, but uninquisitive. At times beneath the lace-hemmed snowy skirts might be seen the toe of a tiny slipper, and perhaps the gleam of a silver buckle upon the arch of an instep, but thence imagination retired, baffled, but enthralled. In olden times the sweetest singers among the poets sang to their lutes of those Lilliputian members, and romance struck a lofty note when it wove the deathless legend of Cinderella and the slipper of glass. Courtiers have held aloft the silken slipper of the adored one filled with champagne and drank her health. Where is the bicyclist hero who would undertake the task of draining to the good health of his lady love her bicycle gaiter filled with beer?

The mysterious and love-lorn damosel no longer chucks roses at us from her latticed window and sighs to us from afar. She has descended, borrowed our clothes, and is our good friend and demands equal rights. We no longer express our admiration by midnight serenades and sonnets. We slap her on the back and feel we have gained a good comrade.

But we feel like inserting the following want ad in every paper in the land:

LOST—A maiden dressed in long skirts: blushes sometimes, and wears a placard round her neck, which says, "hands off". A liberal reward will be paid for her return.

* * *

The other day the Post Man saw a nice, clean-minded old gentleman, who is of the old school of cavaliers, and who is loath to see woman come down from the pedestal on which he has always viewed her.

He was watching a lady bicycle rider go by. The Post Man asked him what he thought.

"I never see a lady on a bicycle," said he, "but I am reminded of God, for they certainly move in a mysterious way their wonders to perform."

46

Led Astray

THERE was no happier family in all Houston than the O'Malleys. Mr. O'Malley held a responsible position in one of our large breweries, and was a thrifty citizen and an indulgent husband and father. His son Pat was part owner of a flourishing little grocery, and also played the E flat horn in the band that discourses sweet music Sunday afternoons in a building on one of our quietest unpaved avenues.

The light and hope of the family was the youngest daughter Kathleen, an ebon-haired girl of 19, with Madonna-like features, and eyes as black as the wings of the crow. They lived in a little rose-embowered cottage near the corner where the street car turns.

Kathleen was engaged to be married to Fergus O'Hollihan, a stalwart and handsome young man, who came to see her every night, with exquisitely washed hands and face, and wet hair, brushed down low upon a forehead that did not exactly retreat, but seemed to rather fall back for reinforcements. On Sunday nights Kathleen and Fergus would wander arm in arm over to the Gesundheit Bier Garten, and while the string band in the pavilion played the dear Old Fatherland melodies they would sit at a little round table in some dark corner and click glasses in the most friendly and lover-like manner. The marriage was to come off in June, and Kathleen, after the custom of her people, had already prepared her bridal trousseau and housekeeping effects. In her wardrobe were great piles of beautifully embroidered things in fine linen and damask, heaps of table cloths, napkins and towels, and in the big drawers of her bureau were piles of dainty, lace-trimmed garments that Kathleen, being a modest Irish maiden and not a New York millionairess, kept shyly hidden from view, instead of having their description printed in the *Post.* Kathleen had made these garments herself, working with loving care and patience, and they were intended as a guarantee of good faith, and not for publication. The girls in the neighbourhood all envied Kathleen her good luck, for Fergus was a fine-looking young man, and his business was prospering. He could drink more whisky, tell funnier jokes and sing "The Wearin' of the Green" so you could hear it farther on a still night than could any other young man of their acquaintance.

So, dark-haired Kathleen was happy, bending over her work with rosy cheeks and smiling lips, while, alas! already the serpent was at work that was to enter her Eden.

* * *

One day Kathleen was sitting at her window, half hidden by the climbing honeysuckle vines, when she saw Fergus pass down the street with another man, a low-browed, treacherous-looking person, with shifty eyes and a snake-like manner.

It was with a deep foreboding and a strange sinking of the heart that she recognized Fergus' companion as a notorious member of the Young Men's Christian Association of Houston. From that moment Kathleen's peace of mind fled. When Fergus came to see her that night he seemed abstracted and different. His hand trembled when he took the glass of rye she handed him, and when he sang for her,

> Let the huntsman graze his hounds
> As the farmer does his grounds,

that sad and melancholy old song that Irishmen always sing when they feel particularly jolly, his voice sounded plaintive and full of pathos.

Kathleen was far too wise to chide him. She tried to be gay and cheerful, though the change in Fergus made her heart very sad. Again the next day, and once more the following day but one, did she see him with the low-browed tempter that had wrought the change.

Day by day Fergus grew morose and pale. His once jolly

and laughing face grew stern and thoughtful. He rarely spoke to any one, and once when Mr. O'Malley handed him a big schooner from a keg fresh from the brewery, he heaved such a deep and mournful sigh that the foam flew half across the room.

"Kathleen," said her papa one day, "what's the matter wid that long-legged omadhaun Fergus? He looks like he was walking over his own grave."

"Oh, papa," said Kathleen, bursting into tears, "I do not know, he seems to be full of bayou water."

Let us follow Fergus and the sinister stranger, and see what spell is upon our hero.

* * *

William K. Meeks was a member of the notorious Young Men's Christian Association. His parents were honest and reputable citizens of Houston, and they had tried to inculcate in him the best principles, and train him to be a good and useful citizen. When about 18 years of age he met a man on the street one night who persuaded him to visit the rooms of the association.

After taking a bath and joining in the singing of a hymn, he was led into a game of checkers by some smooth-talking young man, and finally threw all reserve to the winds and, without a thought of his mother or his home, sank back into an arm-chair and began to read the editorials in a religious newspaper.

After that his progress in the same direction was easy. He cultivated side whiskers and white ties and fell so swiftly into the alluring ways of his companions that no ice cream and strawberry sociable or Evening of Song in the hall of the association was complete without Mr. Meeks. He became what is known as a "capper" for the hall, and many poor wandering young fellows strolling aimlessly about the streets of Houston have good cause to remember the sly, suave, plausible voice of the low-browed William Meeks, as he addressed them in insinuating tones, and invited them to the gorgeously lighted rooms of the Young Men's Christian Association.

William Meeks had for a long time had his eye upon Fergus O'Hollihan. The innocent straightforwardness of the young Irishman seemed to mark him as an easy prey.

One day he entered Fergus' store, made some trifling purchase, and then invited him to the hall.

"All right," said Fergus, "I'll walk up with you, as trade is a little dull. Hadn't we better take along a bottle of whisky to help pass away the time?"

"No," said William, with a sly smile. "There is no need. We have plenty to drink up there."

They passed down the street together, and then it was that Kathleen saw them, and the cloud began to gather over her happy young life.

William led Fergus to the door of the steps leading up to the hall, gave a sharp glance around to see whether they were observed, and they ascended the stairs.

"What do you fellows do up there?" asked Fergus, gazing around the hall in wonder.

"We read and sing and pray," said William. "Now, come over here, Mr. O'Hollihan, I have something to show you."

William went to a large water cooler in the corner, drew a brimming glass of ice water, and with a cold and cruel smile curling his lips, handed it to Fergus.

Ah, little Kathleen, in thy rose-twined cottage, thy dark eyes have many a tear in waiting. Could love be omnipresent, that sparkling glass of water would be dashed to the floor ere it touched thy lover's lips!

Fergus took the glass and gazed with wonder at its transparent contents; then seized with some sudden impulse he drained the glass of water to the last drop. As he drank, William Meeks, with a diabolical look of triumph on his face, rubbed his clammy hands together and exulted.

"What is this stuff?" asked Fergus; "this cold, refreshing liquid that with such exquisite freshness thrills through my heated frame? What nectar is this, tasteless, colourless and sweet as the morning air that quenches thirst, and does not excite the senses? Speak, Mr. Meeks, is it to be found elsewhere?"

"It is water," said William, softly, "and it can be had in plenty."

"I have often sailed on the bayou," said Fergus, "and have washed my hands at the hydrant at home, but I have never before seen any water."

Fergus drank glass after glass from the cooler, and finally suffered William to lead him, reluctant, from the hall.

They parted at the door, and as Fergus went down the street like one in some happy dream, saying softly to himself at intervals: "Water!" "Water!" William Meeks looked after him with a smile of devilish satisfaction upon his dark face.

* * *

That evening after he closed the store Fergus started home and suddenly felt an imperious thirst come upon him. He was already a slave to this wonderful new liquid that refreshed him so.

He entered a little corner saloon, where he had been in the habit of stopping to get a drink. The bartender seized a mug and reached for the bottle under the counter.

"Hold on," said Fergus; "don't be so fast. Give me a glass of water, please."

"You owe me ein dollar und five cents," he said. "Blease, Mr. Hollihan, bay me now pefore you go py yourself too much grazy to him remember, und I pe mooch obliged."

Fergus then threw the money upon the counter and staggered out of the saloon.

He did not go to see Kathleen that night—he was feeling too badly. He was wandering about in an agony of thirst, when he saw a piece of ice as large as a coconut fall from an ice wagon. He seized it in both hands, and hiding himself behind a pile of lumber sucked the ice greedily, with bloodshot eyes and trembling hands.

After that he kept a jug of water in the store behind some barrels under the counter, and when no one was looking he would stoop down, and holding up the jug, let the cursed stuff that was driving the light from Kathleen's dark eyes trickle down his burning throat.

* * *

It was Kathleen's wedding night. The parlour of the little cottage was brilliantly lit, and roses and evergreens were draped upon the walls. Cape jessamines filled the house with their delicious perfume and wreaths of white lilies were hung upon picture frames and the backs of chairs. The ceremony was to take place at 9 p.m., and by seven o'clock the guests had begun to assemble, for the smell of the good things Mrs. O'Malley was cooking pervaded the whole neighbourhood.

In the parlour, standing on a trestle decorated with violets and evergreens, stood a keg of whisky as cold as ice, and on the centre table were several beautifully decorated imported glasses, with quite a wedding-like polish upon their shining sides.

Kathleen's heart grew lighter as the hour approached. "I will be so loving and sweet to him that this strange melancholy will leave him. If it doesn't, I will pull his hair out."

The minutes crept by, and at half-past eight, Kathleen, blushing and timid-eyed, and looking like the Lorelei that charmed men's souls from their bodies on the purple heights of the Rhine, took her stand by the keg, and shyly drew for her father's guests glass after glass of the ruby liquid, scarcely less red than the glow upon her own fair cheek.

At a quarter to nine Fergus had not come, and all hands began to grow anxious.

At ten minutes to nine, Mr. O'Malley brought in his shot-gun and carefully loaded it. Kathleen burst into tears.

Where was Fergus O'Hollihan?

* * *

In the garish halls of the Young Men's Christian Association were gathered a group of gay young men.

Little do the majority of our citizens know what scenes go on in places of this kind. Our police well know that these resorts exist, but such is our system of city government that rarely do the guardians of peace set foot in establishments of the kind. Two or three young men were playing checkers, feverishly crowning the kings of their opponents, and watching the board with that hollow-eyed absorption and compressed lips so often noted in men of that class. Another played upon the guitar, while in a corner harsh ribald laughter broke from the lips of a man who was reading the Austin *Statesman.*

At a little table at one side of the room sat Fergus O'Hollihan and William Meeks. Before them, on a waiter, were two large glasses of ice water. William Meeks was speaking in a low, treacherous voice, and Fergus was listening with an abandoned and reckless look upon his face.

"Sobriety," said William, insinuatingly, as his snaky eyes were fixed upon the open and ingenuous countenance of Fergus, "sobriety is one of our cardinal virtues. Why should a man debase himself, destroy his brain, deaden his conscience and forge chains that eventually will clog his best efforts and ruin his fondest hopes? Let us be men and live temperate and cleanly lives. Believe me, Mr. O'Hollihan, it is the better plan."

Fergus' unsteady hand went out to the glass of water and he tossed it down his throat. "More," he gasped, gazing with feverish eyes. A member of the association in passing by stopped and laid his hand on William's shoulder.

"Old man," he said in a whisper, "the boys know you've struck a soft thing, but don't carry it too far. We don't want to have to bore another artesian well."

William shot a glance of displeasure at the young man, and he went away.

Just then a quartette began to sing "Come, Thou Fount", and Fergus, forgetting all his associations and best impulses, joined in with his strong tenor, and William Meeks' face wore a look of fiendish gloating.

At this moment Kathleen was weeping in her mother's arms. Mr. O'Malley was just ramming down the wad on the buckshot in his gun, and the beautiful wedding supper was growing cold upon the banquet table.

Suddenly in the street before the hall a brass band began to play an air that was Kathleen's favourite. It brought Fergus to his senses. He sprang to his feet and overturned the table and William Meeks. William sprang to his feet, rushed to the cooler and drawing a glass of water thrust it into Fergus' hands. Fergus hurled the glass to the floor and made a dash for the door. The secretary of the association met him there with the water hose and turned it full in his face. Fergus shut his mouth tightly, put the secretary to sleep with one on the point of his chin, and dashed down the stairs into the street.

* * *

As the clock struck nine, Mr. O'Malley placed two caps on his gun and one upon his head and started to find his son-in-law elect. The door burst open and Fergus rushed in. Kathleen ran to meet him with open arms, but he waved her sternly aside.

"I have first," he said, "a duty to perform." He knelt before the whisky keg, closed his mouth over the faucet and turned on the handle.

Sing, happy birds, in the green trees, but your songs make not half the melody that ripples in the glad heart of little Kathleen.

When Fergus arose from the keg, he was the same old Fergus once more. He gathered his bride to his heart, and Mr. O'Malley fired both barrels of his gun into the ceiling with joy. Fergus was rescued.

47

Makes the Whole World Kin

THE burglar stepped inside the window quickly, and then he took his time. A burglar who respects his art always takes his time before taking anything else.

The house was a private residence. By its boarded front door and untrimmed Boston ivy the burglar knew that the mistress of it was sitting on some ocean-side piazza telling a sympathetic man in a yachting cap that no one had ever understood her sensitive, lonely heart. He knew by the light in the third-storey front windows, and by the lateness of the season, that the master of the house had come home, and would soon extinguish his light and retire. For it was September of the year and of the soul, in which season the house's good man comes to consider roof-gardens and stenographers as vanities, and to desire the return of his mate and the more durable blessings of decorum and the moral excellences.

The burglar lighted a cigarette. The guarded glow of the match illuminated his salient points for a moment. He belonged to the third type of burglars.

This third type has not yet been recognized and accepted. The police have made us familiar with the first and second. Their classification is simple. The collar is the distinguishing mark.

When a burglar is caught who does not wear a collar, he is described as a degenerate of the lowest type, singularly vicious and depraved, and is suspected of being the desperate criminal who stole the handcuffs out of Patrolman Hennessy's pocket in 1878 and walked away to escape arrest.

The other well-known type is the burglar who wears a collar. He is always referred to as a Raffles in real life. He is invariably a gentleman by daylight, breakfasting in a dress suit, and posing as a paperhanger, while after dark he plies his nefarious occupation of burglary. His mother is an extremely wealthy and respected resident of Ocean Grove, and when he is conducted to his cell he asks at once for a nail file and the *Police Gazette*. He always has a wife in every State in the Union and fiancées in all the Territories, and the newspapers print his matrimonial gallery out of their stock of cuts of the ladies who were cured by only one bottle after having been given up by five doctors, experiencing great relief after the first dose.

The burglar wore a blue sweater. He was neither a Raffles nor one of the chiefs from Hell's Kitchen. The police would have been baffled had they attempted to classify him. They have not yet heard of the respectable, unassuming burglar who is neither above nor below his station.

This burglar of the third class began to prowl. He wore no masks, dark lanterns, or gum shoes. He carried a ·38-calibre revolver in his pocket, and he chewed peppermint gum thoughtfully.

The furniture of the house was swathed in its summer dust-protectors. The silver was far away in safe-deposit vaults. The burglar expected no remarkable "haul". His objective point was that dimly lighted room where the master of the house should be sleeping heavily after whatever solace he had sought to lighten the burden of his loneliness. A "touch" might be made there to the extent of legitimate, fair professional profits—loose money, a watch, a jewelled stick-pin—nothing exorbitant or beyond reason. He had seen the window left open and had taken the chance.

The burglar softly opened the door of the lighted room. The gas was turned low. A man lay in the bed asleep. On the dresser lay many things in confusion—a crumpled roll of bills, a watch, keys, three poker chips, crushed cigars, a pink silk hair bow, and an unopened bottle of bromo-seltzer for a bulwark in the morning.

The burglar took three steps toward the dresser. The man in the bed suddenly uttered a squeaky groan and opened his eyes. His right hand slid under his pillow, but remained there.

"Lay still," said the burglar in conversational tone. Burglars of the third type do not hiss. The citizen in the bed looked at the round end of the burglar's pistol and lay still.

"Now hold up both your hands," commanded the burglar.

The citizen had a little, pointed, brown-and-grey beard, like that of a painless dentist. He looked solid, esteemed, irritable, and disgusted. He sat up in bed and raised his right hand above his head.

"Up with the other one," ordered the burglar. "You might be amphibious and shoot with your left. You can count two, can't you? Hurry up, now."

"Can't raise the other one," said the citizen, with a contortion of his lineaments.

"What's the matter with it?"

"Rheumatism in the shoulder."

"Inflammatory?"

"Was. The inflammation has gone down."

The burglar stood for a moment or two, holding his gun on the afflicted one. He glanced at the plunder on the dresser and then, with a half-embarrassed air, back at the man in the bed. Then he, too, made a sudden grimace.

"Don't stand there making faces," snapped the citizen, bad-humouredly. "If you've come to burgle, why don't you do it? There's some stuff lying around."

"'Scuse me," said the burglar, with a grin; "but it just socked me one, too. It's good for you that rheumatism and me happens to be old pals. I got it in my left arm too. Most anybody but me would have popped you when you wouldn't hoist that left claw of yours."

"How long have you had it?" inquired the citizen.

"Four years. I guess that ain't all. Once you've got it, it's you for a rheumatic life—that's my judgment."

"Ever try rattlesnake oil?" asked the citizen, interestedly.

"Gallons," said the burglar. "If all the snakes I've used the oil of was strung out in a row they'd reach eight times as far as Saturn, and the rattles could be heard at Valparaiso, Indiana, and back."

"Some use Chiselum's Pills," remarked the citizen.

"Fudge!" said the burglar. "Took 'em five months. No good. I had some relief the year I tried Finkelham's Extract, Balm of Gilead poultices and Pott's Pain Pulverizer; but I think it was the buckeye I carried in my pocket what done the trick."

"Is yours worse in the morning or at night?" asked the citizen.

"Night," said the burglar; "just when I'm busiest. Say, take down that arm of yours—I guess you won't—— Say! did you ever try Blickerstaff's Blood Builder?"

"I never did. Does yours come in paroxysms or is it a steady pain?"

The burglar sat down on the foot of the bed and rested his gun on his crossed knee.

"It jumps," said he. "It strikes me when I ain't looking for it. I had to give up second-storey work because I got stuck sometimes half-way up. Tell you what—I don't believe the bloomin' doctors know what is good for it."

"Same here. I've spent a thousand dollars without getting any relief. Yours swell any?"

"Of mornings. And when it's goin' to rain—great Christopher!"

"Me too," said the citizen. "I can tell when a streak of humidity the size of a tablecloth starts from Florida on its way to New York. And if I pass a theatre where there's an *East Lynne* matinée going on, the moisture starts my left arm jumping like a toothache."

"It's undiluted—hades!" said the burglar.

"You're dead right," said the citizen.

The burglar looked down at his pistol and thrust it into his pocket with an awkward attempt at ease.

"Say, old man," he said constrainedly, "ever try opodeldoc?"

"Slop!" said the citizen angrily. "Might as well rub on restaurant butter."

"Sure," concurred the burglar. "It's a salve suitable for little Minnie when the kitty scratches her finger. I'll tell you what! We're up against it. I only find one thing that eases her up. Hey? Little old sanitary, ameliorating, lest-we-forget

Booze. Say—this job's off—'scuse me—get on your clothes and let's go out and have some. 'Scuse the liberty, but—ouch! There she goes again!"

"For a week," said the citizen. "I haven't been able to dress myself without help. I'm afraid Thomas is in bed, and——"

"Climb out," said the burglar. "I'll help you get into your duds."

The conventional returned as a tidal wave and flooded the citizen. He stroked his brown-and-grey beard.

"It's very unusual——" he began.

"Here's your shirt," said the burglar, "fall out. I knew a man who said Omberry's Ointment fixed him in two weeks so he could use both hands in tying his four-in-hand."

As they were going out the door the citizen turned and started back.

"'Liked to forget my money," he explained; "laid it on the dresser last night."

The burglar caught him by the right sleeve.

"Come on," he said bluffly. "I ask you. Leave it alone. I've got the price. Ever try witch hazel and oil of wintergreen?"

48

Hygeia at the Solito

IF you are knowing in the chronicles of the ring, you will recall to mind an event in the early 'nineties when, for a minute and sundry odd seconds, a champion and a "would-be" faced each other on the alien side of an international river. So brief a conflict had rarely imposed upon the fair promise of true sport. The reporters made what they could of it, but, divested of padding, the action was sadly fugacious. The champion merely smote his victim, turned his back upon him, remarking, "I know what I done to dat stiff," and extended an arm like a ship's mast for his glove to be removed.

Which accounts for a trainload of extremely disgusted gentlemen in an uproar of fancy vests and neckwear being spilled from their Pullmans in San Antonio in the early morning following the fight. Which also partly accounts for the unhappy predicament in which "Cricket" McGuire found himself as he tumbled from his car and sat upon the depôt platform, torn by a spasm of that hollow, racking cough so familiar to San Antonian ears. At that time, in the uncertain light of dawn, that way passed Curtis Raidler, the Nueces County cattleman—may his shadow never measure under six feet two.

The cattleman, out thus early to catch the southbound for his ranch station, stopped at the side of the distressed patron of sport, and spoke in the kindly drawl of his ilk and region, "Got it pretty bad, bud?"

"Cricket" McGuire, ex-feather-weight prize-fighter, tout, jockey, follower of the "ponies", all-round sport, and manipulator of the gum balls and walnut shells, looked up pugnaciously at the imputation cast by "bud".

"G'wan," he rasped, "telegraph pole. I didn't ring for yer."

Another paroxysm wrung him, and he leaned limply against a convenient baggage truck. Raidler waited patiently, glancing around at the white hats, short overcoats, and big cigars thronging the platform. "You're from the No'th, ain't you, bud?" he asked when the other was partially recovered. "Come down to see the fight?"

"Fight!" snapped McGuire. "Puss-in-the-corner! 'Twas a hypodermic injection. Handed him just one like a squirt of dope, and he's asleep, and no tan-bark needed in front of his residence. Fight!" He rattled a bit, coughed, and went on, hardly addressing the cattleman, but rather for the relief of voicing his troubles. "No more dead sure t'ings for me. But Rus Sage himself would have snatched at it. Five to one dat de boy from Cork wouldn't stay t'ree rounds is what I invested in. Put my last cent on, and could already smell the sawdust in dat all-night joint of Jimmy Delaney's on T'irty-seventh Street I was goin' to buy. And den—say, telegraph pole, what a gazaboo a guy is to put his whole roll on one turn of the gaboozlum!"

"You're plenty right," said the big cattleman; "more 'specially when you lose. Son, you get up and ight out for a hotel. You got a mighty bad cough. Had it long?"

"Lungs," said McGuire comprehensively. "I got it. The croaker says I'll come to time for six months longer—maybe a year if I hold my gait. I wanted to settle down and take care of myself. Dat's why I speculated on dat five to one perhaps. I had a t'ousand iron dollars saved up. If I winned I was goin' to buy Delaney's café. Who'd a t'ought dat stiff would take a nap in de foist round—say?"

"It's a hard deal," commented Raidler, looking down at the diminutive form of McGuire crumpled against the truck. "But you go to a hotel and rest. There's the Menger and the Maverick, and——"

"And the Fi'th Av'noo, and the Waldorf-Astoria," mimicked McGuire. "Told you I went broke. I've got one dime left. Maybe a trip to Europe or a sail in me private yacht would fix me up—pa-per!"

He flung his dime at a newsboy, got his *Express*, propped his back against the truck, and was at once rapt in the account of his Waterloo, as expanded by the ingenious press.

Curtis Raidler interrogated an enormous gold watch, and laid his hand on McGuire's shoulder.

"Come on, bud," he said. "We got three minutes to catch the train."

Sarcasm seemed to be McGuire's vein.

"You ain't seen me cash in any chips or call a turn since I told you I was broke, a minute ago, have you? Friend, chase yourself away."

"You're going down to my ranch," said the cattleman, "and stay till you get well. Six months'll fix you good as new." He lifted McGuire with one hand, and half dragged him in the direction of the train.

"What about the money?" said McGuire, struggling weakly to escape.

"Money for what?" asked Raidler, puzzled. They eyed each other, not understanding, for they touched only as at the gear of bevelled cog-wheels—at right angles, and moving upon different axles.

Passengers on the south-bound saw them seated together, and wondered at the conflux of two such antipodes. McGuire was five feet one, with a countenance belonging to either Yokohama or Dublin. Bright-beady of eye, bony of cheek and jaw, scarred, toughened, broken and reknit, indestructible, grisly, gladiatorial as a hornet, he was a type neither new nor unfamiliar. Raidler was the product of a different soil. Six feet two in height, miles broad, and no deeper than a crystal brook, he represented the union of the West and South. Few accurate pictures of his kind have been made, for art galleries are so small and the mutoscope is as yet unknown in Texas. After all, the only possible medium of portrayal of Raidler's kind would be the fresco—something high and simple and cool and unframed.

They were rolling southward on the International. The timber was huddling into little, dense green motts at rare distances before the inundation of the downright, vert prairies. This was the land of the ranchers; the domain of the kings of the kine.

McGuire sat, collapsed into his corner of the seat, receiving with acid suspicion the conversation of the cattleman. What was the "game" of this big "geezer" who was carrying him off? Altruism would have been McGuire's last guess. "He ain't no farmer," thought the captive, "and he ain't no con man, for sure. W'at's his lay? You trail in, Cricket, and see how many cards he draws. You're up against it, anyhow. You got a nickel and gallopin' consumption, and you better lay low. Lay low and see w'at's his game."

At Rincon, a hundred miles from San Antonio, they left the train for a buckboard which was waiting there for Raidler. In this they travelled the thirty miles between the station and their destination. If anything could, this drive should have stirred the acrimonious McGuire to a sense of his ransom. They sped upon velvety wheels across an exhilarant savanna. The pair of Spanish ponies struck a nimble, tireless trot, which gait they occasionally relieved by a wild, untrammelled gallop. The air was wine and seltzer, perfumed, as they absorbed it, with the delicate redolence of prairie flowers. The road perished, and the buckboard swam the uncharted billows of the grass itself, steered by the practised hand of Raidler, to whom each tiny distant mott of trees was a signboard, each convolution of the low hills a voucher of course and distance. But McGuire reclined upon his spine, seeing nothing but a desert, and receiving the cattleman's advances with sullen distrust. "W'at's he up to?" was the burden of his thoughts; "w'at kind of a gold brick has the big guy got to sell?" McGuire was only applying the measure of the streets he had walked to a range bounded by the horizon and the fourth dimension.

A week before, while riding the prairies, Raidler had come upon a sick and weakling calf deserted and bawling. Without dismounting he had reached and slung the distressed bossy across his saddle and dropped it at the ranch for the boys to attend to. It was impossible for McGuire to know or comprehend that, in the eyes of the cattleman, his case and that of the calf were identical in interest and demand upon his assistance. A creature was ill and helpless; he had the power to render aid—these were the only postulates required for the cattleman to act. They formed his system of logic and the most of his creed. McGuire was the seventh invalid whom Raidler had picked up thus casually in San Antonio, where so many thousands go for the ozone that is said to linger about its contracted streets. Five of them had been guests of Solito Ranch until they had been able to leave, cured or better, and exhausting the vocabulary of tearful gratitude. One came too late, but rested very comfortably, at last, under a ratama tree in the garden.

So, then, it was no surprise to the ranchhold when the buckboard spun to the door, and Raidler took up his debile *protégé* like a handful of rags and set him down upon the gallery.

McGuire looked upon things strange to him. The ranch-house was the best in the county. It was built of brick hauled one hundred miles by wagon, but it was of but one storey, and its four rooms were completely encircled by a mud floor "gallery". The miscellaneous setting of horses, dogs, saddles, wagons, guns, and cowpunchers' paraphernalia oppressed the metropolitan eye of the wrecked sportsman.

"Well, here we are at home," said Raidler cheeringly.

"It's a h——l of a looking place," said McGuire promptly, as he rolled upon the gallery floor in a fit of coughing.

"We'll try to make it comfortable for you, buddy," said the cattleman gently. "It ain't fine inside; but it's the out-doors, anyway, that'll do you the most good. This'll be your room, in here. Anything we got, you ask for it."

He led McGuire into the east room. The floor was bare and clean. White curtains waved in the gulf breeze through the open windows. A big willow rocker, two straight chairs, a long table covered with newspapers, pipes, tobacco, spurs, and cartridges stood in the centre. Some well-mounted heads of deer and one of an enormous black javeli projected from the walls. A wide, cool cot-bed stood in a corner. Nueces County people regarded this guest chamber as fit for a prince. McGuire showed his eyeteeth at it. He took out his nickel and spun it up to the ceiling.

"T'ought I was lyin' about the money, did ye? Well, you can frisk me if you wanter. Dat's the last simoleon in the treasury. Who's goin' to pay?"

The cattleman's clear grey eyes looked steadily from under his grizzly brows into the huckleberry optics of his guest. After a little he said simply, and not ungraciously, "I'll be much obliged to you, son, if you won't mention money any more. Once was quite a plenty. Folks I ask to my ranch don't have to pay anything, and they very scarcely ever offers it. Supper'll be ready in half an hour. There's water in the pitcher, and some, cooler, to drink, in that red jar hanging on the gallery."

"Where's the bell?" asked McGuire, looking about.

"Bell for what?"

"Bell to ring for things. I can't—see here," he exploded in a sudden, weak fury, "I never asked you to bring me here. I never held you up for a cent. I never give you a hard-luck story till you asked me. Here I am fifty miles from a bell-boy or a cocktail. I'm sick. I can't hustle. Gee! but I'm up against it!" McGuire fell upon the cot and sobbed shiveringly.

Raidler went to the door and called. A slender, bright-complexioned Mexican youth about twenty came quickly. Raidler spoke to him in Spanish—

"Ylario, it is in my mind that I promised you the position of *vaquero* on the San Carlos range at the fall *rodea.*"

"*Si, señor*, such was your goodness."

"Listen. This *señorito* is my friend. He is very sick. Place yourself at his side. Attend to his wants at all times. Have much patience and care with him. And when he is well, or—and when he is well, instead of *vaquero* I will make you *mayordomo* of the Rancho de las Piedras. *Esta bueno?*"

"*Si, si—mil gracias, señor.*" Ylario tried to kneel upon the floor in his gratitude, but the cattleman kicked at him benevolently, growling, "None of your opery-house antics, now."

Ten minutes later Ylario came from McGuire's room and stood before Raidler.

"The little *señor*," he announced, "presents his compliments" (Raidler credited Ylario with the preliminary) "and desires some pounded ice, one hot bath, one gin feez-z, that the windows be all closed, toast, one shave, one Newyork-heral', cigarettes, and to send one telegram."

Raidler took a quart bottle of whisky from his medicine cabinet. "Here, take him this," he said.

Thus was instituted the reign of terror at the Solito Ranch. For a few weeks McGuire blustered and boasted and swaggered before the cowpunchers who rode in for miles around to see this latest importation of Raidler's. He was an absolutely new experience to them. He explained to them all the intricate points of sparring and the tricks of training and defence. He opened to their minds' view all the indecorous life of a tagger after professional sports. His jargon of slang was a continuous joy and surprise to them. His gestures, his strange poses, his frank ribaldry of tongue and principle fascinated them. He was like a being from a new world.

Strange to say, this new world he had entered did not exist to him. He was an utter egoist of bricks and mortar. He had dropped out, he felt, into open space for a time, and all it contained was an audience for his reminiscences. Neither the limitless freedom of the prairie days nor the grand hush of the close-drawn, spangled nights touched him. All the hues of Aurora could not win him from the pink pages of a sporting journal. "Get something for nothing", was his mission in life; "T'irty-seventh" Street was his goal.

Nearly two months after his arrival he began to complain that he felt worse. It was then that he became the ranch's incubus, its harpy, its Old Man of the Sea. He shut himself in his room like some venomous kobold or flibbertigibbet, whining, complaining, cursing, accusing. The keynote of his plaint was that he had been inveigled into a gehenna against his will; that he was dying of neglect and lack of comforts. With all his dire protestations of increasing illness, to the eyes of others he remained unchanged. His currant-like eyes were as bright and diabolic as ever; his voice was as rasping; his callous face, with the skin drawn tense as a drum-head, had no flesh to lose. A flush on his prominent cheek-bones each afternoon hinted that a clinical thermometer might have revealed a symptom, and percussion might have established the fact that McGuire was breathing with only one lung, but his appearance remained the same.

In constant attendance upon him was Ylario, whom the coming reward of the *mayordomo*ship must have greatly stimulated, for McGuire chained him to a bitter existence. The air—the man's only chance for life—he commanded to be kept out by closed windows and drawn curtains. The room was always blue and foul with cigarette smoke; whosoever entered it must sit, suffocating, and listen to the imp's interminable gasconade concerning his scandalous career.

The oddest thing of all was the relation existing between McGuire and his benefactor. The attitude of the invalid toward the cattleman was something like that of a peevish, perverse child toward an indulgent parent. When Raidler would leave the ranch McGuire would fall into a fit of malevolent, silent sullenness. When he returned, he would be met by a string of violent and stinging reproaches. Raidler's attitude towards his charge was quite inexplicable in its way. The cattleman seemed actually to assume and feel the character assigned him by McGuire's intemperate accusations—the character of tyrant and guilty oppressor. He seemed to have adopted the responsibility of the fellow's condition, and he always met his tirades with a pacific, patient, and even remorseful kindness that never altered.

One day Raidler said to him, "Try more air, son. You can have the buckboard and a driver every day if you'll go. Try a week or two in one of the cow camps. I'll fix you up plum comfortable. The ground, and the air next to it—them's the things to cure you. I knowed a man from Philadelphy, sicker than you are, got lost on the Guadalupe, and slept on the bare grass in sheep camps for two weeks. Well, sir, it started him getting well, which he done. Close to the ground—that's where the medicine in the air stays. Try a little hossback riding now. There's a gentle pony——"

"What've I done to yer?" screamed McGuire. "Did I ever doublecross yer? Did I ask you to bring me here? Drive me out to yer camps if you wanter; or stick a knife in me and save trouble. Ride! I can't lift my feet. I couldn't sidestep a jab from a five-year-old kid. That's what your d——d ranch has done for me. There's nothing to eat, nothing to see, and nobody to talk to but a lot of Ruebens who don't know a punching bag from a lobster salad."

"It's a lonesome place, for certain," apologized Raidler abashedly. "We got plenty, but it's rough enough. Anything you think of you want, the boys'll ride up and fetch it down for you."

It was Chad Murchison, a cowpuncher from the Circle Bar outfit, who first suggested that McGuire's illness was fraudulent. Chad had brought a basket of grapes for him thirty miles, and four out of his way, tied to his saddle-horn. After remaining in the smoke-tainted room for a while, he emerged and bluntly confided his suspicions to Raidler.

"His arm," said Chad, "is harder'n a diamond. He interduced me to what he called a shore-perplexus punch, and 'twas like being kicked twice by a mustang. He's playin' it low down on you, Curt. He ain't no sicker'n I am. I hate to say it, but the runt's workin' you for range and shelter."

The cattleman's ingenuous mind refused to entertain Chad's view of the case, and when, later, he came to apply the test, doubt entered not into his motives.

One day, about noon, two men drove up to the ranch, alighted, hitched, and came in to dinner; standing and general invitations being the custom of the country. One of them was a great San Antonio doctor, whose costly services had been engaged by a wealthy cowman who had been laid low by an accidental bullet. He was now being driven to the station to take the train back to town. After dinner Raidler took him aside, pushed a twenty-dollar bill against his hand, and said—

"Doc., there's a young chap in that room I guess has got a bad case of consumption. I'd like for you to look him over and see just how bad he is, and if we can do anything for him."

"How much was that dinner I just ate, Mr. Raidler?" said the doctor bluffly, looking over his spectacles. Raidler returned the money to his pocket. The doctor immediately entered McGuire's room, and the cattleman seated himself upon a heap of saddles on the gallery, ready to reproach himself in the event the verdict should be unfavourable.

In ten minutes the doctor came briskly out. "Your man," he said promptly, "is as sound as a new dollar. His lungs are better than mine. Respiration, temperature, and pulse normal. Chest expansion four inches. Not a sign of weakness anywhere. Of course I didn't examine for the bacillus, but it isn't there. You can put my name to the diagnosis. Even cigarettes and a vilely close room haven't hurt him. Coughs, does he? Well, you tell him it isn't necessary. You asked if there is anything we could do for him. Well, I advise you to set him digging postholes or breaking mustangs. There's our team ready. Good day, sir." And like a puff of wholesome, blustery wind the doctor was off.

Raidler reached out and plucked a leaf from a mesquite bush by the railing, and began chewing it thoughtfully.

The branding season was at hand, and the next morning Ross Hargis, foreman of the outfit, was mustering his force of some twenty-five men at the ranch, ready to start for the San Carlos range, where the work was to begin. By six o'clock the horses were all saddled, the grub wagon ready, and the cowpunchers were swinging themselves upon their mounts, when Raidler bade them wait. A boy was bringing up an extra pony, bridled and saddled, to the gate. Raidler walked to McGuire's room, and threw open the door. McGuire was lying on his cot, not yet dressed, smoking.

"Get up," said the cattleman, and his voice was clear and brassy, like a bugle.

"How's that?" asked McGuire, a little startled.

"Get up and dress. I can stand a rattlesnake, but I hate a liar. Do I have to tell you again?" He caught McGuire by the neck and stood him on the floor.

"Say, friend," cried McGuire wildly, "are you mad? I'm sick—see? I'll croak if I got to hustle. What've I done to yer?" —he began his chronic whine—"I never asked yer to——"

"Put on your clothes," called Raidler in a rising tone.

Swearing, stumbling, shivering, keeping his amazed, shiny eyes upon the now menacing form of the aroused cattleman, McGuire managed to tumble into his clothes. Then Raidler took him by the collar and shoved him out and across the yard to the extra pony hitched at the gate. The cowpunchers lolled in their saddles, open-mouthed.

"Take this man," said Raidler to Ross Hargis, "and put him to work. Make him work hard, sleep hard, and eat hard. You boys know I done what I could for him, and he was welcome. Yesterday the best doctor in San Antone examined him, and says he's got the lungs of a burro and the constitution of a steer. You know what to do with him, Ross."

Ross Hargis only smiled grimly.

"Aw," said McGuire, looking intently at Raidler, with a peculiar expression upon his face, "the croaker said I was all right, did he? Said I was fakin', did he? You put him on to me. You t'ought I wasn't sick. You said I was a liar. Say, friend, I talked rough, I know, but I didn't mean most of it. If you felt like I did—aw! I forgot—I ain't sick, the croaker says. Well, friend, now I'll go work for yer. Here's where you play even."

He sprang into the saddle easily as a bird, got the quirt from the horn, and gave his pony a slash with it. "Cricket," who once brought in Good Boy by a neck at Hawthorne—and a 10 to 1 shot—had his foot in the stirrups again.

McGuire led the cavalcade as they dashed away for San Carlos, and the cowpunchers gave a yell of applause as they closed in behind his dust.

But in less than a mile he had lagged to the rear, and was last man when they struck the patch of high chaparral below the horse pens. Behind a clump of this he drew rein, and held a handkerchief to his mouth. He took it away drenched with bright, arterial blood, and threw it carefully into a clump of prickly pear. Then he slashed with his quirt again, gasped "G'wan" to his astonished pony, and galloped after the gang.

That night Raidler received a message from his old home in Alabama. There had been a death in the family; an estate was to divide, and they called for him to come. Daylight found him in the buckboard, skimming the prairies for the station. It was two months before he returned. When he arrived at the ranch-house he found it well-nigh deserted save for Ylario, who acted as a kind of steward during his absence. Little by little the youth made him acquainted with the work done while he was away. The branding camp, he was informed, was still doing business. On account of many severe storms the cattle had been badly scattered, and the branding had been accomplished but slowly. The camp was now in the valley of the Guadalupe, twenty miles away.

"By the way," said Raidler, suddenly remembering, "that fellow I sent along with them—McGuire—is he working yet?"

"I do not know," said Ylario. "Mans from the camp come verree few times to the ranch. So plentee work with the leetle calves. They no say. Oh, I think that fellow McGuire he dead much time ago."

"Dead!" said Raidler. "What you talking about?"

"Verree sick fellow, McGuire," replied Ylario, with a shrug of his shoulder. "I theenk he no live one, two months when he go away."

"Shucks!" said Raidler. "He humbugged you, too, did he? The doctor examined him and said he was sound as a mesquite knot."

"That doctor," said Ylario, smiling, "he tell you so? That doctor no see McGuire."

"Talk up," ordered Raidler. "What the devil do you mean?"

"McGuire," continued the boy tranquilly, "he getting drink water outside when that doctor come in room. That doctor take me and pound me all over here with his fingers"—putting his hand to his chest—"I not know for what. He put his ear here and here and here, and listen—I not know for what. He put little glass stick in my mouth. He feel my arm here. He make me count like whisper—so—twenty, *treinta, cuarenta.* Who knows," concluded Ylario, with a deprecating spread of his hands, "for what that doctor do those verree droll and such-like things?"

"What horses are up?" asked Raidler shortly.

"Paisano is grazing but behind the little corral, *señor.*"

"Saddle him for me at once."

Within a very few minutes the cattleman was mounted and

away. Paisano, well named after that ungainly but swift-running bird, struck into his long lope that ate up the road like a strip of macaroni. In two hours and a quarter Raidler, from a gentle swell, saw the branding camp by a water-hole in the Guadalupe. Sick with expectancy of the news he feared, he rode up, dismounted, and dropped Paisano's reins. So gentle was his heart that at that moment he would have pleaded guilty to the murder of McGuire.

The only being in the camp was the cook, who was just arranging the hunks of barbecued beef, and distributing the tin coffee cups for supper. Raidler evaded a direct question concerning the one subject in his mind.

"Everything all right in camp, Pete?" he managed to inquire.

"So, so," said Pete conservatively. "Grub give out twice. Wind scattered the cattle, and we've had to rake the brush for forty mile. I need a new coffee-pot. And the mosquitoes is some more hellish than common."

"The boys—all well?"

Pete was no optimist. Besides, inquiries concerning the health of cow-punchers were not only superfluous, but bordered on flaccidity. It was not like the boss to make them.

"What's left of 'em don't miss no calls to grub," the cook conceded.

"What's left of 'em?" repeated Raidler in a husky voice. Mechanically he began to look around for McGuire's grave. He had in his mind a white slab such as he had seen in the Alabama churchyard. But immediately he knew that was foolish.

"Sure," said Peter; "what's left. Cow camps change in two months. Some's gone."

Raidler nerved himself.

"That—chap—I sent along—McGuire—did—he——"

"Say," interrupted Pete, rising with a chunk of corn bread in each hand, "that was a dirty shame, sending that poor, sick, kid to a cow camp. A doctor that couldn't tell he was graveyard meat ought to be skinned with a cinch buckle. Game as he was, too—it's a scandal among snakes—lemme tell you what he done. First night in camp the boys started to initiate him in the leather breeches degree. Ross Hargis busted him one swipe with his chaparreras, and what do you reckon the poor child did? Got up, the little skeeter, and licked Ross. Licked Ross Hargis. Licked him good. Hit him plenty and everywhere and hard. Ross'd just get up and pick out a fresh place to lay down on agin.

"Then that McGuire goes off there and lays down with his head in the grass and bleeds. A hem'ridge they calls it. He lays there eighteen hours by the watch, and they can't budge him. Then Ross Hargis, who loves any man who can lick him, goes to work and damns the doctors from Greenland to Poland Chiny; and him and Green Branch Johnson they gets McGuire in a tent, and spells each other feedin' him chopped raw meat and whisky.

"But it looks like the kid ain't got no appetite to git well, for they misses him from the tent in the night and finds him rootin' in the grass, and likewise a drizzle fallin'. 'Gwan,' he says, 'lemme go and die like I wanter. He said I was a liar and a fake and I was playin' sick. Lemme alone.'

"Two weeks," went on the cook, "he laid around, not noticin' nobody, and then——"

A sudden thunder filled the air, and a score of galloping centaurs crashed through the brush into camp.

"Illustrious rattlesnakes!" exclaimed Pete, springing all ways at once; "here's the boys come, and I'm an assassinated man if supper ain't ready in three minutes."

But Raidler saw only one thing. A little, brown-faced, grinning chap, springing from his saddle in the full light of the fire. McGuire was not like that, and yet——

In another instant the cattleman was holding him by the hand and shoulder.

"Son, son, how goes it?" was all he found to say.

"Close to the ground, says you," shouted McGuire, crunching Raidler's fingers in a grip of steel; "and dat's where I found it—healt' and strengt', and tumbled to what a cheap skate I been actin'. T'anks fer kickin' me out, old man. And—say! de joke's on dat croaker, ain't it? I looked t'rough the window and see him plain' tag on dat Dago kid's solar plexus."

"You son of a tinker," growled the cattleman, "whyn't you talk up and say the doctor never examined you?"

"Aw—gwan!" said McGuire, with a flash of his old asperity, "nobody can't bluff me. You never ast me. You made your spiel, and you t'rowed me out, and I let it go at dat. And, say, friend, dis chasin' cows is outer sight. Dis is de whitest bunch of sports I ever travelled with. You'll let me stay, won't yer, old man?"

Raidler looked wonderingly toward Ross Hargis.

"That cussed little runt," remarked Ross tenderly, "is the Jo-dartin'est hustler—and the hardest hitter in anybody's cow camp."

49

The Princess and the Puma

THERE had to be a king and queen, of course. The king was a terrible old man who wore six-shooters and spurs, and shouted in such a tremendous voice that the rattlers on the prairie would run into their holes under the prickly pear. Before there was a royal family they called the man "Whispering Ben". When he came to own 50,000 acres of land and more cattle than he could count, they called him O'Donnell "the Cattle King".

The queen had been a Mexican girl from Laredo. She made a good, mild, Colorado-claro wife, and even succeeded in teaching Ben to modify his voice sufficiently in the house to keep the dishes from being broken. When Ben got to be king she would sit on the gallery of Espinosa Ranch and weave rush mats. When wealth became so irresistible and oppressive that upholstered chairs and a centre table were brought down from San Antone in the wagons, she bowed her smooth, dark head, and shared the fate of the Danaë.

To avoid *lèse-majesté* you have been presented first to the king and queen. They do not enter the story, which might be called "The Chronicle of the Princess, the Happy Thought, and the Lion that Bungled his Job".

Josefa O'Donnell was the surviving daughter, the princess. From her mother she inherited warmth of nature and a dusky, semi-tropic beauty. From Ben O'Donnell the royal she acquired a store of intrepidity, common sense, and the faculty of ruling. The combination was one worth going miles to see. Josefa while riding her pony at a gallop could put five out of six bullets through a tomato-can swinging at the end of a string. She could play for hours with a white kitten she owned, dressing it in all manner of absurd clothes. Scorning a pencil, she could tell you out of her head what 1,545 two-year-olds would bring on the hoof, at $8.50 per head. Roughly speaking, the Espinosa Ranch is forty miles long and thirty broad—but mostly leased land. Josefa, on her pony, had prospected over every mile of it. Every cow-puncher on the range knew her by sight and was a loyal vassal. Ripley Givens, foreman of one of the Espinosa outfits, saw her one day, and made up his mind to form a royal matrimonial alliance. Presumptuous? No. In those days in the Nueces country a man was a man. And, after all, the title of cattle king does not presuppose blood royal. Often it only signifies that its owner wears the crown in token of his magnificent qualities in the art of cattle stealing.

One day Ripley Givens rode over to the Double-Elm Ranch to inquire about a bunch of strayed yearlings. He was late in setting out on his return trip, and it was sundown when he struck the White Horse Crossing of the Nueces. From there to his own camp it was sixteen miles. To the Espinosa ranch-house it was twelve. Givens was tired. He decided to pass the night at the Crossing.

There was a fine water-hole in the river-bed. The banks were thickly covered with great trees, undergrown with brush. Back from the water-hole fifty yards was a stretch of curly mesquite grass—supper for his horse and bed for himself. Givens staked his horse, and spread out his saddle blankets to dry. He sat down with his back against a tree and rolled a cigarette. From somewhere in the dense timber along the river came a sudden, rageful, shivering wail. The pony danced at the end of his rope and blew a whistling snort of comprehending fear. Givens puffed at his cigarette, but he reached leisurely for his pistol-belt, which lay on the grass, and twirled the cylinder of his weapon tentatively. A great gar plunged with a loud splash into the water-hole. A little brown rabbit skipped around a bunch of cat-claw and sat twitching his whiskers and looking humorously at Givens. The pony went on eating grass.

It is well to be reasonably watchful when a Mexican lion sings soprano along the arroyos at sundown. The burden of his song may be that young calves and fat lambs are scarce, and that he has a carnivorous desire for your acquaintance.

In the grass lay an empty fruit can, cast there by some former sojourner. Givens caught sight of it with a grunt of satisfaction. In his coat pocket tied behind his saddle was a handful or two of ground coffee. Black coffee and cigarettes! What ranchero could desire more?

In two minutes he had a little fire going clearly. He started, with his can, for the water-hole. When within fifteen yards of its edge he saw, between the bushes, a side-saddled pony with down-dropped reins cropping grass a little distance to his left. Just rising from her hands and knees on the brink of the water hole was Josefa O'Donnell. She had been drinking water, and she brushed the sand from the palms of her hands. Ten yards away, to her right, half concealed by a clump of sacuista, Givens saw the crouching form of the Mexican lion. His amber eyeballs glared hungrily; six feet from them was the tip of the tail stretched straight, like a pointer's. His hind-quarters rocked with the motion of the cat tribe preliminary to leaping.

Givens did what he could. His six-shooter was thirty-five yards away lying on the grass. He gave a loud yell, and dashed between the lion and the princess.

The "rucus", as Givens called it afterward, was brief and somewhat confused. When he arrived on the line of attack he saw a dim streak in the air, and heard a couple of faint cracks. Then a hundred pounds of Mexican lion plumped down upon his head and flattened him, with a heavy jar, to the ground. He remembered calling out: "Let up, now—no fair gouging!" and then he crawled from under the lion like a worm, with his mouth full of grass and dirt, and a big lump on the back of his head where it had struck the root of a water-elm. The lion lay motionless. Givens, feeling aggrieved, and suspicious of fouls, shook his fist at the lion, and shouted: "I'll rastle you again for twenty——" and then he got back to himself.

Josefa was standing in her tracks, quietly reloading her silver-mounted ·38. It had not been a difficult shot. The lion's head made an easier mark than a tomato-can swinging at the end of a string. There was a provoking, teasing, maddening smile upon her mouth and in her dark eyes. The would-be rescuing knight felt the fire of his fiasco burn down to his soul. Here had been his chance, the chance that he had dreamed of; and Momus, and not Cupid, had presided over it. The satyrs in the wood were, no doubt, holding their sides in hilarious, silent laughter. There had been something like vaudeville—say Signor Givens and his funny knockabout act with the stuffed lion.

"Is that you, Mr. Givens?" said Josefa, in her deliberate, saccharine contralto. "You nearly spoiled my shot when you yelled. Did you hurt your head when you fell?"

"Oh, no," said Givens quietly; "that didn't hurt." He stooped ignominiously and dragged his best Stetson hat from under the beast. It was crushed and wrinkled to a fine comedy effect. Then he knelt down and softly stroked the fierce, open-jawed head of the dead lion.

"Poor old Bill!" he exclaimed mournfully.

"What's that?" asked Josefa sharply.

"Of course you didn't know, Miss Josefa," said Givens, with an air of one allowing magnanimity to triumph over grief. "Nobody can blame you. I tried to save him, but I couldn't let you know in time."

"Save who?"

"Why, Bill. I've been looking for him all day. You see, he's been our camp pet for two years. Poor old fellow, he wouldn't have hurt a cotton-tail rabbit. It'll break the boys all up when they hear about it. But you couldn't tell, of course, that Bill was just trying to play with you."

Josefa's black eyes burned steadily upon him. Ripley Givens met the test successfully. He stood rumpling the yellow-brown curls on his head pensively. In his eyes was regret, not unmingled with a gentle reproach. His smooth features were set to a pattern of indisputable sorrow. Josefa wavered.

"What was your pet doing here?" she asked, making a last stand. "There's no camp near the White Horse Crossing."

"The old rascal ran away from camp yesterday," answered Givens readily. "It's a wonder the coyotes didn't scare him to death. You see, Jim Webster, our horse wrangler, brought a little terrier pup into camp last week. The pup made life miserable for Bill—he used to chase him around and chew his hind legs for hours at a time. Every night when bedtime came Bill would sneak under one of the boys' blankets and sleep to keep the pup from finding him. I reckon he must have been worried pretty desperate or he wouldn't have run away. He was always afraid to get out of sight of camp."

Josefa looked at the body of the fierce animal. Givens gently patted one of the formidable paws that could have killed a yearling calf with one blow. Slowly a red flush widened upon the dark olive face of the girl. Was it the signal of shame of the true sportsman who has brought down ignoble quarry? Her eyes grew softer, and the lowered lids drove away all their bright mockery.

"I'm very sorry," she said humbly; "but he looked so big, and jumped so high that——"

"Poor old Bill was hungry," interrupted Givens, in defence of the deceased. "We always made him jump for his supper in camp. He would lie down and roll over for a piece of meat. When he saw you he thought he was going to get something to eat from you."

Suddenly Josefa's eyes opened wide.

"I might have shot you!" she exclaimed. "You ran right in between. You risked your life to save your pet! That was fine, Mr. Givens. I like a man who is kind to animals."

Yes; there was even admiration in her gaze now. After all, there was a hero rising out of the ruins of the anti-climax. The look on Givens's face would have secured him a high position in the S.P.C.A.

"I always loved 'em," said he; "horses, dogs, Mexican lions, cows, alligators——"

"I hate alligators," instantly demurred Josefa; "crawly, muddy things!"

"Did I say alligators?" said Givens. "I meant antelopes, of course."

Josefa's conscience drove her to make further amends. She held out her hand penitently. There was a bright, unshed drop in each of her eyes.

"Please forgive me, Mr. Givens, won't you? I'm only a

girl, you know, and I was frightened at first. I'm very, very sorry I shot Bill. You don't know how ashamed I feel. I wouldn't have done it for anything."

Givens took the proffered hand. He held it for a time while he allowed the generosity of his nature to overcome his grief at the loss of Bill. At last it was clear that he had forgiven her.

"Please don't speak of it any more, Miss Josefa. 'Twas enough to frighten any young lady the way Bill looked. I'll explain it all right to the boys."

"Are you really sure you don't hate me?" Josefa came closer to him impulsively. Her eyes were sweet—oh, sweet and pleading with gracious penitence. "I would hate any one who would kill my kitten. And how daring and kind of you to risk being shot when you tried to save him! How very few men would have done that!" Victory wrested from defeat! Vaudeville turned into drama! Bravo, Ripley Givens!

It was now twilight. Of course Miss Josefa could not be allowed to ride on to the ranch-house alone. Givens resaddled his pony in spite of that animal's reproachful glances, and rode with her. Side by side they galloped across the smooth grass, the princess and the man who was kind to animals. The prairie odours of fruitful earth and delicate bloom were thick and sweet around them. Coyotes yelping over there on the hill! No fear. And yet——

Josefa rode closer. A little hand seemed to grope. Givens found it with his own. The ponies kept an even gait. The hands lingered together, and the owner of one explained—

"I never was frightened before, but just think! How terrible it would be to meet a really wild lion! Poor Bill! I'm so glad you came with me!"

O'Donnell was sitting on the ranch gallery.

"Hallo, Rip!" he shouted—"that you?"

"He rode in with me," said Josefa. "I lost my way and was late."

"Much obliged," called the cattle king. "Stop over, Rip, and ride to camp in the morning."

But Givens would not. He would push on to camp. There was a bunch of steers to start off on the trail at daybreak. He said good night, and trotted away.

An hour later, when the lights were out, Josefa, in her night-robe, came to her door and called to the king in his own room across the brick-paved hallway—

"Say, pop, you know that old Mexican lion they call the 'Gotch-eared Devil'—the one that killed Gonzales, Mr. Martin's sheep herder, and about fifty calves on the Salado range? Well, I settled his hash this afternoon over at the White Horse Crossing. Put two balls in his head with my ·38 while he was on the jump. I knew him by the slice gone from his left ear that old Gonzales cut off with his machete. You couldn't have made a better shot yourself, daddy."

"Bully for you!" thundered Whispering Ben from the darkness of the royal chamber.

50

Tobin's Palm

TOBIN and me, the two of us, went down to Coney one day, for there was four dollars between us, and Tobin had need of distractions. For there was Katie Mahorner, his sweetheart, of County Sligo, lost since she started for America three months before with two hundred dollars, her own savings, and one hundred dollars from the sale of Tobin's inherited estate, a fine cottage and pig on the Bog Shannaugh. And since the letter that Tobin got saying that she had started to come to him not a bit of news had he heard or seen of Katie Mahorner. Tobin advertised in the papers, but nothing could be found of the colleen.

So, to Coney me and Tobin went, thinking that a turn at the chutes and the smell of the popcorn might raise the heart in his bosom. But Tobin was a hard-headed man, and the sadness stuck in his skin. He ground his teeth at the crying balloons; he cursed the moving pictures; and, though he would drink whenever asked, he scorned Punch and Judy, and was for licking the tintype men as they came.

So I gets him down a side way on a board walk where the attractions were some less violent. At a little six by eight stall Tobin halts, with a more human look in his eye.

"'Tis here," says he, "I will be diverted. I'll have the palm of me hand investigated by the wonderful palmist of the Nile, and see if what is to be will be."

Tobin was a believer in signs and the unnatural in nature. He possessed illegal convictions in his mind along the subject of black cats, lucky numbers, and the weather predictions in the papers.

We went into the enchanted chicken coop, which was fixed mysterious with red cloth and pictures of hands with lines crossing 'em like a railroad centre. The sign over the door says it is Madame Zozo the Egyptian Palmist. There was a fat woman inside in a red jumper with pothooks and beasties embroidered upon it. Tobin gives her ten cents and extends one of his hands. She lifts Tobin's hand, which is own brother to the hoof of a dray-horse, and examines it to see whether 'tis a stone in the frog or a cast shoe he has come for.

"Man," says this Madame Zozo, "the line of your fate shows——"

"'Tis not me foot at all," says Tobin, interrupting. "Sure, 'tis, no beauty, but ye hold the palm of me hand."

"The line shows," says the Madame, "that ye've not arrived at your time of life without bad luck. And there's more to come. The mount of Venus—or is that a stone bruise?—shows that ye've been in love. There's been trouble in your life on account of your sweetheart."

"'Tis Katie Mahorner she has references with," whispers Tobin to me in a loud voice to one side.

"I see," says the palmist, "a great deal of sorrow and tribulation with one whom ye cannot forget. I see the lines of designation point to the letter K and the letter M in her name."

"Whist!" says Tobin to me; "do ye hear that?"

"Look out," goes on the palmist, "for a dark man and a light woman; for they'll both bring ye trouble. Ye'll make a voyage upon the water very soon, and have a financial loss. I see one line that brings good luck. There's a man coming into your life who will fetch ye good fortune. Ye'll know him when ye see him by his crooked nose."

"Is his name set down?" asks Tobin. "'Twill be convenient in the way of greeting when he backs up to dump off the good luck."

"His name," says the palmist, thoughtful-looking, "is not spelled out by the lines, but they indicate 'tis a long one, and the letter 'o' should be in it. There's no more to tell. Good evening. Don't block up the door."

"'Tis wonderful how she knows," says Tobin as we walk to the pier.

As we squeezed through the gates a nigger man sticks his

lighted segar against Tobin's ear, and there is trouble. Tobin hammers his neck, and the women squeal, and by presence of mind I drag the little man out of the way before the police comes. Tobin is always in an ugly mood when enjoying himself.

On the boat going back, when the man calls "Who wants the good-looking waiter?" Tobin tried to plead guilty, feeling the desire to blow the foam off a crock of suds, but when he felt in his pocket he found himself discharged for lack of evidence. Somebody had disturbed his change during the commotion. So we sat, dry, upon the stools, listening to the Dagoes fiddling on deck. If anything, Tobin was lower in spirits and less congenial with his misfortunes than when we started.

On a seat against the railing was a young woman dressed suitable for red automobiles, with hair the colour of an unsmoked meerschaum. In passing by, Tobin kicks her foot without intentions, and, being polite to ladies when in drink, he tries to give his hat a twist while apologizing. But he knocks it off, and the wind carries it overboard.

Tobin came back and sat down, and I began to look out for him, for the man's adversities were becoming frequent. He was apt, when pushed so close by hard luck, to kick the best-dressed man he could see, and try to take command of the boat.

Presently Tobin grabs my arm and says, excited: "Jawn," says he, "do ye know what we're doing? We're taking a voyage upon the water."

"There now," says I; "subdue yeself. The boat'll land in ten minutes more."

"Look," says he, "at the light lady upon the bench. And have ye forgotten the nigger man that burned me ear? And isn't the money I had gone—a dollar sixty-five it was?"

I thought he was no more than summing up his catastrophes so as to get violent with good excuse, as men will do, and I tried to make him understand such things was trifles.

"Listen," says Tobin. "Ye've no ear for the gift of prophecy or the miracles of the inspired. What did the palmist lady tell ye out of me hand? 'Tis coming true before your eyes. 'Look out,' says she, 'for a dark man and a light woman; they'll bring ye trouble.' Have ye forgot the nigger man, though he got some of it back from me fist? Can ye show me a lighter woman than the blonde lady that was the cause of me hat falling in the water? And where's the dollar sixty-five I had in me vest when we left the shooting gallery?"

The way Tobin put it, it did seem to corroborate the art of prediction, though it looked to me that these accidents could happen to anyone at Coney without the implication of palmistry.

Tobin got up and walked around on deck, looking close at the passengers out of his little red eyes. I asked him the interpretation of his movements. Ye never know what Tobin has in his mind until he begins to carry it out.

"Ye should know," says he, "I'm working out the salvation promised by the lines in me palm. I'm looking for the crooked nose man that's to bring the good luck. 'Tis all that will save us. Jawn, did ye ever see a straighter-nosed gang of hellions in the days of your life?"

'Twas the nine-thirty boat, and we landed and walked uptown, through Twenty-second Street, Tobin being without his hat.

On a street corner, standing under a gaslight and looking over the elevated road at the moon, was a man. A long man he was, dressed decent, with a segar between his teeth, and I saw that his nose made two twists from bridge to end, like the wriggle of a snake. Tobin saw it at the same time, and I heard him breathe hard like a horse when you take the saddle off. He went straight up to the man, and I went with him.

"Good night to ye," Tobin says to the man. The man takes his segar and passes the compliments, sociable.

"Would ye hand us your name," asks Tobin, "and let us look at the size of it? It may be our duty to become acquainted with ye."

"My name," says the man, polite, "is Friedenhausman—Maximus G. Friedenhausman."

"'Tis the right length," says Tobin. "Do you spell it with an 'o' anywhere down the stretch of it?"

"I do not," says the man.

"*Can* ye spell it with an 'o'?" inquires Tobin, turning anxious.

"If your conscience," says the man with the nose, "is indisposed toward foreign idioms ye might, to please yourself, smuggle the letter into the penultimate syllable."

"'Tis well," says Tobin. "Ye're in the presence of Jawn Malone and Daniel Tobin."

"'Tis highly appreciated," says the man, with a bow. "And now since I cannot conceive that ye would hold a spelling bee upon the street corner, will ye name some reasonable excuse for being at large?"

"By the two signs," answers Tobin, trying to explain, "which ye display according to the reading of the Egyptian palmist from the sole of me hand, ye've been nominated to offset with good luck the lines of trouble leading to the nigger man and the blonde lady with her feet crossed in the boat, besides the financial loss of a dollar sixty-five, all so far fulfilled according to Hoyle."

The man stopped smoking and looked at me.

"Have ye any amendments," he asks, "to offer to that statement, or are ye one too? I thought by the looks of ye ye might have him in charge."

"None," says I to him, "except that as one horseshoe resembles another so are ye the picture of good luck as predicted by the hand of me friend. If not, then the lines of Danny's hand may have been crossed, I don't know."

"There's two of ye," says the man with the nose, looking up and down for the sight of a policeman. "I've enjoyed your company immense. Good night."

With that he shoves his segar in his mouth and moves across the street, stepping fast. But Tobin sticks close to one side of him and me at the other.

"What!" says he, stopping on the opposite sidewalk and pushing back his hat; "do ye follow me? I tell ye," he says, very loud, "I'm proud to have met ye. But it is my desire to be rid of ye. I am off to me home."

"Do," says Tobin, leaning against his sleeve. "Do be off to your home. And I will sit at the door of it till ye come out in the morning. For the dependence is upon ye to obviate the curse of the nigger man and the blonde lady and the financial loss of the one-sixty-five."

"'Tis a strange hallucination," says the man, turning to me as a more reasonable lunatic. "Hadn't ye better get him home?"

"Listen, man," says I to him. "Daniel Tobin is as sensible as he ever was. Maybe he is a bit deranged on account of having drink enough to disturb but not enough to settle his wits, but he is no more than following out the legitimate path of his superstitions and predicaments, which I will explain to you." With that I relates the facts about the palmist lady and how the finger of suspicion points to him as an instrument of good fortune. "Now, understand," I concludes, "my position in this riot. I am the friend of me friend Tobin, according to me interpretations. 'Tis easy to be a friend to the prosperous, for it pays; 'tis not hard to be a friend to the poor, for ye get puffed up by gratitude and have your picture printed standing in front of a tenement with a scuttle of coal and an orphan in each hand. But it strains the art of friendship to be true friend to a born fool. And that's what I'm doing," says I, "for, in my opinion, there's no fortune to be read from the palm of me hand that wasn't printed there with the handle of a pick. And, though ye've got the crookedest nose in New York City, I misdoubt that all the fortune-tellers doing business could milk good luck from ye. But the lines of Danny's hand pointed to ye fair, and I'll assist him to experiment with ye until he's convinced ye're dry."

After that the man turns, sudden, to laughing. He leans against a corner and laughs considerable. Then he claps me and Tobin on the backs of us and takes us by an arm apiece.

"'Tis my mistake," says he. "How could I be expecting anything so fine and wonderful to be turning the corner upon me? I came near being found unworthy. Hard by," says he, "is a café, snug and suitable for the entertainment of idiosyncrasies. Let us go there and have drink while we discuss the unavailability of the categorical."

So saying, he marched me and Tobin to the back room of a saloon, and ordered the drinks, and laid the money on the table. He looks at me and Tobin like brothers of his, and we have the segars.

"Ye must know," says the man of destiny, "that me walk in life is one that is called the literary. I wander abroad be night seeking idiosyncrasies in the masses and truth in the heavens above. When ye came upon me I was in contemplation of the elevated road in conjunction with the chief luminary of night. The rapid transit is poetry and art: the moon but a tedious, dry body, moving by rote. But these are private opinions, for, in the business of literature, the conditions are reversed. 'Tis me hope to be writing a book to explain the strange things I have discovered in life."

"Ye will put me in a book," says Tobin, disgusted; "will ye put me in a book?"

"I will not," says the man, "for the covers will not hold ye. Not yet. The best I can do is to enjoy ye meself, for the time is not ripe for destroying the limitations of print. Ye would look fantastic in type. All alone by meself must I drink this cup of joy. But, I thank ye, boys; I am truly grateful."

"The talk of ye," says Tobin, blowing through his moustache and pounding the table with his fist, "is an eyesore to me patience. There was good luck promised out of the crook of your nose, but ye bear fruit like the bang of a drum. Ye resemble, with your noise of books, the wind blowing through a crack. Sure, now, I would be thinking the palm of me hand lied but for the coming true of the nigger man and the blonde lady and——"

"Whist!" says the long man; "would ye be led astray by physiognomy? Me nose will do what it can within bounds. Let us have these glasses filled again, for 'tis good to keep idiosyncrasies well moistened, they being subject to deterioration in a dry moral atmosphere."

So, the man of literature makes good, to my notion, for he pays, cheerful, for everything, the capital of me and Tobin being exhausted by prediction. But Tobin is sore, and drinks quiet, with the red showing in his eye.

By and by we moved out, for 'twas eleven o'clock, and stands a bit upon the sidewalk. And then the man says he must be going home, and invites me and Tobin to walk that way. We arrives on a side street two blocks away where there is a stretch of brick houses with high stoops and iron fences. The man stops at one of them and looks up at the top windows which he finds dark.

"'Tis me humble dwelling," says he, "and I begin to perceive by the signs that me wife has retired to slumber. Therefore I will venture a bit in the way of hospitality. 'Tis me wish that ye enter the basement-room, where we dine, and partake of a reasonable refreshment. There will be some fine cold fowl and cheese and a bottle or two of ale. Ye will be welcome to enter and eat, for I am indebted to ye for diversions."

The appetite and conscience of me and Tobin was congenial to the proposition, though 'twas sticking hard in Danny's superstitions to think that a few drinks and a cold lunch should represent the good fortune promised by the palm of his hand.

"Step down the steps," says the man with the crooked nose, "and I will enter by the door above and let ye in. I will ask the new girl we have in the kitchen," says he, "to make ye a pot of coffee to drink before ye go. 'Tis fine coffee Katie Mahorner makes for a green girl just landed three months. Step in," says the man, "and I'll send her down to ye."

51

A Bird of Bagdad

WITHOUT doubt much of the spirit and genius of the Caliph Harun Al Rashid descended to the Margrave August Michael von Paulsen Quigg.

Quigg's restaurant is in Fourth Avenue—that street that the city seems to have forgotten in its growth. Fourth Avenue—born and bred in the Bowery—staggers northward full of good resolutions.

Where it crosses Fourteenth Street it struts for a brief moment proudly in the glare of the museums and cheap theatres. It may yet become a fit mate for its high-born sister boulevard to the west, or its roaring, polyglot, broad-waisted cousin to the east. It passes Union Square; and here the hoofs of the dray horses seem to thunder in unison, recalling the tread of marching hosts—Hooray! But now come the silent and terrible mountains—buildings square as forts, high as the clouds, shutting out the sky, where thousands of slaves bend over desks all day. On the ground floors are only little fruit-shops and laundries and bookshops, where you see copies of *Littell's Living Age* and G. W. M. Reynolds's novels in the windows. And next—poor Fourth Avenue!—the street glides into a mediaeval solitude. On each side are the shops devoted to "Antiques".

Let us say it is night. Men in rusty armour stand in the windows and menace the hurrying cars with raised, rusty iron gauntlets. Hauberks and helms, blunderbusses, Cromwellian breastplates, matchlocks, creeses, and the swords and daggers of an army of dead-and-gone gallants gleam dully in the ghostly light. Here and there from a corner saloon (lit with Jack-o'-lanterns or phosphorus) stagger forth shuddering, home-bound citizens, nerved by the tankards within to their fearsome journey adown that eldrich avenue lined with the bloodstained weapons of the fighting dead. What street could live enclosed by these mortuary relics, and trod by these spectral citizens in whose sunken hearts scarce one good whoop or tra-la-la remained?

Not Fourth Avenue. Not after the tinsel but enlivening glories of the Little Rialto—not after the echoing drum-beats of Union Square. There need be no tears, ladies and gentlemen; 'tis but the suicide of a street. With a shriek and a crash Fourth Avenue dives headlong into the tunnel at Thirty-fourth and is never seen again.

Near the sad scene of the thoroughfare's dissolution stood the modest restaurant of Quigg. It stands there yet if you care to view its crumbling red-brick front, its show window heaped with oranges, tomatoes, layer cakes, pies, canned asparagus—its papier-mâché lobster and two Maltese kittens asleep on a bunch of lettuce—if you care to sit at one of the little tables upon whose cloth has been traced in the yellowest of coffee stains the trail of the Japanese advance—to sit there with one eye on your umbrella and the other upon the bogus bottle from which you drop the counterfeit sauce foisted upon us by the cursed charlatan who assumes to be our dear old lord and friend, the "Nobleman in India".

Quigg's title came through his mother. One of her ancestors was a Margravine of Saxony. His father was a Tammany brave. On account of the dilution of his heredity he found that he could neither become a reigning potentate nor get a job in the City Hall. So he opened a restaurant. He was a man full of thought and reading. The business gave him a living, though he gave it little attention. One side of his house bequeathed to him a poetic and romantic nature. The other gave him the restless spirit that made him seek adventure. By day he was Quigg, the restaurateur. By night he was the Margrave—the Caliph—the Prince of Bohemia—going about the city in search of the odd, the mysterious, the inexplicable, the recondite.

One night at nine, at which hour the restaurant closed, Quigg set forth upon his quest. There was a mingling of the foreign, the military and the artistic in his appearance as he buttoned his coat high up under his short-trimmed brown and grey beard and turned westward toward the more central life conduits of the city. In his pocket he had stored an assortment of cards, written upon, without which he never stirred out of doors. Each of those cards was good at his own restaurant for its face value. Some called simply for a bowl of soup or sandwiches and coffee; others entitled their bearer to one, two, three or more days of full meals; a very few were for single regular meals; a very few were, in effect, meal tickets good for a week.

Of riches and power Margrave Quigg had none; but he had a Caliph's heart—it may be forgiven him if his head fell short of the measure of Harun Al Rashid's. Perhaps some of the gold pieces in Bagdad had put less warmth and hope into the complainants among the bazaars than had Quigg's beef stew among the fishermen and one-eyed calenders of Manhattan.

Continuing his progress in search of romance to divert him, or of distress that he might aid, Quigg became aware of a fast-gathering crowd that whooped and fought and eddied at a corner of Broadway and the crosstown street that he was traversing. Hurrying to the spot he beheld a young man of an exceedingly melancholy and preoccupied demeanour engaged in the pastime of casting silver money from his pockets to the middle of the street. With each motion of the generous one's hand the crowd huddled upon the falling largesse with yells of joy. Traffic was suspended. A policeman in the centre of the mob stooped often to the ground as he urged the blockaders to move on.

The Margrave saw at a glance that here was food for his hunger after knowledge concerning abnormal workings of the human heart. He made his way swiftly to the young man's side and took his arm. "Come with me at once," he said, in the low but commanding voice that his waiters had learned to fear.

"Pinched," remarked the young man, looking up at him with expressionless eyes. "Pinched by a painless dentist. Take me away, flatty, and give me gas. Some lay eggs and some lay none. When is a hen?"

Still deeply seized by some inward grief, but tractable, he

allowed Quigg to lead him away and down the street to a little park.

There, seated on a bench, he upon whom a corner of the great Caliph's mantle has descended, spake with kindness and discretion, seeking to know what evil had come upon the other, disturbing his soul and driving him to such ill-considered and ruinous waste of his substance and stores.

"I was doing the Monte Cristo act as adopted by Pompton, N.J., wasn't I?" asked the young man.

"You were throwing small coins into the street for the people to scramble after," said the Margrave.

"That's it. You buy all the beer you can hold, and then you throw chicken feed to—— Oh, curse that word chicken, and hens, feathers, roosters, eggs, and everything connected with it!"

"Young sir," said the Margrave kindly, but with dignity, "though I do not ask your confidence, I invite it. I know the world and I know humanity. Man is my study, though I do not eye him as the scientist eyes a beetle or as the philanthropist gazes at the objects of his bounty—through a veil of theory and ignorance. It is my pleasure and distraction to interest myself in the peculiar and complicated misfortunes that life in a great city visits upon my fellow-men. You may be familiar with the history of that glorious and immortal ruler, the Caliph Harun Al Rashid, whose wise and beneficent excursions among his people in the city of Bagdad secured him the privilege of relieving so much of their distress. In my humble way I walk in his footsteps. I seek for romance and adventure in city streets—not in ruined castles or in crumbling palaces. To me the greatest marvels of magic are those that take place in men's hearts when acted upon by the furious and diverse forces of a crowded population. In your strange behaviour this evening I fancy a story lurks. I read in your act something deeper than the wanton wastefulness of a spendthrift. I observe in your countenance the certain traces of consuming grief or despair. I repeat—I invite your confidence. I am not without some power to alleviate and advise. Will you not trust me?"

"Gee, how you talk!" exclaimed the young man, a gleam

of admiration supplanting for a moment the dull sadness of his eyes. "You've got the Astor Library skinned to a synopsis of preceding chapters. I mind that old Turk you speak of. I read *The Arabian Nights* when I was a kid. He was a kind of Bill Devery and Charlie Schwab rolled into one. But, say, you might wave enchanted dish-rags and make copper bottles smoke up coon giants all night without ever touching me. My case won't yield to that kind of treatment."

"If I could hear your story," said the Margrave, with his lofty, serious smile.

"I'll spiel it in about nine words," said the young man, with a deep sigh, "but I don't think you can help me any. Unless you're a peach at guessing it's back to the Bosphorus for you on your magic lineoleum."

THE STORY OF THE YOUNG MAN AND THE HARNESS MAKER'S RIDDLE

"I work in Hildebrant's saddle and harness shop down in Grand Street. I've worked there five years. I get $18 a week. That's enough to marry on, ain't it? Well, I'm not going to get married. Old Hildebrant is one of these funny Dutchmen —you know the kind—always getting off bum jokes. He's got about a million riddles and things that he faked from Rogers Brothers' great-grandfather. Bill Watson works there, too. Me and Bill have to stand for them chestnuts day after day. Why do we do it? Well, jobs ain't to be picked off every Anheuser bush—— And then there's Laura.

"What? The old man's daughter. Comes in the shop every day. About nineteen, and the picture of the blonde that sits on the palisades of the Rhine and charms the clam-diggers into the surf. Hair the colour of straw matting, and eyes as black and shiny as the best harness blacking—think of that!

"Me? Well, it's either me or Bill Watson. She treats us both equal. Bill is all to the psychopathic about her; and me?—well, you saw my plating the road-bed of the Great Maroon Way with silver to-night. That was on account of Laura. I was spiflicated, Your Highness, and I wot not of what I wouldst.

"How? Why, old Hildebrant says to me and Bill this afternoon: 'Boys, one riddle have I for you gehabt haben. A young man who cannot riddles antworten, he is not so good by business for ein family to provide—is not that—hein?' And he hands us a riddle—a conundrum, some calls it—and he chuckles interiorly and gives both of us till to-morrow morning to work out the answer to it. And he says whichever of us guesses the repartee end of it goes to his house o' Wednesday night to his daughter's birthday party. And it means Laura for whichever of us goes, for she's naturally aching for a husband, and it's either me or Bill Watson, for old Hildebrant likes us both, and wants her to marry somebody that'll carry on the business after he's stitched his last pair of traces.

"The riddle? Why, it was this: 'What kind of a hen lays the longest?' Think of that! What kind of a hen lays the longest? Ain't it like a Dutchman to risk a man's happiness on a fool proposition like that? Now what's the use? What I don't know about hens would fill several incubators. You say you're giving imitations of the old Arab guy that gave way—libraries in Bagdad. Well, now, can you whistle up a fairy that'll solve this hen query, or not?"

When the young man ceased the Margrave arose and paced to and fro by the park bench for several minutes. Finally he sat again, and said, in grave and impressive tones:

"I must confess, sir, that during the eight years that I have spent in search of adventure and in relieving distress I have never encountered a more interesting or a more perplexing case. I fear that I have overlooked hens in my researches and observations. As to their habits, their times and manner of laying, their many varieties and cross-breedings, their span of life, their——"

"Oh, don't make an Ibsen drama of it!" interrupted the young man flippantly. "Riddles—especially old Hildebrant's riddles—don't have to be worked out seriously. They are light themes such as Sim Ford and Harry Thurston Peck like to handle. But, somehow, I can't just strike the answer. Bill Watson may, and he may not. To-morrow will tell. Well, Your

Majesty, I'm glad anyhow that you butted in and whiled the time away. I guess Mr. Al Rashid himself would have bounced back if one of his constituents had conducted him up against this riddle. I'll say good night. Peace fo' yours, and what-you-may-call-its of Allah."

The Margrave, with a gloomy air, held out his hand.

"I cannot express my regret," he said sadly. "Never before have I found myself unable to assist in some way. 'What kind of a hen lays the longest?' It is a baffling problem. There is a hen, I believe, called the Plymouth Rock that——"

"Cut it out," said the young man. "The Caliph trade is a mighty serious one. I don't suppose you'd even see anything funny in a preacher's defence of John D. Rockefeller. Well, good night, Your Nibs."

From habit the Margrave began to fumble in his pockets. He drew forth a card and handed it to the young man.

"Do me the favour to accept this, anyhow," he said. "The time may come when it might be of use to you."

"Thanks!" said the young man, pocketing it carelessly. "My name is Simmons."

* * *

Shame to him who would hint that the reader's interest shall altogether pursue the Margrave August Michael von Paulsen Quigg. I am indeed astray if my hand fail in keeping the way where my peruser's heart would follow. Then let us, on the morrow, peep quickly in at the door of Hildebrant, harness maker.

Hildebrant's 200 pounds reposed on a bench, silver-buckling a raw leather martingale.

Bill Watson came in first.

"Vell," said Hildebrant, shaking all over with the vile conceit of the joke-maker, "haf you guessed him? 'Vat kind of a hen lays der longest?'"

"Er—why, I think so," said Bill, rubbing a servile chin. "I think so, Mr. Hildebrant—the one that lives the longest—— Is that right?"

"Nein!" said Hildebrant, shaking his head violently. "You haf not guessed der answer."

Bill passed on and donned a bed-tick apron and bachelorhood.

In came the young man of the Arabian Night's fiasco—pale, melancholy, hopeless.

"Vell," said Hildebrant, "haf you guessed him? 'Vat kind of a hen lays der longest?'"

Simmons regarded him with dull savagery in his eye. Should he curse this mountain of pernicious humour—curse him and die? Why should—— But there was Laura.

Dogged, speechless, he thrust his hands into his coat pockets and stood. His hand encountered the strange touch of the Margrave's card. He drew it out and looked at it, as men about to be hanged look at a crawling fly. There was written on it in Quigg's bold, round hand: "Good for one roast chicken to bearer."

Simmons looked up with a flashing eye.

"A dead one!" said he.

"Goot!" roared Hildebrant, rocking the table with giant glee. "Dot is right! You gome at mine house at eight o'clock to der party."

52

The Missing Chord

I STOPPED overnight at the sheep-ranch of Rush Kinney, on the Sandy Fork of the Nueces. Mr. Kinney and I had been strangers up to the time when I called "Hallo!" at his hitching-rack; but from that moment until my departure on the next morning we were, according to the Texas code, undeniable friends.

After supper the ranchman and I lugged our chairs outside the two-room house, to its floorless gallery roofed with chaparral and sacuista grass. With the rear legs of our chairs sinking deep into the hard-packed loam, each of us reposed against an elm pillar of the structure and smoked El Toro tobacco, while we wrangled amicably concerning the affairs of the rest of the world.

As for conveying adequate conception of the engaging charm of that prairie evening, despair waits upon it. It is a bold chronicler who will undertake the description of a Texas night in the early spring. An inventory must suffice.

The ranch rested upon the summit of a lenient slope. The ambient prairie, diversified by arroyos and murky patches of brush and pear, lay around us like a darkened bowl at the bottom of which we reposed as dregs. Like a turquoise cover the sky pinned us there. The miraculous air, heady with ozone and made memorably sweet by leagues of wild flowerets, gave tang and savour to the breath. In the sky was a great round, mellow searchlight which we knew to be no moon, but the dark lantern of summer, who came to hunt northward the cowering spring. In the nearest corral a flock of sheep lay silent until a groundless panic would send a squad of them huddling together with a drumming rush. For other sounds a shrill family of coyotes yapped beyond the shearing-pen, and whippoorwills twittered in the long grass. But even these dissonances hardly rippled the clear torrent of the mocking-birds' notes that fell from a dozen neighbouring shrubs and trees. It would not have been preposterous for one to tiptoe and essay to touch the stars, they hung so bright and imminent.

Mr. Kinney's wife, a young and capable woman, we had left in the house. She remained to busy herself with the domestic round of duties, in which I had observed that she seemed to take a buoyant and contented pride. In one room we had supped. Presently, from the other, as Kinney and I sat without, there burst a volume of sudden and brilliant music. If I could justly estimate the art of piano-playing, the construer of that rollicking fantasia had creditably mastered the secrets of the keyboard. A piano, and one so well played, seemed to me to be an unusual thing to find in that small and unpromising ranch-house. I must have looked my surprise at Rush Kinney, for he laughed in his soft, Southern way, and nodded at me through the moonlit haze of our cigarettes.

"You don't often hear as agreeable a noise as that on a sheep-ranch," he remarked; "but I never see any reason for not playing up to the arts and graces just because we happen to live out in the brush. It's a lonesome life for a woman; and if a little music can make it any better, why not have it? That's the way I look at it."

"A wise and generous theory," I assented. "And Mrs. Kinney plays well. I am not learned in the science of music, but I should call her an uncommonly good performer. She has technic and more than ordinary power."

The moon was very bright, you will understand, and I saw upon Kinney's face a sort of amused and pregnant expression, as though there were things behind it that might be expounded.

"You came up the trail from the Double-Elm Fork," he said promisingly. "As you crossed it you must have seen an old deserted *jacal* to your left under a comma mott."

"I did," said I. "There was a drove of *javalis* rooting around it. I could see by the broken corrals that no one lived there."

"That's where this music proposition started," said Kinney. "I don't mind telling you about it while we smoke.

That's where old Cal Adams lived. He had about eight hundred graded merinos and a daughter that was solid silk and as handsome as a new stake-rope on a thirty-dollar pony. And I don't mind telling you that I was guilty in the second degree of hanging around old Cal's ranch all the time I could spare away from lambing and shearing. Miss Marilla was her name; and I had figured it out by the rule of two that she was destined to become the châtelaine and lady superior of Rancho Lomito, belonging to R. Kinney, Esq., where you are now a welcome and honoured guest.

"I will say that old Cal wasn't distinguished as a sheepman. He was a little, old, stoop-shouldered *hombre* about as big as a gun scabbard, with scraggy white whiskers, and condemned to the continuous use of language. Old Cal was so obscure in his chosen profession that he wasn't even hated by the cowmen. And when a sheepman don't get eminent enough to acquire the hostility of the cattlemen, he is mighty apt to die unwept and considerably unsung.

"But that Marilla girl was a benefit to the eye. And she was the most elegant kind of a housekeeper. I was the nearest neighbour, and I used to ride over to the Double-Elm anywhere from nine to sixteen times a week with fresh butter or a quarter of venison or a sample of new sheep-dip just as a frivolous excuse to see Marilla. Marilla and me got to be extensively inveigled with each other, and I was pretty sure I was going to get my rope around her neck and lead her over to the Lomito. Only she was so everlastingly permeated with filial sentiments toward old Cal that I never could get her to talk about serious matters.

"You never saw anybody in your life that was as full of knowledge and had less sense than old Cal. He was advised about all the branches of information contained in learning, and he was up to all the rudiments of doctrines and enlightenment. You couldn't advance him any ideas on any of the parts of speech or lines of thought. You would have thought he was a professor of the weather and politics and chemistry and natural history and the origin of derivations. Any subject you brought up old Cal could give you an abundant synopsis of it from the Greek root up to the time it was sacked and on the market.

"One day just after the fall shearing I rides over to the Double-Elm with a lady's magazine about fashions for Marilla and a scientific paper for old Cal.

"While I was tying my pony to a mesquite, out runs Marilla, 'tickled to death' with some news that couldn't wait.

"'Oh, Rush,' she says, all flushed up with esteem and gratification, 'what do you think! Dad's going to buy me a piano. Ain't it grand! I never dreamed I'd ever have one.'

"'It's sure joyful,' says I. 'I always admired the agreeable uproar of a piano. It'll be lots of company for you. That's mighty good of Uncle Cal to do that.'

"'I'm all undecided,' says Marilla, 'between a piano and a organ. A parlour organ is nice.'

"'Either of 'em,' says I, 'is first-class for mitigating the lack of noise around a sheep-ranch. For my part,' I says, 'I shouldn't like anything better than to ride home of an evening and listen to a few waltzes and jigs, with somebody about your size sitting on the piano-stool and rounding up the notes.'

"'Oh, hush about that,' says Marilla, 'and go on in the house. Dad hasn't rode out to-day. He's not feeling well.'

"Old Cal was inside, lying on a cot. He had a pretty bad cold and a cough. I stayed to supper.

"'Going to get Marilla a piano, I hear,' says I to him.

"'Why, yes, something of the kind, Rush,' says he. 'She's been hankering for music for a long spell; and I allow to fix her up with something in that line right away. The sheep sheared six pounds all round this fall; and I'm going to get Marilla an instrument if it takes the price of the whole clip to do it.'

"'*Star wayno*,' says I. 'The little girl deserves it.'

"'I'm going to San Antone on the last load of wool,' says Uncle Cal, 'and select an instrument for her myself.'

"'Wouldn't it be better,' I suggest, 'to take Marilla along and let her pick out one that she likes?'

"I might have known that would set Uncle Cal going. Of

course, a man like him, that knew everything about everything, would look at that as a reflection on his attainments.

"'No, sir, it wouldn't,' says he, pulling at his white whiskers. 'There ain't a better judge of musical instruments in the whole world than what I am. I had an uncle,' says he, 'that was a partner in a piano factory, and I've seen thousands of 'em put together. I know all about musical instruments from a pipe-organ to a corn-stalk fiddle. There ain't a man lives, sir, that can tell me any news about any instrument that has to be pounded, blowed, scraped, grinded, picked, or wound with a key.'

"'You get me what you like, dad,' says Marilla, who couldn't keep her feet on the floor from joy. 'Of course you know what to select. I'd just as lief it was a piano or a organ or what.'

"'I see in St. Louis once what they call a orchestrion,' says Uncle Cal, 'that I judged was about the finest thing in the way of music ever invented. But there ain't room in this house for one. Anyway, I imagine they'd cost a thousand dollars. I reckon something in the piano line would suit Marilla the best. She took lessons in that respect for two years over at Birdstail. I wouldn't trust the buying of an instrument to anybody else but myself. I reckon if I hadn't took up sheep-raising I'd have been one of the finest composers or piano-and-organ manufacturers in the world.'

"That was Uncle Cal's style. But I never lost any patience with him, on account of his thinking so much of Marilla. And she thought just as much of him. He sent her to the academy over at Birdstail for two years when it took nearly every pound of wool to pay the expenses.

"Along about Tuesday Uncle Cal put out for San Antone on the last wagonload of wool. Marilla's uncle Ben, who lived in Birdstail, come over and stayed at the ranch while Uncle Cal was gone.

"It was ninety miles to San Antone, and forty to the nearest railroad station, so Uncle Cal was gone about four days. I was over at the Double-Elm when he come rolling back one evening about sundown. And up there in the wagon, sure enough, was a piano or a organ—we couldn't tell which—

all wrapped up in woolsacks, with a wagon-sheet tied over it in case of rain. And out skips Marilla, hollering, 'Oh, oh!' with her eyes shining and her hair a-flying. 'Dad—dad,' she sings out, 'have you brought it—have you brought it?'—and it right there before her eyes, as women will do.

"'Finest piano in San Antone,' says Uncle Cal, waving his hand, proud. 'Genuine rosewood, and the finest, loudest tone you ever listened to. I hear the storekeeper play it, and I took it on the spot and paid cash down.'

"Me and Ben and Uncle Cal and a Mexican lifted it out of the wagon and carried it in the house and set it in a corner. It was one of them upright instruments, and not very heavy or very big.

"And then all of a sudden Uncle Cal flops over and says he's mighty sick. He's got a high fever, and he complains of his lungs. He gets into bed, while me and Ben goes out to unhitch and put the horses in the pasture, and Marilla flies around to get Uncle Cal something hot to drink. But first she puts both arms on that piano and hugs it with a soft kind of a smile, like you see kids doing with their Christmas toys.

"When I came in from the pasture, Marilla was in the room where the piano was. I could see by the strings and wool sacks on the floor that she had had it unwrapped. But now she was tying the wagon-sheet over it again, and there was a kind of solemn, whitish look on her face.

"'Ain't wrapping up the music again, are you, Marilla?' I asks. 'What's the matter with just a couple of tunes for to see how she goes under the saddle?'

"'Not to-night, Rush,' says she. 'I don't want to play any to-night. Dad's too sick. Just think, Rush, he paid three hundred dollars for it—nearly a third of what the wool-clip brought!'

"'Well, it ain't anyways in the neighbourhood of a third of what you are worth,' I told her. 'And I don't think Uncle Cal is too sick to hear a little agitation of the piano-keys just to christen the machine.'

"'Not to-night, Rush,' says Marilla, in a way that she had when she wanted to settle things.

"But it seems that Uncle Cal was plenty sick, after all. He

got so bad that Ben saddled up and rode over to Birdstail for Doc Simpson. I stayed around to see if I'd be needed for anything.

"When Uncle Cal's pain let up on him a little he called Marilla and says to her: 'Did you look at your instrument, honey? And do you like it?'

"'It's lovely, dad,' says she, leaning down by his pillow; 'I never saw one so pretty. How dear and good it was of you to buy it for me!'

"'I haven't heard you play on it any yet,' says Uncle Cal; 'and I've been listening. My side don't hurt quite so bad now—won't you play a piece, Marilla?'

"But no; she puts Uncle Cal off and soothes him down like you've seen women do with a kid. It seems she's made up her mind not to touch that piano at present.

"When Doc Simpson comes over he tells us that Uncle Cal has pneumonia the worst kind; and as the old man was past sixty and nearly on the lift anyhow, the odds was against his walking on grass any more.

"On the fourth day of his sickness he calls for Marilla again and wants to talk piano. Doc Simpson was there, and so was Ben and Mrs. Ben, trying to do all they could.

"'I'd have made a wonderful success in anything connected with music,' says Uncle Cal. 'I got the finest instrument for the money in San Antone. Ain't that piano all right in every respect, Marilla?'

"'It's just perfect, dad,' says she. 'It's got the finest tone I ever heard. But don't you think you could sleep a little while now, dad?'

"'No, I don't,' says Uncle Cal. 'I want to hear that piano. I don't believe you've even tried it yet. I went all the way to San Antone and picked it out for you myself. It took a third of the fall clip to buy it; and I don't mind that if it makes my good girl happier. Won't you play a little bit for dad, Marilla?'

"Doc Simpson beckoned Marilla to one side and recommended her to do what Uncle Cal wanted, so it would get him quieted. And her uncle Ben and his wife asked her, too.

"'Why not hit out a tune or two with the soft pedal on?' I asks Marilla. 'Uncle Cal has begged you so often. It would please him a good deal to hear you touch up the piano he's bought for you. Don't you think you might?'

"But Marilla stands there with big tears rolling down from her eyes and says nothing. And then she runs over and slips her arm under Uncle Cal's neck and hugs him tight.

"'Why, last night, dad,' we heard her say, 'I played ever so much. Honest—I have been playing it. And it's such a splendid instrument, you don't know how I love it. Last night I played "Bonnie Dundee" and the "Anvil Polka" and the "Blue Danube"—and lots of pieces. You must surely have heard me playing a little, didn't you, dad? I didn't like to play loud when you was so sick.'

"'Well, well,' says Uncle Cal, 'maybe I did. Maybe I did and forgot about it. My head is a little cranky at times. I heard the man in the store play it fine. I'm mighty glad you like it, Marilla. Yes, I believe I could go to sleep a while if you'll stay right beside me till I do.'

"There was where Marilla had me guessing. Much as she thought of that old man, she wouldn't strike a note on that piano that he'd bought her. I couldn't imagine why she told him she'd been playing it, for the wagon-sheet hadn't ever been off it since she put it back on the same day it came. I knew she could play a little anyhow, for I'd once heard her snatch some pretty fair dance-music out of an old piano at the Charco Largo Ranch.

"Well, in about a week the pneumonia got the best of Uncle Cal. They had the funeral over at Birdstail, and all of us went over. I brought Marilla back home in my buckboard. Her uncle Ben and his wife were going to stay there a few days with her.

"That night Marilla takes me in the room where the piano was, while the others were out on the gallery.

"'Come here, Rush,' says she; 'I want you to see this now.'

"She unties the rope, and drags off the wagon-sheet.

"If you ever rode a saddle without a horse, or fired off a gun that wasn't loaded, or took a drink out of an empty bottle, why, then you might have been able to scare an opera or two out of the instrument Uncle Cal had bought.

"Instead of a piano, it was one of them machines they've invented to play the piano with. By itself it was about as musical as the holes of a flute without the flute.

"And that was the piano that Uncle Cal had selected; and standing by it was the good, fine, all-wool girl that never let him know it.

"And what you heard playing a little while ago," concluded Mr. Kinney, "was that same deputy-piano machine; only just at present it's shoved up against a six-hundred-dollar piano that I bought for Marilla as soon as we was married."

53

Schools and Schools

I

OLD Jerome Warren lived in a hundred-thousand-dollar house at 35 East Fifty-Soforth Street. He was a downtown broker, so rich that he could afford to walk for his health a few blocks in the direction of his office every morning and then call a cab.

He had an adopted son, the son of an old friend named Gilbert—Cyril Scott could play him nicely—who was becoming a successful painter as fast as he could squeeze the paint out of his tubes. Another member of the household was Barbara Ross, a step-niece. Man is born to trouble; so, as old Jerome had no family of his own, he took up the burdens of others.

Gilbert and Barbara got along swimmingly. There was a tacit and tactical understanding all round that the two would stand up under a floral bell some high noon, and promise the minister to keep old Jerome's money in a state of high commotion. But at this point complications must be introduced.

Thirty years before, when old Jerome was young Jerome, there was a brother of his named Dick. Dick went West to seek his or somebody else's fortune. Nothing was heard of him until one day old Jerome had a letter from his brother. It was badly written on ruled paper that smelled of salt bacon and coffee-grounds. The writing was asthmatic and the spelling St. Vitusy.

It appeared that instead of Dick having forced Fortune to stand and deliver, he had been held up himself, and made to give hostages to the enemy. That is, as his letter disclosed, he was on the point of pegging out with a complication of disorders that even whisky had failed to check. All that his thirty years of prospecting had netted him was one daughter, nineteen years old, as per invoice, whom he was shipping East, charges prepaid, for Jerome to clothe, feed, educate, comfort, and cherish for the rest of her natural life or until matrimony should them part.

Old Jerome was a board-walk. Everybody knows that the world is supported by the shoulders of Atlas; and that Atlas stands on a rail-fence; and that the rail-fence is built on a turtle's back. Now, the turtle has to stand on something; and that is a board-walk made of men like old Jerome.

I do not know whether immortality should accrue to man; but if not so, I would like to know when men like old Jerome get what is due them?

They met Nevada Warren at the station. She was a little girl, deeply sunburned and wholesomely good-looking, with a manner that was frankly unsophisticated, yet one that not even a cigar-drummer would intrude upon without thinking twice. Looking at her, somehow you would expect to see her in a short skirt and leather leggings, shooting glass balls or taming mustangs. But in her plain white waist and black skirt she sent you guessing again. With an easy exhibition of strength she swung along a heavy valise, which the uniformed porters tried in vain to wrest from her.

"I am sure we shall be the best of friends," said Barbara, pecking at the firm, sunburned cheek.

"I hope so," said Nevada.

"Dear little niece," said old Jerome, "you are as welcome to my house as if it were your father's own."

"Thanks," said Nevada.

"And I am going to call you 'cousin'," said Gilbert, with his charming smile.

"Take the valise, please," said Nevada. "It weighs a million pounds. It's got samples from six of dad's old mines in it," she explained to Barbara. "I calculate they'd assay about nine cents to the thousand tons, but I promised him to bring them along."

II

It is a common custom to refer to the usual complication between one man and two ladies, or one lady and two men, or a lady and a man and a nobleman, or—well, any of those problems—as the triangle. But they are never unqualified triangles. They are always isosceles—never equilateral. So, upon the coming of Nevada Warren, she and Gilbert and Barbara Ross lines up into such a figurative triangle; and of that triangle Barbara formed the hypotenuse.

One morning old Jerome was lingering long after breakfast over the dullest morning paper in the city before setting forth to his down-town fly-trap. He had become quite fond of Nevada, finding in her much of his dead brother's quiet independence and unsuspicious frankness.

A maid brought in a note for Miss Nevada Warren.

"A messenger-boy delivered it at the door, please," she said. "He's waiting for an answer."

Nevada, who was whistling a Spanish waltz between her teeth, and watching the carriages and autos roll by in the street, took the envelope. She knew it was from Gilbert, before she opened it, by the little gold palette in the upper left-hand corner.

After tearing it open she pored over the contents for a while, absorbedly. Then, with a serious face, she went and stood at her uncle's elbow.

"Uncle Jerome, Gilbert is a nice boy, isn't he?"

"Why, bless the child!" said old Jerome, crackling his paper loudly; "of course he is. I raised him myself."

"He wouldn't write anything to anybody that wasn't exactly—I mean that everybody couldn't know and read, would he?"

"I'd just like to see him try it," said uncle, tearing a handful from his newspaper. "Why, what——"

"Read this note he just sent me, uncle, and see if you think it's all right and proper. You see, I don't know much about city people and their ways."

Old Jerome threw his paper down and set both his feet upon it. He took Gilbert's note and fiercely perused it t ice, and then a third time.

"Why, child," said he, "you had me almost excited, although I was sure of that boy. He's a duplicate of his father, and he was a gilt-edged diamond. He only asks if you and Barbara will be ready at four o'clock this afternoon for an automobile drive over to Long Island. I don't see anything to criticize in it except the stationery. I always did hate that shade of blue."

"Would it be all right to go?" asked Nevada, eagerly.

"Yes, yes, yes, child; of course. Why not? Still, it pleases me to see you so careful and candid. Go, by all means."

"I didn't know," said Nevada demurely. "I thought I'd ask you. Couldn't you go with us, uncle?"

"I? No, no, no, no! I've ridden once in a car that boy was driving. Never again! But it's entirely proper for you and Barbara to go. Yes, yes. But I will not. No, no, no, no!"

Nevada flew to the door, and said to the maid:

"You bet we'll go. I'll answer for Miss Barbara. Tell the boy to say to Mr. Warren, 'You bet we'll go.'"

"Nevada," called old Jerome, "pardon me, my dear, but wouldn't it be as well to send him a note in reply? Just a line would do."

"No, I won't bother about that," said Nevada, gaily. "Gilbert will understand—he always does. I never rode in an automobile in my life; but I've paddled a canoe down Little Devil River through the Lost Horse Cañon, and if it's any livelier than that I'd like to know!"

III

Two months are supposed to have elapsed.

Barbara sat in the study of the hundred-thousand-dollar house. It was a good place for her. Many places are provided in the world where men and women may repair for the purpose of extricating themselves from divers difficulties. There are cloisters, wailing-places, watering-places, confessionals, hermitages, lawyers' offices, beauty-parlours, airships, and studies; and the greatest of these are studies.

It usually takes a hypotenuse a long time to discover that it is the longest side of a triangle. But it's a long line that has no turning.

Barbara was alone. Uncle Jerome and Nevada had gone to the theatre. Barbara had not cared to go. She wanted to stay at home and study in the study. If you, miss, were a stunning New York girl, and saw every day that a brown, ingenuous Western witch was getting hobbles and a lasso on the young man you wanted for yourself, you, too, would lose taste for the oxidized silver setting of a musical comedy.

Barbara sat by the quartered-oak library table. Her right arm rested upon the table, and her dextral fingers nervously manipulated a sealed letter. The letter was addressed to Nevada Warren; and in the upper left-hand corner of the envelope was Gilbert's little gold palette. It had been delivered at nine o'clock, after Nevada had left.

Barbara would have given her pearl necklace to know what the letter contained; but she could not open and read it by the aid of steam, or a pen-handle, or a hairpin, or any of the generally approved methods because her position in society forbade such an act. She had tried to read some of the lines of the letter by holding the envelope up to a strong light and pressing it hard against the paper, but Gilbert had too good a taste in stationery to make that possible.

At eleven-thirty the theatre-goers returned. It was a delicious winter night. Even so far as from the cab to the door they were powdered thickly with the big flakes downpouring diagonally from the east. Old Jerome growled good-naturedly about villainous cab service and blockaded streets. Nevada, coloured like a rose, with sapphire eyes, babbled of the stormy nights in the mountains around dad's cabin. During all these wintry apostrophes, Barbara, cold at heart, sawed wood—the only appropriate thing she could think of to do.

Old Jerome went immediately upstairs to hot-water bottles and quinine. Nevada fluttered into the study, the only cheerful lighted room, subsided into an arm-chair, and while at the interminable task of unbuttoning her elbow gloves, gave oral testimony as to the demerits of the "show".

"Yes, I think Mr. Fields is really amusing—sometimes," said Barbara. "Here is a letter for you, dear, that came by special delivery just after you had gone."

"Who is it from?" asked Nevada, tugging at a button.

"Well, really," said Barbara, with a smile, "I can only

guess. The envelope has that queer little thing in one corner that Gilbert calls a palette, but which looks to me rather like a gilt heart on a schoolgirl's valentine."

"I wonder what he's writing to me about," remarked Nevada listlessly.

"We're all alike," said Barbara; "all women. We try to find out what is in a letter by studying the postmark. As a last resort we use scissors, and read it from the bottom upward. Here it is."

She made a motion as if to toss the letter across the table to Nevada.

"Great catamounts!" exclaimed Nevada. "These centre-fire buttons are a nuisance. I'd rather wear buckskins. Oh, Barbara, please shuck the hide off that letter and read it. It'll be midnight before I get these gloves off!"

"Why, dear, you don't want me to open Gilbert's letter to you? It's for you, and you wouldn't wish anyone else to read it, of course!"

Nevada raised her steady, calm, sapphire eyes from her gloves.

"Nobody writes me anything that everybody mightn't read," she said. "Go on, Barbara. Maybe Gilbert wants us to go out in his car again to-morrow."

Curiosity can do more things than kill a cat; and if emotions, well recognized as feminine, are inimical to feline life, then jealousy would soon leave the whole world catless. Barbara opened the letter, with an indulgent, slightly bored air.

"Well, dear," she said, "I'll read if it you want me to."

She slit the envelope, and read the missive with swift-travelling eyes; read it again, and cast a quick, shrewd glance at Nevada, who, for the time, seemed to consider gloves as the world of her interest, and letters from rising artists as no more than messages from Mars.

For a quarter of a minute Barbara looked at Nevada with a strange steadfastness; and then a smile so small that it widened her mouth only the sixteenth part of an inch, and narrowed her eyes no more than a twentieth flashed like an inspired thought across her face.

Since the beginning no woman has been a mystery to another woman. Swift as light travels, each penetrates the chart and mind of another, sifts her sister's words of their cunningest disguises, reads her most hidden desires, and plucks the sophistry from her wiliest talk like hairs from a comb, twiddling them sardonically between her thumb and fingers before letting them float away on the breezes of fundamental doubt. Long ago Eve's son rang the door-bell of the family residence in Paradise Park, bearing a strange lady on his arm, whom he introduced. Eve took her daughter-in-law aside and lifted a classic eyebrow.

"The Land of Nod," said the bride, languidly flirting the leaf of a palm. "I suppose you've been there, of course?"

"Not lately," said Eve, absolutely unstaggered. "Don't you think the apple-sauce they serve over there is execrable? I rather like that mulberry-leaf tunic effect, dear; but, of course, the real fig goods are not to be had over there. Come over behind this lilac-bush while the gentlemen split a celery tonic. I think the caterpillar-holes have made your dress open a little in the back."

So, then and there—according to the records—was the alliance formed by the only two who's-who ladies in the world. Then it was agreed that women should for ever remain as clear as a pane of glass—though glass was yet to be discovered—to other women, and that she should palm herself off on man as a mystery.

Barbara seemed to hesitate.

"Really, Nevada," she said, with a little show of embarrassment, "you shouldn't have insisted on my opening this. I—I'm sure it wasn't meant for anyone else to know."

Nevada forgot her gloves for a moment.

"Then read it aloud," she said. "Since you've already read it, what's the difference? If Mr. Warren has written to me something that anyone else oughtn't to know, that is all the more reason why everybody should know it."

"Well," said Barbara, "this is what it says: 'Dearest Nevada—Come to my studio at twelve o'clock to-night. Do not fail.'" Barbara rose and dropped the note in Nevada's lap. "I'm awfully sorry," she said, "that I knew. It isn't like

Gilbert. There must be some mistake. Just consider that I am ignorant of it, will you, dear? I must go upstairs now, I have such a headache. I'm sure I don't understand the note. Perhaps Gilbert has been dining too well, and will explain. Good night!"

IV

Nevada tiptoed to the hall, and heard Barbara's door close upstairs. The bronze clock in the study told the hour of twelve was fifteen minutes away. She ran swiftly to the front door, and let herself out into the snowstorm. Gilbert Warren's studio was six squares away.

By aerial ferry the white silent forces of the storm attacked the city from beyond the sullen East River. Already the snow lay a foot deep on the pavements, the drifts heaping themselves like scaling-ladders against the walls of the besieged town. The Avenue was as quiet as a street in Pompeii. Cabs now and then skimmed past like white-winged gulls over a moonlit ocean; and less frequent motor-cars—sustaining the comparison—hissed through the foaming waves like submarine boats on their jocund, perilous journeys.

Nevada plunged like a wind-driven storm-petrel on her way. She looked up at the ragged sierras of cloud-capped buildings that rose above the streets, shaded by the night lights and the congealed vapours to grey, drab ashen, lavender, dun, and cerulean tints. They were so like the wintry mountains of her Western home that she felt a satisfaction such as the hundred-thousand-dollar house had seldom brought her.

A policeman caused her to waver on a corner just by his eye and weight.

"Hello, Mabel!" said he. "Kind of late for you to be out, ain't it?"

"I—I am just going to the drug store," said Nevada, hurrying past him.

The excuse serves as a passport for the most sophisticated. Does it prove that woman never progresses, or that she sprang from Adam's rib, full-fledged in intellect and wiles?

Turning eastward, the direct blast cut down Nevada's speed one half. She made zigzag tracks in the snow; but she was as tough as a piñon sapling, and bowed to it as gracefully. Suddenly the studio-building loomed before her, a familiar landmark, like a cliff above some well-remembered cañon. The haunt of business and its hostile neighbour, art, was darkened and silent. The elevator stopped at ten.

Up eight flights of Stygian stairs Nevada climbed, and rapped firmly at the door numbered "89". She had been there many times before, with Barbara and Uncle Jerome.

Gilbert opened the door. He had a crayon pencil in one hand, a green shade over his eyes, and a pipe in his mouth. The pipe dropped to the floor.

"Am I late?" asked Nevada. "I came as quick as I could. Uncle and me were at the theatre this evening. Here I am, Gilbert!"

Gilbert did a Pygmalion-and-Galatea act. He changed from a statue of stupefaction to a young man with a problem to tackle. He admitted Nevada, got a whisk-broom, and began to brush the snow from her clothes. A great lamp, with a green shade, hung over an easel, where the artist had been sketching in crayon.

"You wanted me," said Nevada simply, "and I came. You said so in your letter. What did you send for me for?"

"You read my letter?" inquired Gilbert, sparring for wind.

"Barbara read it to me. I saw it afterward. It said: 'Come to my studio at twelve to-night, and do not fail.' I thought you were sick, of course, but you don't seem to be."

"Aha!" said Gilbert irrelevantly. "I'll tell you why I asked you to come, Nevada. I want you to marry me immediately—to-night. What's a little snowstorm? Will you do it?"

"You might have noticed that I would, long ago," said Nevada. "And I'm rather stuck on the snow-storm idea myself. I surely would hate one of these flowery church noon-weddings. Gilbert, I didn't know you had grit enough to propose it this way. Let's shock 'em—it's our funeral, ain't it?"

"You bet!" said Gilbert. "Where did I hear that expression?" he added to himself. "Wait a minute, Nevada; I want to do a little 'phoning."

He shut himself in a little dressing-room, and called upon the lightnings of the heavens—condensed into unromantic numbers and districts.

"That you, Jack? You confounded sleepy-head! Yes, wake up; this is me—or I—oh, bother the difference in grammar! I'm going to be married right away. Yes! Wake up your sister—don't answer me back; bring her along, too—you *must*. Remind Agnes of the time I saved her from drowning in Lake Ronkonkoma—I know it's caddish to refer to it, but she *must* come with you. Yes! Nevada is here, waiting. We've been engaged quite a while. Some opposition among the relatives, you know, and we have to pull it off this way. We're waiting here for you. Don't let Agnes out-talk you—bring her! You will? Good old boy! I'll order a carriage to call for you, double-quick time. Confound you, Jack, you're all right!"

Gilbert returned to the room where Nevada waited.

"My old friend, Jack Peyton, and his sister were to have been here at a quarter to twelve," he explained; "but Jack is so confoundedly slow. I've just 'phoned them to hurry. They'll be here in a few minutes. I'm the happiest man in the world, Nevada! What did you do with the letter I sent you to-day?"

"I've got it cinched here," said Nevada, pulling it out from beneath her opera-cloak.

Gilbert drew the letter from the envelope and looked it over carefully. Then he looked at Nevada thoughtfully.

"Didn't you think it rather queer that I should ask you to come to my studio at midnight?" he asked.

"Why, no," said Nevada, rounding her eyes. "Not if you needed me. Out West, when a pal sends you a hurry call—ain't that what you say here?—we get there first and talk about it after the row is over. And it's usually snowing there, too, when things happen. So I didn't mind."

Gilbert rushed into another room, and came back burdened with overcoats warranted to turn wind, rain, or snow.

"Put this raincoat on," he said, holding it for her. "We

have a quarter of a mile to go. Old Jack and his sister will be here in a few minutes." He began to struggle into a heavy coat. "Oh, Nevada," he said, "just look at the headlines on the front page of that evening paper on the table, will you? It's about your section of the West, and I know it will interest you."

He waited a full minute, pretending to find trouble in the getting on of his overcoat and then turned. Nevada had not moved. She was looking at him with strange and pensive directness. Her cheeks had a flush on them beyond the colour that had been contributed by the wind and snow; but her eyes were steady.

"I was going to tell you," she said, "anyhow, before—you —before we—before—well, before anything. Dad never gave me a day of schooling. I never learned to read or write a darned word. Now if——"

Pounding their uncertain way upstairs, the feet of Jack, the somnolent, and Agnes, the grateful, were heard.

V

When Mr. and Mrs. Gilbert Warren were spinning softly homeward in a closed carriage, after the ceremony, Gilbert said:

"Nevada, would you really like to know what I wrote you in the letter that you received to-night?"

"Fire away!" said his bride.

"Word for word," said Gilbert, "it was this: 'My dear Miss Warren—You were right about the flower. It was a hydrangea, and not a lilac.'"

"All right," said Nevada. "But let's forget it. The joke's on Barbara, anyway!"

54

The Clarion Call

HALF of this story can be found in the records of the Police Department; the other half belongs behind the business counter of a newspaper office.

One afternoon two weeks after Millionaire Norcross was found in his apartment, murdered by a burglar, the murderer, while strolling serenely down Broadway, ran plump against Detective Barney Woods.

"Is that you, Johnny Kernan?" asked Woods, who had been near-sighted in public for five years.

"No less," cried Kernan, heartily. "If it isn't Barney Woods, late and early of old Saint Jo! You'll have to show me! What are you doing East? Do the green-goods circulars get out that far?"

"I've been in New York some years," said Woods. "I'm on the city detective force."

"Well, well!" said Kernan, breathing smiling joy and patting the detective's arm.

"Come into Muller's," said Woods, "and let's hunt a quiet table. I'd like to talk to you a while."

It lacked a few minutes to the hour of four. The tides of trade were not yet loosed, and they found a quiet corner of the café. Kernan, well dressed, slightly swaggering, self-confident, seated himself opposite the little detective, with his pale, sandy moustache, squinting eyes, and ready-made cheviot suit.

"What business are you in now?" asked Woods. "You know you left Saint Jo a year before I did."

"I'm selling shares in a copper mine," said Kernan. "I may establish an office here. Well, well! and so old Barney is a New York detective. You always had a turn that way. You were on the police in Saint Jo after I left there, weren't you?"

P

"Six months," said Woods. "And now there's one more question, Johnny. I've followed your record pretty close ever since you did that hotel job in Saratoga, and I never knew you to use your gun before. Why did you kill Norcross?"

Kernan stared for a few moments with concentrated attention at the slice of lemon in his highball; and then he looked at the detective with a sudden, crooked, brilliant smile.

"How did you guess it, Barney?" he asked, admiringly. "I swear I thought the job was as clean and as smooth as a peeled onion. Did I leave a string hanging out anywhere?"

Woods laid upon the table a small gold pencil intended for a watch-charm.

"It's the one I gave you the last Christmas we were in Saint Jo. I've got your shaving mug yet. I found this under a corner of the rug in Norcross's room. I warn you to be careful what you say. I've got it put on to you, Johnny. We were old friends once, but I must do my duty. You'll have to go to the chair for Norcross."

Kernan laughed.

"My luck stays with me," said he. "Who'd have thought old Barney was on my trail!" He slipped one hand inside his coat. In an instant Woods had a revolver against his side.

"Put it away," said Kernan, wrinkling his nose. "I'm only investigating. Aha! It takes nine tailors to make a man, but one can do a man up. There's a hole in that vest pocket. I took that pencil off my chain and slipped it in there in case of a scrap. Put up your gun Barney, and I'll tell you why I had to shoot Norcross. The old fool started down the hall after me, popping at the buttons on the back of my coat with a peevish little ·22, and I had to stop him. The old lady was a darling. She just lay in bed and saw her $12,000 diamond necklace go without a chirp, while she begged like a panhandler to have back a little thin gold ring with a garnet worth about $3. I guess she married old Norcross for his money, all right. Don't they hang on to the little trinkets from the Man Who Lost Out, though? There were six rings, two brooches, and a chatelaine watch. Fifteen thousand would cover the lot."

"I warned you not to talk," said Woods.

"Oh, that's all right," said Kernan. "The stuff is in my suit-case at the hotel. And now I'll tell you why I'm talking. Because it's safe. I'm talking to a man I know. You owe me a thousand dollars, Barney Woods, and even if you wanted to arrest me your hand wouldn't make the move."

"I haven't forgotten," said Woods. "You counted out twenty fifties without a word. I'll pay it back some day. That thousand saved me, and—well, they were piling my furniture out on the sidewalk when I got back to the house."

"And so," continued Kernan, "you being Barney Woods, born as true as steel, and bound to play a white man's game, can't lift a finger to arrest the man you're indebted to. Oh, I have to study men as well as Yale locks and window fastenings in my business. Now, keep quiet while I ring for the waiter. I've had a thirst for a year or two that worries me a little. If I'm ever caught, the lucky sleuth will have to divide honours with old boy Booze. But I never drink during business hours. After a job I can crook elbows with my old friend Barney with a clear conscience. What are you taking?"

The waiter came with the little decanters and the siphon and left them alone again.

"You've called the turn," said Woods, as he rolled the little gold pencil about with a thoughtful forefinger. "I've got to pass you up. I can't lay a hand on you. If I'd a-paid that money back—but I didn't, and that settles it. It's a bad break I'm making, Johnny, but I can't dodge it. You helped me once, and it calls for the same."

"I knew it," said Kernan, raising his glass, with a flushed smile of self-appreciation. "I can judge men. Here's to Barney, for—'he's a jolly good fellow'."

"I don't believe," went on Woods quietly, as if he were thinking aloud, "that if accounts had been square between you and me, all the money in all the banks in New York could have bought you out of my hands to-night."

"I know it couldn't," said Kernan. "That's why I knew I was safe with you."

"Most people," continued the detective, "look sideways at my business. They don't class it among the fine arts and the professions. But I've always taken a kind of fool pride in it.

And here is where I go 'busted'. I guess I'm a man first and a detective afterward. I've got to let you go, and then I've got to resign from the force. I guess I can drive an express wagon. Your thousand dollars is farther off than ever, Johnny."

"Oh, you're welcome to it," said Kernan, with a lordly air. "I'd be willing to call the debt off, but I know you wouldn't have it. It was a lucky day for me when you borrowed it. And now, let's drop the subject. I'm off to the West on a morning train. I know a place out there where I can negotiate the Norcross sparks. Drink up, Barney, and forget your troubles. We'll have a jolly time while the police are knocking their heads together over the case. I've got one of my Sahara thirsts on to-night. But I'm in the hands—the unofficial hands—of my old friend Barney, and I won't even dream of a cop."

And then, as Kernan's ready finger kept the button and the waiter working, his weak point—a tremendous vanity and arrogant egotism—began to show itself. He recounted story after story of his successful plunderings, ingenious plots and infamous transgressions until Woods, with all his familiarity with evildoers, felt growing within him a cold abhorrence toward the utterly vicious man who had once been his benefactor.

"I'm disposed of, of course," said Woods, at length. "But I advise you to keep under cover for a spell. The newspapers may take up this Norcross affair. There has been an epidemic of burglaries and manslaughter in town this summer."

The word sent Kernan into a high glow of sullen and vindictive rage.

"To h——l with the newspapers," he growled. "What do they spell but brag and blow and boodle in box-car letters? Suppose they do take up a case—what does it amount to? The police are easy enough to fool; but what do the newspapers do? They send a lot of pin-head reporters around to the scene; and they make for the nearest saloon and have beer, while they take photos of the bartender's oldest daughter in evening dress, to print as the fiancée of the young man in the tenth storey, who thought he heard a noise below on the night of the murder. That's about as near as the newspapers ever come to running down Mr. Burglar."

"Well, I don't know," said Woods, reflecting. "Some of the papers have done good work in that line. There's the *Morning Mars*, for instance. It warmed up two or three trails, and got the man after the police had let 'em get cold."

"I'll show you," said Kernan, rising, and expanding his chest. "I'll show you what I think of newspapers in general, and your *Morning Mars* in particular."

Three feet from their table was the telephone booth. Kernan went inside and sat at the instrument, leaving the door open. He found a number in the book, took down the receiver, and made his demand upon Central. Woods sat still, looking at the sneering, cold, vigilant face waiting close to the transmitter, and listened to the words that came from the thin, truculent lips curved into a contemptuous smile.

"That the *Morning Mars*? . . . I want to speak to the managing editor. . . . Why, tell him it's some one who wants to talk to him about the Norcross murder.

"You the editor? . . . All right. . . . I am the man who killed old Norcross. . . . Wait! Hold the wire; I'm not the usual crank. . . . Oh, there isn't the slightest danger. I've just been discussing it with a detective friend of mine. I killed the old man at 2.30 a.m. two weeks ago to-morrow. . . . Have a drink with you? Now, hadn't you better leave that kind of talk to your funny man? Can't you tell whether a man's guying you or whether you're being offered the biggest scoop your dull dish-rag of a paper ever had? . . . Well, that's so; it's a bobtail scoop—but you can hardly expect me to 'phone in my name and address. . . . Why? Oh, because I heard you make a speciality of solving mysterious crimes that stump the police. . . . No, that's not all. I want to tell you that your rotten, lying, penny sheet is of no more use in tracking an intelligent murderer or highwayman than a blind poodle would be. . . . What? . . . Oh, no, this isn't a rival newspaper office; you're getting it straight. I did the Norcross job, and I've got the jewels in my suit-case at—'the name of the hotel could not be learned'—you recognize that phrase, don't you? I thought so. You've used it often enough. Kind of rattles you, doesn't it, to have the mysterious villain call up your great, big, all-powerful organ of right and justice and good government and tell you what a helpless old gas-bag you are? . . . Cut that out; you're not that big a fool—no, you don't think I'm a fraud. I can tell it by your voice. . . . Now, listen, and I'll give you a pointer that will prove it to you. Of course, you've had this murder case worked over by your staff of bright young blockheads. Half of the second button on old Mrs. Norcross's nightgown is broken off. I saw it when I took the garnet ring off her finger. I thought it was a ruby. . . . Stop that! it won't work."

Kernan turned to Woods with a diabolic smile.

"I've got him going. He believes me now. He didn't quite cover the transmitter with his hand when he told somebody to call up Central on another 'phone and get our number. I'll give him just one more dig, and then we'll make a 'get-away'.

"Hello! . . . Yes. I'm here yet. You didn't think I'd run from such a little subsidized turn-coat rag of a newspaper, did you? . . . Have me inside of forty-eight hours? Say, will you quit being funny? Now, you let grown men alone, and attend to your business of hunting up divorce cases and street-car accidents, and printing the filth and scandal that you make your living by. Good-bye, old boy—sorry I haven't time to call on you. I'd feel perfectly safe in your sanctum asinorum. Tra-la!"

"He's as mad as a cat that's lost a mouse," said Kernan, hanging up the receiver and coming out. "And now, Barney, my boy, we'll go to a show and enjoy ourselves until a reasonable bedtime. Four hours' sleep for me, and then the west-bound."

The two dined in a Broadway restaurant. Kernan was pleased with himself. He spent money like a prince of fiction. And then a weird and gorgeous musical comedy engaged their attention. Afterward there was a late supper in a grill-room, with champagne, and Kernan at the height of his complacency.

Half-past three in the morning found them in a corner of an all-night café, Kernan still boasting in a vapid and rambling way, Woods thinking moodily over the end that had come to his usefulness as an upholder of the law.

But, as he pondered, his eye brightened with a speculative light.

"I wonder if it's possible," he said to himself, "I won-der if it's pos-si-ble!"

And then outside the café the comparative stillness of the early morning was punctured by faint, uncertain cries that seemed mere fireflies of sound, some growing louder, some fainter, waxing and waning amid the rumble of milk-wagons and infrequent cars. Shrill cries they were when near—well-known cries that conveyed many meanings to the ears of those of the slumbering millions of the great city who waked to hear them. Cries that bore upon their significant, small volume the weight of a world's woe and laughter and delight and stress. To some, cowering beneath the protection of a night's ephemeral cover, they brought news of the hideous, bright day; to others, wrapped in happy sleep, they announced a morning that would dawn blacker than sable night. To many of the rich they brought a besom to sweep away what had been theirs while the stars shone; to the poor they brought—another day.

All over the city the cries were starting up, keen and sonorous, heralding the chances that the slipping of one cog-wheel in the machinery of time had made; apportioning to the sleepers while they lay at the mercy of fate, the vengeance, profit, grief, reward, and doom that the new figure in the calendar had brought them. Shrill and yet plaintive were the cries, as if the young voices grieved that so much evil and so little good was in their irresponsible hands. Thus echoed in the streets of the helpless city the transmission of the latest decrees of the gods, the cries of the newsboys—the Clarion Call of the Press.

Woods flipped a dime to the waiter, and said:

"Get me a *Morning Mars*."

When the paper came he glanced at its first page, and then tore a leaf out of his memorandum book and began to write on it with the little gold pencil.

"What's the news?" yawned Kernan.

Woods flipped over to him the piece of writing:

The New York *Morning Mars*:

Please pay to the order of John Kernan the one thousand dollars reward coming to me for his arrest and conviction.

BARNARD WOODS.

"I kind of thought they would do that," said Woods, "when you were jollying 'em so hard. Now, Johnny, you'll come to the police station with me."

55

The Hiding of Black Bill

A LANK, strong, red-faced man with a Wellington beak and small, fiery eyes tempered by flaxen lashes, sat on the station platform at Los Pinos swinging his legs to and fro. At his side sat another man, fat, melancholy, and seedy, who seemed to be his friend. They had the appearance of men to whom life had appeared as a reversible coat—seamy on both sides.

"Ain't seen you in about four years, Ham," said the seedy man. "Which way you been travelling?"

"Texas," said the red-faced man. "It was too cold in Alaska for me. And I found it warm in Texas. I'll tell you about one hot spell I went through there.

"One morning I steps off the International at a water-tank and lets it go on without me. 'Twas a ranch country, and fuller of spite-houses than New York City. Only out there they build 'em twenty miles away so you can't smell what they've got for dinner, instead of running 'em up two inches from their neighbours' windows.

"There wasn't any roads in sight, so I footed it 'cross country. The grass was shoe-top deep, and the mesquite timber looked just like a peach orchard. It was so much like a gentleman's private estate that every minute you expected a kennelful of bulldogs to run out and bite you. But I must have walked twenty miles before I came in sight of a ranch-house. It was a little one, about as big as an elevated railroad station.

"There was a little man in a white shirt and brown overalls and a pink handkerchief around his neck rolling cigarettes under a tree in front of the door.

"'Greetings,' says I. 'Any refreshment, welcome, emoluments, or even work for a comparative stranger?"

"'Oh, come in,' says he, in a refined tone. 'Sit down on that stool, please. I didn't hear your horse coming.'

"'He isn't near enough yet,' says I. 'I walked. I don't want to be a burden, but I wonder if you have three or four gallons of water handy.'

"'You do look pretty dusty,' says he; 'but our bathing arrangements——'

"'It's a drink I want,' says I. 'Never mind the dust that's on the outside.'

"He gets me a dipper of water out of a red jar hanging up, and then goes on:

"'Do you want work?'

"'For a time,' says I. 'This is a rather quiet section of the country, isn't it?'

"'It is,' says he. 'Sometimes—so I have been told—one sees no human being pass for weeks at a time. I've been here only a month. I bought the ranch from an old settler who wanted to move farther west.'

"'It suits me,' says I. 'Quiet and retirement are good for a man sometimes. And I need a job. I can tend bar, salt mines, lecture, float stock, do a little middle-weight slugging, and play the piano.'

"'Can you herd sheep?' asks the little ranchman.

"'Do you mean *have* I heard sheep?' says I.

"'Can you herd 'em—take charge of a flock of 'em?' says he.

"'Oh,' says I, 'now I understand. You mean chase 'em around and bark at 'em like collie dogs. Well, I might,' says I. 'I've never exactly done any sheep-herding, but I've often seen 'em from car windows masticating daisies, and they don't look dangerous.'

"'I'm short a herder,' says the ranchman. 'You never can depend on the Mexicans. I've only got two flocks. You may take out my bunch of muttons—there are only eight hundred of 'em—in the morning, if you like. The pay is twelve dollars a month and your rations furnished. You camp in a tent on the prairie with your sheep. You do your own cooking, but wood and water are brought to your camp. It's an easy job.'

"'I'm on,' says I. 'I'll take the job even if I have to garland my brow and hold on to a crook and wear a loose effect and play on a pipe like the shepherds do in pictures.'

"So the next morning the little ranchman helps me drive the flock of muttons from the corral to about two miles out and let 'em graze on a little hillside on the prairie. He gives me a lot of instructions about not letting bunches of them stray off from the herd, and driving 'em down to a water-hole to drink at noon.

"'I'll bring out your tent and camping outfit and rations in the buckboard before night,' says he.

"'Fine,' says I. 'And don't forget the rations. Nor the camping outfit. And be sure to bring the tent. Your name's Zollicoffer, ain't it?'

"'My name,' says he, 'is Henry Ogden.'

"'All right, Mr. Ogden,' says I. 'Mine is Mr. Percival Saint Clair.'

"I herded sheep for five days on the Rancho Chiquito; and then the wool entered my soul. That getting next to Nature certainly got next to me. I was lonesomer than Crusoe's goat. I've seen a lot of persons more entertaining as companions than those sheep were. I'd drive 'em to the corral and pen 'em every evening, and then cook my corn-bread and mutton and coffee, and lie down in a tent the size of a tablecloth, and listen to the coyotes and whip-poor-wills singing around the camp.

"The fifth evening, after I had corralled my costly but uncongenial muttons, I walked over to the ranch-house and stepped in the door.

"'Mr. Ogden,' says I, 'you and me have got to get sociable. Sheep are all very well to dot the landscape and furnish eight-dollar cotton suitings for man, but for table-talk and fireside companions they rank along with five-o'clock teazers. If you've got a deck of cards, or a parcheesi outfit, or a game of authors, get 'em out, and let's get on a mental basis. I've got to do something in an intellectual line, if it's only to knock somebody's brains out.'

"This Henry Ogden was a peculiar kind of ranchman. He wore finger-rings and a big gold watch and careful neckties. And his face was calm, and his nose-spectacles was kept very shiny. I saw once, in Muscogee, an outlaw hung for murdering six men, who was a dead ringer for him. But I knew a preacher in Arkansas that you would have taken to be his brother. I didn't care much for him either way; what I wanted was some fellowship and communion with holy saints or lost sinners—anything sheepless would do.

"'Well, Saint Clair,' says he, laying down the book he was reading, 'I guess it must be pretty lonesome for you at first. And I don't deny that it's monotonous for me. Are you sure you corralled your sheep so they won't stray out?'

"'They're shut up as tight as the jury of a millionaire murderer,' says I. 'And I'll be back with them long before they'll need their trained nurse.'

"So Ogden digs up a deck of cards, and we play casino. After five days and nights of my sheep-camp it was like a toot on Broadway. When I caught big casino I felt as excited as if I had made a million in Trinity. And when H. O. loosened up a little and told the story about the lady in the Pullman car I laughed for five minutes.

"That showed what a comparative thing life is. A man may see so much that he'd be bored to turn his head to look at a $3,000,000 fire or Joe Weber or the Adriatic Sea. But let him herd sheep for a spell, and you'll see him splitting his ribs laughing at 'Curfew Shall Not Ring To-night', or really enjoying himself playing cards with ladies.

"By and by Ogden gets out a decanter of Bourbon, and then there is a total eclipse of sheep.

"'Do you remember reading in the papers, about a month ago,' says he, 'about a train hold-up on the M.K. & T.? The express agent was shot through the shoulder and about $15,000 in currency taken. And it's said that only one man did the job.'

"'Seems to me I do,' says I. 'But such things happen so often they don't linger long in the human Texas mind. Did they overtake, overhaul, seize, or lay hands upon the despoiler?'

"'He escaped,' says Ogden. 'And I was just reading in a paper to-day that the officers have tracked him down into this part of the country. It seems the bills the robber got were all the first issue of currency to the Second National Bank of Espinosa City. And so they've followed the trail where they've been spent, and it leads this way.'

"Ogden pours out some more Bourbon, and shoves me the bottle.

"'I imagine,' says I, after ingurgitating another modicum of the royal booze, 'that it wouldn't be at all a disingenuous idea for a train-robber to run down into this part of the country to hide for a spell. A sheep-ranch, now,' says I, 'would be the finest kind of a place. Who'd ever expect to find such a desperate character among these song-birds and muttons and wild flowers? And, by the way,' says I, kind of looking H. Ogden over, 'was there any description mentioned of this single-handed terror? Was his lineaments or height and thickness or teeth fillings or style of habiliments set forth in print?'

"'Why no,' says Ogden; 'they say nobody got a good sight of him because he wore a mask. But they know it was a train-robber called Black Bill, because he always works alone and because he dropped a handkerchief in the express-car that had his name on it.'

"'All right,' says I. 'I approve of Black Bill's retreat to the sheep-ranges. I guess they won't find him.'

"'There's one thousand dollars reward for his capture,' says Ogden.

"'I don't need that kind of money,' says I, looking Mr. Sheepman straight in the eye. 'The twelve dollars a month you pay me is enough. I need a rest, and I can save up until I get enough to pay my fare to Texarkana, where my widowed mother lives. If Black Bill,' I goes on, looking significantly at Ogden, 'was to have come down this way—say, a month ago—and bought a little sheep-ranch and——'

"'Stop,' says Ogden, getting out of his chair and looking pretty vicious. 'Do you mean to insinuate——'

"'Nothing,' says I; 'no insinuations. I'm stating a hypodermical case. I say, if Black Bill had come down here and bought a sheep-ranch, and hired me to Little-Boy-Blue 'em and treated me square and friendly, as you've done, he'd never have anything to fear from me. A man is a man, regardless of any complications he may have with sheep or railroad trains. Now we know where I stand.'

"Ogden looks black as camp-coffee for nine seconds, and then he laughs, amused.

"'You'll do, Saint Clair,' says he. 'If I *was* Black Bill I wouldn't be afraid to trust you. Let's have a game or two of seven-up to-night. That is, if you don't mind playing with a train-robber.'

"'I've told you,' says I, 'my oral sentiments, and there's no strings to 'em.'

"While I was shuffling after the first hand, I asks Ogden, as if the idea was a kind of casualty, where he was from.

"'Oh,' says he, 'from the Mississippi Valley.'

"'That's a nice little place,' says I. 'I've often stopped over there. But didn't you find the sheets a little damp and the food poor? Now, I hail,' says I, 'from the Pacific Slope. Ever put up there?'

"'Too draughty,' says Ogden. 'But if you're ever in the Middle West just mention my name, and you'll get foot-warmers and dripped coffee.'

"'Well,' says I, 'I wasn't exactly fishing for your private telephone number and the middle name of your aunt that carried off the Cumberland Presbyterian minister. It don't matter. I just want you to know you are safe in the hands of your shepherd. Now, don't play hearts on spades, and don't get nervous.'

"'Still harping,' says Ogden, laughing again. 'Don't you suppose that if I was Black Bill and thought you suspected me, I'd put a Winchester bullet into you and stop my nervousness if I had any?'

"'Not any,' says I. 'A man who's got the nerve to hold up a train single-handed wouldn't do a trick like that. I've knocked about enough to know that them are the kind of men who put a value on a friend. Not that I can claim being a friend of yours, Mr. Ogden,' says I, 'being only your sheep-herder; but under more expeditious circumstances we might have been.'

"'Forget the sheep temporarily, I beg,' says Ogden, 'and cut for deal.'

"About four days afterward, while my muttons was nooning on the water-hole and I deep in the interstices of making a pot of coffee, up rides softly on the grass a mysterious person in the garb of the being he wished to represent. He was dressed somewhere between a Kansas City detective, Buffalo Bill, and the town dog-catcher of Baton Rouge. His chin and eye wasn't moulded on fighting lines so I knew he was only a scout.

"'Herdin' sheep?' he asks me.

"'Well,' says I, 'to a man of your evident gumptional endowments, I wouldn't have the nerve to state that I am engaged in decorating old bronzes or oiling bicycle sprockets.'

"You don't talk or look like a sheep-herder to me,' says he.

"'But you talk like what you look like to me,' says I.

"And then he asks me who I was working for, and I shows him Rancho Chiquito, two miles away, in the shadow of a low hill, and he tells me he's a deputy sheriff.

"'There's a train-robber called Black Bill supposed to be somewhere in these parts,' says the scout. 'He's been traced as far as San Antonio, and may be farther. Have you seen or heard of any strangers around here during the past month?'

"'I have not,' says I, 'except a report of one over at the Mexican quarters of Loomis' ranch, on the Frio.'

"'What do you know about him?' asks the deputy.

"'He's three days old,' says I.

"'What kind of a looking man is the man you work for?' he asks. 'Does old George Ramey own this place yet? He's run sheep here for the last ten years, but never had no success.'

"'The old man has sold out and gone West,' I tells him. 'Another sheep-fancier bought him out about a month ago.'

"'What kind of a looking man is he?' asks the deputy again.

"'Oh,' says I, 'a big, fat kind of a Dutchman with long whiskers and blue specs. I don't think he knows a sheep from a ground-squirrel. I guess old George soaked him pretty well on the deal,' says I.

"After indulging himself in a lot more non-communicative information and two-thirds of my dinner, the deputy rides away.

"That night I mentions the matter to Ogden.

"'They're drawing the tendrils of the octopus around Black Bill,' says I. And then I told him about the deputy sheriff and how I'd described him to the deputy, and what the deputy said about the matter.

"'Oh, well,' says Ogden, 'let's don't borrow any of Black Bill's troubles. We've a few of our own. Get the Bourbon out of the cupboard and we'll drink to his health—unless,' says he, with his little cackling laugh, 'you're prejudiced against train-robbers.'

"'I'll drink,' says I, 'to any man who's a friend to a friend. And I believe that Black Bill,' I goes on, 'would be that. So here's to Black Bill, and may he have good luck.'

"And both of us drank.

"About two weeks later comes shearing-time. The sheep had to be driven up to the ranch, and a lot of frowzy-headed Mexicans would snip the fur off of them with back-action scissors. So the afternoon before the barbers were to come I hustled my underdone muttons over the hill, across the dell, down by the winding brook, and up to the ranch-house, where I penned 'em in a corral and bade 'em my nightly adieus.

"I went from there to the ranch-house. I find H. Ogden, Esquire, lying asleep on his little cot bed. I guess he had been overcome by anti-insomnia or diswakefulness or some of the diseases peculiar to the sheep business. His mouth and vest were open, and he breathed like a second-hand bicycle pump. I looked at him and gave vent to just a few musings. 'Imperial Caesar,' says I, 'asleep in such a way, might shut his mouth and keep the wind away.'

"A man asleep is certainly a sight to make angels weep. What good is all his brain, muscle, backing, nerve, influence, and family connections? He's at the mercy of his enemies, and more so of his friends. And he's about as beautiful as a cab-horse leaning against the Metropolitan Opera House at 12.30 a.m. dreaming of the plains of Arabia. Now, a woman asleep you regard as different. No matter how she looks, you know it's better for all hands for her to be that way.

"Well, I took a drink of Bourbon and one for Ogden,

and started in to be comfortable while he was taking his nap. He had some books on his table on indigenous subjects, such as Japan and drainage and physical culture—and some tobacco, which seemed more to the point.

"After I'd smoked a few, and listened to the sartorial breathing of H. O., I happened to look out of the window towards the shearing-pens, where there was a kind of a road coming up from a kind of a road across a kind of a creek farther away.

"I saw five men riding up to the house. All of 'em carried guns across their saddles, and among 'em was the deputy that had talked to me at my camp.

"They rode up careful, in open formation, with their guns ready. I set apart with my eye the one I opinionated to be the boss muckraker of this law-and-order cavalry.

"'Good evening, gents,' says I. 'Won't you 'light and tie your horses?'

"The boss rides up close, and swings his gun over till the opening in it seems to cover my whole front elevation.

"'Don't you move your hands none,' says he, 'till you and me indulge in a adequate amount of necessary conversation.'

"'I will not,' says I. 'I am no deaf-mute, and therefore will not have to disobey your injunctions in replying.'

"'We are on the look out,' says he, 'for Black Bill, the man that held up the Katy for $15,000 in May. We are searching the ranches and everybody on 'em. What is your name, and what do you do on this ranch?'

"'Captain,' says I, 'Percival Saint Clair is my occupation, and my name is sheep-herder. I've got my flock of veals—no, muttons—penned here to-night. The searchers are coming to-morrow to give them a hair-cut—with baa-a-rum, I suppose.'

"'Where's the boss of this ranch?' the captain of the gang asked me.

"'Wait just a minute, cap'n,' says I. 'Wasn't there a kind of a reward offered for the capture of this desperate character you have referred to in your preamble?'

"'There's a thousand dollars reward offered,' says the

captain, 'but it's for his capture and conviction. There don't seem to be no provision made for an informer.'

"'It looks like it might rain in a day or so,' says I, in a tired way, looking up at the cerulean blue sky.

"'If you know anything about the locality, disposition, or secretiveness of this here Black Bill,' says he, in a severe dialect, 'you are amiable to the law in not reporting it.'

"'I heard a fence-rider say,' says I, in a desultory kind of voice, 'that a Mexican told a cowboy named Jake over at Pidgin's store on the Nueces that he heard that Black Bill had been seen in Matamoras by a sheepman's cousin two weeks ago.'

"'Tell you what I'll do, Tight Mouth,' says the captain, after looking me over for bargains. 'If you put us on so we can scoop Black Bill, I'll pay you a hundred dollars out of my own—out of our own—pockets. That's liberal,' says he. 'You ain't entitled to anything. Now, what do you say?'

"'Cash down now?' I asked.

"The captain has a sort of discussion with his helpmates, and they all produce the contents of their pockets for analysis. Out of the general results they figured up $102.30 in cash and $31 worth of plug tobacco.

"'Come nearer, capitan meeo,' says I, 'and listen.' He so did.

"'I am mighty poor and low down in the world,' says I. 'I am working for twelve dollars a month trying to keep a lot of animals together whose only thought seems to be to get asunder. Although,' says I, 'I regard myself as some better than the State of South Dakota, it's a come-down to a man who has heretofore regarded sheep only in the form of chops. I'm pretty far reduced in the world on account of foiled ambitions and rum and a kind of cocktail they make along the P.R.R. all the way from Scranton to Cincinnati—dry gin, French vermouth, one squeeze of a lime, and a good dash of orange bitters. If you're ever up that way, don't fail to let one try you. And, again,' says I, 'I have never yet went back on a friend. I've stayed by 'em when they had plenty, and when adversity's overtaken me I've never forsook 'em.

"'But,' I goes on, 'this is not exactly the case of a friend.

Twelve dollars a month is only bowing-acquaintance money. And I do not consider brown beans and cornbread the food of friendship. I am a poor man,' says I, 'and I have a widowed mother in Texarkana. You will find Black Bill,' says I 'lying asleep in this house on a cot in the room to your right. He's the man you want, as I know from his words and conversation. He was in a way a friend,' I explains, 'and if I was the man I once was the entire product of the mines of Gondola would not have tempted me to betray him. But,' says I, 'every week half of the beans was wormy, and not nigh enough wood in camp.

"'Better go in careful, gentlemen,' says I. 'He seems impatient at times, and when you think of his late professional pursuits one would look for abrupt actions if he was come upon sudden.'

"So the whole posse unmounts and ties their horses, and unlimbers their ammunition and equipments, and tiptoes into the house. And I follows, like Delilah when she set the Philip Steins on to Samson.

"The leader of the posse shakes Ogden and wakes him up. And then he jumps up, and two more of the reward-hunters grab him. Ogden was mighty tough with all his slimness, and he gives 'em as neat a single-footed tussle against odds as I ever see.

"'What does this mean?' he says, after they had him down.

"'You're scooped in, Mr. Black Bill,' says the captain. 'That's all.'

"'It's an outrage,' says H. Ogden, madder yet.

"'It was,' says the peace-and-good-will man. 'The Katy wasn't bothering you, and there's a law against monkeying with express packages.'

"And he sits on H. Ogden's stomach and goes through his pockets symptomatically and careful.

"'I'll make you perspire for this,' says Ogden, perspiring some himself. 'I can prove who I am.'

"'So can I,' says the captain, as he draws from H. Ogden's inside coat-pocket a handful of new bills of the Second National Bank of Espinosa City. 'Your regular engraved

Tuesdays-and-Fridays visiting-card wouldn't have a louder voice in proclaiming your indemnity than this here currency. You can get up now and prepare to go with us and expatriate your sins.'

"H. Ogden gets up and fixes his necktie. He says no more after they have taken the money off of him.

"'A well-greased idea,' says the sheriff captain, admiring, 'to slip off down here and buy a little sheep-ranch where the hand of man is seldom heard. It was the slickest hide-out I ever see,' says the captain.

"So one of the men goes to the shearing-pen and hunts up the other herder, a Mexican they call John Sallies, and he saddles Ogden's horse, and the sheriffs all ride up close around him with their guns in hand, ready to take their prisoner to town.

"Before starting, Ogden puts the ranch in John Sallies' hands and gives him orders about the shearing and where to graze the sheep, just as if he intended to be back in a few days. And a couple of hours afterward one Percival Saint Clair, an ex-sheep-herder of the Rancho Chiquito, might have been seen, with a hundred and nine dollars—wages and blood-money—in his pocket, riding south on another horse belonging to said ranch."

The red-faced man paused and listened. The whistle of a coming freight-train sounded far away among the low hills.

The fat, seedy man at his side sniffed, and shook his frowzy head slowly and disparagingly.

"What is it, Snipy?" asked the other. "Got the blues again?"

"No, I ain't," said the seedy one, sniffing again. "But I don't like your talk. You and me have been friends, off and on, for fifteen year; and I never yet knew or heard of you giving anybody up to the law—not no one. And here was a man whose saleratus you had et and at whose table you had played games of cards—if casino can be so called. And yet you inform him to the law and take money for it. It never was like you, I say."

"This H. Ogden," resumed the red-faced man, "through a

lawyer, proved himself free by alibis, and other legal terminalities, as I so heard afterward. He never suffered no harm. He did me favours, and I hated to hand him over.

"How about the bills they found in his pocket?" asked the seedy man.

"I put 'em there," said the red-faced man, "while he was asleep, when I saw the posse riding up. I was Black Bill. Look out, Snipy, here she comes! We'll board her on the bumpers when she takes water."

56

The Girl and the Habit

Habit—a tendency or aptitude acquired by custom or frequent repetition.

The critics have assailed every source of inspiration save one. To that one we are driven for our moral theme. When we levied upon the masters of old they gleefully dug up the parallels to our columns. When we strove to set forth real life they approved us for trying to imitate Henry George, Washington, George Washington Irving, and Irving Bacheller. We wrote of the West and the East, and they accused us of both Jesse and Henry James. We wrote from our heart —and they said something about a disordered liver. We took a text from Matthew or—yes, Deuteronomy, but the preachers were hammering away at the inspiration idea before we could get into type. So, driven to the wall, we go for our subject-matter to the reliable, old, moral, unassailable vade mecum—the unabridged dictionary.

Miss Merriam was cashier at Hinkle's. Hinkle's is one of the big downtown restaurants. It is in what the papers call the "financial district". Each day from twelve o'clock to two Hinkle's was full of hungry customers—messenger-boys, stenographers, brokers, owners of mining stock, promoters, inventors with patents pending—and also people with money.

The cashiership at Hinkle's was no sinecure. Hinkle egged and toasted and griddle-caked and coffeed a good many customers; and he lunched (as good a word as "dined") many more. It might be said that Hinkle's breakfast crowd was a contingent, but his luncheon patronage amounted to a horde.

Miss Merriam sat on a stool at a desk enclosed on three

sides by a strong, high fencing of woven brass wire. Through an arched opening at the bottom you thrust your waiter's check and the money, while your heart went pit-a-pat.

For Miss Merriam was lovely and capable. She could take 45 cents out of a $2 bill and refuse an offer of marriage before you could—Next!—lost your chance—please don't shove. She could keep cool and collected while she collected your check, give you the correct change, win your heart, indicate the toothpick stand, and rate you to a quarter of a cent better than Bradstreet could to a thousand in less time than it takes to pepper an egg with one of Hinkle's casters.

There is an old and dignified allusion to the "fierce light beats upon a throne". The light that beats upon the young lady cashier's cage is also something fierce. The other fellow is responsible for the slang.

Every male patron of Hinkle's, from the A.D.T. boys up to the kerbstone brokers, adored Miss Merriam. When they paid their checks they wooed her with every wile known to Cupid's art. Between the meshes of the brass railing went smiles, winks, compliments, tender cows, invitations to dinner, sighs, languishing looks and merry banter that was wafted pointedly back by the gifted Miss Merriam.

There is no coign of vantage more effective than the position of young lady cashier. She sits there, easily queen of the court of commerce; she is duchess of dollars and devoirs, countess of compliments and coin, leading lady of love and luncheon. You take from her a smile and a Canadian dime, and you go your way uncomplaining. You count the cheery word or two that she tosses you as misers count their treasures; and you pocket the change for a five uncomputed. Perhaps the brass-bound inaccessibility multiplies her charms—anyhow, she is a shirt-waisted, angel, immaculate, trim, manicured, seductive, bright-eyed, ready, alert—Psyche, Circe and Ate in one, separating you from your circulating medium after your sirloin medium.

The young men who broke bread at Hinkle's never settled with the cashier without an exchange of badinage and open compliment. Many of them went to greater lengths and dropped promissory hints of theatre tickets and chocolates.

The older men spoke plainly of orange blossoms, generally withering the tentative petals by after-allusions to Harlem flats. One broker, who had been squeezed by copper, proposed to Miss Merriam more regularly than he ate.

During a brisk luncheon hour Miss Merriam's conversation, while she took money for checks, would run something like this:

"Good morning, Mr. Haskins—sir?—it's natural, thank you—don't be quite so fresh. . . . Hallo, Johnny—ten, fifteen, twenty—chase along now or they'll take the letters off your cap . . . Beg pardon—count it again, please—oh, don't mention it . . . Vaudeville?—thanks; not on your moving picture . . I was to see Carter in Hedda Gabler on Wednesday night with Mr. Simmons . . . 'Scuse me, I thought that was a quarter . . . Twenty-five and seventy-five's a dollar—got that ham-and-cabbage habit yet? I see, Billy . . . Who are you addressing? say—you'll get all that's coming to you in a minute . . . Oh, fudge! Mr. Bassett—you're always fooling—no——? Well, maybe I'll marry you some day—three, four and sixty-five is five . . . Kindly keep them remarks to yourself, if you please . . . Ten cents?—'scuse me; the check calls for seventy—well, maybe it is a one instead of a seven . . . Oh, do you like it that way, Mr. Saunders?—some prefer a pomp; but they say this Cleo de Merody does suit refined features . . . and ten is fifty . . . Hike along there, buddy; don't take this for a Coney Island ticket booth . . . Huh?—why, Macy's —don't it fit nice? Oh no, it isn't too cool—these light-weight fabrics is all the go this season . . . Come again, please—that's the third time you've tried to—what?—forget it—that lead quarter is an old friend of mine . . . Sixty-five?—must have had your salary raised, Mr. Wilson . . . I seen you on Sixth Avenue Tuesday afternoon, Mr. De Forest—swell?—oh, my! —who is she? . . . What's the matter with it?—why, it ain't money—what?—Colombian half?—well, this ain't South America . . . Yes, I like the mixed best—Friday?—awfully sorry, but I take my ju-jitsu lesson on Friday—Thursday, then . . . Thanks—that's sixteen times I've been told that this morning—I guess I must be beautiful . . . Cut that out, please —who do you think I am? . . . Why, Mr. Westbrook—do you really think so?—the idea!—one—eighty and twenty's a dollar—thank you ever so much; but I don't ever go automobile riding with gentlemen—your aunt?—well, that's different—perhaps . . . Please don't get fresh—your check was fifteen cents, I believe—kindly step aside and let . . . Hallo, Ben—coming around Thursday evening?—there's a gentleman going to send around a box of chocolates, and . . . forty and sixty is a dollar, and one is two . . ."

About the middle of one afternoon the dizzy goddess Vertigo—whose other name is Fortune—suddenly smote an old, wealthy and eccentric banker while he was walking past Hinkle's, on his way to a street car. A wealthy and eccentric banker who rides in street cars is—move up, please; there are others.

A Samaritan, a Pharisee, a man and a policeman who were first on the spot lifted Banker McRamsey and carried him into Hinkle's restaurant. When the aged but indestructible banker opened his eyes he saw a beautiful vision bending over him with a pitiful, tender smile, bathing his forehead with beef tea and chafing his hands with something *frappé* out of a chafing-dish. Mr. McRamsey sighed, lost a vest button, gazed with deep gratitude upon his fair preserveress, and then recovered consciousness.

To the Seaside Library all who are anticipating a romance! Banker McRamsey had an aged and respected wife, and his sentiments toward Miss Merriam were fatherly. He talked to her for half an hour with interest—not the kind that went with his talks during business hours. The next day he brought Mrs. McRamsey down to see her. The old couple were childless—they had only a married daughter living in Brooklyn.

To make a short story shorter, the beautiful cashier won the hearts of the good old couple. They came to Hinkle's again and again; they invited her to their old-fashioned but splendid home in one of the East Seventies. Miss Merriam's winning loveliness, her sweet frankness and impulsive heart took them by storm. They said a hundred times that Miss Merriam reminded them so much of their lost daughter. The Brooklyn matron, *née* Ramsey, had the figure of Buddha and a face like the ideal of an art photographer. Miss Merriam was a combination of curves, smiles, rose leaves, pearls, satin and hair-tonic posters. Enough of the fatuity of parents.

A month after the worthy couple became acquainted with Miss Merriam, she stood before Hinkle one afternoon and resigned her cashiership.

"They're going to adopt me," she told the bereft restaurateur. "They're funny old people, but regular dears. And the swell home they have got! Say, Hinkle, there isn't any use of talking—I'm on the *à la carte* to wear brown duds and goggles in a whiz wagon, or marry a duke at least. Still, I somehow hate to break out of the old cage. I've been cashiering so long I feel funny doing anything else. I'll miss joshing the fellows awfully when they line up to pay for the buckwheats. But I can't let this chance slide. And they're awfully good, Hinkle; I know I'll have a swell time. You owe me nine-sixty-two and a half for the week. Cut out the half if it hurts you, Hinkle."

And they did. Miss Merriam became Miss Rosa McRamsey. And she graced the transition. Beauty is only skin-deep, but the nerves lie very near to the skin. Nerve—but just here will you oblige by perusing again the quotation with which the story begins?

The McRamseys poured out money like domestic champagne to polish their adopted one. Milliners, dancing masters and private tutors got it. Miss—er—McRamsey was grateful, loving, and tried to forget Hinkle's. To give ample credit to the adaptability of the American girl, Hinkle's did fade from her memory and speech most of the time.

Not everyone will remember when the Earl of Hitesbury came to East Seventy—— Street, America. He was only a fair-to-medium earl, without debts, and he created little excitement. But you will surely remember the evening when the Daughters of Benevolence held their bazaar in the W——f-A——a Hotel. For you were there, and you wrote a note to Fannie on the hotel paper, and mailed it, just to show her that—you did not? Very well; that was the evening the baby was sick, of course.

At the Bazaar the McRamseys were prominent. Miss Mer

—er—McRamsey was exquisitely beautiful. The Earl of Hitesbury had been very attentive to her since he dropped in to have a look at America. At the charity bazaar the affair was supposed to be going to be pulled off to a finish. An earl is as good as a duke. Better. His standing may be lower, but his outstanding accounts are also lower.

Our ex-young-lady-cashier was assigned to a booth. She was expected to sell worthless articles to nobs and snobs at exorbitant prices. The proceeds of the bazaar were to be used for giving to the poor children of the slums a Christmas din——Say! did you ever wonder where they get the other 364?

Miss McRamsey—beautiful, palpitating, excited, charming, radiant—fluttered about in her booth. An imitation brass network, with a little arched opening, fenced her in.

Along came the Earl, assured, delicate, accurate, admiring—admiring greatly, and faced the open wicket.

"You look chawming, you know—'pon my word you do—my deah," he said beguilingly.

Miss McRamsey whirled around.

"Cut that joshing out," she said, coolly and briskly. "Who do you think you are talking to? Your check, please. Oh, lordy!——"

Patrons of the bazaar became aware of a commotion and pressed around a certain booth. The Earl of Hitesbury stood near by pulling a pale blond and puzzled whisker.

"Miss McRamsey has fainted," some one explained.

57

Bo-Peep, of the Ranches

"AUNT ELLEN," said Octavia cheerfully, as she threw her black kid gloves carefully at the dignified Persian cat on the window-seat, "I'm a pauper."

"You are so extreme in your statements, Octavia, dear," said Aunt Ellen mildly, looking up from her paper. "If you find yourself temporarily in need of some small change for bonbons, you will find my purse in the drawer of the writing-desk."

Octavia Beaupree removed her hat and seated herself on a footstool near her aunt's chair, clasping her hands about her knees. Her slim and flexible figure, clad in a modish mourning costume, accommodated itself easily and gracefully to the trying position. Her bright and youthful face, with its pair of sparkling, life-enamoured eyes, tried to compose itself to the seriousness that the occasion seemed to demand.

"You good auntie, it isn't a case of bonbons; it is abject, staring, unpicturesque poverty, with ready-made clothes, gasolined gloves, and probably one o'clock dinners all waiting with the traditional wolf at the door. I've just come from my lawyer, auntie, and, 'Please, ma'am, I ain't got nothink 't all. Flowers, lady? Buttonhole, gentleman? Pencils, sir, three for five, to help a poor widow?' Do I do it nicely, auntie, or, as a bread-winner accomplishment, were my lessons in elocution entirely wasted?"

"Do be serious, my dear," said Aunt Ellen, letting her paper fall to the floor, "long enough to tell me what you mean. Colonel Beaupree's estate——"

"Colonel Beaupree's estate," interrupted Octavia, emphasizing her words with appropriate dramatic gestures, "is of Spanish castellar architecture. Colonel Beaupree's resources are—wind. Colonel Beaupree's stocks are—water. Colonel

Breaupree's income is—all in. The statement lacks the legal technicalities to which I have been listening for an hour, but that is what it means when translated."

"Octavia!" Aunt Ellen was now visibly possessed by consternation. "I can hardly believe it. And it was the impression that he was worth a million. And the De Peysters themselves introduced him!"

Octavia rippled out a laugh, and then became properly grave.

"*De mortuis nil*, auntie—not even the rest of it. The dear old colonel—what a gold brick he was, after all! I paid for my bargain fairly—I'm all here, am I not?—items: eyes, fingers, toes, youth, old family, unquestionable position in society as called for in contract—no wild-cat stock here." Octavia picked up the morning paper from the floor. "But I'm not going to 'squeal'—isn't that what they call it when you rail at Fortune because you've lost the game?" She turned the pages of the paper calmly. "'Stock market'—no use for that. 'Society's doings'—that's done. Here is my page—the wish column. A Van Dresser could not be said to 'want' for anything, of course. 'Chambermaids, cooks, canvassers, stenographers——'"

"Dear," said Aunt Ellen, with a little tremor in her voice, "please do not talk in that way. Even if your affairs are in so unfortunate a condition, there is my three thousand——"

Octavia sprang up lithely, and deposited a smart kiss on the delicate cheek of the prim little elderly maid.

"Blessed auntie, your three thousand is just sufficient to ensure your hyson to be free from willow leaves and keep the Persian in sterilized cream. I know I'd be welcome, but I prefer to strike bottom like Beelzebub rather than hang around like the Peri listening to the music from the side entrance. I'm going to earn my own living. There's nothing else to do. I'm a—Oh, oh, oh!—I had forgotten. There's one thing saved from the wreck. It's a corral—no, a ranch in—let me see—Texas; an asset, dear old Mr. Bannister called it. How pleased he was to show me something he could describe as unencumbered! I've a description of it among those stupid papers he made me bring away with me from his office. I'll try to find it."

Octavia found her shopping-bag, and drew from it a long envelope filled with typewritten documents.

"A ranch in Texas," sighed Aunt Ellen. "It sounds to me more like a liability than an asset. Those are the places where the centipedes are found, and cowboys, and fandangos."

"'The Rancho de las Sombras,'" read Octavia from a sheet of violently purple typewriting, "'is situated one hundred and ten miles south-east of San Antonio, and thirty-eight miles from its nearest railroad station, Nopal, on the I. and G.N. Ranch consists of 7,680 acres of well-watered land, with title conferred by State patents, and twenty-two sections, or 14,080 acres, partly under yearly running lease and partly bought under State's twenty-year-purchase act. Eight thousand graded merino sheep, with the necessary equipment of horses, vehicles and general ranch paraphernalia. Ranch-house built of brick, with six rooms comfortably furnished according to the requirements of the climate. All within a strong barbed-wire fence.

"'The present ranch manager seems to be competent and reliable, and is rapidly placing upon a paying basis a business that, in other hands, had been allowed to suffer from neglect and misconduct.

"'This property was secured by Colonel Beaupree in a deal with a Western irrigation syndicate, and the title to it seems to be perfect. With careful management, and the natural increase of land values, it ought to be made the foundation for a comfortable fortune for its owner.'"

When Octavia ceased reading, Aunt Ellen uttered something as near a sniff as her breeding permitted.

"The prospectus," she said, with uncompromising metropolitan suspicion, "doesn't mention the centipedes, or the Indians. And you never did like mutton, Octavia. I don't see what advantage you can derive from this—desert."

But Octavia was in a trance. Her eyes were steadily regarding something quite beyond their focus. Her lips were parted, and her face was lighted by the kindling furor of the explorer, the ardent, stirring disquiet of the adventurer. Suddenly she clasped her hands together exultantly.

"The problem solves itself, auntie," she cried. "I'm going to that ranch. I'm going to live on it. I'm going to learn to like mutton, and even concede the good qualities of centipedes—at a respectful distance. It's just what I need. It's a new life that comes when my old one is just ending. It's a release, auntie; it isn't a narrowing. Think of the gallops over those leagues of prairies, with the wind tugging at the roots of your hair, the coming close to the earth and learning over again the stories of the growing grass and the little wild flowers without names! Glorious is what it will be. Shall I be a shepherdess with a Watteau hat, and a crook to keep the bad wolves from the lambs, or a typical Western ranch girl, with short hair, like the pictures of her in the Sunday papers? I think the latter. And they'll have my picture, too, with the wild-cats I've slain, single-handed, hanging from my saddle-horn. 'From the Four Hundred to the Flocks' is the way they'll head-line it, and they'll print photographs of the old Van Dresser mansion and the church where I was married. They won't have my picture, but they'll get an artist to draw it. It'll be wild and woolly, and I'll grow my own wool."

"Octavia!" Aunt Ellen condensed into the one word all the protests she was unable to utter.

"Don't say a word, auntie. I'm going. I'll see the sky at night fit down on the world like a big butter-dish cover, and I'll make friends again with the stars that I haven't had a chat with since I was a wee child. I wish to go. I'm tired of all this. I'm glad I haven't any money. I could bless Colonel Beaupree for that ranch, and forgive him for all his bubbles. What if the life will be rough and lonely! I—I deserve it. I shut my heart to everything except that miserable ambition. I—oh, I wish to go away, and forget—forget!"

Octavia swerved suddenly to her knees, laid her flushed face in her aunt's lap, and shook with turbulent sobs.

Aunt Ellen bent over her, and smoothed the coppery-brown hair.

"I didn't know," she said gently; "I didn't know—that. Who was it, dear?"

* * *

When Mrs. Octavia Beaupree, *née* Van Dresser, stepped from the train at Nopal, her manner lost, for the moment, some of that easy certitude which had always marked her movements. The town was of recent establishment, and seemed to have been hastily constructed of undressed lumber and flapping canvas. The element that had congregated about the station, though not offensively demonstrative, was clearly composed of citizens accustomed to and prepared for rude alarms.

Octavia stood on the platform, against the telegraph office, and attempted to choose by intuition, from the swaggering, straggling string of loungers, the manager of the Rancho de las Sombras, who had been instructed by Mr. Bannister to meet her there. That tall, serious-looking, elderly man in the blue flannel shirt and white tie she thought must be he. But no; he passed by, removing his gaze from the lady as hers rested on him, according to the Southern custom. The manager, she thought, with some impatience at being kept waiting, should have no difficulty in selecting her. Young women wearing the most recent thing in ash-coloured travelling suits were not so plentiful in Nopal!

Thus keeping a speculative watch on all persons of possible managerial aspect, Octavia, with a catching breath and a start of surprise, suddenly became aware of Teddy Westlake hurrying along the platform in the direction of the train—of Teddy Westlake or his sun-browned ghost in cheviot, boots and leather-girdled hat—Theodore Westlake, Jr., amateur polo (almost) champion, all-round butterfly and cumberer of the soil; but a broader, surer, more emphasized and determined Teddy than the one she had known a year ago when last she saw him.

He perceived Octavia at almost the same time, deflected his course, and steered for her in his old, straightforward way. Something like awe came upon her as the strangeness of his metamorphosis was brought into closer range; the rich, red-brown of his complexion brought out so vividly his straw-coloured moustache and steel-grey eyes. He seemed more grown-up, and, somehow, farther away. But, when he spoke, the old, boyish Teddy came back again. They had been friends from childhood.

"Why, 'Tave!" he exclaimed, unable to reduce his perplexity to coherence. "How—what—when—where?"

"Train," said Octavia; "necessity; ten minutes ago; home. Your complexion's gone, Teddy. Now, how—what—when—where?"

"I'm working down here," said Teddy. He cast side glances about the station as one does who tries to combine politeness with duty.

"You didn't notice on the train," he asked, "an old lady with grey curls and a poodle, who occupied two seats with her bundles and quarrelled with the conductor, did you?"

"I think not," answered Octavia, reflecting. "And you haven't, by any chance, noticed a big, grey-moustached man in a blue shirt and six-shooters, with little flakes of merino wool sticking in his hair, have you?"

"Lots of 'em," said Teddy, with symptoms of mental delirium under the strain. "Do you happen to know any such individual?"

"No; the description is imaginary. Is your interest in the old lady whom you describe a personal one?"

"Never saw her in my life. She's painted entirely from fancy. She owns the little piece of property where I earn my bread and butter—The Rancho de las Sombras. I drove up to meet her according to arrangement with her lawyer."

Octavia leaned against the wall of the telegraph office. Was this possible? And didn't he know?

"Are you the manager of that ranch?" she asked weakly.

"I am," said Teddy, with pride.

"I am Mrs. Beaupree," said Octavia faintly; "but my hair never would curl, and I was polite to the conductor."

For a moment that strange, grown-up look came back and removed Teddy miles away from her.

"I hope you'll excuse me," he said, rather awkwardly. "You see, I've been down here in the chaparral a year. I hadn't heard. Give me your checks, please, and I'll have your traps loaded into the wagon. José will follow with them. We travel ahead in the buckboard."

Seated by Teddy in a feather-weight buckboard, behind a pair of wild, cream-coloured Spanish ponies, Octavia abandoned all thought for the exhilaration of the present. They swept out of the little town and down the level road toward the south. Soon the road dwindled and disappeared, and they struck across a world carpeted with an endless reach of curly mesquite grass. The wheels made no sound. The tireless ponies bounded ahead at an unbroken gallop. The temperate wind, made fragrant by thousands of acres of blue and yellow wild flowers, roared gloriously in their ears. The motion was aerial, ecstatic, with a thrilling sense of perpetuity in its effect. Octavia sat silent, possessed by a feeling of elemental, sensual bliss. Teddy seemed to be wrestling with some internal problem.

"I'm going to call you madama," he announced as the result of his labours. "That is what the Mexicans will call you —they're nearly all Mexicans on the ranch, you know. That seems to me about the proper thing."

"Very well, Mr. Westlake," said Octavia primly.

"Oh, now," said Teddy, in some consternation, "that's carrying the thing too far, isn't it?"

"Don't worry me with your beastly etiquette. I'm just beginning to live. Don't remind me of anything artificial. If only this air could be bottled! This much alone is worth coming for. Oh, look! there goes a deer!"

"Jack-rabbit," said Teddy, without turning his head.

"Could I—might I drive?" suggested Octavia, panting, with rose-tinted cheeks and the eye of an eager child.

"On one condition. Could I—might I smoke?"

"For ever!" cried Octavia, taking the lines with solemn joy. "How shall I know which way to drive?"

"Keep her sou' by sou'east, and all sail set. You see that black speck on the horizon under that lower-most Gulf cloud? That's a group of live-oaks and a landmark. Steer half-way between that and the little hill to the left. I'll recite you the whole code of driving rules for the Texas prairies:

keep the reins from under the horses' feet, and swear at 'em frequent."

"I'm too happy to swear, Ted. Oh, why do people buy yachts or travel in palace-cars, when a buckboard and a pair of plugs and a spring morning like this can satisfy all desire?"

"Now, I'll ask you," protested Teddy, who was futilely striking match after match on the dashboard, "not to call those denizens of the air plugs. They can kick out a hundred miles between daylight and dark." At last he succeeded in snatching a light for his cigar from the flame held in the hollow of his hands.

"Room!" said Octavia intensely. "That's what produces the effect. I know now what I've wanted—scope—range—room!"

"Smoking-room," said Teddy unsentimentally. "I love to smoke in a buckboard. The wind blows the smoke into you and out again. It saves exertion."

The two fell so naturally into their old-time good-fellowship that it was only by degrees that a sense of the strangeness of the new relations between them came to be felt.

"Madama," said Teddy wonderingly, "however did you get it into your head to cut the crowd and come down here? Is it a fad now among the upper classes to trot off to sheep ranches instead of to Newport?"

"I was broke, Teddy," said Octavia sweetly, with her interest centred upon steering safely between a Spanish dagger plant and a clump of chaparral; "I haven't a thing in the world but this ranch—not even any other home to go to."

"Come, now," said Teddy, anxiously but incredulously, "you don't mean it?"

"When my husband," said Octavia, with a shy slurring of the word, "died three months ago I thought I had a reasonable amount of the world's goods. His lawyer exploded that theory in a sixty-minute fully illustrated lecture. I took to the sheep as a last resort. Do you happen to know of any fashionable caprice among the gilded youth of Manhattan that induces them to abandon polo and club windows to become managers of sheep ranches?"

"It's easily explained in my case," responded Teddy promptly. "I had to go to work. I couldn't have earned my board in New York, so I chummed a while with old Sandford, one of the syndicate that owned the ranch before Colonel Beaupree bought it, and got a place down here. I wasn't manager at first. I jogged around on ponies and studied the business in detail, until I got all the points in my head. I saw where it was losing and what the remedies were, and then Sandford put me in charge. I get a hundred dollars a month, and I earn it."

"Poor Teddy!" said Octavia, with a smile.

"You needn't. I like it. I save half my wages, and I'm as hard as a water-plug. It beats polo."

"Will it furnish bread and tea and jam for another outcast from civilization?"

"The spring shearing," said the manager, "just cleaned up a deficit in last year's business. Wastefulness and inattention have been the rule heretofore. The autumn clip will leave a small profit over all expenses. Next year there will be jam."

When, about four o'clock in the afternoon, the ponies rounded a gentle, brush-covered hill, and then swooped, like a double cream-coloured cyclone, upon the Rancho de las Sombras, Octavia gave a little cry of delight. A lordly grove of magnificent live-oaks cast an area of grateful, cool shade, whence the ranch had drawn its name, "de las Sombras"—of the shadows. The house, of red brick, one storey, ran low and long beneath the trees. Through its middle, dividing its six rooms in half, extended a broad, arched passage-way, picturesque with flowering cactus and hanging red earthen jars. A "gallery", low and broad, encircled the building. Vines climbed about it, and the adjacent ground was, for a space, covered with transplanted grass and shrubs. A little lake, long and narrow, glimmered in the sun at the rear. Farther away stood the shacks of the Mexican workers, the corrals, wool sheds and shearing pens. To the right lay the low hills, splattered with dark patches of chaparral; to the left the unbounded green prairie blending against the blue heavens.

"It's a home, Teddy," said Octavia, breathlessly; "that's what it is—it's a home."

"Not so bad for a sheep ranch," admitted Teddy, with excusable pride. "I've been tinkering on it at odd times."

A Mexican youth sprang from somewhere in the grass, and took charge of the creams. The mistress and the manager entered the house.

"Here's Mrs. MacIntyre," said Teddy, as a placid, neat, elderly lady came out upon the gallery to meet them. "Mrs. Mac, here's the boss. Very likely she will be wanting a hunk of bacon and a dish of beans after her drive."

Mrs. MacIntyre, the housekeeper, as much a future on the place as the lake or the live-oaks, received the imputation of the ranch's resources of refreshment with mild indignation, and was about to give it utterance when Octavia spoke.

"Oh, Mrs. MacIntyre, don't apologize for Teddy. Yes, I call him Teddy. So does every one whom he hasn't duped into taking him seriously. You see, we used to cut paper dolls and play jackstraws together ages ago. No one minds what he says."

"No," said Teddy, "no one minds what he says, just as he doesn't do it again."

Octavia cast one of those subtle, sidelong glances toward him from beneath her lowered eyelids—a glance that Teddy used to describe as an uppercut. But there was nothing in his ingenuous, weather-tanned face to warrant a suspicion that he was making an allusion—nothing. Beyond a doubt, thought Octavia, he had forgotten.

"Mr. Westlake likes his fun," said Mrs. MacIntyre, as she conducted Octavia to her rooms. "But," she added loyally, "people around here usually pay attention to what he says when he talks in earnest. I don't know what would have become of this place without him."

Two rooms at the east end of the house had been arranged for the occupancy of the ranch's mistress. When she entered them a slight dismay seized her at their bare appearance and the scantiness of their furniture; but she quickly reflected that the climate was a semi-tropical one, and was moved to appreciation of the well-conceived efforts to conform to it.

The sashes had already been removed from the big windows, and white curtains waved in the Gulf breeze that streamed through the wide jalousies. The bare floor was simply strewn with cool rugs; the chairs were inviting, deep, dreamy willows; the walls were papered with a light, cheerful olive. One whole side of her sitting-room was covered with books on smooth, unpainted pine shelves. She flew to these at once. Before her was a well-selected library. She caught glimpses of titles of volumes of fiction and travel not yet seasoned from the dampness of the press.

Presently, recollecting that she was now in a wilderness given over to mutton, centipedes and privations, the incongruity of these luxuries struck her, and, with intuitive feminine suspicion, she began turning to the fly-leaves of volume after volume. Upon each one was inscribed in fluent characters the name of Theodore Westlake, Jr.

Octavia, fatigued by her long journey, retired early that night. Lying upon her white, cool bed, she rested deliciously, but sleep coquetted long with her. She listened to faint noises whose strangeness kept her faculties on the alert—the fractious yelping of the coyotes, the ceaseless, low symphony of the wind, the distant booming of the frogs about the lake, the lamentation of a concertina in the Mexicans' quarters. There were many conflicting feelings in her heart—thankfulness and rebellion, peace and disquietude, loneliness and a sense of protecting care, happiness and an old, haunting pain.

She did what any other woman would have done—sought relief in a wholesome tide of unreasonable tears, and her last words, murmured to herself before slumber, capitulating, came softly to woo her, were, "He has forgotten."

The manager of the Rancho de las Sombras was no dilettante. He was a "hustler". He was generally up, mounted, and away of mornings before the rest of the household were awake, making the rounds of the flocks and camps. This was the duty of the major-domo, a stately old Mexican with a princely air and manner, but Teddy seemed to have a great deal of confidence in his own eyesight. Except in the busy seasons, he nearly always returned to the ranch to breakfast at eight o'clock, with Octavia and Mrs. MacIntyre, at the little table set in the central hallway, bringing with him a tonic and breezy cheerfulness full of the health and flavour of the prairies.

A few days after Octavia's arrival he made her get out of one of her riding-skirts, and curtail it to a shortness demanded by the chaparral brakes.

With some misgivings she donned this and the pair of buckskin leggings he prescribed in addition, and, mounted upon a dancing pony, rode with him to view her possessions. He showed her everything—the flocks of ewes, muttons and grazing lambs, the dipping vats, the shearing pens, the uncouth merino rams in their little pasture, the water-tanks prepared against the summer drought—giving account of his stewardship with a boyish enthusiasm that never flagged.

Where was the old Teddy that she knew so well? This side of him was the same, and it was a side that pleased her; but this was all she ever saw of him now. Where was his sentimentality—those old, varying moods of impetuous love-making, of fanciful, quixotic devotion, of heart-breaking gloom, of alternating, absurd tenderness and haughty dignity? His nature had been a sensitive one, his temperament bordering closely on the artistic. She knew that, besides being a follower of fashion and its fads and sports, he had cultivated tastes of a finer nature. He had written things, he had tampered with colours, he was something of a student in certain branches of art, and once she had been admitted to all his aspirations and thoughts. But now—and she could not avoid the conclusion—Teddy had barricaded against her every side of himself except one—the side that showed the manager of the Rancho de las Sombras and a jolly chum who had forgiven and forgotten. Queerly enough the words of Mr. Bannister's description of her property came into her mind—"all enclosed within a strong barbed-wire fence."

"Teddy's fenced, too," said Octavia to herself.

It was not difficult for her to reason out the cause of his fortifications. It had originated one night at the Hammersmiths' ball. It occurred at a time soon after she had decided to accept Colonel Beaupree and his million, which was no more than her looks and the entrée she held to the inner circles were worth. Teddy had proposed with all his impetuosity and fire, and she looked him straight in the eyes, and said, coldly and finally: "Never let me hear any such silly nonsense from you again." "You won't," said Teddy, with a new expression around his mouth, and—now Teddy was enclosed within a strong barbed-wire fence.

It was on this first ride of inspection that Teddy was seized by the inspiration that suggested the name of Mother Goose's heroine, and he at once bestowed it upon Octavia. The idea, supported by both a similarity of names and identity of occupations, seemed to strike him as a peculiarly happy one, and he never tired of using it. The Mexicans on the ranch also took up the name, adding another syllable to accommodate their lingual incapacity for the final "p", gravely referring to her as "La Madama Bo-Peepy". Eventually it spread, and "Madame Bo-Peep's ranch" was as often mentioned as the "Rancho de las Sombras".

Came the long, hot season from May to September, when work is scarce on the ranches. Octavia passed the days in a kind of lotus-eater's dream. Books, hammocks, correspondence with a few intimate friends, a renewed interest in her old water-colour box and easel—these disposed of the sultry hours of daylight. The evenings were always sure to bring enjoyment. Best of all were the rapturous horseback rides with Teddy, when the moon gave light over the wind-swept leagues, chaperoned by the wheeling night-hawk and the startled owl. Often the Mexicans would come up from their shacks with their guitars and sing the weirdest of heartbreaking songs. There were long, cosy chats on the breezy gallery, and an interminable warfare of wits between Teddy and Mrs. MacIntyre, whose abundant Scotch shrewdness often more than overmatched the lighter humour in which she was lacking.

And the nights came, one after another, and were filed away by weeks and months—nights soft and languorous and fragrant, that should have driven Strephon to Chloe over wires however barbed, that might have drawn Cupid himself to hunt, lasso in hand, among those amorous pastures—but Teddy kept his fences up.

One July night Madama Bo-Peep and her ranch manager were sitting on the east gallery. Teddy had been exhausting the science of prognostication as to the probabilities of a price of twenty-four cents for the autumn clip, and had then subsided into an anaesthetic cloud of Havana smoke. Only as incompetent a judge as a woman would have failed to note long ago that at least a third of his salary must have gone up in the fumes of those imported Regalias.

"Teddy," said Octavia suddenly, and rather sharply, "what are you working down here on a ranch for?"

"One hundred per," said Teddy glibly, "and found."

"I've a good mind to discharge you."

"Can't do it," said Teddy, with a grin.

"Why not?" demanded Octavia, with argumentative heat.

"Under contract. Terms of sale respect all unexpired contracts. Mine runs until 12 p.m., December thirty-first. You might get up at midnight on that date and fire me. If you try it sooner I'll be in a position to bring legal proceedings."

Octavia seemed to be considering the prospects of litigation.

"But," continued Teddy cheerfully, "I've been thinking of resigning, anyway."

Octavia's rocking-chair ceased its motion. There were centipedes in this country, she felt sure; and Indians; and vast, lonely, desolate, empty wastes; all within strong barbed-wire fence. There was a Van Dresser pride, but there was also a Van Dresser heart. She must know for certain whether or not he had forgotten.

"Ah, well, Teddy," she said, with a fine assumption of polite interest, "it's lonely down here; you're longing to get back to the old life—to polo and lobsters and theatres and balls."

"Never cared much for balls," said Teddy virtuously.

"You're getting old, Teddy. Your memory is failing. Nobody ever knew you to miss a dance, unless it occurred on the same night with another one which you attended. And you showed such shocking bad taste, too, in dancing too often with the same partner. Let me see, what was that

Forbes girl's name—the one with wall eyes—Mabel, wasn't it?"

"No; Adèle. Mabel was the one with the bony elbows. That wasn't wall in Adèle's eyes. It was soul. We used to talk sonnets together, and Verlaine. Just then I was trying to run a pipe from the Pierian spring."

"You were on the floor with her," said Octavia, undeflected, "five times at the Hammersmiths'."

"Hammersmiths' what?" questioned Teddy vacuously.

"Ball—ball," said Octavia viciously. "What were we talking of?"

"Eyes, I thought," said Teddy, after some reflection; "and elbows."

"Those Hammersmiths," went on Octavia, in her sweetest society prattle, after subduing an intense desire to yank a handful of sunburnt, sandy hair from the head lying back contentedly against the canvas of the steamer chair, "had too much money. Mines, wasn't it? It was something that paid something to the ton. You couldn't get a glass of plain water in their house. Everything at that ball was dreadfully overdone."

"It was," said Teddy.

"Such a crowd there was!" Octavia continued, conscious that she was talking the rapid drivel of a schoolgirl describing her first dance. "The balconies were as warm as the rooms. I—lost—something at that ball." The last sentence was uttered in a tone calculated to remove the barbs from miles of wire.

"So did I," confessed Teddy in a lower voice.

"A glove," said Octavia, falling back as the enemy approached her ditches.

"Caste," said Teddy, halting his firing line without loss. "I hobnobbed half the evening with one of Hammersmiths' miners, a fellow who kept his hands in his pockets, and talked like an archangel about reduction plants and drifts and levels and sluice-boxes."

"A pearl-grey glove, nearly new," sighed Octavia mournfully.

"A bang-up chap, that McArdle," maintained Teddy

approvingly. "A man who hated olives and elevators; a man who handled mountains as croquettes, and built tunnels in the air; a man who never uttered a word of silly nonsense in his life. Did you sign those lease-renewal applications yet, madama? They've got to be on file in the land office by the thirty-first."

Teddy turned his head lazily. Octavia's chair was vacant.

* * *

A certain centipede, crawling along the lines marked out by fate, expounded the situation. It was early one morning while Octavia and Mrs. MacIntyre were trimming the honeysuckle on the west gallery. Teddy had risen and departed hastily before daylight in response to word that a flock of ewes had been scattered from their bedding ground during the night by a thunderstorm.

The centipede, driven by destiny, showed himself on the floor of the gallery, and then, the screeches of the two women giving his cue, he scuttled with all his yellow legs through the open door into the farthermost west room, which was Teddy's. Arming themselves with domestic utensils selected with regard to their length, Octavia and Mrs. MacIntyre, with much clutching of skirts and skirmishing for the position of rear guard in the attacking force, followed.

Once outside, the centipede seemed to have disappeared, and his prospective murderers began a thorough but cautious search for their victim.

Even in the midst of such a dangerous and absorbing adventure Octavia was conscious of an awed curiosity on finding herself in Teddy's sanctum. In that room he sat alone, silently communing with those secret thoughts that he now shared with no one, dreamed there whatever dreams he now called on no one to interpret.

It was the room of a Spartan or a soldier. In one corner stood a wide, canvas-covered cot; in another a small bookcase; in another, a grim stand of Winchesters and shot-guns. An immense table, strewn with letters, papers and documents and surmounted by a set of pigeon-holes, occupied one side.

The centipede showed genius in concealing himself in such bare quarters. Mrs. MacIntyre was poking a broom-handle behind the bookcase. Octavia approached Teddy's cot. The room was just as the manager had left it in his hurry. The Mexican maid had not yet given it her attention. There was his big pillow with the imprint of his head still in the centre. She thought the horrid beast might have climbed the cot and hidden itself to bite Teddy. Centipedes were thus cruel and vindictive toward managers.

She cautiously overturned the pillow, and then parted her lips to give the signal for reinforcements at sight of a long, slender, dark object lying there. But, repressing it in time, she caught up a glove, a pearl-grey glove, flattened—it might be conceived—by many, many months of nightly pressure beneath the pillow of the man who had forgotten the Hammersmiths' ball. Teddy must have left so hurriedly that morning that he had, for once, forgotten to transfer it to its resting-place by day. Even managers, who are notoriously wily and cunning, are sometimes caught up with.

Octavia slid the grey glove into the bosom of her summery morning gown. It was hers. Men who put themselves within a strong, barbed-wire fence, and remember Hammersmith balls only by the talk of miners about sluice-boxes, should not be allowed to possess such articles.

After all, what a paradise this prairie country was! How it blossomed like the rose when you found things that were thought to be lost! How delicious was that morning breeze coming in the windows, fresh and sweet with the breath of the yellow ratama blooms! Might one not stand, for a minute, with shining, far-gazing eyes, and dream that mistakes might be corrected?

Why was Mrs. MacIntyre poking about so absurdly with a broom.

"I've found it," said Mrs. MacIntyre, banging the door. "Here it is."

"Did you lose something?" asked Octavia, with sweetly polite non-interest.

"The little devil!" said Mrs. MacIntyre, driven to violence. "Ye've no forgotten him alretty?"

Between them they slew the centipede. Thus was he rewarded for his agency toward the recovery of things lost at the Hammersmiths' ball.

It seems that Teddy, in due course, remembered the glove, and when he returned to the house at sunset made a secret but exhaustive search for it. Not until evening, upon the moonlit eastern gallery, did he find it. It was upon the hand that he had thought lost to him for ever, and so he was moved to repeat certain nonsense that he had been commanded never, never to utter again. Teddy's fences were down.

This time there was no ambition to stand in the way, and the wooing was as natural and successful as should be between ardent shepherd and gentle shepherdess.

The prairies changed to a garden. The Rancho de las Sombras became the Ranch of Light.

A few days later Octavia received a letter from Mr. Bannister, in reply to one she had written to him asking some questions about her business. A portion of the letter ran as follows:

I am at a loss to account for your references to the sheep ranch. Two months after your departure to take up your residence upon it, it was discovered that Colonel Beaupree's title was worthless. A deed came to light showing that he disposed of the property before his death. The matter was reported to your manager, Mr. Westlake, who at once repurchased the property. It is entirely beyond my powers of conjecture to imagine how you have remained in ignorance of this fact. I beg that you will at once confer with that gentleman, who will, at least, corroborate my statement.

Octavia sought Teddy, with battle in her eye.

"What are you working on this ranch for?" she asked once more.

"One hundred——" he began to repeat, but saw in her face that she knew. She held Mr. Bannister's letter in her hand. He knew that the game was up.

"It's my ranch," said Teddy, like a schoolboy detected in

evil. "It's a mighty poor manager that isn't able to absorb the boss's business if you give him time."

"Why were you working down here?" pursued Octavia, still struggling after the key to the riddle of Teddy.

"To tell the truth, 'Tave," said Teddy, with quiet candour, "it wasn't for the salary. That about kept me in cigars and sunburn lotions. I was sent south by my doctor. 'Twas that right lung that was going to the bad on account of over-exercise and strain at polo and gymnastics. I needed climate and ozone and rest and things of that sort."

In an instant Octavia was close against the vicinity of the affected organ. Mr. Bannister's letter fluttered to the floor.

"It's—it's well now, isn't it, Teddy?"

"Sound as a mesquite chunk. I deceived you in one thing. I paid fifty thousand for your ranch as soon as I found you had no title. I had just about that much income accumulated at my banker's while I've been herding sheep down here, so it was almost like picking the thing up on a bargain-counter for a penny. There's another little surplus of unearned increment piling up there, 'Tave. I've been thinking of a wedding trip in a yacht with white ribbons tied to the mast, through the Mediterranean, and then up among the Hebrides and down Norway to the Zuyder Zee."

"And I was thinking," said Octavia softly, "of a wedding gallop with my manager among the flocks of sheep and back to a wedding breakfast with Mrs. MacIntyre on the gallery, with, maybe, a sprig of orange blossom fastened to the red jar above the table."

Teddy laughed, and began to chant:

Little Bo-Peep has lost her sheep,
And doesn't know where to find 'em.
Let 'em alone, and they'll come home,
And——

Octavia drew his head down and whispered in his ear. But that is one of the tales they brought behind them.

58

The Dream

[This was the last work of O. Henry. The *Cosmopolitan Magazine* had ordered it from him and, after his death, the unfinished manuscript was found in his room, on his dusty desk.]

MURRAY dreamed a dream.

Both psychology and science grope when they would explain to us the strange adventures of our immaterial selves when wandering in the realm of "Death's twin brother, Sleep". This story will not attempt to be illuminative; it is no more than a record of Murray's dream. One of the most puzzling phases of that strange waking sleep is that dreams which seem to cover months or even years may take place within a few seconds or minutes.

Murray was waiting in his cell in the ward of the condemned. An electric arc-light in the ceiling of the corridor shone brightly upon his table. On a sheet of white paper an ant crawled wildly here and there as Murray blocked its way with an envelope. The electrocution was set for eight o'clock in the evening. Murray smiled at the antics of the wisest of insects.

There were seven other condemned men in the chamber. Since he had been there Murray had seen three taken out to their fate; one gone mad and fighting like a wolf caught in a trap; one, no less mad, offering up a sanctimonious lip-service to Heaven; the third, a weakling, collapsed and strapped to a board. He wondered with what credit to himself his own heart, foot, and face would meet his punishment; for this was his evening. He thought it must be nearly eight o'clock.

Opposite his own in the two rows of cells was the cage of Bonifacio, the Sicilian slayer of his betrothed and of two officers who came to arrest him. With him Murray had played checkers many a long hour, each calling his move to his unseen opponent across the corridor.

Bonifacio's great booming voice with its indestructible singing quality called out:

"Eh, Meestro Murray; how you feel—all-a right—yes?"

"All right, Bonifacio," said Murray steadily, as he allowed the ant to crawl upon the envelope and then dumped it gently on the stone floor.

"Dat's good-a, Meestro Murray. Men like us, we must-a die-a men. My time come nex'-a week. All-a right. Remember, Meestro Murray, I beat-a you dat las' game of de check. Maybe we play again some-a time. I don'-a know. Maybe we have to call-a de move damn-a loud to play de check where dey goin' send us."

Bonifacio's hardened philosophy, followed closely by his deafening, musical peal of laughter, warmed rather than chilled Murray's numbed heart. Yet Bonifacio had until next week to live.

The cell-dwellers heard the familiar, loud click of the steel bolts as the door at the end of the corridor was opened. Three men came to Murray's cell and unlocked it. Two were prison guards; the other was "Len"—no; that was in the old days; now the Reverend Leonard Winston, a friend and neighbour from their barefoot days.

"I got them to let me take the prison chaplain's place," he said, as he gave Murray's hand one short, strong grip. In his left hand he held a small Bible, with his forefinger marking a page.

Murray smiled slightly and arranged two or three books and some penholders orderly on his small table. He would have spoken, but no appropriate words seemed to present themselves to his mind.

The prisoners had christened this cellhouse, eighty feet long, twenty-eight feet wide, Limbo Lane. The regular guard of Limbo Lane, an immense, rough, kindly man, drew a pint bottle of whisky from his pocket and offered it to Murray saying:

"It's the regular thing, you know. All has it who feel like

they need a bracer. No danger of it becoming a habit with 'em, you see."

Murray drank deep into the bottle.

"That's the boy!" said the guard. "Just a little nerve tonic, and everything goes smooth as silk."

They stepped into the corridor, and each one of the doomed seven knew. Limbo Lane is a world on the outside of the world; but it had learned, when deprived of one or more of the five senses, to make another sense supply the deficiency. Each one knew that it was nearly eight, and that Murray was to go to the chair at eight. There is also in the many Limbo Lanes an aristocracy of crime. The man who kills in the open, who beats his enemy or pursuer down, flushed by the primitive emotions and the ardour of combat, holds in contempt the human rat, the spider, and the snake.

So, of the seven condemned only three called their farewells to Murray as he marched down the corridor between the two guards—Bonifacio, Marvin, who had killed a guard while trying to escape from the prison, and Bassett, the train-robber, who was driven to it because the express-manager wouldn't raise his hands when ordered to do so. The remaining four smouldered, silent, in their cells, no doubt feeling their social ostracism in Limbo Lane society more keenly than they did the memory of their less picturesque offences against the law.

Murray wondered at his own calmness and nearly indifference. In the execution room were about twenty men, a congregation made up of prison officers, newspaper reporters, and lookers-on who had succeeded

Here, in the very middle of a sentence, the hand of Death interrupted the telling of O. Henry's last story. He had planned to make this story different from his others, the beginning of a new series in a style he had not previously attempted. "I want to show the public," he said, "that I can write something new—new for me, I mean—a story without slang, a straightforward dramatic plot treated in a way that will come nearer my idea of real story-writing." Before starting to write the present story he outlined briefly how he intended to develop it: Murray, the criminal accused and convicted of the brutal murder of his sweetheart—a murder prompted by jealous rage—at first faces the death penalty, calm, and, to all outward appearances, indifferent to his fate. As he nears the electric chair he is overcome by a revulsion of feeling. He is left dazed, stupefied, stunned. The entire scene in the death-chamber—the witnesses, the spectators, the preparations for execution—become unreal to him. The thought flashes through his brain that a terrible mistake is being made. Why is he being strapped to the chair? What has he done? What crime has he committed? In the few moments while the straps are being adjusted a vision comes to him. He dreams a dream. He sees a little country cottage, bright, sunlit, nestling in a bower of flowers. A woman is there, and a little child. He speaks with them and finds that they are his wife, his child—and the cottage their home. So, after all, it is a mistake. Someone has frightfully, irretrievably blundered. The accusation, the trial, the conviction, the sentence to death in the electric chair—all a dream. He takes his wife in his arms and kisses the child. Yes, here is happiness. It was a dream. Then—at a sign from the prison warden the fatal current is turned on.

Murray had dreamed the wrong dream.